YESTERDAY IS DEAD

A five gallon water bottle inverted on its stand beside the kitchen door exploded in a shower of glass and water. The second shot shattered a window just above it. The thirty-eight sounded strangely toylike in the quiet house.

'Stop, you son of a bitch,' Collison shouted as the man raced from the back of the house toward a cement block wall at the rear of the wide yard. He never broke stride. When he reached the wall, Collison and Mattingly fired. Fragments and chips danced from the wall in white puffs as the man dropped from sight on the other side.

'We got 'em,' Mattingly exclaimed, 'We got the bastard.'

'What 'da you mean we,' Collison scorned. 'All you killed was the goddamned wall.'

'Horse shit,' Mattingly argued, shaking mud from his arm. 'I didn't hit the wall.'

'Where's he at?' The Fox shouted from the corner of the house.

The Fox raced to the five foot wall, jumped, and pulled himself to the top, gun still in hand. Peering over it, he quickly surveyed the littered alley. 'He's gone,' he shouted.

About the Author

Dallas Barnes is a veteran of the Los Angeles
police department, currently assigned to Southwest homicide division.

He is also the author of two previous novels,
See the Woman and *Badge of Honor*. Barnes
has also written episodes for television's
'Kojak,' 'Joe Forrester,' and 'Crunch.'

He and his wife JoAnne live in Southern
California.

Yesterday Is Dead

Dallas Barnes

CORONET BOOKS
Hodder and Stoughton

First published in Great Britain 1977 by
Hodder and Stoughton Limited

Coronet Edition 1977
Second impression 1980

Printed and bound in Great Britain for
Hodder and Stoughton Paperbacks,
a division of Hodder and Stoughton Ltd.,
Mill Road, Dunton Green, Sevenoaks, Kent
(Editorial Office: 47 Bedford Square, London, WC1 3DP)
by Richard Clay (The Chaucer Press), Ltd.,
Bungay, Suffolk

ISBN 0 340 21826 6

DEDICATED TO THOSE FEW MEN WHO PURSUE
A FADING HOPE.......................................JUSTICE.

TELETYPE/LOCAL

SWD AND SHERIFFS LOCAL 6/21/75
WANTED PERSON/MURDER/RAPE
SUSPECT MALE/NEG., 150-190, SIZE 10½ SHOE.
NFD.

VEH   VW/69-72, WHITE. NFD
M O   SUSPECT REMOVED GLASS LOUVERS
FROM VICTIMS APT. BEDROOM WIN-
DOW LOCATED 2714 MONTCLAIR AVE
—8. BETWEEN 2200 AND 2400 HRS ABV.
DATE AND ENTERED.

SUSPECT RAPED VICTIM. PUBIC HAIRS
RECOVERED FROM VICTIMS GENITAL
AREA IDENTIFY SUSPECT AS ADULT
M/NEG. AUTOPSY REVEALED MALE
SEMEN STOMACH OF VICTIM, EVID.
FORCED ORAL COPULATION.

VICTIMS THROAT AND WRISTS SLASHED
BY POSS/RAZOR OR SHARP KNIFE. SUS-
PECT URINATED ON VICTIM.

SIZE 10 1/2 LEFT FOOT PRINT FOUND
IN VICTIMS BLOOD APT. FLOOR.

POSS/SUSPECT OBS FLEEING SCENE IN
VW SDN, WHT 69-72 E/B MONTCLAIR
AVE.

ATTN; ALL HOMICIDE AND SEX DETAILS
REQUEST ALL INFO ON SIMILAR MO
ANY CASE INVOLVING URINATION BY
SUSPECT.

REFER SOUTHWEST DETECTIVES ATTN/HOL-
LISTER & FOX DR 75-506-719 PD LOS ANGELES
SWD VIA LOP PH

PROLOGUE

In the time it takes you to read these few paragraphs, in this country there will be at least one homicide, six robberies, eight rapes, nine burglaries, fourteen assaults, and twenty-two auto thefts.

Sixty percent of the individuals committing these offenses will never be arrested. Of the forty percent that are apprehended only twenty-two percent will be found guilty. Six percent of the twenty-two percent convicted will be sentenced to confinement. The remainder will rejoin those on the street who were never apprehended.

To quote Justice Douglas R. Staff: "It is better we release a hundred murderers than convict one innocent soul."

This is the story of one man, his crimes, his victims, and his justice. To the police he is known as "The Pisser."

PART ONE

He knew that standing in the dark night shadows of the quiet street was a dangerous luxury. Only nine days out of prison, four miles from his apartment, it would be difficult to explain even to a rookie policeman what he was doing there in the middle of the night. But the hunt demanded the risk. He had been running a long time, so long that it seemed he couldn't remember a day for years when he was not always cautious. He remembered the last time when screams brought neighbors to the apartment door and he had to rush the finish and leave. If he wanted to be more leisurely he knew he could take his time setting her up, following her for a few more days planning the details. The excitement was when they would first realize what was about to happen and their appeal was to a survival instinct deep inside. Only one failed him; she fainted and when he revived her she remained motionless as if she were no longer there. He killed her instantly with no pleasure.

Ellen Shane was her name and she was twenty-eight years old. Since her divorce she lived alone with Dawn, her three-year-old daughter, on the first floor of the Montclair Court Apartments, where Montclair Avenue twisted north to meet Adams Boulevard. The apartment had been remodeled just before she moved in and for one seventy-five a month she didn't think she could do better. It was located in the buffer zone between Los Angeles's hard-core ghetto, south of Adams Boulevard, and the upper-middle-class blacks that lived west of Crenshaw in the rolling Baldwin Hills.

After her separation from Jeff it had taken three months to find a job and that was as a clerk at Thrifty Mart. Jeffrey had offered a threatening laugh and told her she'd be on welfare for the rest of her life.

However, she didn't think of Jeffrey and his drugs much anymore, not since David. On his first six visits to the store he seemed not to notice her. She assumed he lived nearby. He was quiet but athletic looking and his dark eyes excited her. She always hoped that he'd choose her checkout stand, and usually he did, but he usually ignored her overt flirtations. She'd just about convinced herself he was happily married or at least not interested when one night he asked if she would like a drink after work.

Ellen had decided much earlier that she would go to bed with this man. There had been no one since Jeff. "Would you like to come in for a drink?" she had asked with the most suggestive smile she could manage after unlocking the door.

"I'd like that very much," David answered, taking her hand, "but I've got a long day tomorrow." Then he left without even a kiss.

The next day when he didn't return to the store, she felt utterly depressed. She recalled how Jeffrey in a rage would say, "You're only half a woman . . . a bum piece of ass . . . not fit to be a whore." When she left the store that night David was waiting in front.

David was a Los Angeles policeman. He was twenty-six and he'd been a cop for three years. When she and David first made love it was on the living-room floor. She had cried out, in the middle of her orgasm, that she loved him. He answered the same.

She'd been home for an hour now. David was getting off at midnight and it had been their routine now for almost six months that he would stop for some Chinese food or pizza and then come by for a few hours. Dawn was in bed asleep. The FM station was playing a (Gladys Pips?) song as she walked into her bedroom, kicked off her sandals, and switched on the light.

He had been outside for nearly forty minutes now after following Ellen home from Thrifty Mart for the third time. Once he waited the forty minutes he was convinced the other man she usually slept with was not coming by. He moved along the stucco wall from the side window to the rear as she disappeared from sight. He knew she was in the bedroom. Kneeling next to the bedroom window, he peered through the bottom of the venetian blind. His heart quickened as he found her standing near the far side of the bed. The light was on, not like the other times when all he could see were dark figures moving in a darker room and all he could hear was the sounds of their lovemaking. Now he could see everything.

As she pulled the yellow blouse up over her head his hand moved to his erection. His breathing became labored. He pushed closer to the window. Arching her shoulders back, Ellen reached behind and unsnapped her bra, letting it slide down her arms and fall to the floor. Her breasts were firm and brown with walnut-colored nipples. "You whore," he whispered, "you beautiful whore." Hooking her thumbs inside her white bell-bottom slacks, Ellen pushed both panties and slacks to the floor in a smooth motion, bending slightly to step out of them. Her breasts swayed as she moved. The man unzipped his trousers.

Ellen admired herself in the bedroom dresser mirror. She studied for a moment, drew in a breath, twisted, eyeing her stomach, patted it, checking firmness. "Not bad," Ellen smiled, pleased with her reflection. She turned, now humming along with the Friends of Distinction, switched off the light, and headed for the bath. It was eleven-ten.

The bathroom window was high, small, and screened, but it was open. Standing beneath it he could hear the sound of running water. After a few minutes the water stopped. He stood with penis in hand, massaging himself gently. He had to have her and he knew she'd want him. Anyway she was just a whore and whores were always ready to fuck. She had probably seen him, which explained why she had undressed like that. It was a come-on. He knew her kind.

Ellen had just about dozed off in her oil bath when she heard the noise. Opening her eyes she listened. "Damn it, Dawn, don't you wake up." She waited. There was no more, only the soft music of the FM. She relaxed. Another five minutes and she would have to get out. She wondered if David had ever made love in a bathtub. She smiled as she thought of it.

The man, using a long folding pocket-knife, had already removed five of the glass louvers from the side of the bedroom window, when he dropped one. It scraped along the stucco wall and fell on the others he had stacked neatly on the ground. He froze, fearing discovery. After a few minutes he was convinced no one had heard. He went back to work, carefully sliding the blade along the edge of the glass where the louvered slats met the metal frame on both sides, then pulling it silently away.

After removing another two in the darkness, he knew he had room to climb in. Reaching inside the darkened room, his gloved hand slid along the side of the window until it touched a hanging cord. Wrapping his hand gently around it he pulled. The blind swayed slightly and then folded quietly toward the top.

Ellen pushed the chrome drain control to open with her

big toe, splashed some of the hot water over her breasts,
then climbed out of the tub. Drying her hands first, she
paused to light a Silva Thin, set it in the ashtray on the
back of the bowl, then toweled herself dry. Finishing, she
powdered in the spots she knew David enjoyed, picked up
her cigarette, glanced at the tub, deciding to return and
rinse it later, and headed for the bedroom.

He waited just inside the open bedroom door, his back to
the wall, the open knife in his right hand. He lowered the
venetian blind again. He tensed as the bathroom light
switched off.

Ellen opened the door to Dawn's room quietly. In the
soft glow of the green night light she could see that her
daughter was sleeping soundly. She eased the door closed.
He waited, his nerves making his legs tremble.

She reached the door to her room when the telephone
rang. She paused. He pressed closer to the wall, able to see
her now framed in the hallway light. She was wrapped in a
blue bath towel. Her left breast was exposed. The phone rang
again.

Kneeling beside the end table in the living room, she
turned down the FM and picked up the phone on the third
ring. "Hello."

"Hello, baby," the male voice answered. It was Jeffrey.

"Jeff," she said in a tone that left no chance for misun-
derstanding. "I gave you my number because you're the father of my daughter. Not so you could call here when you
damn please. This is the second time, Jeff. . . . You do it
again and I swear I'll change the number and you won't get
it."

"Hey," he countered with a slur. "I got a right to call and
check on my baby. . . . My daughter . . . you understand . . .
I'm her goddamned father."

"Well, then call at a decent hour. Call when you can talk
to her. I know what you want Jeff. The answer is no. You're
not coming over tonight or any other night. It's over."

There was an awkward pause on the line followed by a
plastic click. She hung up the receiver carefully, studying the
phone for a moment. Jeffrey frightened her. She was always
afraid that after one of those calls he would come over,
break in, and beat her. Her fear had eased some since meeting David, even though she hadn't yet told him.

Adjusting the bath towel she walked to the bedroom,
determined not to let his call ruin her night. Reaching the

doorway she pulled the towel away, tossing it toward the bed. She reached for the light switch. A gloved hand slapped into the left side of her face from the rear, leaving her ear ringing and burning.

The hand slid forward, covering her mouth and nose. Her scream sounded distant and hollow to her, as if it came from someone else.

He forced her forward before she could resist and they fell face forward onto the bed, his weight pushing her into the mattress. She could feel the coarseness of his trousers and shirt on her flesh. She struggled, trying to scream through the musty glove that covered her face.

He pulled back hard on her head, and her neck muscles stretched painfully. Her stomach jerked, and she felt as if she were going to urinate. "Listen," he said. Another scream came from deep inside her. He pulled harder on her neck. "Listen," he warned again, breathing heavily in her ear. "You fight anymore and I'll kill your baby."

It had to be a dream. Her mind was a jumble of terror and fear. "David . . . Oh, David, help me."

"Did you hear me?" he asked, jerking on her neck. Lights flashed inside her closed eyes as her neck cracked. He eased the grip slightly. "You scream and I'll kill the baby. So help me I will." His voice was distant, hollow, her neck pained terribly, she felt as if she were drowning, she gasped for breath and tried to speak but couldn't. She nodded her head.

"Good . . . Good," the man breathed into her ear, as he ground his pelvis against her buttocks. She could smell his alcoholic breath. The stubble of his beard raked along her ear and cheek. "All I wanna do is give you what you want," he breathed heavily. "I just wanna screw you. You'll like that, won't you?" He licked at her ear. She began to cry as he shifted his weight to unzip his trousers. Then stiffened as his erection touched her.

"Felton," Dorease Clark whispered to her husband who lay beside her in bed watching the eleven o'clock news.

Her husband didn't respond.

"Felton," she said again, this time nudging him.

"What?"

"Something's wrong next door," she said, pushing up slightly in the bed.

"What goes on over there ain't none of our business," he answered.

"But, I heard her scream."

"She's got a phone. If she needs help, she can call the police."

"But Felton? She lives alone."

"You hear anything now?"

"No."

"Then forget it."

"Felton!"

"Dammit, let me watch the sports. Then I'll give you something to clear your mind."

"Felton, you're terrible."

David Wilson glanced at his watch as he pushed through the double doors at the rear of Southwest Station. It was twelve-ten. It had been busy for a Thursday night, but he was pleased that he was getting off on time. Summer was on its way, which meant his work day, like every other cop's in the city, would get longer as the summer temperatures rose. He wondered why heat did that to people. Must be hell being a cop in Panama.

He glanced at the morning watch crew as they spread across the parking lot to the black and whites parked along the west side of the station. They were laughing, smiling, loading shotguns, storing their helmets in the trunks. How could anyone be in such a good mood when they worked from eleven-fifteen to 8:00 A.M.? He had tried it. His days had become a blur. Sleeping all day, up all night, having a big meal at four in the morning. After six weeks he gave it up and requested P.M.'s.

A final wave to the poor bastards that had drawn station security for the night at the rear gate and he gunned the 240Z west on Santa Barbara, then north on Western Avenue. Giving in to his hunger, he turned east on Adams, deciding to pick up some Golden Bird Fried Chicken. After the arrest there hadn't been time for any chow. Stopping at LaSalle for a red light a blond-wigged prostitute offered him a warm smile from the bus stop. He smiled back. An hour ago she had turned away when he and his partner had rolled by in their black-and-white.

After picking up the box of chicken and two red sodas he raced west on Adams, cheating a little at the traffic light at Western Avenue, and two minutes later down-shifted to turn left onto Montclair.

There was a tattered Volkswagen pulling from the curb in

front of the Montclair Courts as Dave approached. The VW pulled out and sped away quickly. Dave shook his head. "Crazy bastard." He backed into the spot and shut off his car.

The courtyard was quiet. Here and there a curtained window spilled soft light onto the walkway. Tucking the box of chicken under his arm he pushed the bell. "Chicken man's here," he smiled, glancing at the sky. "Hey, a star. Damn pretty night." He pushed the bell again. After waiting a second, he glanced at the window. There were lights on, along with music.

He rapped lightly on the door. "Ellen . . . Ellen." Digging in his pocket he pulled out his key.

The bedroom was dark. He closed the front door quietly behind him. Setting the chicken and drinks on the kitchen bar, he pulled the two-inch thirty-eight from his waistband, putting it on top of the refrigerator. "Ellen," he said, pushing off his shoes. "I'm gonna come in there and bite you in the neck."

His eyes weren't accustomed to the room's darkness, but he could see she was on her stomach and nude. He sat down on the edge of the bed. "Don't get the idea I'm this easy with every girl," he smiled, leaning toward her. It was his left hand that felt the wetness on her back. Then the right, along her neck and cheek. "My God!" he gasped, realizing it was her blood. "Ellen," he screamed, grabbing her. Dawn, awakened by the shout, let out a shrill cry.

"God damn people fightin' all night. I gotta work tomorrow," Felton Clark mumbled, walking through the darkness of his apartment to the kitchen phone.

"Hurry, honey," his wife urged, joining him. "The baby's still screaming and so is that man."

Dave reeled from the bedroom, his jaw slack, mouth open. "No, Ellen . . . No . . . No . . ." he moaned, scarcely hearing Dawn's cries, his hands and arms wet with blood. He sank to the floor near the phone, smearing the white wall with her blood.

"Police Department."

"I'm a police officer," Dave cried in near hysteria. "I'm a police officer and somebody's killed Ellen."

The officer working the complaint board straightened in his chair. "Where do you work?" He was skeptic.

"Here, Los Angeles," he sobbed into the phone, "and I need help."

"Okay . . . all right. Where are you?"

"On Montclair . . . twenty-seven fourteen Montclair. . . . She's all cut up. You've got to get me an ambulance."

"Help's on the way. But stay on the line. Keep talking."

"SOUTHWEST UNITS IN THE VICINITY AND THREE ADAM TWENTY-ONE. ADDITIONAL ON YOUR UNKNOWN TROUBLE CALL AT TWENTY-SEVEN FOURTEEN MONTCLAIR, APARTMENT EIGHT. IT IS NOW, OFFICER NEEDS HELP. THREE ADAM TWENTY-ONE YOUR CALL IS CODE THREE. USE CAUTION THE OFFICER IS OFF DUTY. NO DESCRIPTION."

Forty seconds later the first black-and-white roared onto the block from the east. Its red lights on, electronic siren piercing the night. As it rocked to a halt in front of the Montclair Courts, two more patrol cars raced in from the west. Leaving their cars, the officers, shotguns in hand, moved cautiously through the shadows of the courtyard.

"Hear anything?" one whispered as they crouched near the front door of the apartment.

"Just a kid crying," came a hushed reply.

"Knock," another urged.

They moved away from the door. One of the officers, his back to the wall, stretched and rapped heavily on the door. His partner, on the other side of the door, called, "Police officers. Open up."

The child's crying increased.

After a few seconds: "Police officers. You've got ten seconds to open the door."

"Kick it in," a voice barked from the shadows, after they got no response.

Two of the biggest officers centered themselves on the door and, with a nod, kicked in unison. The prefab door exploded into a shower of splinters.

"Jesus Christ!" one of the officers grimaced as their flashlights illuminated Dave sitting in the dark room on the edge of the bed, cradling Ellen's torn bloody body, talking softly to an unhearing ear. Dawn, crying hysterically, clung to her mother's limp leg.

Lee Hollister was kissing her right breast. Moving the moist erect nipple slowly back and forth across his mouth, teasing it with a tongue, when he heard the Tonight Show theme. She moaned softly as he paused. He resumed, moving

with two soft kisses to the left breast. "Damn news," he silently told himself as her fingers caressed the back of his
neck. If the news hadn't bored him he wouldn't have started
this until after Carson's monologue. "Where was it?" he
wondered. "The weather." It was during the weather fore-
cast he had laid his head on her chest and that did it. She
pushed a long leg under his. He wondered if he could make
love to her and listen to the monologue at the same time.
That wouldn't work, he decided. She'd notice he was quiet,
and she had once asked why he was so quiet when he made
love to her. He wasn't certain how to answer that. It seemed
to him if things were all right you didn't need conversation.

"Here's Johnny," Ed McMahan said, as she pushed her leg
further under his. He moved from breast to mouth. Her
tongue found his. He slid his hand beneath the elastic of her
panties and over her ass. The telephone rang.

"Oh, shit," Janice hissed.

He moved back to a breast. She pushed into him. The
phone rang again. "What time is it?" he mumbled, not moving from the breast.

She twisted slightly to see the lighted clock radio. "Almost
. . . Almost one," she said with effort.

"Damn it," he groaned as the phone rang for the third
time. Giving her breast what he was sure was a good-night
kiss, he pushed up and reached over her for the phone. He
and his partner were the on-call homicide team for Southwest Division this week. A call at this hour meant nothing
else.

"Hollister," he said, picking up the phone.

"Good morning, Lee. This is Kline on the desk. Hope I
didn't wake you."

Janice pulling him down, ran her tongue along his jaw.
He tried his best to ignore it. "It's okay, Kline. I had to get
up to answer the phone anyway."

"Got one for you on Montclair," Kline went on. "Policeman involved."

"Policeman killed?" Hollister stiffened.

Janice stopped.

"No . . . possible suspect. D.H.Q.'s at the scene now. How
soon can you get in?"

" 'Bout twenty minutes. You called Fox yet?"

"No, just about to."

"Okay," Hollister agreed. "And you better call the skipper.

If we've got an officer suspect, he's gonna want in from the ground level."

He put the receiver back and let his weight sink on her, burying his head in the tangle of long hair at her shoulder. Her finger tips worked their way across his back. "It wouldn't take long," she whispered in his ear.

He considered it as she shifted beneath him, her fingers moving to the back of his neck. No, he couldn't. Fox would be waiting at the station. "Could you wait?" he tried tactfully, not yet moving.

"Like last time, Lee?" she asked, her tone cool, moving her hands away. He kissed softly along the line of her neck. "No," she went on. "I don't want to wake up in the morning here . . . alone."

He pushed up onto his elbows. "I'm sorry, lady," he said to her blue eyes. She managed less than a hearty smile. "I love you, dummy." He thanked her with a grin. "But, I'm going home," she added, "and you've got to take me to dinner tomorrow night to make up for this."

"You've got a deal."

"And then," she smiled, pulling his head down on her breasts, "we'll start earlier."

Eight minutes later he was on the freeway. He hadn't yet put on his tie. Avoid that as long as he could, but with the skipper coming in it was inevitable. For some crazy god-damned reason the L.A.P.D. had the idea you couldn't do detective work without wearing a tie.

He glanced at his watch. It was one-twenty. Janice would almost be home. She lived only eight blocks away. He had tried hard to talk her into moving in with him but she'd have no part of it. "You want me to live with you, marry me," she had said flatly. "That's bigamy," he answered. "Then wait until your divorce is final," she argued.

His marriage with Carol had been good, but after twelve years it had just wound down. They had a nice home in Huntington Beach, two cars, and a boat. The kids were attending good schools, money was no problem, but he was unhappy and not sure why. There wasn't another woman then. He just wasn't comfortable.

It had been a morning like so many others. He was sitting at the kitchen table working on coffee and a cigarette, scanning the morning paper. Carol, after getting the children up, joined him at the table as she always did. "Judy put a dent in their new car yesterday," she said, sipping her coffee.

He didn't know why, maybe he had been considering it for a long time without realizing it, but it hit him. He put down the paper.

"I'm going to leave."

"I know that," she smiled.

"No, I mean for keeps. I want out."

She studied him for a long moment. "You're serious, aren't you?"

He was surprised that she hadn't pleaded with him to stay. Maybe if she had . . . Well, it didn't matter now. One day he was there and the next he was gone. The first two months had been the worst, the loneliness was nearly unbearable, and to combat it he found himself going to bed each night with the television on. Returning to the empty apartment each day was depressing. He tried leaving the radio on but it didn't help. He bought goldfish and they quickly died. But as the days turned to weeks and the weeks to months the loneliness faded, replaced by the growing daily routine of life alone. A brief affair with the nineteen-year-old in Two-C helped.

It was a month or more after his separation that his being thirty-six seemed particularly important, even distressing. He took to jogging each morning and exercising each night. His medicine cabinet became crammed with a variety of vitamins which he took religiously each morning. A close look at himself in the bathroom mirror one morning showed his once sandy brown hair was now sprinkled with streaks of gray, and the corners of his eyes and forehead showed lines he just hadn't seen before. It worried him. He bought some face cream the next day although he never did use it.

Living alone he found wasn't all that bad once he had made it through the first few months. The proper separation of laundry was a hard lesson. He now had the distinction of being the only L.A.P.D. detective with pink tee shirts and shorts after washing them with a red sweater. Getting fed was another constant problem but he learned to enjoy, reluctantly, frozen dinners. Much to his genuine surprise he found he drank less when he was alone.

Still not many months after his divorce he began thinking of remarriage, even though he didn't know to whom. Living without a woman was possible, but to him, living with one was far more comfortable. Returning to Carol was a thought he seldom considered, and then never seriously. He wasn't really sure why he'd left her. He was certain it wasn't something she'd done. Perhaps, he told himself, it was the things she hadn't done. Thinking of it brought a pain that kept him from getting a clear mental focus. He hoped time would bring an answer. For now when he was asked why he'd left her, he'd laugh and say it was her cooking or snoring at night. The real reason that he wouldn't share with anyone was that he was bored with marriage. That, in his opinion, was an immoral reason to leave his wife and children. But yet it was the real one. He and Carol had run out of goals. Life had leveled off and they simply waited for the years to pass while the children grew up. He was sick of television movies, the weekly card game with Bill and Judy, and pizza every Friday night. He'd tried every way he could to let Carol know he was bored. She wouldn't change, she was a creature of habit who found great security in all the maddening sameness. He was thoroughly convinced that a man could love a woman a lot more than he could know her. When their love died, he realized how little he had in common with her or she with him.

His greatest shock had been when he drove home one night without calling, to see the kids. He saw the station wagon parked in front of the house when he'd turned onto the block. It was Bill and Judy's. They'd been friends for years. If he went in now he knew it would be awkward for everybody. Deciding to wait until they left, he parked down the street.

As the minutes turned into hours, his mind made suggestions to him he wasn't willing to accept, but he couldn't leave. At ten-thirty the lights went out, but no one left the house. He wept in the darkness.

By midnight, his sorrow had turned to rage. He sat waiting, gun in hand. When the outside light flashed on, he crushed out his cigarette. He looked away as the two shadows embraced in the darkened doorway. When he looked back, Bill was at his car. He sat quietly as Bill got in and drove away. It had been two months. He pushed the thirty-eight back in his waistband. Wiping his cheek, he started the car and drove away. He slept well that night. Now the divorce wasn't just his.

Janice had been a long-time friend of Carol's and the two had worked together several years ago. Janice's husband was a deputy sheriff, so the two women had a common bond. Hollister had been standing in line at the bank when Janice said from behind, "Gonna rob the bank, fella?"

They chatted for a few minutes as the line moved and then she asked how Carol and the kids were. With some embarrassment he stammered through telling her they were separated. Janice didn't pry. After he told her she shifted the conversation.

As the two walked from the bank, Janice explained she was on her lunch break.

"Lunch break," Hollister said.

"Yes, I'm a working woman again. With two little ones I have to."

"I thought Chuck didn't want you working," he said.

She smiled, or was it a smile? He wasn't sure. "Chuck is gone. He fell in love with some female deputy. He left me three months ago."

Deciding that two lost souls should share something, he bought her lunch. He never really remembered looking at her before, but now that he had, he knew it wouldn't end with lunch.

The Adams Boulevard off-ramp flashed by. His exit was coming up next. Easing off the gas he moved to the right-hand lane. Exposition Boulevard, one quarter mile. Fox would probably be at the station waiting on him. Virgil Fox, or just the Fox, as Hollister and most other policemen knew him was always waiting on something. He was the most impatient man Hollister knew.

Virgil Fox had been Hollister's partner for eighteen months now. Hollister had raised hell when Fox had first been assigned to him. He dreaded the idea of being saddled with a do-nothing black partner. He'd seen too many other black policemen heave their guts out at the sight of the coroner's bone saw buzzing through hair and skull to dig out a dead brain. "They just can't stomach working homicide," he had argued to Lieutenant Purington. His request had been denied.

Hollister treated his black partner as less than an equal for their first few weeks. It was during the second month of their partnership that the Fox proved his stomach was superior to Hollister's. Hollister had grimaced and covered his mouth as the Fox helped a deputy coroner pull a two-foot broom handle out of a dead fruit's ass after he had succumbed to a drug overdose in the middle of his masochistic act. From that day on, Hollister figured the Fox had earned his way into the fraternal order of homicide detectives.

He turned the mustang south on Denker from Exposition,

moved quickly through three sleepy residential blocks, and stopped for a red light at Santa Barbara. Southwest Station sat quietly across the intersection from him, bathed in its soft night light. Looking as sleepy and peaceful as any of the other buildings on the street.

Parking on the east side of the station's lot, he walked toward the rear door. The morning's darkness was cool and refreshing. He enjoyed it for a moment; even a few of the brighter stars sprinkled the sky, which was rare in Los Angeles. Pausing to light a cigarette at the door, he remembered his tie in the car.

Hollister, as he knew he would, found the Fox waiting in the detective squad room. He smiled; as always the Fox looked like he had just walked out of Harris and Franks, in a new suit. The Fox was the type of man—square shoulders, straight back, strong neck—who looked good in a suit.

The Fox was talking with a uniformed sergeant and lieutenant near his and Hollister's desk.

"What the hell do you do?" Hollister asked as he reached them. "Sit near the phone dressed like that waiting for a call?"

Fox offered a wide white smile. "Mom always taught me to respect the dead."

"I swear, man," Hollister added, "I think you moonlight as a goddamned undertaker."

"Just referrals," the Fox countered.

"I was just telling the Fox what we've got out on Montclair," Lieutenant Bowen, the uniformed watch commander said. Hollister felt a bit guilty about his attempt at humor. The lieutenant looked worried.

"Go ahead," Hollister agreed, pushing onto the edge of the desk.

"We had a help call come out from an off-duty officer at about twelve thirty-five, at twenty-seven fourteen Montclair. Our units rolled. They found a dark apartment——"

"What number?" The Fox interrupted.

"Eight . . . number eight. They heard a kid screaming inside. They knocked. Nothing. So they booted it in. They found Wilson." He nodded toward an interview room along the west wall of the squad room. An officer sat outside it. Hollister guessed that this Wilson was inside. "He was sitting on the bed in the dark holding this cut-up broad. She was nude."

"He say anything?" Hollister asked, glancing at the closed door and the officer outside it.

"No," the lieutenant said, "and we haven't asked. We know this would be a sensitive one . . . anyway, he's still pretty upset."

"We did get him to clean up a bit," the uniformed sergeant added. "He was covered with blood."

Hollister looked to Fox. "Wanna go out there before we talk with him?"

"Think that would be best," the Fox answered.

Hollister finished his cigarette. "Where's Wilson work?"

"Here," the sergeant answered. "P.M. Watch. He got off at midnight."

Hollister massaged his chin with the back of his hand, wishing he had had time to shave. Being unshaven he knew he'd feel tired in a couple of hours. "Anyone told Wilson he's under arrest?" he asked.

"No," the lieutenant said flatly.

"Has he asked for anything?" Fox added.

"Nothing."

"Where's the officers that were in the apartment?" Hollister asked.

"Two here," the lieutenant answered, "down in the coffee room. Sergeant Mason, here, was there. There's still two at the scene with the dicks from D.H.Q. and the other unit is in the field, but we can get 'em when you need them."

"We'll wanna talk with them later," Hollister explained.

Turning to the Fox, Hollister pushed off the desk. "Let's talk to the desk crew, then get down there."

"What shall we do with Wilson?" the sergeant asked.

Hollister again glanced at the closed door. He wondered who and what this Wilson was. "Keep him isolated. No talk about what happened and no phone calls. Give him a coffee if he wants it. We'll talk to 'im when we get back."

"Is he under arrest?" the sergeant asked.

Hollister glanced at him. "Did you arrest him?"

"No."

"Neither have we."

They talked to the men working the night-watch detective desk. Kline had called the captain. He was on his way in. They left the station and drove north on Western toward Montclair. The same route Wilson had taken.

"What'd ya think," the Fox asked as Hollister drove the plain brown Plymouth.

"I think the butler did it," Hollister said sarcastically.

"Fuck you."

"Well, how in the hell should I know?"

"What do your instincts tell you?" the Fox questioned.

"The only instincts I have," Hollister said, slowing for a red light, lighting a cigarette, "are sexual, and they got ripped off tonight."

The Fox chuckled as they rolled forward on the green.

"I wonder," Hollister exhaled a puff of smoke, "if the annual F.B.I. report on crime statistics for this country reflects how many times a homicide interrupts a detective getting laid."

They had no problem finding the address. A black-and-white sat in front, double parked, its lights blinking out a red pulse every few seconds, casting the smell of violence on the darkness. Two plain, bland-colored detective cars crowded the street behind it.

After parking, they walked into the courtyard. Most of the apartments were now lit. A group of tenants stood whispering in a small cluster, peering at the shattered door of apartment 8.

"I hope for Wilson's sake," Fox whispered as they moved through the courtyard, "that the butler did it."

Hollister tossed away his cigarette as they neared the door. A uniformed officer stood outside. He clicked on his flashlight, then switched it off. "You'll have to stay outside, fellas," he said in the darkness.

Hollister smiled. The officer was doing his job well. "I'm Sergeant Hollister. This is my partner, Fox. We're handling this case. Is D.H.Q. inside?"

"Yeah, but Sergeant Case said not to let anyone in," the officer said.

"Good," Hollister agreed. "Call 'im to the door."

The officer leaned into the open doorway. "Sergeant Case."

"Yeah," came the reply from inside.

"Southwest is here," he called.

"Let 'em in."

The officer stepped aside. Hollister and Fox moved inside. As they crossed the living room into a room off to the left, they saw a second uniformed officer sitting on the edge of a bed, book in hand, hat off, reading to a small black girl.

The two detectives in the bedroom let Hollister and Fox look for a moment before saying anything. The once-pretty young woman lay face up and nude, sprawled awkwardly across the bed. Her unseeing eyes wide, mouth open. Heavy globs of coagulated blood hung from a slash across her neck. More blood covered her wrists and hands in random streaks. The pale blue sheet was stained and wet.

"I'm Case, D.H.Q., Morning Watch," the tall, graying detective said, extending a hand to Hollister. "That's my partner, Butler."

"Hollister from Southwest. That's my helper, Virgil Fox." The Fox frowned.

Case glanced at his watch. "We've only been here about thirty minutes. Haven't touched anything. Just been baby-sitting the body."

Hollister was looking around the room as the detective spoke.

"The suspect was already gone when we got here," Case went on. "Understand he was a cop from Southwest."

"Uh huh," Hollister agreed. "That's what they tell us."

Fox moved by Hollister and around to the window, watching where he walked. Avoiding a partial bloody footprint. Pulling the curtain aside, he grabbed the cord; the venetian blind folded and pulled up with a soft hush, exposing the wide gap in the louvered side window.

"Thought I felt a draft," the Fox smiled.

"Fox," Hollister said, studying the window, "get these guys' names, serial numbers, and unit. Then we can cut 'em loose. I'll get on the phone and call prints, photos, and the coroner."

Hollister moved into the living room. He was relieved. He wondered if he'd ever get used to the sight of a lifeless body. There was some strange mysterious fascination about them. He didn't really want to see them, but yet he couldn't suppress his desire to look. He wondered if he was some kind of pervert.

Some day he'd ask Fox how he felt about it. Maybe he felt the same. He hoped he did.

Case and his partner left while Hollister was still on the phone, to the photo lab. He waved his thanks to them. After finishing his calls he rejoined Fox in the bedroom.

The Fox was hanging out the gap in the louvered window, peering into the morning's darkness.

"Find anything?" Hollister asked, glancing at the body. He silently wished she were face down, or at least her eyes closed.

"Yeah," the Fox said, pulling inside, brushing dust from a sleeve.

"All the glass he took out is stacked on the ground. And if he stacked the louvers, he's a neat glove-wearing son of a bitch."

"No doubt," Hollister agreed. Then asked, "What ya think? Rape. Burglary . . . What?"

"Don't see any evidence of ransack," the Fox answered. "Looks like rape."

Hollister drew on his cigarette, then glanced at it. "Tastes shitty," he complained.

"It's the smell," the Fox said, moving to a night stand beside the bed.

"What smell?"

"Piss. . . . Urine," the Fox said, eyeing the assortment of feminine odds and ends on the night stand. Picking up an envelope: "That's what's all over the sheet." He gestured to the body. "See, her navel's still full of it."

Hollister stepped closer, looking. "Sure looks it. What ya think? Hers?"

The Fox chuckled. "Now, how in the hell is she gonna piss in her own navel?"

"Good point," Hollister smiled a boyish embarrassed grin.

The Fox, studying the envelope he picked up from the table, said, "She was Ellen Shane."

Hollister touched a lifeless foot, squeezing gently. "Hasn't been dead for long."

Hollister had the two patrol officers take the little girl to the station, as he and Fox worked at making a diagram of the apartment, the position of the body, window sizes, and room dimensions. They found the blue steel thirty-eight on top of the refrigerator, and the box of chicken on the kitchen bar.

"Think it's Wilson's?" The Fox asked, picking the gun up by the trigger guard.

Hollister shrugged as he noted where it was found on his drawing. "I'd guess it is."

"If you were gonna rip off some broad, would you take your gun off?" Fox wondered aloud.

"Pretty hard to get laid wearing a gun," Hollister smiled.

"Hard," Fox agreed, "but not impossible."

"You'd know," Hollister said, studying his drawing, satisfied it was complete. He laid the notebook on the kitchen bar.

"Hey," a voice called from the shattered front door. "Anybody home?"

Hollister looked to the door from the kitchen. It was the photo lab. The man was graying, looked tired; his suit hung loose on his long angular frame. He had camera in hand, an equipment bag around his neck. "Come on in," Hollister answered.

"Wilks, from the photo lab," he said, pulling the bag from around his neck, looking with a question before setting it on the kitchen bar.

"It's okay," Hollister said. The man slid the bag onto the bar.

Hollister didn't feel like introducing himself. What the hell did it matter who he was, or who this sleepy-looking cameraman was. All he wanted to do was take his pictures and get back to Parker Center. He didn't care that some good-looking young broad got raped and murdered. All he cared about was how this had screwed up his night. He'd have something to tell his wife in the morning, Hollister thought.

The Fox spoke. "I'm Fox, this is Hollister. We're from Southwest Dicks'."

Wilks extended a hand to Fox. Hollister walked away. Not really sure why he was angry. Maybe if he had laid Janice? If he got off by five, he'd go see her, he decided. She enjoyed being awakened by him.

He hoped that would last.

"Let's start in the bedroom," he heard the Fox saying. "Then we'll work our way through the rest. Catch the outside last."

Hollister went back to his notebook on the bar. Pretending to recheck it.

"Whew," he heard Wilks say from the bedroom. "Real messy one." Then he laughed loudly. "Look. . . . Look, there's a fly on her cunt. Want an eight by ten of that?"

It was too much. Hollister couldn't take it. A warm flush of anger swept over his ears as he rushed for the bedroom.

The Fox saw Hollister coming, but couldn't reach him before he had grabbed the cameraman and driven him backwards into the wall. "Lee," he cried as Hollister pushed on Wilks's neck. A small cry came from Wilks's throat.

"Lee," Fox pleaded, grabbing his arms from behind. "Come on, Lee, let 'em go."

"I'm gonna kick his ignorant ass. He's a fucking creep, and I'm gonna kick his ass."

The Fox pulled harder. Wilks pushed, thrashing his arms and camera. "Come on, Lee. You dumb son of a bitch," Fox growled. "Think of what the fuck you're doing."

Hollister let go. Wilks moved away along the wall, massaging his throat. "You saw that," he gasped. "He assaulted me. . . . He's crazy."

"You're lucky I didn't kill you, you son of a bitch," Hollister breathed.

"You won't get away with this," Wilks answered with a pointed finger.

"Shut up, man," the Fox snapped. Then taking Hollister by the arm: "Come on, Lee. Go outside and have a smoke, okay?"

His hands shook as he lit the cigarette. It tasted bitter, but the fresh air helped. Janice wanted him to quit smoking; he told himself he would soon. A few curious neighbors still stood in a tight cluster a few doors away. He studied them as he drew on the cigarette. "Hey, buzzards," he called silently. "You wanna come look? Wanna see death up close? You wanna see what all the little muscles and cords in a slashed throat look like?"

He was taking a final drag on his cigarette when he recognized the figure of Captain Slack enter the courtyard's shadows. Lieutenant Purington was with him.

Hollister tossed away the butt as they reached him. Damn it, he wished he hadn't forgotten his tie.

"Good morning, gentlemen," he said.

"Hollister," the captain nodded, eyeing the open shirt collar. Hollister took mental note. He knew nothing more would be said of it.

The captain glanced inside as a flash from the photographer's camera cast hard shadows across the dim courtyard for a split second. "What have we got other than an officer as a suspect?" he asked.

"Not much yet," Hollister explained. "The victim's a female Negro, I'd guess twenty-five to twenty-eight. Looks like she lived here along with her kid, maybe two or three. . . . No male clothing in the apartment, no shaving gear, you know?"

The captain and lieutenant nodded.

Hollister went on. "Our bad guy, whomever he is, used a sharp blade. Ear to ear on the neck, and both wrists. She's nude on the bed now. Face up, but we don't know if that's where she was. We'll have to talk to Wilson, and the seven other cops that were in here after the help call came out."

"Not gonna help you with prints, is it?" the captain snorted, with a frown.

"No," Hollister agreed, "but we're still gonna give it a go. One good one would do it. Prints should be here pretty soon."

"Motive," Captain Slack asked, digging out a smoke, offering one to Hollister. "No thanks," Hollister said. "I'd guess rape. She was a good-lookin' broad. Young, nice body."

"You talked to the officer yet?" the captain said, exhaling a puff of smoke, shaking out his match.

"No," Hollister answered. "We thought it would be best to get the picture out here first. That way we'd know a bit more about what we're talking about."

"Anything point at Wilson yet?" Lieutenant Purington asked as he peered into the apartment. The camera's flash washed them in intense light every minute or so as Fox directed Wilks around inside.

Hollister considered it for a moment. "No . . . nothing more than his being here."

"How do you explain that?" Captain Slack asked, glancing at the group of waiting neighbors.

"Well, we found a two-inch thirty-eight on top of the refrigerator and a box of chicken sitting on the bar. It looks like Wilson came in, took off his gun, set down the chicken, and then discovered the body."

"Could he have just as well come in, took off the gun, set down the chicken, and killed her?"

"No," Hollister disagreed. "Our bad guy took the louvers out of the bedroom window and climbed in. At least, that's the way it looks. Not likely Wilson climbed in with a box of chicken."

"Maybe she brought in the chicken?" Captain Slack suggested.

"Don't think so," Hollister shook his head. "She wouldn't have let it sit on the bar."

"Maybe she didn't get a chance to eat it," Purington added.

"Don't agree," Hollister said. "Her clothes are stacked neatly on a chair in the bedroom. Not torn or anything. Looks like she took 'em off."

"Why do you think rape?" the captain asked.

"No ransack. Doesn't look like anything's missing, and the suspect pissed all over the body."

"Pissed on her!" Slack said with distaste, pulling the cigarette from his mouth.

"Right, pissed on her."

"Jesus Christ!"

"Why?" Purington asked.

"I'll ask 'em that when we find him, Lieutenant."

Captain Slack took a final drag on his cigarette, dropped it on the cement, and ground it out with a heel. "Wilson, unlike anyone else, being a policeman is going to be guilty until proven innocent. Not having enough evidence to convict him isn't gonna do it. If he's dirty, let's run him up the goddamned flagpole, but if he's innocent, let's prove it beyond anybody's doubt, and the only way you're gonna do that is to catch the son of a bitch that did it. Until you do get him, Wilson's gonna be dirty in the public's eye. You can bet your ass that this caper is going to be wall-to-wall news across southern California tomorrow. You're going to have a hell of a lot of people looking over your shoulder, Hollister, and they'll be there until you get this . . . this goddamned animal that likes to piss on bodies."

Hollister said nothing. He knew all this shit. Maybe if he had his tie on, the captain wouldn't have spouted all this Jack Webb bullshit. He fought a smile that the thought provoked. "Fox and I will find him," he said. What the hell else could he say. It was the answer that Slack wanted to hear.

"Couple more out here and we'll be done," the Fox said as he and Wilks moved toward the front door.

Hollister tensed. Wilks would no doubt tell Slack that he had choked and cursed him. Wilks paused in the doorway to adjust his camera settings. Hollister shifted nervously, moving aside.

"Morning," the Fox said, giving the captain and Lieutenant Purington his untiring grin.

"Fox," the captain smiled in return. Fox was wearing a tie. Hollister was sure that helped the captain's smile.

"Can we get a look inside?" Purington asked.

Fox looked to Hollister.

"Sure," he shrugged.

"Why don't you show 'em, Lee," the Fox said. "I'll help Wilks here finish up. We wanna get a couple of the glass out back and the windows."

"Okay," Hollister agreed, glancing cautiously at Wilks. Wilks showed no expression, his face relaxed.

"Ready, Wilks?" Fox asked.

"Sure," he said, patting his camera, following Fox into the shadows and around the corner of the apartment.

Hollister led Slack and Purington to the door of the bedroom. He leaned against the wall as the two men gazed into the room.

"Jesus Christ!" the captain breathed.

Purington said nothing.

A few seconds later the captain turned away. Purington followed. Hollister pushed away from the wall and joined them in the living room.

The captain looked awkward, embarrassed. He glanced about the room, struggling for something to say. "I . . . we'd better get back to the station, Tom," he said. "I've got some calls to make. Duty deputy chief's gonna want to know what's happening."

Hollister wished they'd leave. He and the Fox had shared many dead bodies, but this was the first he'd seen with the captain. The uncomfortable and awkward feeling was unnerving. It was a kind of intimacy and he didn't like it. "The sooner you go, the sooner we'll get done," he said.

Purington flashed Hollister a heated glance.

Captain Slack glanced at him. "You're right." Then to Purington: "Come on, Tom. Let's get the hell outta their road."

Hollister, not sure if he'd overstepped himself, said nothing more as the two men left. He knew he'd hear from Purington later.

Fox came in smiling. "Which one of 'em did you choke?" he kidded. "The skipper or Purington?"

Hollister grinned. "I'm sorry about that. The son of a bitch just caught me at a bad moment. What did you do? Bribe or threaten his ass to keep 'em quiet."

"I just reasoned with him," the Fox smiled, "but," he cautioned, "calm down a little. Relax."

Hollister drew in a deep breath and gave the Fox his boyish grin. "I will," he promised.

"Hollister," a voice called from the front door.

They looked. Hollister knew the man. It was Swan from latent prints. He was fiftyish, well dressed, very detective-looking, carrying a large black box. "Come on in, Swan."

Swan sat the box on the living room floor as he glanced

around the apartment. Hollister knew his interest was academic. Working Morning Watch prints, Swan, he knew, was called to the scene of nearly every homicide in the city.

"How many rooms you want done?" he asked as his visual survey continued.

"Full bore on the bedroom," Hollister said in an apologetic tone, knowing it was a difficult task. "Then, we'll be selective in the others."

"Okay," Swan agreed, reaching for the box on the floor. "Any do's or don't's in there?" he asked, glancing ahead to the bedroom.

"No," Hollister said. "We've been through it. There's a footprint on the left side of the bed, that's all."

"Uh huh, okay, I'll be careful."

"Got a gun you can take back with you," the Fox added.

"I'll get it on the way out," he said, picking up his equipment box and heading for the bedroom.

In the bathroom cabinet they found a bottle of eye medication with an eyedropper in it. The Fox washed it clean with hot water in the sink. "We can use this to collect the urine."

"Tub's still wet," Hollister said, looking at the beads of water around the drain.

The Fox shook the bottle and blew in it to dry it. "Explains why she was nude," he said, holding the bottle up to the light, studying it.

"Uh huh," Hollister agreed, looking at his reflection in the mirror. The Fox now worked at flushing the eyedropper clean. His eyes met Hollister's in the mirror. "Besides not having a tie, needing a shave, you don't look too bad."

Hollister ran a hand over his cheek and chin. "You're just jealous because you Indians don't grow beards."

The Fox smiled, shaking water from the eyedropper. "That's very white of you."

They moved back to the bedroom. Swan was kneeling beside a night stand, small brush in one hand, a jar of black powder in the other. A larger dresser, a lamp, and a variety of bottles and creams had already been dusted and were now a flat, dusty, dirty-looking black. He glanced up as the two men entered. He had his jacket off now, shirt sleeves rolled up. "Hell of a lot of prints in here," he said, preparing to lift another from the polished surface of the night stand with a strip of heavy, clear Scotch tape. "It's gonna take me awhile to make 'em all."

"It's all right," Hollister shrugged. "We won't pressure you."

"Here. Hold this," the Fox said, offering the washed bottle to Hollister. He leaned over the body and carefully moved the eyedropper toward the reservoir of yellow urine in the navel's depression.

Hollister watched. The smooth brown skin of Ellen's stomach was unmoving. The Fox waved a hand at a fly that buzzed above the fluff of pubic hair.

Inserting the eyedropper into the navel, the Fox released the pressure he held on the rubber bulb. The yellow liquid quickly filled the clear glass tube. He glanced to her eyes and then smiled slightly at his stupidity. She wasn't gonna move. Her wide eyes were glazed and drying.

Hollister held the bottle near. The Fox squeezed the dropper into it. "One more should do it."

"What the hell are you two doing?" Swan asked, pausing from his dusting.

"Taking a urine specimen," the Fox answered, moving the dropper back to the navel.

"From her navel?"

"It's not hers," Hollister explained. "The crook pissed on her."

"Son of a bitch," Swan breathed. "Pissed on her, huh? Ha," he laughed. "Hell of a defense. He's thinking, he'll claim he's got a few cards missing from his deck and some pea-brained judge will commit the bastard to a mental hospital so he can be helped."

Hollister said nothing. The Fox squeezed another dropper full of urine into the bottle. "Should do it." Hollister gave the bottle to the Fox and he twisted the cap in place. Taking out a felt-tip pen, the Fox wrote "The Pisser" on the paper label and then slipped the bottle into a jacket pocket.

The two men wandered back into the kitchen. The Fox opened a cabinet door and eyed the contents. Hollister, leaning on the refrigerator, dug out his cigarettes. Squeezing the pack, he found it empty. "Son of a bitch," he complained.

"What's wrong?" the Fox asked, glancing over his shoulder.

"Why the hell don't you smoke?" Hollister said, crumpling the empty pack, throwing it to the floor.

The Fox noticed. "You okay?"

"Let's go talk to the neighbors. Somebody should have heard something," the Fox suggested.

Hollister nodded agreement.

Felton Clark and his wife were still standing in their open doorway when the two detectives walked out of apartment number eight. They looked toward the Clarks.

"You keep quiet, like I said," Felton whispered to his wife as the two men walked toward them.

"Good morning," the Fox smiled as they reached them. "My name's Investigator Fox, this is Sergeant Hollister. We're from Southwest Detectives. We're investigating a homicide. We'd like to ask you a few questions."

"I knew it," Dorease blurted, looking to her husband. "I told you, Felton. I told you."

"You told him what, ma'am?" the Fox asked.

She hesitated. "I . . . I told him . . . I told him with this many police somebody . . . somebody must'a been killed."

The Fox studied her face. She looked away. "You live right next door to—" The Fox deliberately paused, pretending to struggle for the name.

"Ellen," Dorease said. "Ellen Shane."

"Right," he smiled. "Ellen. Did you know her?"

"Not much," Felton Clark said with a shake of the head. "We both work, you know. Keep to ourselves. Don't butt in other people's affairs."

"But, you have talked with her?" the Fox suggested.

"Yeah, sure." Clark nodded. "We're friendly. But, we're married you know. She's divorced. We spoke, but she had her life and we got ours. You know?"

"How'd ya know she was divorced?"

"Ah . . . Dorease told me. Yeah, my wife told me," he answered awkwardly.

"Uh huh," the Fox said. "Did you hear or see anything unusual over there tonight?"

They answered together. "No, we were asleep," he said. "We had the TV on and couldn't hear any of the noise over there," her voice trailing away, her embarrassment obvious.

Hollister was angry.

"Which is it?" the Fox asked. "Were you asleep, or watching TV?"

There was an awkward pause. Felton Clark shifted nervously in his push-on slippers. His wife gripped his arm tighter. Her eyes pleading with him.

"You do understand, that somebody broke into Ellen's apartment, raped, and killed her," the Fox said in a slow deliberate tone.

"We didn't hear anything," Clark said without looking at him.

It was too much for Hollister. He, like the Fox, knew they were lying. "You better hope somebody hears something when he breaks into your apartment and rapes your wife," Hollister warned with sarcasm.

Dorease moved her hand to her mouth. Clark slid an arm around her shoulders. "You got no right to scare my wife like that," he shot back.

"How close to home does it have to hit for you people to get involved? A young woman's been killed. Don't you care?"

"We didn't hear nothing," Clark repeated

Hollister stepped closer, pointing a finger at Clark's face. "Mister," he grated, "I don't know why, but you're a god-damned liar. I hope you sleep well the rest of the night." He turned and walked away.

"Do you work for him?" Clark said with a sneer to the Fox.

"No," the Fox smiled. "I work for you. Good night."

They talked to six other people. Nobody had heard or seen anything. They walked back to number 8.

"Doesn't help Wilson any, does it?" the Fox said.

"No, sure as hell doesn't," Hollister agreed, then asked: "Can you figure that guy next door?"

"Clark?"

"Yeah."

"Yeah," the Fox said thoughtfully. "I understand him."

"Well?" Hollister asked.

"He knows that odds are we'll never catch the pisser. He knows that if he says he or his wife saw or heard anything, that somehow the press is going to find out and fifteen news-men will be following him around wanting a story. He's afraid the suspect will come back and rip him off. It's hap-pened before. I'll bet in three days he'll be moved."

"You know we wouldn't say shit about any wits."

"He doesn't know that, and how many times have you seen our P.R.-minded press relations officer cough up info that we had a wit, a lead, just to pacify the goddamned press? You know it happens."

Hollister's silence agreed. "But he could save Wilson's ass . . . maybe."

"He's more concerned with his own," the Fox countered. "Don't get me wrong. I don't agree with the chicken-shit son of a bitch. I just understand him. He's betting we can solve it without him."

A well-dressed middle-aged black man came into the courtyard pulling a four-wheeled chrome-railed stretcher by a long strap. He carried a small black bag. The stretcher's swivel wheels squeaked as they twisted and turned on the rough cement.

"Sergeant Hollister?" the man asked as he reached them at the door. His voice cool, unemotional.

"Yeah, I'm Hollister."

"I'm Raymond T. Simmons. Deputy coroner. I understand there's been a homicide here." His expression was sober.

Hollister couldn't believe it. He glanced to the Fox and then back to the men. "Where's Fat Bill?" Fat Bill was the round-faced overweight deputy coroner he and the Fox were used to seeing.

"If you mean Mr. Tatum, he's off work tonight with a stomach discomfort. As I said, I am also a deputy coroner, well qualified and equally experienced."

Hollister just stared at him. "A faggot. Gotta be a faggot," he silently told himself.

The Fox smiled. "We didn't think you were the Avon lady."

Deputy coroner Simmons did not return the smile. "Could we please be about the task at hand?"

"It's a girl," Hollister said with a slight grin.

Simmons's lips narrowed to a straight line. "Sergeant Hollister," he said, letting the name roll out in a slow controlled tone, "the sex of the deceased is of no interest to me. I think a personality conflict at this time is only going to make both our jobs a bit more difficult. I assure you I am competent. Whether or not you care for me is irrelevant, but I would prefer you keep your comments and opinions to yourself, at least while I'm present."

Hollister studied him for a moment. Simmons didn't look away. A fruit that didn't deny being a fruit. Plus, he made it clear he wasn't about to accept their ridicule. That made him more acceptable, at least in Hollister's opinion.

"Okay, Deputy Simmons," Hollister agreed. No more bullshit. "Come on, the body's in the bedroom."

"Lemme help you with that thing," the Fox said, grabbing the other end of the wheeled stretcher.

Swan was in the living room, kneeling next to his equipment case. Fox and the coroner squeezed by.

"Finished?" Hollister asked, pausing.

"Yeah," Swan said, wiping his hands clean with a cloth, tossing it back inside the case. "I hit out here where I thought the crook might touch." He pushed to his feet. "You know. Door knob level on the doors, bottle of cold duck there on the bar, photo album on the end table."

"How long do you think, Swan?"

"Before I can put a name on all these?"

"No," Hollister smiled. "And quit trying to get me to flatter you. I know you're good. You know where and what the crook touched in there. How long?"

Swan slipped on his jacket. "I got about nine different sets. . . . At least. I can cut that down to three or four quick possibles."

"Any from the window or louvers?"

"Yeah, couple. I'll give you a call at the station as soon as I can."

When Swan left, Hollister joined the Fox and the coroner in the bedroom.

The Fox was digging in a beige purse beside the bed as Simmons made notes on a small yellow pad. "Here's her driver's license," the Fox said, handing the license to the deputy.

The coroner's bag was sitting on the floor, open. Beside Ellen's body on the wrinkled sheets and spread lay a chromed thermometer with a long pointed shank. Hollister knew what it was.

Simmons laid his notebook on the night stand. Extending his thumb he reached and probed along Ellen's jaw and cheek with it. "We're starting to get rigor mortis here in the face and jaw," he looked up at them. "Do you have a time of death?" he asked.

"No," the Fox answered. "Body was discovered sometime after midnight."

"Uh huh," Simmons said, moving from the body's face to the shoulder and arm. Squeezing the fleshy part of her upper arm, he said, "The rigor hasn't spread here yet."

"Which means death within the past three .to five hours. Right?" the Fox suggested.

Simmons picked up his pad and added to his notes. "Generally that would be true," he agreed, "but here we have a victim who has bled considerably. That will retard rigor."

"What's your guess?" the Fox asked.

"It's damned important to a suspect we have."

Simmons put the notebook down again. Grabbing a shoulder and pushing on the hip he pushed the body onto its side. A lifeless arm swung awkwardly, folding at the elbow, and its bloody fingers touched against a gaping mouth.

"See here. Along her buttocks," Simmons said, still holding onto the shoulder to keep the body from rolling. The Fox moved to where he could see.

The buttocks were a blotchy deep purple. "That's postmortem lividity," Simmons explained. "Simply blood settling to the lowest point in the body. This begins one to two hours after death."

Simmons pushed with a finger against the discolored skin. "See, no change when I push."

"Uh huh," the Fox said. "What's that mean?"

Simmons released the shoulder. The body fell to its back. The arm at the mouth jerked and came to rest in the groin.

Simmons explained, "When I applied pressure to the buttock it didn't cause any blanching. That means the blood has clotted. She's been dead four or five hours."

Hollister glanced at his watch. It was five minutes after four. Five hours helped Wilson but four hours was marginal. "Can't you hit any closer than that?"

"I'd be guessing," Simmons shrugged, "and I'd rather not." Hollister said nothing.

"A complete autopsy will show us the degree of digestion of her stomach contents," Simmons said. "Then, if you can find out when she last ate, you'll pin down the time pretty close."

Picking up the thermometer from the surface of the bed, Simmons recorded the reading on his pad. Then holding the pointed shank in his right hand, he ran his left hand down over Ellen's rib cage below her breasts. His fingers probing expertly. Finding the spot he sought, he held it with one finger while driving the shank of the thermometer through the skin, with a sharp jab pushing it deep into her liver. A trace of blood lathered around the top of the thermometer shaft.

The Fox watched with seemingly little interest. Hollister pretended it didn't bother him either.

Knowing the coroner's task was nearly completed, he said, "Hey, Fox, I'm gonna find out who the apartment manager is and get him over here to button up this place."

Hollister walked outside. The stubble of his beard was beginning to itch. The courtyard was quiet. Most of the apartments were again dark, although he was certain not many were asleep. He wished he had a smoke. He hadn't really been able to get his mind into it this morning. Usually he would be concentrating only on the homicide and its investigation, but now his mind wandered from Janice to Carol and the kids, to last summer, next summer, how old he was, and why he couldn't remember the last time he really felt good.

A gray-haired old lady in number 12, who asked God to bless him, gave him the manager's telephone number. He walked back to number 8.

The Fox and Simmons were pulling the body, now covered with a red wool blanket and strapped into the low stretcher, out the front door. "I'm gonna help Simmons load up and I'll be back," the Fox said.

Hollister nodded.

He had let the phone ring nine times and was about to hang up when the sleepy male answered.

"Hello."

"Mr. Krentzman?"

"Yes . . . who is this?"

"This is Sergeant Hollister, Southwest Detectives, L.A.P.D., and I'm calling——"

"The police! . . . What's happened?"

"Do you own an apartment building on Montclair Avenue?"

"Yes, yes, I do."

"Well, sir, there's been a homicide here in apartment 8."

"My God . . . those people."

"Anyhow, Mr. Krentzman, the door's been broken and a window's been removed and we were wondering if you could come down and secure things."

"The door's been broken . . . and a window. I just remodeled that apartment. Don't they know those things cost money?"

"Will you come down, sir, and close the place up?" Hollister's irritation was leaking into his tone.

"I don't know. I live in west Los Angeles. That's a long drive . . . and into that neighborhood. . . . Couldn't you do . . ."

"No," Hollister said flatly. "I'm a police officer, not a carpenter. If you don't care if *these people* carry off your range or refrigerator, that's up to you."

"Now look, Sergeant. I pay taxes for police protection,

and I think it's only reasonable that you assign a couple of
men to guard my property until——"

"Look, Krentzman," Hollister snarled. "We've gotta couple
serious things to work on this morning, like a murder. Not
me, not some other policeman is gonna sit here and guard
your precious refrigerator. Now, get somebody down here."

"Yes. . . . Well, you needn't get angry, Sergeant. My son
lives much closer than me. I'll call him. I'm sure he'll come
by."

"How long will that take?"

"Perhaps twenty minutes. He lives near Wilshire. Will
someone be there to meet him? I want him to be safe."

"I'll be here."

"Well . . . fine. I would worry you understand. Him down
there with those people after they've murdered someone."

"Mr. Krentzman."

"Yes."

"I'm one of those people," he lied.

"Yes. . . . Well, what I meant by those people was . . .
was that element that even you don't respect. I certainly
didn't mean all blacks. You're different, you're a policeman.
I have respect for you."

"Thank you, Mr. Krentzman."

"Get a hold of someone?" the Fox asked, returning.

"Yeah," Hollister answered. "He'll be here in about twenty
minutes."

"Well," the Fox said, "let's hit the bedroom."

"Be with you as soon as I take a leak."

Standing in the small, girlish, perfumed bathroom, reliev-
ing himself, Hollister found the pack of Silva Thins on the
top of the bowl. Finishing, he zipped up and picked up the
pack. They were much milder than he was used to, but it
was a smoke.

The Fox was balling up the bloody sheets and spread.
"Didn't find anything else in here that would help us," he
said. "Went over it ceiling to floor."

"Okay, I'll hit the living room and kitchen."

In a kitchen drawer Hollister found the divorce papers.
He read them. Ellen Shane, formerly Ellen Dukes, had
sought the divorce from Jefferson Davis Shane. "Maybe a
clue," he thought, stuffing the papers into a pocket.

Next to the telephone he found her address book. He
opened it to the S's. Mrs. Bertha Shane, twelve-o-six West
Thirty-eighth Place, 296-0976, mother-in-law, grandmother

he guessed. Jeff Shane, 727-4471, no address. She didn't care what the address was, he concluded. Had to be her ex. They would take the address book too.

Thumbing through the photo album, he found a picture of Ellen, a baby, and a man he guessed would be Jefferson. They were sitting on the floor in front of a Christmas tree, surrounded by gifts. On the margin was written: Jeff, Dee Dee, and me. Christmas 1970. The photo album would go.

It was nearly five o'clock when the owner's thirty-year-old son arrived. They told him what the situation was and explained that they wanted the apartment undisturbed until further notice.

He promised it would be. In twenty minutes he had the louvered window repaired and the shattered door patched with a piece of plywood.

Hollister and the Fox plastered the windows and doors with evidence seals, thanked young Krentzman, and left. Felton Clark in apartment 9 watched from his darkened kitchen as the two detectives walked from the courtyard. The black one carrying a bundle of sheets, the other, several books. He was worried.

Hollister was in the car behind the wheel. The Fox slammed the trunk lid closed, after throwing in the sheets. "Wait a minute," he called to Hollister.

"What?"

"Wanna get a few license numbers," the Fox said, walking to the driver's side. "Who knows, maybe this crazy bastard has still got his ride parked here."

"Could be," Hollister agreed.

The Fox walked up and down the dark street for a half block on each side. He recorded twelve license numbers in his notebook.

Hollister slouched behind the steering wheel, halfway through another cigarette, watching for the Fox with interest. He was sharp. He hadn't thought of the possibility that the pisser's car might still be there. That is, if he came in a car. He yawned, then glanced at his watch. It was five thirty-five. The morning sky was a chalky gray light. He took a final drag on his cigarette as Fox slid in the other side. "Fun's over. Let's go to work."

Hollister twisted the key and the car growled to life. "What number is this?" His tone was matter of fact.

"Number?" Fox questioned with a yawn, relaxing in the seat.

"Homicides. . . . How many we handled this year?"

Fox thought for a moment. "Seventeen, I think."

"You know," Hollister said, shaking his head, "I can't remember most of them."

Fox studied him for a moment in the car's half light. "Why would you want to?" His interest was sincere.

"Seems like I should . . . or we should." Hollister shrugged.

"Just bodies," Fox said, searching for a comfortable spot in the seat.

"They were people," Hollister countered, slowing for a stop sign.

"All people become bodies," Fox said, resting his head on the back of the seat. "Sooner or later."

"What do you think when you see one?" Hollister questioned.

"Who killed it," Fox answered quickly.

"Is that all?"

"Uh huh."

"I sometimes wonder what they were like alive," Hollister offered.

"I wonder why someone wanted them dead," Fox answered.

"You're full of shit," Hollister snapped. "You get that answer from watching Hawaii Five-O."

The Fox straightened in the seat. "Okay," he said, looking to Hollister. "I'll level with you. I'm scared of death. I'd like to believe in all that God crap about heaven and hell, but after seeing how one human can rip apart another, while our loving God watches over all . . . well, it's a crock of shit. There ain't no God. Death hurts and it's goddamned final, and there isn't shit after it. That's why I think motherfuckers that kill folks should be in jail." He relaxed in his seat again. "I once gave it some hard thought . . . you know . . . about who we are, what we're doing, and the thought came to me that maybe we chase those that kill so we won't become the killed. Chase death so he can't chase us. You know?"

Hollister didn't answer.

They were quiet the rest of their ride back to the station. The streets were starting to fill with early morning traffic. A variety of milk, bread, and fresh produce trucks wormed their way over the streets, others crowded the corner donut shops as the drivers pushed down the sweet stale pastries and hot coffee.

"Ah, sunrise in the big city," the Fox sighed. "Who knows what this day holds as the first rays of sun sift through the haze of dawn and wake the sleeping giant."

Hollister glanced at him. "When's your vacation?"

"Why?"

"Cause you're going bug fuck."

The Fox laughed. "I always get philosophical at dawn."

"Is that what that was?"

"Sure."

Hollister stopped at the gate at the west end of the station, after turning onto LaSalle Avenue. The officer working station security walked to them. He looked red-eyed and tired.

Hollister glanced at his name tag. "You been here all night, Tate?"

"Yes, sir," the officer yawned. "And, who knows how many angry militants bent on destroying this fascist establishment were turned away by the presence of this ever-ready sentinel in blue?"

"Jesus Christ," Hollister complained, "are you related to Fox?"

"Who?"

"Forget it. Do you know Dave Wilson from P.M.'s?"

"Yeah," Tate answered, his young face turning sober as he leaned on the car. "I know 'em, and I know what you're gonna ask. I saw him. He left a little after midnight in his 240Z. It's a pretty yellow. He waved to me."

"You're sure about that? It's important," the Fox added.

"I know," Tate nodded. "Hell, everybody knows. There's more brass here tonight than I've ever seen, and I'm sure. He left a little after midnight."

"How about putting that on a 15.7 and sending it back to us before you get off this morning?" Hollister asked.

"My watch commander already had me do that. I gave it to Lieutenant Purington back in detectives."

"Okay, thanks, Tate."

They parked along the east side and walked to the rear of the station. Fox could see the group of polished staff cars parked near the detective entrance. "Lots of brass, like the man said."

"Just what we need," Hollister complained, once again remembering he was tieless. He considered going to his car to get it, but then decided not to.

The detective squad room, usually quiet at this hour of

the morning, was crowded. Hollister recognized about four or five of them.

Deputy Chief Spear, the South Bureau commander, stood drinking coffee, talking with Captain Slack and Commander Cockran, the Detective Bureau commander.

Lieutenant Purington, standing near the head of the room with several uniformed captains and lieutenants, saw Hollister and the Fox come in. He moved toward them.

"Lot of people interested, huh?" the Fox said, surveying the group.

Hollister nodded his agreement.

"Come on," Purington said, reaching them. "I'll buy you a coffee."

They walked down the polished hall in the rear of the station, past the girls in records, the patrol watch commander's windowed office, the jail and into the coffee room.

Purington dug out some change and dropped it into the machine. "Learn anything more out there?" he asked.

"Cream and sugar," Hollister said. Purington pushed the button.

"Victim had been dead for about four or five hours at four A.M.," the Fox said. "That's the coroner's best guess."

When they all had their coffee, they sat down at one of the tables. Purington sipped his. "Four hours doesn't help Wilson much, does it?"

"Wilson didn't do it," the Fox said, staring into his coffee.

"I know," Purington agreed.

Hollister dug out one of the Silva Thins.

Lighting it up, he asked, "What changed your mind, Tom?"

"Well, anyone who thinks Wilson did it only has to listen to the tape from Communications. Wilson called at twelve thirty-three. He was hysterical, crying that someone had killed Ellen. Wait till you hear it," Purington said, shaking his head. "It'll give you a chill."

"How's he doing?" the Fox asked.

"I've checked on him a couple times. Got him a coffee but he hasn't touched it. He's just sittin' in there staring at the floor. He looks completely washed out."

"Where's the kid?" Hollister asked, taking a deep drink of his coffee.

"Asleep in the cot room. A patrol cop's with her."

"We'll have to call someone in the family to come get her," the Fox suggested.

"Got her dad's phone number in an address book we

brought back," Hollister said. "We'll release her to him, if he's not our suspect."

"Think he could be?" Purington asked.

"Uh huh."

"Rape his own wife?" the lieutenant added.

"Ex-wife," the Fox said.

"You know," Purington said, running a hand back over his short black hair, "about three years ago. Yeah. . . . It was in seventy, I think. We had a hot prowl rapist like this. He hit twice in Wilshire Division, once in Southwest. Stryker and West worked on it then. The son of a bitch never hit again before Stryker was killed, and before that they didn't have clue one. West will be in at eight. Might be worth your while to talk to 'em."

Hollister pushed up from the table. "I think Fox should talk to Wilson and we'd better tape it. I'll start interviewing the patrol cops that were at the scene. That's gonna take awhile."

"It's been done," Purington said. "And don't worry. I did it right. I used to be a policeman myself. The reports are typed and on your desk."

Hollister turned to walk from the coffee room.

"Hey, Hollister," Purington called. "Where in the hell's your tie?"

"I got behind in the payments and it was repossessed."

The Fox eased open the door to the interview room. Wilson, slouched in one of the two chairs at the small wooden table, digging at one thumb nail with another, didn't look up.

Closing the door behind him, the Fox slid into the chair across from Wilson. As Wilson looked up, Fox could see that his eyes were red and swollen.

The Fox sat quietly for a moment and then folded his hands on the table in front of him. "Dave, my name's Virgil Fox. My partner and I have been assigned to the case."

Wilson said nothing. His brown face expressionless. Breathing shallow, controlled.

"Before we talk, Dave," Fox said in a warm yet firm tone, "I have to do something you'll find painful, but it's necessary. You have the right to remain silent. If you give up the right to remain silent anything you say can and will be used against you in a court of law. You have the right to speak with an attorney and to have the attorney present during questioning. If you so desire and cannot afford one, an attorney will be appointed for you without charge before

questioning. Do you understand each of these rights I've explained to you?"

Wilson showed no sign of acknowledgment.

The Fox studied him. Waiting. After a long moment:
"Okay, nigger." The Fox growled. "You stuck your head in
the sand. Don't worry about us catching this motherfucker
that ripped off your woman. You just sit in here and pity
your own black ass." He pushed his chair back about to get
up.

Wilson quickly grabbed Fox's arm. "Wait, I'll talk."

The Fox adjusted his chair. "Okay . . . but no bullshit. I
know you're hurting. And I'm sorry about that, brother, but
you're not just some dude off the street, you're the man.
Somebody got a piece of you. Now, do you understand your
rights?"

"Yeah," Wilson seemed almost to laugh. "I'll talk to you
and I don't want an attorney." He looked up at the Fox.
"Never thought I'd ever have to say that. . . . You know?"

"I know," the Fox nodded.

"Now, why don't you start with the time you left the station and follow on through."

The Fox listened as Dave took him step by step through
his actions from the time he got off duty until the moment he
found Ellen's body. They went over it time and time again.
The Fox prying for details, times, places, over and over
again. Hollister sat in the cramped dim tape room monitor-
ing the conversation and occasionally making a note or two
on a yellow pad.

After ninety minutes the Fox was once again taking Dave
back to when he arrived on Montclair Avenue. "How about
when you parked, man," the Fox asked. "Did you see anything then?"

"No . . . I didn't see anyone. Nobody . . ." He paused
momentarily. "Wait a minute. There was a white VW when
I pulled up. I took his spot.

"He sat high in the seat. Musta been a tall dude. Looked
like he had on a knit cap. Pulled out and left. I took his
spot."

"You know the year? The license?"

"No . . . No," he said shaking his head. "Then it was just
a car pulling out."

"I think that's enough for now, Dave," the Fox said. "I'll
get somebody to give you a ride home."

Wilson shifted and looked up at him. Shaking his head he

said, "Lemme get a coffee. I don't wanna go home yet. Not just yet. I'll catch a ride with one of the guys from Morning Watch."

"Okay," the Fox agreed. "But there's going to be a lot of people wanting to hear your story. I want you to sit on it. Think of it, and if you come up with anything call me. I'll be here all day. I'll talk with you again later."

Wilson nodded. "Can I sit here for a few minutes?"

"Sure," the Fox said, pushing out of his chair. He patted Wilson on the shoulder and left the room, leaving the door half open.

Hollister was sitting with Captain Slack at their desk. At another table a handcuffed youth sat across from two patrol officers working on reports. The crowd was gone. "Where'd everybody go?"

"Bed or breakfast, if they had any brains. It's almost seven now," Captain Slack said. "How's Wilson feeling?"

"Pretty good, considering what he's been through. He doesn't wanna go home yet."

"Learn anything?" Hollister said, leaning back in his chair.

"Maybe," the Fox sat down on the top of a desk, next to theirs. "He saw a VW pull out as he got there. Thinks it was white. Don't know what year. Remembers the driver as tall, with a knit cap."

"What?" Hollister said, straightening in his chair.

"I said——"

"I heard, I heard," Hollister said, grabbing the photo album, opening it up. He thumbed through it hurriedly.

"Here, look at this," Hollister said. The others crowded around him. In the small snapshot a tall, slender black man stood smiling, with his elbow resting on top of a white VW sedan. On the margin of the picture was written "Jeffrey."

"I'll be damned," the Fox smiled.

"Do you know where he's at?" the captain asked.

"We've got his phone number," Hollister said.

"Who is he?" Purington asked.

"Her ex," the Fox smiled. "And the son of a bitch has got a white VW."

"And Wilson saw a white VW leaving," Purington said.

"Makes him a suspect, doesn't it," Hollister breathed, studying the picture.

"Best we have," the captain said. "Let's get him outta bed."

Hollister picked up the phone and pushed a button for an outside line.

Dave Wilson pulled open the door to the interview room and walked out. They fell silent as Wilson moved along the west wall and into the rear hallway. He said nothing.

"Think he heard?" Purington asked, watching Wilson walk down the long hall.

"I doubt it," the Fox said.

Hollister dialed information. "Operator, do you have a listing for a Jefferson Davis Shane?" After a few seconds he penciled out the number on a pad in front of him. "What address do you show for him?" He added the address below the number.

"Give it to me," Captain Slack said. "I'll get Lieutenant Bowen to have a couple of his units pick 'em up. Unless you wanna go get 'em."

Hollister glanced to the Fox. The Fox shrugged. "Fine," Hollister agreed. "Here, take the picture too."

The captain and Purington with the address and picture walked down the hall to the patrol watch commander's office.

The Fox sat down at the desk across from Hollister. "You look tired, officer," the Fox smiled at him.

Hollister lit up the last of the Silva Thins. "Tired, hungry, horny, and tieless."

"I'm different," the Fox said.

"Just a shade," Hollister smiled.

"No," the Fox chuckled. "I mean other than that."

"How?"

"I've got a tie."

Jefferson Davis Shane sat up sharply in the bed. The pounding on the door continued. Swinging his feet to the floor he walked cautiously to the living room dressed only in his shorts. "Who is it?" he asked in a frightened tone.

"Police officers. Open the door."

"Wait a minute," he turned and darted for the kitchen.

"Open the door," the voice outside demanded.

Jerking open a kitchen cabinet, Shane dug wildly through a pile of dishes and pots. Several fell crashing to the floor. Finding the several wax-paper lids of marijuana he sought, he grabbed them from the shelf and raced for the bathroom.

He was crossing the living room when the door, with a loud bang, swung in, sending splinters of wood and plaster flying across the room.

"Freeze," a voice screamed at him. Glancing back over his shoulder he saw the barrel of the gray shotgun aimed at his back by a uniformed officer. He stopped. Dropping the packages to the floor.

"Put your hands on the wall."

Dave Wilson was feeling better. Several of his buddies from the Morning Watch had drifted into the coffee room and were sharing coffee and war stories. They knew what had happened, but there was no talk of it.

Four uniformed officers, with a handcuffed man, came in the rear door adjacent to the coffee room. The man, tall and slender, complained vigorously. "You people kick in my door, point guns at me, just because some detective wants to talk to me. You people are in a lot of trouble. I know my rights and you're all gonna pay."

"The detectives will tell you what it's all about, Shane," one of the officers said as they moved down the hallway.

Wilson heard the name and knew who he must be. The voices of the men at the table became distant. Blood pounded in his ears and his eyes narrowed.

"You okay, Dave?" one of the three officers with him asked. He didn't answer.

"Abbott," another suggested, watching Wilson. "Go get Lieutenant Bowen."

The officer pushed away from the table and was standing up when Dave grabbed the four-inch thirty-eight from his holster and bolted into the hallway.

"Dave, stop."

"Wilson, don't."

"Stop him!"

A roaring buzzing in his ears drowned out the shouts behind him in the hallway. With gun in hand he raced for the detective bureau.

Jefferson Davis Shane had just been set down in a chair across the desk from Hollister, a defiant look on his face. Fox stood with arms folded nearby.

Captain Slack was on the telephone at the head of the room. Purington sat nearby working on a coffee, feet propped up.

The four patrol officers were milling toward the door. Joking, laughing, pleased with the excitement of kicking in a door.

Hollister looked to the hallway when he heard the shouts. The Fox unfolded his arms.

Wilson burst into the room. The officers chasing, shouting from behind.

The four uniformed officers near the doorway seeing him first scattered, knocking over chairs, diving behind desks.

"My God!" Purington gasped, dropping his feet to the floor.

"Wilson, don't!" the Fox shouted.

Dave didn't hear, he didn't see anyone, only Jefferson Davis Shane who sat wide-eyed and frightened, staring at Wilson.

Hollister pushed over backwards, his chair crashing to the floor as he saw Wilson take aim.

The first shot sent splinters of wood and bits of paper flying from the center of the desk, its sound deafening in the squadroom. The second tore into Shane's left jaw, spraying shattered teeth and blood, twisting him violently in the chair. The third ripped low into the base of his neck, gushing blood out of his mouth, throwing him crashing to the floor.

Shane's body jerked on the tile as Wilson fired three more shots into him.

The six shots had come in rapid succession, leaving a shrill ring in the air with a blue-gray acrid haze.

But the momentary silence that followed seemed more deafening. No one moved while the police radio near the lieutenant's desk continued pouring out its never-ending string of calls.

Hollister's cheek lay against the cool tile floor. As he rolled over carefully he saw Shane facing him, eyes half open, tongue extended through a torn bleeding mouth, hands still handcuffed behind him. A puddle of urine appeared from Shane's crotch and snaked its way across the floor.

"Get him!" A voice shouted.

"Wilson, don't!"

"Stop him!" The shots came in a rush as Hollister scrambled to his feet. Wilson stood with the thirty-eight pressed at his skull. The hammer pushed back, poised, and fell forward with a quick metallic snap. The gun was empty.

One of the officers jerked the gun violently from his hand. Another grabbed Wilson around the neck from behind. "Let me die," Wilson growled, clawing savagely at the arm. The officer tightened his hold, shutting off the air. "Let me die."

Wilson's knees shook, then parted, unable to support his weight as the oxygen-starved brain slipped into unconsciousness. The officer lowered him to the floor as another snapped a handcuff over his wrists.

The Fox moved quickly to where Shane lay. "He's dead," Hollister said, brushing at his trousers, as he pushed up off the floor.

"Jesus Christ," Captain Slack said, staring over Hollister's desk at Shane's body.

Other uniformed officers began to pour into the squad room from the hall, crowding around the body and Wilson.

"All right, listen up," Lieutenant Purington said, eyeing the group. "If you weren't in here when the shooting went down, get out. We've got enough confusion already."

"You," Hollister said, taking a uniformed officer by the arm and pointing to the hall door. "Cover that door and don't let anyone else in here. No one!"

To another: "You take the door at the front desk."

"I never saw anybody killed before," the blond-haired officer muttered, his voice barely audible.

"Just cover the door like I told you," Hollister added, pulling at him.

Wilson stirred on the floor, pulling at the handcuffs that held his arms behind his back.

The Fox looked at him, then to the officers standing over him. "Take 'em into one of the interrogation rooms."

They nodded. One handing the thirty-eight to Fox. Then the two lifted Wilson gently to his feet. The circle of officers moved back. Wilson's usually square shoulders were hunched forward, his head low.

"Come on," Hollister said in a loud voice, "you heard the lieutenant. Let's move it out."

As Purington and Hollister moved the crowd of curious out of the squad room, Captain Slack walked stiff-legged to one of the lieutenant's desks along the wall and sank into a chair. Having a policeman a suspect in a homicide had created enough of a furor. Now he was no longer a suspect. Now he had shot and killed a handcuffed suspect in custody.

The Fox, hanging up one of the phones, walked to where Hollister stood, near the hall door. Purington joined them. "I got an ambulance on the way," the Fox said. "Called the coroner too."

"God damn," Purington whispered, wiping his face. Hollister and the Fox looked at him; the lieutenant was visibly shaken. "God damn, how did we let it happen?"

"Did you notice," Hollister said, glancing toward the body,

"there were eight of us in here? We all have guns. Nobody pulled one."

"It all happened too fast," Fox suggested.

"When did you ever see a slow shooting?" Hollister replied.

"Well, the really bad thing is that we lost a cop tonight, a good one," the Fox answered.

Captain Slack hung up wearily after calling Investigative Headquarters Division to ask for the officer-involved shooting team from robbery-homicide, the special problem unit from internal affairs, and the duty deputy chief. He pushed away from the desk and walked in a wide circle through the rows of desks to where Hollister and the others stood, never looking at the body.

"You know," he paused to light a cigarette. Hollister noticed the captain's hand tremble. "It's nights like this I wish the hell I'd joined the fire department." He took a long look at the body. "When I made the notifications the duty deputy chief nearly hit the ceiling. Couldn't believe we let it happen. He's coming down."

Hollister studied the cluster of uniformed patrol officers at the rear of the squad room. There were six of them. They were talking quietly, as if expected to, standing in a tight group. "Fox," he said, "why don't you take those people across the hall to narcotics. There's no one in there now. They can relax in there, until someone gets their statements."

"Take the ones on the doors too," Purington added. "But leave the two with Wilson."

The Fox nodded. "The gun's on the desk over there. I think it's empty."

"I'll call Ellen's mother," Hollister said. "Get her to come pick up the kid. Then I'll be over."

Outside the whine of a siren grew near. "Should be our ambulance," the Fox said, moving toward the patrol officers. "Come on, fellas. I'll let you buy me a cup of coffee."

Captain Slack took a final drag on his cigarette, dropped it to the floor and ground it out. "There's a team on the way from Robbery-Homicide. They're going to have to handle this since we're all wits." He massaged his chin. "It's going to be a long day."

Hollister walked back to his desk and picked up Ellen's address book. When he shook it, several wood splinters fell from its cover to the desk top. He studied the jagged hole

Wilson's first shot had torn in the desk top, then reached and pulled open the center drawer. There he saw that the flattened lead had ripped through a polaroid snapshot of his wife, Carol, and the two kids. He pushed the drawer shut.

Sliding into a chair at another desk, Hollister pulled a phone to him and punched a button on one of the clear lines. Following a hunch, he opened the address book to M and found the entry, Mother, 296-6552.

Pausing for a moment, he rubbed his eyes. They were beginning to burn. Running a hand over his face, he could feel and hear the scratch of his beard. He was getting tired.

He sat quietly for a moment, one hand on the phone, as the sound of the siren they had heard approaching stoppped in what he guessed was the front of the station. He waited, deciding to light a smoke. He had got out the cigarette, lit up, and was taking a second drag when they knocked on the hall door of the squad room. He glanced at it.

Lieutenant Purington opened the door. As Hollister expected, it was the white-uniformed ambulance crew. One carrying the customary black bag. He wondered why they carried black bags. They wore white uniforms, with white shoes, but always carried black bags. He wondered if any ambulance attendant had ever carried a white bag, or a blue one, maybe even a red one. He supposed not. Ambulance attendants had no imagination, he decided, or they wouldn't be ambulance attendants.

"Just one for you to pronounce," he heard Purington tell them.

The two attendants looked to the body. "How'd it happen?" the heavier one asked.

"Shot," Purington said without explanation.

"Here . . . in the station?"

"Let us worry about how," Purington said, his irritation showing. "You just tell us what we already know."

The attendant, sensing the subject was sensitive, nodded and moved with his partner to the body. Kneeling next to it, opening their bag, one of them asked, "You wanna uncuff him for us?"

"No," Purington said. "Ain't gonna make a damn now."

The two men looked at the body, then to each other. "Why bother?" the big one said, closing the bag. The other pulled a notebook from his rear pocket. "What's the deceased's name?"

As Purington provided the ambulance attendants with the

answers they needed for their records, Hollister turned his
attention back to the phone. Crushing out his cigarette pre-
maturely in a nicotine-stained tin ashtray, he drew in a
breath and carefully dialed the number.

Waiting for a ring at the other end of the line, Hollister
looked at his watch. "Six-forty . . . Jesus Christ." On the fifth
ring a middle-aged female voice answered.

"Hello." The voice was crisp, awake, with a trace of South
in it.

"Good morning, ma'am, this is Sergeant Hollister from
Southwest Detectives, L.A.P.D. Do you have a daughter by
the name of Ellen Shane?" His tone was emotionless and
flat. The question was phrased to prompt a quick answer
without allowing her time to think.

"Yes . . . yes, she lives on Montclair."

"What's your name, ma'am?"

"Has something happened?"

"May I have your name, ma'am?"

"Mrs. Harrison . . . Mrs. Jewel Harrison . . . Could you
please——"

Hollister stopped the question. "Mrs. Harrison, could you
come down to the station? We're located at Santa Barbara
and Western. We have your granddaughter here."

"Is my . . . is Ellen there?"

"No, ma'am, she's not." Again it was short, emotionless.
He added another question: "How long will it take you to
get here?"

"About ten . . . maybe fifteen minutes. Jewel's already
gone to work, but I have a car. Could you tell me . . . ?"

"I'll explain everything when you arrive, ma'am. I don't
think it's appropriate for the telephone. I could have a car
pick you up."

"It's . . . It's bad, isn't it?" her voice was now edged with
fear. He knew he had to end it.

"I'll explain when you arrive, ma'am. Would you like a
car to pick you up?"

"No, Sergeant, I'll drive . . . I won't be long. What was
your name again?"

"Hollister . . . Sergeant Hollister. I'll be at the desk waiting
on you."

"Is Ellen okay . . . has she been in an accident?"

"Mrs. Harrison, I really can't discuss it on the phone."

"All right . . . I should call Jewel, he'd——"

"You can call him from here, ma'am."

"All right, I'll be there as soon as I can, Sergeant."

"Thank you, ma'am."

He hung up the phone carefully. She knows, he thought. He had told her without telling her. He knew from experience that mothers, more than anyone else, could sense tragedy. By the time she reached the station, she'd be prepared for the shock that was now half expected. After telling her, a granddaughter in her arms would fill the void, and demand some control. "It's a sick goddamned logic," he told himself, shaking his head slowly. A half laugh came from deep inside and chilled him as it crossed his lips.

"What's so funny?" Purington asked from behind.

"Nothing," Hollister sighed. "Nothing at all."

The station's hallways were filled with officers and conversation. The remainder of the detectives assigned to the division were beginning to arrive for the day's work, only to find their squad room locked. They mingled with the patrol officers who were about to change watch.

"What the hell happened?" a frustrated robbery detective asked, finding the squad room locked.

"Friday's been canceled due to lack of interest," a patrol officer smiled.

"Very funny."

"There's been a shooting in there," another said seriously.

"In the squad room?" the detective said with alarm.

"Yeah, Berry," another detective called from a few feet away. "It's all part of the chief's program to take crime off the streets."

A splattering of laughter rippled through the crowded hall.

"Makes it easy for homicide too," someone added. "They don't lose time driving to the scene."

A uniformed lieutenant pushed open the door to the detective reception desk. "Is the captain in there?" he asked, glancing to Slack's office.

"Yeah," Lieutenant Purington answered from behind the counter. "What do you need?"

"I've got three reporters and two camera crews in the lobby," the lieutenant complained, "and they're driving me nuts on the phone too. . . . What do I tell them?"

"How in the hell do they find out so fast?" Purington grated.

"I didn't ask," the lieutenant said with sarcasm, leaning on the counter.

The door behind the lieutenant pushed open again. Purington recognized the stout figure and quickly straightened in his chair.

"Where's the captain?" Deputy Chief Yearling asked as he pushed on through the half-door at the end of the counter.

"Good morning, sir," Purington said, and immediately regretted it. "He's in his office."

Deputy Chief Yearling walked into Slack's office and pushed the door closed. Sitting down in a chair in front of the captain's desk, he studied Slack, who returned the look from the other side.

Yearling was younger than Slack by several years. His hair was cropped short. Brown eyes set deep under heavy brows. He was the department's youngest deputy chief. He had the reputation for being a head hunter. Slack did not welcome him now.

"How in the hell did you let this happen, Captain!"

Slack rocked forward, resting his elbows on the desk. "Let's set one thing straight, Chief," he said in a near-warning tone. "I didn't let it happen, and neither did anybody else. If we could have foreseen this, we sure as hell would have stopped it. We had a very unique situation in which a patrol officer, in what I have no doubt was an insane rage, shot a suspect that had raped and killed his fiancée. I have no doubt that if you'd been here it still would have gone down the same way."

"Come off it, Captain," Yearling shot back. "You get paid to avert situations like this. This is your detective bureau and when something goes wrong, you're responsible."

"And when something goes right, who gets the credit? The goddamned bureau commander! Okay, now, it's gone wrong. Why didn't some of you supersmart, carpeted, office assholes foresee this and send out a directive on how to handle officers who have their fiancées raped and murdered?"

Yearling studied him for a moment. Slack's face reddened slightly, his jaw was set. "Watch your mouth, Captain," he warned.

"Bullshit," Slack shouted, banging his desk with a fist. "You haven't asked how the officer is. . . . You haven't asked his name. All you care about is what this is going to do to the department's image. You came down here looking for some scapegoat to throw to the wolves. Well, screw you, *sir*. We haven't got any volunteers. You want somebody's ass, you're gonna have to work for it. No one's gonna hand it to you."

"Now, you listen to me, Captain," Yearling said, straightening in his chair. "I haven't asked the officer's name because right now I don't want to know it. I don't want to see him, I don't want to know anything about him. That way it's easier to hang 'em out to dry. I can't afford the luxury of caring.

"As for looking for somebody's ass. . . . You bet I am. This isn't Chicago or New York. Shit like this shouldn't happen, and when it does, it's because someone exercised poor judgment. In Los Angeles that doesn't get pushed under the rug.

"I've listened to you run off at the mouth. You've been up all night, you're tired. You got a body in your squad room, and I understand why you're angry, but now let's take personalities out of it and get some answers. I've got to call Chief Peck by 8:00 A.M. So let's take it from the beginning and lay it out to me."

"Sergeant Hollister," a uniformed officer called from the entrance to the coffee room.

"Yeah," Hollister answered, looking up from a cup of coffee he wasn't really interested in.

"There's a Mrs. Harrison at the desk. She says you called her."

"Okay, thanks."

"Victim's mother?" the Fox asked from the other side of the crowded table.

"Uh huh," Hollister answered, looking up and down the table at the other detectives. "Mattingly," he called to one at the other end.

"What?"

"Give me your tie."

"What!"

"Let me borrow your tie."

"Why?"

"I wanna polish my shoes."

"Where's yours?"

"In my pocket. I like yours so much better. It's so breathtakingly beautiful."

Mattingly frowned but quickly undid the knot and pulled off the tie. "Take care of it. I only have two others."

Hollister stopped at a rest room in the rear hallway to put on the tie. On the third try he came up with a knot that was less than perfect. "Fuck it," he growled at the twisted knot in

the mirror. He glanced at the Fox who stood nearby waiting. "How in the hell do you do it?"

"Carefully," the Fox smiled.

"Where do you want to take her?" Hollister asked as they
moved down the hall.

"How about the community relations office, upstairs," the
Fox suggested. "Everything else is crowded."

"Sounds good," Hollister agreed. "I'll get her. You get the
people out of the office."

"Right."

Hollister crossed through the patrol watch commander's
office, where a uniformed lieutenant was on one telephone as
two other lines were ringing. His assistant, a gray-haired sergeant, with an arm full of hash marks, ignored the phones
and concentrated on a pile of reports before him.

Out in the front hallway Hollister found himself quickly
surrounded by a noisy crowd of reporters, some thrusting
microphones into his face.

"Could we have your name, detective?"

"Would you comment on the shooting here at Southwest
this morning?"

"Is it true, one of your officers went berserk, raped a woman and her child, and then shot and killed another officer here
at the station after being arrested?"

Hollister ignored the questions as he scanned the lobby
looking for Mrs. Harrison. A camera's floodlights flashed intense white.

"Did an officer shoot someone here in the station?"

"Mrs. Harrison," Hollister called, squinting as the camera
light moved around in front of him. He could hear the electric whine and the rhythmic clicking of the camera's shutter.

When a small elderly black woman wearing a floppy wide-
brimmed hat that looked too large for her, answered, Hollister pushed toward her. The reporters and camera lights
quickly focussed their attention on the woman. She pushed
up off the bench, holding her purse to her chest, looking a
little bewildered.

"Mrs. Harrison, are you the mother of the officer?"

"Did the police call you here, ma'am?"

"Yes, my granddaughter's here."

"Has she been raped?"

As Hollister reached her, he took her by the arm. "I'm
Sergeant Hollister, Mrs. Harrison."

"Has Dawn been hurt?" the woman asked in a frightened tone as the reporters encircled them.

Hollister led her toward the hall. "No, ma'am, she's fine."

"Is she here to identify the officer?" one of the reporters asked as they continued to press around them as they moved.

The woman, catching a foot in one of the microphone leads, stumbled. Hollister quickly caught her by the arm. The circle of reporters pulled back. The camera lights faded. "Sergeant," she whispered to him. "What is all this? I'm worried. Please tell me. Where is Ellen and Dawn?"

Hollister, ignoring her, turned back toward the reporters. "You people get back into the lobby or I'll personally throw you out of the station."

A well-dressed young man who looked to Hollister more like a male model than a reporter adjusted his tie, ran a hand back over his hair, and signaled the camera crew. The lights flashed on.

"Turn that off," Hollister demanded.

"Now wait a minute," the reporter said, stepping to the front of the group, and on camera. "I'm Darren Clark, Channel Three News. We are all legitimate and reputable representatives of the media and have a right to be here gathering information for broadcast."

"You wait a minute, Slick," Hollister shot back, sticking a finger in Clark's face. The reporter stiffened. "You wanna talk about rights, okay, how about her right to privacy? How about her right to not be asked a multitude of thoughtless, insulting, frightening questions? How about my right to conduct an investigation without interference . . . forget all that did you? . . . or is it more important to gather something for your nightly sell-a-thon you call a news broadcast?"

"Who's your boss, Sergeant?" Clark demanded in less than his usual forceful tone.

"You are, sir." He turned, took the woman by the arm, and moved away.

The reporters stood quietly for a moment, watching. The camera lights died quickly. "Smart son of a bitch," Darren Clark snarled.

The community relations office on the second floor was a. large spacious room whose walls were covered with posters urging community involvement. Fox noted the' aroma of freshly brewed coffee as he stepped into the office.

"Good morning, troops." The three male officers and one female were all black and dressed in mod fashion. A tall slender man about thirty years old who was holding a cup of coffee was the only one who returned his smile.

"How's Wilson?"

The Fox shrugged. He didn't know how to answer the question.

The girl twisted her chair around toward him. "Will he be booked?" she asked.

He could see her almond eyes were red and tearing. "No doubt. But he didn't know what he was doing."

"You think a jury will buy that?"

"Well, I hope so," the Fox answered. "His police career is certainly over and it's gonna take 'em a long time to gather up the pieces, but if you'd seen what that son of a bitch did to his woman you'd know why he snapped. That bastard really did a number on her." He stopped as his eyes met hers.

"You know that and I know it," the girl said with growing tension, "because we're police officers. The black community will understand it because they know there isn't any justice in the courts, and the white community will see it as just one nigger killing another one."

"Anyway", the Fox said, folding his arms and leaning back against a file cabinet, "what I come up for is, we'd like to borrow your office for a couple minutes. We wanna talk to the girls' mother and it's kinda crowded downstairs".

"Sure", the officer with the coffee assured. "We'll get outta your road".

The woman, now in tears, mopped her eyes with a tissue as Hollister led her slowly up the stairs. The uniformed officers and detectives in the hallway watch quietly.

"Who in the hell's she?" one whispered.

"Shut up!" another snapped.

The Fox moved a chair from behind one of the desks as Hollister closed the door. She sat down. "Would you like a coffee, Ma'am"?

"No . . . No, thank you", she sniffed through the tissue.

Hollister pulled a chair near and sat down, leaning his elbows on his knees. The Fox sat down on the edge of a desk.

"Mrs. Harrison," Hollister began, interweaving his fingers, glancing to her, then to the floor. "I'm afraid the news of Ellen is not good."

She tightened the grip on a tissue, leaning forward until her face was buried against her knees. Hollister shifted nervously in his chair. He wished she'd cry, but the only sound in the room was the perking coffeepot.

Straightening in his chair, Hollister pulled out his cigarettes so that he had something to do with his hands until
she moved. He glanced at the Fox, who caught his look,
shrugged, and then spoke. "Mrs. Harrison, we have your
granddaughter here. She's fine." She looked up. Her eyes
were red and tearing, a few strands of gray hair clung to her
wet cheek.

"Will I be able to see her?"

"Of course. You can take her home with you."

"Oh, God . . . My poor Ellen . . . My poor baby."

"Mrs. Harrison," Hollister asked as she lowered her head
again, "do you know anyone that has threatened your daughter, or may have wanted to harm her?"

"No." She shook her head without looking up. "No one.
Ellen was a beautiful girl. Everyone liked her."

"When's the last time you talked with her?"

She thought for a moment. "Yesterday . . . Yesterday before she went to work."

"Everything seem all right then?"

"Yes, she . . . she was going to come over Saturday morning. Her dad was going to look at her car. The battery's been
going dead on it."

"She hasn't had any problems with anyone you know of?"

"No . . . No one."

"How about her ex-husband?"

"She hasn't mentioned Jeffrey in weeks," she sobbed.

"Did he ever give her a bad time?"

"Just threats."

"What kind of threats, ma'am?"

"Well . . ." she mopped an eye, "he said he was going to
take Dawn and run away with her."

"Is that all?"

"That's all she ever told me."

"Can you think of anything else?"

She sniffed. "No, that's all . . . Oh, wait a minute. Once,
about two months ago, he took her car. My husband went
and got it back. Jewel told him never to go near her or Dawn
again or he'd beat him to a pulp. Do you think he did this?"

"We don't know, ma'am." He twisted and ground out his
cigarette in an ashtray on the desk behind him.

"Does Jeffrey still have his white VW?" the Fox asked.

"No," she answered. "It was repossessed several months
ago. That's why he took her car."

Suddenly Hollister felt very tired, empty. "Mrs. Harrison,"

he said, hoping it wasn't all a tragic error, "do you know if Jeffrey has a car now?"

"I just don't know," she sobbed.

"Ellen ever mention Dave Wilson to you, Mrs. Harrison?" the Fox asked.

"David, yes. He's an officer you know. We've had them over to dinner several times. Do you know him?"

"Yeah, we know 'em," the Fox smiled.

Hollister pressed forward. "Do you think your former son-in-law could?"

"I don't think . . . I mean, oh, I just don't know. I don't know how anyone could. How could anyone? . . . Why Ellen? . . . What did . . ." She couldn't go on.

The Fox pushed off the desk. "Mrs. Harrison, would you like to see Dawn?"

"Yes," she said, inhaling deeply and straightening in the chair, as if to prove she was in control. "We'll take good care of her."

"Fine," the Fox smiled, moving toward the door. "I'll get her."

Hollister watched him, wondering how in the hell he did it. The Fox still looked fresh and bright-eyed while he felt like a soiled towel, unshaven and tired.

"Sergeant," she said softly, after the Fox closed the door.

"Yeah?"

"Will Jeffrey get Dawn now that . . . ?"

"No, ma'am," he sighed. "He won't get her."

"I always thought that if one parent was . . . was dead, the other got custody."

"That's the law," he said flatly, hoping she'd drop it. He didn't want to tell her more. How could it be explained? It all made sense to him, but it was too complex. He didn't want to explain now.

"Well . . . if that's the law——"

"He's dead, Mrs. Harrison," he grated, looking to the floor. Silently damning her.

"Jeffrey's dead!"

He didn't answer.

"My God!"

"I'm sorry, Mrs. Harrison." He didn't look at her, hoping she could take it. He wished he could just go home, lie down, and sleep for twelve hours. Not in his apartment, but home, to Carol and the kids. He could remember when he first went to Homicide, working ten or twelve hours straight till he was exhausted, followed by a long raw drive home in the morning sun. Sitting on the edge of the bed, Carol used to pull off his shoes, unbutton his shirt, and kiss him good night. When he awoke it was often to the sound of the kids coming home from school in the afternoon. He wondered if she still loved him.

"Here's sleeping beauty," the Fox said, pushing through the door, carrying the sleeping child in his arms, accompanied by a black policewoman with a natural.

"Oh, the poor baby," Mrs. Harrison sobbed, stretching out her arms.

Hollister watched as the Fox gently handed the limp form to her. "Oh, Dawn . . . poor sweet Dawn," she cried, cradling her. "Gramma's gonna take real good care of you, baby. Gramma won't let anything hurt you."

Once the policewoman escorted Mrs. Harrison and her granddaughter out, Hollister walked to the coffeepot. From across the room he said, "Fox, I think we're in a world of shit."

In the hallway Lieutenant Purington intercepted Lee and told him that Deputy Chief Yearling wanted to see him about threatening some reporter in the station lobby.

Purington warned, "You had better get your story straight before we get down there or Yearling will have you working autos in Seventy-Seventh Division next month."

They worked their way through the crowded hallway to the front detective desk. As Purington knocked lightly on the captain's door, Hollister watched a photographer through the glass partition that separated the reception desk from the squad room move about taking a number of flash photographs, presumably of Shane's body, which was obscured by a desk. The familiar, most times comforting, squad room looked somehow foreign.

Inside Deputy Chief Yearling was behind Captain Slack's desk, on the telephone, while the captain sat in a chair in front. He glanced angrily up at Hollister and told him to sit down.

Hollister eased into the one remaining chair which was furthest from the deputy chief. He wished he had kept his mouth shut.

Once the deputy chief hung up, he straightened some in his chair, and Hollister noted that Purington, who was now seated next to Slack, did the same.

"Is this Hollister?" Yearling asked as he gazed at Lee.

"Yes, sir," Hollister heard Purington answer.

"Sergeant Hollister, isn't it?" Yearling questioned.

Hollister swallowed and looked up. "Yes, sir." His throat was dry.

Yearling studied him for a long moment. Hollister looked away.

"Either three members of the press are liars, Sergeant," Yearling said in a flat tone, "or you're an idiot!"

Hollister folded his hands together. "I'm no idiot," he answered in what he feared wasn't a convincing tone.

"You calling them liars?" Yearling asked, drumming his fingers on the desk top.

Hollister's eyes met his. "I have no idea what they told you, sir."

Yearling leaned into the desk. "They told me a Sergeant Hollister threatened to throw them out of the station so they couldn't gather information for their nightly sell-a-thon. Is that right, Sergeant?"

"Part of it is true, sir!"

"I understand you're the investigator in charge of the homicide on Montclair, that got this whole ball rolling."

"Yes, sir."

"All right, then, if you want to remain in charge, you go out there and apologize to those men you threatened to throw out."

Hollister was stunned.

"In fact, Sergeant," Yearling continued, "I'm ordering you to. If you refuse, I'll have to suspend you immediately, remove you from the case, have you transferred, and personally file a complaint against you."

Hollister's eyes pleaded with Slack and Purington. They said nothing. He looked back to the deputy chief. "That's it, without even listening to my side of the story."

"We've heard your side and you were wrong."

"And they never are?" Hollister replied.

"They weren't this time, and you were." Hollister sensed he wasn't going to budge.

"You weren't there. You don't know what the hell they did."

"All right, Sergeant," Yearling conceded, rocking back in his chair. "I'll give you that much. Tell me."

Hollister glared at him. Yearling didn't look away. "You son of a bitch," he thought. "No matter what I say, you're not going to change your mind. You're worried about the image."

"Well," Yearling urged.

Hollister shook his head. "I don't have anything to say."

"Then go apologize."

Lee felt embarrassed, humiliated. He wanted to take out his badge and gun, drop them on the floor, and walk out. He hated Yearling then. He wondered what the Fox would do and how much would he bend? He wanted time to think. He wanted to stay on the case.

"Either get it done, Sergeant," Yearling threatened, "or give me your badge and gun."

It wasn't a bluff. Lee had to submit. He pushed out of the chair as Yearling watched, waiting for the decision. Hollister inhaled deeply, letting the breath out through his nostrils, and moved for the door.

Yearling relaxed in the chair after Hollister closed the door behind him. "For a minute," he said with half a smile, "I thought he was going to tell me to go to hell."

"He did," Slack said. "You just didn't hear him."

"Any other time," Yearling explained, "I would have handled the complaint myself. I know he's tired, tense, frustrated. But this time we need the press on our side. I know they're a bunch of bastards sometimes . . . but like I said, either they can help us out of this mess or they can nail us to the wall, so this time we apologize."

Hollister paused outside the captain's office, behind the reception counter, to light a cigarette. His hands trembled as he held a match to the end of the Marlboro.

"Been a long night, huh, Lee?" It was a graying, slender desk officer.

"Sure as hell has, Cliff. Sure as hell has."

Moving into the front hallway, he found the group of reporters had grown some as the bizarre news story had spread.

"Is Darren Clark still here?" Hollister called out. Conversation in the group fell off sharply as they turned their attention to him. His shirt collar was sweat-stained and wrinkled and his face now dark with a full day's beard. His eyes looked tired but his jaw was set.

"Hey, Clark," a bearded reporter called over a shoulder as he eyed Hollister.

"Somebody's here to see you."

Hollister surveyed the group. Dress ranged from the faded

levis of the camera crews to the two-hundred-dollar suits of the television reporters. Some were young and looked almost unkempt, others graying, mature, neat appearing. All wore press identification cards clipped to their lapel or collar, which meant they had presented their credentials to the police commission and had undergone a thorough background investigation. He knew that wearing the I.D. card they represented the best of L.A.'s press corps, regardless of what he thought.

Clark pushed through the press of bodies. "Who called me? Oh, yes," Clark, seeing Lee, smiled with practiced charm. "Sergeant Hollister, isn't it?"

"Right," Hollister breathed, with restraint. "We met earlier."

"Well," Clark smiled, as if he knew what the script was, playing his role properly. "What can I do for you?"

Hollister glanced to the others. "I have something to say to Mr. Clark, but you gentlemen may be interested too."

They pressed in closer, pencils pulled out and readied, recorders turned on. Hollister squinted as the floodlights flashed on. Clark removed his smile, taking on a sober expression for the camera.

"I haven't slept in over twenty-four hours," Hollister began, speaking loud enough for all of them to hear, but looking only at Clark. "I've been in these clothes for nine hours now. I haven't had a chance to shave or eat. All my partner and I have had since dinner yesterday is coffee and cigarettes, and he doesn't smoke. I've seen one young woman who had been raped and cut to shreds, and I saw a man get his jaw blown away with a thirty-eight. He's dead too. About forty minutes ago I came into the lobby to get a woman who had come to the station at my request. It was my job to tell her that her daughter and son-in-law were dead. Murdered to be exact. Her motherless granddaughter will go home with her. When I came in to get her, some of you people crowded around us, asking questions. That's your job, your responsibility. My job, my responsibility was to protect her, to make her as comfortable as I could." He paused for a moment.

Clark still stood poised, face relaxed, listening. "I'm tired. I haven't had a pleasant night. You people annoyed me, and I threatened to throw you out . . . though I didn't think any of you men would have taken that remark literally." His eyes searched their faces.

They shook their heads. "No . . . Hell, no . . . It was half our fault too."

"Everybody's a little tense."

"Don't worry about it."

Clark said nothing, remaining calm, almost bored.

"Mr. Clark, here," Hollister continued, "doesn't share that opinion. Mr. Clark took it so seriously that he made a complaint to Deputy Chief Yearling."

Clark reddened slightly as a camera panned toward him. "Now wait a minute. I don't see any need to discuss this under these circumstances."

"Is it true you complained to a deputy chief?" a voice behind the lights asked.

Clark shifted nervously. "Yes! I thought it significant enough to bring to someone's attention."

"Terrific," one of the reporters muttered.

"Outstanding work, Clark," another added.

"As a result of the complaint," Hollister went on, "I'm being removed from the case and suspended from duty . . . unless I—as ordered—apologize to you people."

"That's a bunch of crap."

"Don't let it happen."

"Wait a minute, Sergeant," Clark smiled. It was a worried forced smile. "Like we said, we're all a bit tense." He glanced toward the camera lights. "Jim, could you have your men turn those off?"

"It's okay," a voice replied, "they need the practice."

Several in the group laughed. The lights stayed on.

"Okay," Clark said, turning his attention back to Hollister, trying to mask his irritation. "I think this whole matter has been blown out of proportion. The deputy chief's actions are a bit harsh." Clark continued, unable to recapture his practiced smile: "I think if I explained to him that we've thought over our complaint and—"

"Whose complaint, Clark?" a voice in the midst of the group demanded.

He was visibly shaken. "I . . . I'll talk with Deputy Chief Yearling. I'm sure he . . . I'm sure he'll reconsider his actions."

Hollister waited for a long moment, then turned and walked away.

The handcuffed Wilson was escorted out the back door of the station by two detectives. The men in the hallway, both the uniformed officers and the detectives, watched silently.

In a few brief seconds the hunched figure, sandwiched between the two detectives, was hustled into a waiting car at the rear of the station. The car door banged shut and it pulled away.

The men inside watched as the car rolled across the parking lot, the morning sun glaring from the glass and chrome of the parked cars. "It doesn't seem right that the sun is shining this morning," a voice among the detectives said.

The coroner followed next. Shane's body, wrapped tightly in a red blanket and strapped into the low-wheeled stretcher, jiggled slightly in its new-found freedom as the deputy coroner pulled it forward by a webbed strap. The men in the hall studied the lifeless form outlined by the blanket.

Hollister pushed through the crowded hallway, heading for the restroom, ignoring questions from a few curious cops. One of the station's custodians, a gentle-looking middle-aged Negro, pushed a wheeled bucket and mop slowly down the hall toward the Detective Bureau. Hollister glanced at him. His aging face was expressionless as he moved toward his unpleasant task.

Hollister pushed into the restroom, the salty stinging smell of stale urine greeting him. A huge bulk of a man moved away from the single urinal. "Hey, Lee." The round lined face smiled from beneath the visor set low over the eyes. Zipping up, he stepped aside.

"How ya do'en, Moose?" Hollister smiled, moving in next to the urinal.

The big man turned the water on in the small sink. "What the hell happened down the hall, Lee—Indians attack the fort or something?"

Hollister heard the voice but not the question. Standing and watching his stream of urine spread over the urinal's white enamel toward the soggy cigarette butts in the drain, he thought of the custodian who was probably now mopping up Shane's blood. He had worked Homicide for three years now. Average of seventy murders a year, in Southwest Division alone. The average adult has an average of twelve pints of blood. The average murder yields two, no maybe three, pints, that's . . . lemme see . . . that's two hundred and ten pints per year or an average of fifty-two quarts of spilled blood a year. Who sees the poor bastard that had to clean up the blood? Juries never do. Man, you bleed on a rug and it's a bitch. A mattress? Even worse. Fifty-two quarts a year. Dry cleaners, like undertakers, were getting rich off homicides.

"You okay?" Moose asked with a suspicious glance as he toweled his hands dry.

"Sure," Hollister answered, stepping back, zipping up.

Moose studied him carefully. "Tough one last night?" he asked.

Hollister moved to the sink. "Yeah . . . it was a tough one." He glanced in the water-spotted mirror. His hair was in need of a comb. The stubble of his beard gave his face an unwashed look. He felt very old for his thirty-six years. "Moose," he said, continuing to study his image, "did you ever think of who cleans up all the blood?"

The big man hooked a thumb inside his gun belt as he eyed his polished black shoes. "Nope," he said flatly. "And neither should you." He gave Hollister a big brotherish look. "You start thinking about shit like that and you'll go bug fuck. I taught you better when we worked Morning Watch together. Don't take this crap serious. You'll drive yourself nuts over some shit that everybody else forgets in a couple days. How in the hell do you think I've lasted so long? They're not people, they're victims. It's not blood. It's evidence. And you're not a goddamned philosopher, you're a cop. So it doesn't make a goddamn who cleans up the blood."

"Thanks, Moose," Hollister said with a tired grin.

Traffic in the halls was once again light. The sounds of ringing telephones and teletypes drifted through the corridors. The station had caught its breath and was again resuming its normal seemingly endless task of handling that which was not normal. Reaching the bottom of the stairs, he dug out a cigarette. When he and Fox finished the reports he decided he'd call his wife. That was normal.

Lieutenant Purington was sitting at his desk with the Fox. Hollister worked his way through the crowded squad room. Glancing about the room, he wondered what would happen to Los Angeles if all the phones went out. At least one out of every two men sat with a black phone pressed to the side of his head. He tried to remember the squad room as it looked several hours earlier. Wilson was there, fifteen . . . no maybe eighteen feet into the room. Fired from a raised straight-arm position. The first shot struck Shane . . . no. The first shot struck the victim in the lower left jaw. Good, still thinking like a detective. He glanced to the floor near his desk. It was clean, no blood. His eyes had to search hard to find the smooth rounded depressions the deformed lead bullets had left in the stained hard tile.

The Fox yawned as Purington got up to give Hollister his chair. Hollister was glad to see the Fox was tiring.

"I have some good news and some bad news for ya, partner." Fox spread his palms on the desk.

"The good news is that we don't have to go to the autopsy. They are gonna send down Hanson and Gilmore."

"Swell. I knew she was dead anyway."

"Now the bad news. No prints. Just the victim's, the little girl's, and Wilson's."

It was no surprise. Hollister accepted it as such. "Okay," he said calmly. "Where do we go next?"

Fox reached into a jacket pocket and retrieved the glass vial of urine. "We've got this," he said, holding it up to the light.

"A bottle of piss?" Hollister snorted.

"Sure." The Fox smiled. "All we've gotta do is find out where it came from."

"I can tell you where it came——"

"Okay . . . okay. I'll rephrase that. All we've gotta do is find the *who* it came from." He set the vial carefully on the desk.

Hollister massaged the stubble on his chin. "The autopsy may give us a couple clues too. Pubic hair, male semen. Maybe S.I.D. can help us do something with them."

The Fox nodded thoughtfully. "There's still the white car too. We can run it through the Auto F.I., on the crook too, we can make an M.O. run on him. Maybe we've got an asshole that's made a habit of pissing other places."

Hollister ran a finger carefully over the pencil-sized bullet hole on the wooden desk. A blue circle had been drawn several inches around the hole with a felt-tip pencil. The number one was noted beside it in the same color. He turned his attention back to the Fox. "The woman and the girl, are they . . .?"

"Yeah," the Fox nodded. "The old man works at the Standard station down at Santa Barbara and Vermont. Took 'em about two minutes to get here after I called."

"Lieutenant Purington, line eight-six," a speaker on the wall announced. The lieutenant moved toward his desk.

"What did the captain want?" the Fox asked after Purington was out of earshot.

"Just an up-date," Hollister lied. "For the press I guess."

"Figured," the Fox agreed. "Skipper and Yearling are talking to them now."

Captain Slack stopped in the station's second-story rest-room. He bathed his face with cold water at one of the four white sinks. It helped. For his forty-plus years he didn't feel too bad after missing a night's sleep. He was pleased with that. After toweling his face dry, he checked his image in the full-length mirror. Adjust the tie, pull up the pants a little, and hold in the stomach.

Lieutenant Purington escorted the reporters to the roll call room on the second floor. They were some twenty plus now. Los Angeles's five major television stations were represented along with an even greater number of radio and newspapermen.

The roll call room had the appearance of a large class-room—row after row of blond wooden desks with fixed swivel chairs divided by a wide aisle down the center of the polished tile floor. The walls were lined with posters, graphs, charts, and large framed maps punctured with a rainbow of colored pins.

The group of reporters spread across the room. The camera crews, with the help of their soundmen, shifted back and forth, stopping, pressing an eye to their camera's view finder, moving again, searching for the best angle. The reporters penciled out a few final questions while exchanging greetings with faces unseen since the last major news event.

Lieutenant Purington eased onto the edge of the watch commander's desk, which sat on a raised platform at the head of the room. He was pulling at his shorts, certain that somehow they had twisted into a tight knot that was stran-gling his left nut, when the camera's floodlights washed the shadows from the room. He jerked his hand away. "Just test-ing, Lieutenant," one of the crew smiled.

"Thanks," he breathed with a quick short-lived smile.

Slack pushed in the side door near the front of the room.

"Gentlemen," Purington said, ". . . if we could have your attention, we'll get started."

The cigarettes were smashed out. Equipment given a final quick check. Tape recorders snapped on. Cameras shouldered. Darren Clark brushed some lint from a trouser leg and gave his Press I.D. card on his lapel a final adjust-ment.

Lieutenant Purington moved from the desk to the side

of the room. The Captain stepped onto the platform and centered himself on the desk. Letting his weight rest against it.

The room flushed white. Slack squinted for a second. He could feel the heat from the light. It was an unnerving feeling. He cleared his throat and began. "For those of you that don't know me I'm Captain Slack. I'm the commander of Southwest Detectives. I'm going to give you a summary of this morning's events first, then I'll take a few questions."

The Captain recounted the night's events, starting with the discovery of Ellen Shane's body. He gave addresses, times, described the events, all in the familiar mechanical tone that police use when talking to reporters. He refused to give any of the victims' names, explaining that many of the next of kin were yet to be notified. He moved quickly through his description of the shooting at the station, careful not to show any emotion and speaking of it as if it were any other homicide. When he opened up for questions, a reporter asked, "Captain, were there witnesses to the shooting here in the station?"

"Yes."

"Police officers?"

"Yes, Police officers."

"Captain," the reporter added thoughtfully, "if there were police officers present and, assuming they were armed, couldn't they have prevented this tragedy?"

Slack reddened slightly. "I was one of the officers present," he admitted, taking a deep breath. "Let me explain something," he added, working hard to maintain composure. "We didn't just sit back and watch this officer kill a man. He grabbed a gun from a uniformed patrolman in the coffee room, raced down the hall, burst into the detective squad-room, and shot the man." Without realizing it his voice had raised to an excited tense pitch. He glanced at Purington. The lieutenant stood with his arms folded, staring at the floor. "The whole thing took . . . maybe eight to ten seconds," he added softly.

"Captain Slack," a graying distinguished-looking reporter asked, "would it be fair to assume that as a result of this shooting the black community will lose some of the confidence it had in the police department?"

"No doubt," Slack agreed with a nod. "We'll lose those who'll read only the headline. Black man shot to death in police station. Doesn't sound good, does it? But if they stop to think we won't lose many. The police department didn't kill this man. One enraged man did. He just happened to be a cop."

"Sir," another questioned, "do you think this officer knew what he was doing? I mean the one that shot the ex-husband?"

"Yes," Slack answered carefully. "I think he knew, but knowing what he was doing and being able to control it are two different things."

"Captain," the reporter added, "don't you think that by answering that way you're building a defense for the officer?"

Slack gave the man a hard look. "You asked the question, I answered it. If you think the answer is going to bias anyone, don't use it."

Lieutenant Purington, still standing along the wall, extended his arm and gestured to the watch on his wrist. Slack noticed. "Gentlemen, that's all the time I have for now. When we have new developments in the case we'll be in touch."

"Don't call us. We'll call you, right?" a voice in the midst of the reporters chimed in. The group laughed. Slack joined in.

"Captain."

"Yeah."

"Could we get some pictures in the squad room where the shooting occurred?"

"Tom," Slack said, glancing at Purington, "could you take care of that?"

"Right."

He never fully understood why he felt such a surge of depression after screwing one of them. Perhaps, he thought, it was because it had been so long since the last one. He was the kind of man who always had to shower after sex, but only in his own home, alone. He'd been grooming himself now for over an hour. The clothes from last night would have to go. He had them in a trash sack in the kitchen. She'd been good and he'd gotten so involved that he ruined a good pair of slacks. That angered him. The whore wasn't worth it. Well, he was going out for breakfast, he could shop for a pair of slacks afterward. Had to look good tonight; dinner with his brother and his wife at the Flying Fox at six. He splashed on some Brut, switched off the bathroom light, and headed for the door.

The jail elevator jerked to a halt on the second floor
of Parker Center. The metal doors parted and slid away. Dave
Wilson, his arms locked behind him with chromed handcuffs,
along with four detectives—two from Robbery-Homicide
and two from Internal Affairs—stepped off.

An overweight khaki-clad, graying jailor gave the group
no more than a casual glance, then returned his attention to
the naked long-haired bearded youth before him. "All right,
open your mouth. Wider. Lift your tongue, roll it around."

The young man's arms hung slack at his side. His mouth
was open and a look of desperation filled his hollow bloodshot eyes.

"Okay. Lift your balls."

The man grabbed himself and lifted.

"Okay. Turn around and bend over and spread your
cheeks."

The youth did a shaky about-face, bent forward, reached
back, and spread his buttocks.

"Smile for the camera," a sarcastic voice chuckled behind
the screened booking counter.

The jailor grimaced. "Okay, pick up your clothes . . . and
learn to wipe your ass while you're in our jail."

The long-hair gathered up his soiled and wrinkled clothes
from the gray floor.

"What have you got?" another jailor asked the men with
Wilson from behind the screened booking counter.

"Wait till he gets out of here," one of them answered.

The booking officer glanced at Wilson. His face was without expression, completely passive.

"One in," the heavy jailor called as the long-haired youth
stood holding his clothes to his naked chest facing a row of
heavy bars. Another jailor appeared on the opposite side
and unlocked the heavy gate. "Put your clothes over there
and get in the shower. Use lots of soap." The youth shuffled
through.

When the man was gone, one of the detectives leaned onto the booking counter. "My name is Parks. I'm from Robbery-Homicide, I want you to call downstairs and hold all
other bookings until we're done. I want nobody coming up
on that elevator. I don't want anybody else in the booking
area, and get me your watch commander."

The jailor studied the sober face for a moment.

"No questions," Parks added. "Just do it."

The jailor nodded and stepped to a nearby intercom box.

Keying it he called, "Hey, Reception Desk. No more fish on the elevator till I give the word. No one. The elevator's closed, and send up Lieutenant Bloom."

"Got it. Elevator's closed."

"Okay," the jailor said, giving Parks a curious look. "They got it. Lieutenant will be up."

"Uncuff him," Parks said, turning to the others. One of the men carefully unlocked and removed the handcuffs.

"You want coffee or something, Dave?" Parks asked. Wilson shook his head as he massaged his freed wrists. A uniformed lieutenant appeared at the top of the stairs outside the bars, unlocked the heavy gate, and let himself into the booking area. Removing an unlit chewed cigar stub from his mouth he said, "What's going on?"

"Parks from R.H.D., Lieutenant. Let's step over here." The two men walked to the far end of the booking area. Wilson watched. As Parks spoke, the lieutenant shook his head. Dave seemed to be studying the littered dirty floor when the lieutenant said, "Isolation won't be any problem." Wilson laughed softly. The detectives noticed and tensed. One moved carefully behind him.

"Okay, Dave," Parks said with a forced short-lived grin. "We got things squared away. We'll put you in the north wing. You'll be the only one over there, so don't worry about assholes bothering you."

Wilson nodded his appreciation.

"There's a phone over there. You can have unlimited use of it."

Dave said nothing.

Lieutenant Bloom pulled the chewed cigar from his mouth. "Wilson, you wanna step up to the counter here and empty your pockets. You know the procedure. We'll have to hold onto your property." His tone was sympathetic.

Dave stepped closer. The circle of detectives tightened around him. He glanced at them. "I'm okay . . . I really am . . . I'm not going to do anything." His voice was broken, choppy.

"Relax, guys," Parks said, more for Dave's benefit than theirs. They remained poised, ready, knowing Wilson was a smoldering fuse.

He dug in his trouser pockets and dumped the contents on the counter. Two dimes, one quarter, three pennies, a half roll of spearmint Certs, and a button off a uniform shirt.

"You carrying your badge?" Parks asked from his side.

Wilson reached into his rear pocket and removed the black-leather badge case. Unfolding it, he studied the silver and gold badge.

Parks held out an open hand. Dave folded the badge case shut and handed it to him. A tear spilled from his eye and left a wet trace on his brown cheek as it raced toward his neck. "It's a son of a bitch," he said softly, glancing at Parks. Parks nodded silent agreement.

"We'll need your wallet too," Lieutenant Bloom added.

Dave pulled out his wallet and slid it on the counter. The lieutenant opened it and pulled out the bills. "Five, ten, twenty, twenty-five, twenty-six dollars." The booking officer behind the screen typed the amount on the booking slip. The clatter of the typewriter sounded loud in the otherwise quiet room.

Pushing the bills aside, the lieutenant pulled out Wilson's driver's license and slid it beneath the screen to the booking officer behind the counter.

Parks lit up a cigarette while the officer typed the information from the license onto the booking slip. "How's your kid doing, Henry?" he said to one of the other detectives.

"Fine," Henry answered from behind Wilson. "Doc says he'll have the cast off in another week."

"Good."

The conversation died. The attempt to make small talk failed. None of them were in the mood for it. Parks, drawing heavy on his cigarette, wished he hadn't tried.

"Charge?" The man behind the screen at the typewriter asked without emotion.

"Leave all the rest of that shit blank," Parks snapped.

The booking officer looked to the lieutenant. Bloom nodded his agreement and stuck the cigar back in the corner of his mouth.

"Okay, and this is all his property," the officer said, glancing through the screen at Wilson. "Take off your belt please."

Wilson didn't move.

"He'll keep it," Parks said.

"What the hell do you mean, they're gonna take pictures," Hollister protested angrily, pushing up out of his chair.

"It'll only take five minutes," Purington explained. "You don't even have to move."

"Shit," Hollister hissed through clenched teeth. Picking up a cigarette from a tin ashtray, he walked toward the hall.

The Fox pushed aside several reports and followed.

"Take only five minutes, I promise," Purington called to them.

"Hey, Tom." A detective at the Robbery table smiled at Purington. "Could Berry and me get in the picture? He could send it home to his mom and show he's a real big-city detective."

"Go to hell," Purington growled.

Hollister and the Fox pushed out the station's rear door. Walking another thirty feet, they moved out of the station's shadow and into the bright morning sun. There was little activity in the wide parking lot. Several garage attendants worked at refueling a black-and-white near the maintenance garage, but even they were quiet.

Two pigeons darted down from the top of the station. Flaring their wings, they landed smoothly on the asphalt several feet from the two men. The smaller of the two birds immediately began picking at a discarded morsel it considered eatable. The other, larger and darker, puffed its feathery breast and neck and paraded in circles around the uncaring female, cooing and nodding.

"Must be nice to be a pigeon," Hollister said, enjoying the feel of the bright June sun on his back and neck. "Just fly around and fuck all day."

The Fox, studying the two birds, added thoughtfully, "You know, pigeons are a lot like policemen. They're constantly horny, they eat shit, bother people, and the government protects them."

Hollister took a final drag on his cigarette and flipped it at the two birds. It hit the pavement between them. Wings fluttered and they were gone. "No intercourse on city property," he called to the departing birds.

"Now you've done it," the Fox cautioned. "They're gonna find your car and do a number on it."

"You wanna get some breakfast?" Hollister asked.

"Not before I get my tie back," Mattingly said as he and his partner approached.

"Sorry," Hollister apologized. "I forgot."

"You tie that all by yourself?" Mattingly smiled, eyeing the wrinkled knot.

"It's a cheap tie," Hollister defended. "You can't tie cheap ties right." He pulled it loose and slid it from around his neck.

"Look," Mattingly said, accepting the tie, "I've got a couple more at home. If you need some I'd be——"

"No thanks," Hollister snorted.

"You people going to breakfast?" the Fox asked.

"I wish we were," Mattingly's partner answered. "Gotta go rip off a crook for attempted burglary."

"If he's home," Mattingly added.

"Have fun." The Fox smiled.

"We will. Gonna impound his VW and put 'em in jail. Introduce him to the system of justice in this great country of ours."

Hollister and Fox exchanged a glance as the two men walked away.

"Hey Collison," Hollister called. "What kind of car does your crook have?"

"A VW."

"What color?"

"White." Laying his folder on the back of a detective car, he leafed through a collection of papers. "Here it is." He held up the gray teletype and read it. "It's a nineteen sixty-eight VW sedan. Call license seven one seven, Edward, David, Sam. Registered to Raymond P. Blatts, twelve-o-two West Fifty-second Street."

"Blatts," Fox said. "Name like that, he's gotta be a crook. What did he do?"

"Attempt burglary," Mattingly answered, digging a pink crime report from among the other papers spread on the trunk lid. "Last night at about nine-thirty at thirty-five-four-teen Stocker he removed the screen from a side window and pushed it up. A German shepherd inside convinced him he had picked the wrong house. He ran back to his VW and split."

"Who got the license number?" Hollister asked.

"Neighbor of the victim," Collison said. "He heard the dog barking and growling, looked out and saw the crook running to his ride, and copied down the number. Patrol checked his pad couple times last night but couldn't find the car there."

"Who's the victim?" The Fox asked.

"Shelia Summers," Mattingly answered. "Twenty-five, twenty seven at the most. A schoolteacher. That's why she has Rin Tin Tin to protect her ass."

Collison understood what they were thinking of. "You think maybe this dude is good for your caper?"

"Wilson told me that when he got to his woman's house

last night," the Fox explained, "a white VW pulled out and tore ass out of there. He didn't think anything of it at the time. Now if this turkey of yours was looking to climb in that window and get a little forced ass, but got scared away by the dog, he wouldn't just go home with a hard-on. I think he might have kept shopping until he scored."

"Well," Mattingly invited, "get your shit together and we'll go knock on his door, say good morning. Advise him he doesn't have to talk to us, but if he does he can have six lawyers from the A.C.L.U. there and then we'll ask him if he's carrying a concealed rape tool."

Hollister looked to the Fox and, finding no objection, he said, "Go get our jackets and lock that crap in our desk. I'll get my tie out of the car."

The Fox found the detective squad room jammed with the group of reporters and cameramen. Lieutenant Purington, standing in the bright lights with several microphones held near his face, sweat glistening on his smooth boyish face, was speaking. "After the suspect was brought in for questioning he was escorted in here, to the squad room, for an interview. He had been here, at the most, a minute before the shooting occurred."

The Fox hurriedly gathered the unfinished reports, the address book, the photo album, and the vial of urine from the desk top, placing them all into a drawer.

One of the reporters on the fringe of the group, watching him, moved to the desk as the Fox locked it. "Could I ask you a question, Officer?"

"Sure." The Fox smiled with a friendly white grin as he slipped on his jacket.

"I noticed you at this desk. Does that mean you're one of the investigators assigned to this rape murder?"

"Uh huh."

"I couldn't help but notice what looked like a small bottle of urine sitting on the desk."

The Fox's smile faded. "It's not urine," he said softly, pretending to glance around the room. He motioned for the man to lean closer. "I let it set out by mistake," he whispered. "It's a substance taken from the liver of unborn female calves. It's a test program sponsored by the Sickle Cell Anemia Research Center at the U.C.L.A. School of Medicine." He glanced around again. "If the department found out I was being treated, I'd be relieved." His voice was pleading.

The reporter laid a hand on his shoulder and squeezed gently. "Good luck . . . and I didn't see a thing."

"Thank you." The Fox breathed.

The Fox got into the car and laid Lee's jacket over the back of the seat. Lee had the rear-view mirror twisted toward him as he struggled with his tie. The Fox smiled. "Screw it," Lee growled, leaving the tie in a loose wrinkled knot, with the top button of his shirt undone.

They followed Mattingly and Collison from the parking lot onto Denker Avenue and turned south toward Vernon.

"You tell Purington where we're going?" Hollister asked as they slowed for a red light.

"Didn't get a chance," the Fox answered with a yawn. "He was still playing guest host to the Ghetto Show."

The temperature had climbed to the high seventies. Following the other detective car through the light traffic, Hollister wondered what his children were doing and if they and Carol missed him. He felt an erection growing as he thought of being called out last night. Janice was so damned good. Maybe he could call her at work. She'd come home early. He knew he couldn't sleep soundly after being up so long without getting laid first. Yet if Janice couldn't get off, he'd drive home. He tried to think whether Carol would still go to bed with him. The bedroom was never a problem area for them. He didn't know how you ask a wife you hadn't touched in six months to go to bed with you, but the thought excited him. He'd call her later. He could tell from her voice on the phone if it would be worth his time to go by.

"If this crook isn't home," the Fox said, "I could call Paula, have her fix a good breakfast for us. Beat sitting in a restaurant with a bunch of civilians."

"Huh?"

"I said I'm hungry."

"Me too. We'll get something if this guy's not home."

"Thanks," the Fox smiled.

Dave Wilson had been in the barren cell now for about forty minutes. Sitting on the top bunk with his feet over the edge, he stared blankly at the frosted windows several feet from the heavy bars. Several bright shafts of sunlight sliced through the dust-laden air floating in the gray hallway. Now and then an electric lock buzzed or a metal gate clanged shut, sending an echo reverberating through the metallic cubicles.

Having pulled off his belt, he sat with it balled in his lap, his hands damp and clammy. Once he was certain he could hear no one approaching, he reached up, pushed the end of the leather belt through the heavy wire mesh covering the bulb on the ceiling, and then looped it into a wide loose knot, leaving the buckle end to form a large noose. When he jerked at it, the light blinked, dust filtered down, but it held.

Leaning forward he pushed the leather noose over his head. Pulling with both hands, he forced the loop below his chin, leaving the back of it high on the back of his head.

Then he pushed hard off the high bunk.

His one hundred and eighty pounds snapped the leather belt straight. The metal buckle sliced deep into his jaw and grated along the bone, several bones shattering with a loud crack in the base of his neck. His teeth, jammed together by the weight hanging on the noose, ripped through his tongue as he clawed at the pain instinctively, kicking his feet wildly as one of his shoes fell to the floor in the silence.

"Three-William-Fourteen to Three-William-six." The Fox, opening the glove box, picked up the mike. "Six here. Go, Fourteen."

"Three-William-six Park on Budlong just north of Five-two Street. We'll make a pass. See if his ride's there and then join you."

"Six, Roger."

Hollister eased the unmarked Plymouth to the curb, pushed the selector to park, and turned off the ignition.

Just ahead of where they parked, a female Negro clad in very brief white shorts and a revealing halter worked at watering a lawn as several children darted in and out of the hose's spray, enjoying its coolness.

"You know," the Fox said, laying his head back on the seat, propping his knees on the padded dash, "days like this my brother, Jasper, and I used to walk down to Willow Pond, strip naked, swing out on the tire swing, and drop in. Once ole Benny Watts—he musta weighed a hundred and fifty pounds when he was twelve—swung out on that damn swing and the rope snapped. Man, what a splash. He hit that water like a cannonball. When he came up, he was covered with green mud and slime. Screaming and yelling he thought he was gonna die. All he did do was run off up the hill and headed home, bare-ass naked."

Lee wondered if he had missed something in life by being

white. He believed that blacks somehow got greater physical pleasure out of life. Someday he planned to talk to the Fox about it.

Hollister watched in the rear-view mirror as the other detective car slid quietly to the curb behind them. When Mattingly and Collison climbed out, the girl in shorts spotted the two cars and twisted the nozzle of the hose to off. A few sharp words from her sent the protesting children scurrying to the house. She followed quickly.

Hollister and Fox joined Mattingly on the sidewalk. "Car's there," Mattingly said optimistically.

"It's the second house west of the corner," Collison explained, "on this side of the street. You guys take the rear, John and I will take the front."

"What if he's got a dog back there?" The Fox asked.

"I don't know," Mattingly shrugged. "I'll be at the front." They started their walk to the corner.

"What if he's got a dog, Lee?" The Fox asked Hollister, his tone apprehensive.

"We'll worry about that when we get there."

"I don't like going in the backyard if there's a dog back there. I don't care if it's big or small, meek or bad-ass. I've been bit and chewed up too many times by those K-9 bastards."

"Don't worry about it," Hollister smiled.

They rounded the corner. A heavyset black woman wrapped in a blue robe was picking a morning paper up from the lawn. She saw the four men, then turned to the house.

"That's the house," Collison said in a hushed tone. They picked up the pace, closing the distance to her.

"Ma'am," Mattingly called as she neared the front porch. The front door was standing open.

She paused, holding the folded paper to her chest. Her face was round and smooth, the once black hair was streaked with gray, her eyes suspicious.

As they crossed the strip of grass, Collison pulled out his badge case. "We're police officers, ma'am."

She looked at the silver and gold badge, then to them. "What's this about?"

"You live here at twelve-o-two?"

"Yes, I have for years." She gave them a hard look.

The Fox was listening but watching a curious neighbor across the street. He had come out of his house and walked to a car in the driveway, keys in hand. Then, noticing them, he pocketed the keys and decided to water the lawn. The Fox realized that the man knew they were the police. While he had probably known his neighbor for years, all he would do is stand and watch, content at the moment to let her solve her own problems. The Law of the Ghetto was "Don't get involved, particularly when The Man is involved."

"What's your name, ma'am?" Collison asked.

"Rosey Blatts," she shot back. "Now what's this all about?"

"Who owns the white VW?" Mattingly demanded, gesturing to the driveway. His tone wasn't friendly. Hollister guessed he didn't like her attitude either.

"Why?" She said with some defiance.

Mattingly ignored her question for one of his own: "Where's Raymond at?"

"He's in the house, but—" She stopped. She realized she was answering his question after he had ignored hers. She rested a hand on her hip. "How do you know my boy?"

"I don't know him," Mattingly answered, "but I do know that's his VW."

"Hey, Mama, what's go'en on?" a voice called from inside the open door.

The Fox, like the others, looked to the voice. They couldn't see much. He stood with a hand on the open door. He was young—twenty-three, twenty-five, the Fox guessed—but looking from the bright sunlight into the shadow of the room it was difficult to tell.

"It's okay, baby," the woman answered with the wave of a chubby hand. "Go back inside. It's okay."

The figure didn't move. Hollister called to him. "Hey, Ray, how 'ya do'en, man?"

"Gett'en by, ya know," the shadow answered without hesitation.

"Hey, man," the Fox added, "can I talk with you for a minute?" He moved casually toward the porch. Hollister followed.

The man inside didn't answer. The Fox watched him carefully. He was twenty feet from the porch, Hollister just behind him, when the woman yelled, "It's the police, baby. It's about the car."

The door slammed shut with a window-rattling crash before her voice faded away. The Fox bolted for the porch, knowing Hollister was with him. "Take the back," he heard Hollister shouting to the other two detectives. Now on the porch, both with gun in hand, they glanced at each other. In the tenth of a second they maintained eye contact it was agreed they'd kick the door. The Fox was on the left. He'd be first in. Take everything on the left. Hollister would take the right. If you hear a shot, hit the floor. No firing through walls until you knew where your partner was. Moving as one their feet smashed at the door.

The lock held but the dry hardwood around it exploded in a burst of jagged splinters, and the door swung open, banging against the wall. The metal knob buried itself in the soft plaster wall.

"Raymond," Fox shouted with his thirty-eight poised. He moved cautiously into the living room, finding it difficult to adjust his eyes in the shaded room. "Don't be a fool, man. Don't get your ass killed."

The only movement in the room was the television set. Allen Ludden, with his undying smile, handed the next Pass Word to a worried-looking contestant. The word "door" flashed on the screen for the home audience to see.

Hollister moved by him on the right and disappeared into a room Fox guessed would be a bedroom.

Fox eased through an archway into a brighter dining room. Nothing looked disturbed, no closet big enough for a man to hide in. He moved toward the kitchen.

Pausing just short of the doorway, he watched and heard some movement in another room. He inched closer toward the kitchen. Maybe he heard it first, or saw it, he wasn't sure. He tensed and drew up a forearm to shield his face instinctively. Sunlight filtering through a dining room window flashed in a sharp reflection off the glass coffeepot just before it crashed into the kitchen doorway spewing its hot steaming contents over Fox.

Fox, grimacing as the hot liquid burned the side of his face fired twice in quick succession, seeing only a shadow dive toward the back door.

A five-gallon water bottle inverted on its stand beside the kitchen door exploded in a shower of glass and water. The second shot shattered a window just above it. The thirty-eight sounded strangely toylike in the quiet house.

"Fox," Lee yelled from somewhere deep inside the house.

"He's out back," The Fox answered, wiping at his face.

Mattingly and Collison, struggling with a locked chain-link gate at the side of the house, dove to the ground when they heard the crash inside followed by two shots. Closest to the house Mattingly pressed into a wet, muddy flower bed, covering his jacket with slime.

"Stop, you son of a bitch," Collison shouted as the man raced from the back of the house toward a cement block wall at the rear of the wide yard. He never broke stride. When he reached the wall, Collison and Mattingly fired. Fragments and chips danced from the wall in white puffs as the man dropped from sight on the other side.

"We got 'em," Mattingly exclaimed, pushing up out of the mud. "We got the bastard." Heavy globs of mud slid from his chest, dropping to his shoes.

"What 'da you mean we," Collison scorned. "All you killed was the goddamned wall."

"Horse shit," Mattingly argued, shaking mud from his forearm. "I didn't hit the wall."

"Come on," Collison urged, struggling up the defiant gate.

"Don't kill him," Rosey Blatts screamed from behind them. "My God please don't kill my baby."

"Where's he at?" The Fox shouted from the corner of the house.

Collison, trying hard to wedge his leather shoe into the narrow links in the gate, slipped and slid to the cement. "Son of a bitch."

"Where in the hell did he go?" the Fox demanded.

"Over the wall," Mattingly said, gesturing to the rear of the yard. "Think we hit 'em."

The Fox raced to the five-foot wall, jumped, and pulled himself to the top, gun still in hand. Peering over it, he quickly surveyed the littered alley. "He's gone," he shouted. Pushing his legs over, he dropped down into the alley.

Lee caught a glimpse of the Fox as he dropped out of sight over the wall. Running for the rear of the yard, he shouted to Mattingly and Collison, "Bring a car around. Get us some help."

Collison, having finally reached the top of the gate, looked to Mattingly. "Take the car around, John. See if you can spot 'em . . . and get air-three down here."

Lee scaled the wall and dropped into the alley. The Fox, fifty yards to his left, raised his arms and hunched his shoulders. Then he motioned in the other direction. The Fox nodded agreement. They moved further apart.

Fox wiped again, this time tenderly, at the burn on his face. Sweat teasing at it made it sting. Brushing splinters of glass from his jacket sleeve, he glanced back at Hollister.

He was peering into a garage, now nearly half a block away. Help was on its way, he guessed. Fox moved on, skirting some broken bottles and a puddle, looking for the small openings between the garages and unlocked doors. A siren whined in the distance, still many blocks away.

Reaching a tee intersection in the alley, the Fox looked both directions. To his right a dog barked and growled. He looked back to Lee, considered calling to him. Then moved off at a jog toward the dog.

He wanted this man, not for rape, murder, or burglary but for burning his face and ruining a hundred-dollar suit. He'd shoot the son of a bitch between the eyes and enjoy it.

Spotting several unlocked garages off to his right, he slowed to a walk. The unseen dog continued its barking. He thought of the thirty-eight in his hand. He should have reloaded.

Fox faced the unlocked double-frame garage with two sets of wide double doors. A gray sparrow landed on the edge of the roof and flew away. Making a mental note of the fact that the garage would be at the rear of a Fifty-first Street address, he brushed at the sweat on his left temple.

Choosing the set of doors on the left he studied the ground, which was a maze of tire and footprints. He couldn't tell if any were fresh. Grasping the latch on the door, raising his gun, he pulled it open.

Stepping quickly inside he flattened his back to the wall. The air was cool and musty. The dog's barking became more persistent, its chain rattled against the outside wall. Fox's chest heaved and fell as he stood, rigid, eyes darting about the shaded garage.

Several flies buzzed in aimless circles in a shaft of sunlight that filtered through a dusty side window. A blanket-covered automobile rested a few feet from him and an empty case of soft-drink bottles sat on its hood. He carefully knelt at the rear of the car and peered under it. All he saw was a few bundled oily rags, crumpled papers, and a rusty beer can. Pushing up, he moved carefully along the side of the car toward the front. The dog continued.

Reaching the front of the covered auto, he searched the other car space, which was stacked with an assortment of trunks and boxes. Squeezing by the front of the car, he bumped a lawn mower which hung by its handle from the wall and it dropped, slamming into the Fox's left heel. "Son of a bitch," he cursed, jerking his foot away from it.

He was reaching for his paining foot when the double doors on the other side of the trunks and boxes burst open, flooding the garage with bright sunlight. He caught only a glimpse of the man before he was out of sight.

Fox struggled desperately between the covered auto and the stacked boxes, squinting in the bright sunlight. Several boxes crashed to the floor. As Fox reached the door he forced a shoulder into it and it swung open.

The man, running hard, was nearing the mouth of the alley where it met Fifty-first Street. The Fox centered himself in the cluttered alley, raised the thirty-eight, and steadied it with both hands, centering the front sight blade squarely on the center of the man's bobbing back. With the broad shoulders still dancing in the sights the Fox braced for the shot. It was then a telephone repair truck pulled into the mouth of the alley.

His target darted to the right around the van and out of the alley. Fox ran after him.

"You dumb bastard," the Fox shouted at the bearded repairman as he raced by the van.

He burst onto Fifty-first Street and searched the block. On the other side of the street, still running hard, he spotted his man. With kids playing on the sidewalk he had no chance for a shot. He ran after him. "Police officer . . . Stop."

They ran hard for another block. The man glanced back at the Fox as he crossed Budlong Avenue. The Fox wasn't gaining.

Mattingly raced the brown Plymouth down the alley toward Hollister as he spoke into the mike. "Three-William-fifteen, officer needs help. Shots fired. In the alley rear of twelve-o-two West Fifty-second Street."

Immediately a male voice on the radio responded, overriding the other radio traffic: "SOUTHWEST UNITS IN THE VICINITY AND THREE-ADAM-EIGHTY-EIGHT. OFFICER NEEDS HELP. SHOTS FIRED. IN THE ALLEY AT THE REAR OF TWELVE-O-TWO WEST FIFTY-SECOND STREET. THREE-ADAM-EIGHTY-EIGHT, YOUR CALL IS CODE THREE."

Mattingly stood on the brake and the Plymouth slid to a dusty, grinding halt beside Hollister, who jerked open the door. "He's not down here. The Fox is down at the other end. Let's go."

"What the hell happened? Who did the shooting?" Hollister

asked as Mattingly raced the Plymouth down the cluttered alley.

Mattingly shook his head. "I don't know. We heard a crash, then some shots. Then Asshole came bust'en out the back, running for the wall. Doug and I fired. We thought we got 'em."

"Who shot inside? Does the crook have a gun?" Hollister wanted answers.

"I don't know."

Hollister picked up the mike. "Three-William-fifteen to control. Advise units responding to twelve-o-two West Fifty-second that we need units at Five-two and Budlong, Five-two and Normandie, and Five-o and Normandie. All others to assemble at Five-two and Budlong. The suspect is a male Negro named Raymond Blatts, no further description at this time. Suspect last seen in alley rear of twelve-o-two West Fifty-second. Suspect is possible armed with handgun and is wanted for burglary, rape, and homicide, K.M.A."

A female voice answered, "Three-William-fifteen, Roger."

Hollister keyed the mike again. "Three-William-fifteen, is Air-three up?"

"William-fifteen, negative. Air-three is down at the heliport for refueling."

"Well get 'em up, damn it. We need him."

"Three-William-fifteen . . . Roger."

They reached the tee intersection in the alley. Hollister, glancing to his right, saw the parked telephone company van. "Turn left," he said. "They wouldn't have gone that way." Mattingly turned the car left.

"Lieutenant Purington, may I see you for a moment," a detective called from the head of the squad room near the reception counter.

"Excuse me a moment, gentlemen." Purington left the reporters who were crowded around the desk where the shooting had occurred and walked over toward the sergeant, who took him by the arm, turning him away from the watching reporters. "Mattingly and Collison are down on Fifty-second street and they just put out a Help Call with shots fired." His voice was low but excited. "I heard Hollister on the air too."

"Jesus Christ," Purington grimaced, his dark eyes narrowed. "Okay. Keep an ear on it." He turned and moved toward the reporters. "That's going to have to be it for now, fellows."

Captain Slack walked into the squad room with Inspector Cockeran, the area detective commander. Slack looked worried. "Lieutenant," he called to Purington.

"What's going on down there, Tom?" Slack demanded as Purington reached them.

"I don't know, Skipper," he admitted. "I just heard about it. Pete picked it up on the radio."

"God damn it," Slack complained as his face flushed.

Fox could hear plainly that the sirens were close now. The man was nearing another cross street. "Come on, guys." He couldn't stand the pace much longer. His legs were like lead weights.

As the man neared the intersection a black-and-white patrol car burst into view from the side street, its siren screaming, lights flashing.

The man slowed and staggered to a stop. His arms hung limp. He looked as if he were about to fall.

The Fox was slowing to a walk when he realized the black-and-white wasn't going to stop. They slowed slightly for the intersection, checking for traffic, then raced on. "Hey . . . Hey," the Fox screamed. The police car roared out of sight.

The man looked back at the Fox, his dark skin glistening with sweat. He was gasping for breath.

The Fox, still a quarter of a block away, walked slowly toward him, his pistol raised. "Don't . . . don't move, motherfucker," he coughed.

He studied Fox for a moment, first his face, then the blue steel thirty-eight. He broke, racing across a lawn and up the steps to a house. By the time the Fox found him in the sights, the screen door was swinging shut.

Fox slipped and fell hard in the grass as he ran for the steps. Pushing up he scrambled for the screen door and jerked it open.

A small brown baby in a diaper smiled up at him from the floor. "Truck," he said proudly, holding out a toy.

"What the hell . . . ?" A man appeared in the hallway wearing only boxer trunks and shaving cream.

A door slammed in the rear of the house. Fox bolted after the sound.

The Fox was mad, determined, as the man grabbed a shaky, decaying wooden fence at the rear of the house. He fired, bits and pieces of wood flew, but the man disappeared over it. The Fox fired again through the shabby wood where he hoped his target was.

He labored to the fence at a jog. Pulling himself up he hoped to find the man bleeding on the other side. As his face cleared the top of the fence the man swung the board. It hit the Fox squarely with a loud smack, sending blood and mucous flying from his nose. He reeled back off the fence and collapsed in an awkward sprawl on his back.

Raymond Blatts, after hitting the officer with the board, slid along the rough fence to the ground, exhausted. His breath came in short painful bursts that knotted his stomach. He drew up his knees to find relief. His stomach convulsed and a bitter slime filled his mouth and spilled over his lips. He was too weak to brush it away.

Hollister was out of the car and running to the house before Mattingly got stopped. Rosey Blatts sat, head bowed, crying on her front steps.

"Have you seen the Fox?" he said, grabbing Collison by the arm.

"No," Collison answered, pulling away, looking at him. "I thought he was with you."

"He's not," Hollister raised his voice as more black-and-whites arrived, their sirens whining. "We can't find him."

The Fox opened his eyes, blinking several times as shafts of sunlight danced down through the swaying leaves of a tall palm. He moved a hand tenderly to his bloody nose. Moving his right hand, he found it still holding his gun.

He tried breathing through his nose but couldn't. Much to his surprise the pain wasn't bad yet. He knew the real pain wouldn't be long in coming.

"Control One to Three-William-fifteen," the link operator called.

Collison heard and turned to a nearby patrol car parked in the street. Hollister followed. Collison picked up the mike from the seat. "This is Three-William-fifteen, go ahead."

"Three-William-fifteen, we have a Four Fifteen, man with a gun, running eastbound from eleven-forty-two West Five-One Street. Possible related to your One Eighty-seven suspect. See the woman at that address for further."

Hollister was already headed for his car.

"Take two cars with you," Collison shouted to him. "And switch to tact one. I'll stay here."

Raymond Blatts heard the officer moan when he sat up. He pushed to his feet and ran at a staggered gait down the alley.

Fox struggled to the top of the fence, lost his balance, and crashed to the ground on the other side. Rolling over, he saw the man zigzagging down the alley.

Taking careful aim, still in his prone position, steadying the pistol with both hands, the Fox fired. The thirty-eight jumped in his hands. He watched as the man jerked, slammed into the dusty alley, cartwheeled, and lay still.

The Fox lowered his head. It was quiet. Several birds chattered unseen in a nearby tree, a jet thundered overhead as it neared its final approach to Los Angeles International.

It was time, he decided, to go look at this dead man's face. He had never killed anyone before. Strangely, he wasn't excited, as he had often thought he would be after a shooting. As he raised his head his heart jumped. The man was gone.

Getting up, he raced to the mouth of the alley, forgetting his pain and fatigue.

The Fox watched in disbelief as another black-and-white police car raced by on the street. The man darted across the busy street just behind it.

Reaching the far curb, the man looked back. The Fox yelled, "Stop that man . . . I'm a police officer . . . stop him." Several faces on both sides of the street eyed him suspiciously. None even seemed to notice the gun in his hand. They kept walking. He bolted into the street.

"Get outta the street, nigger," an angry voice shouted from a passing truck as he reached the far sidewalk. The man was moving away fast, nearing another corner. Fox raced on, blood running from his nose, dripping from his chin. Several women screamed as he ran by them.

Fox now was gaining on him, and the man knew it. The quick glances over his shoulder showed the fear on his face. Fox had decided that when he got within twenty feet or so he'd shoot on the run.

Racing along the front of a Better Foods Market, Raymond Blatts noticed a woman shopper, her arms laden with heavy bags, walking out of one of the automatic doors. Without a second thought he crashed into her at a dead run as he stepped through the door into the market.

As Fox neared the doors they folded shut. Realizing they were the exit doors, Fox leaped over a chromed metal rail and the in-doors hissed open. Several women screamed as he ran along the crowded row of checkout stands.

The market manager, hearing the screams, looked up from behind his glass-walled booth to see the Fox racing toward him, face covered with blood and gun in hand. He slammed the cash drawer locked, tramped on a silent alarm button, and grabbed a pistol.

William Banks was terrified. He was forty-five, black and balding, and since becoming the manager of the Better Foods Market at Fifty-first and Vermont, he had been robbed four times. After the last robbery he had bought the gun but he hadn't fired any gun since the Korean War.

Stepping from the glass-lined booth, Banks shouted in a shrill voice as he raised the gun, "Stop . . . stop, or I'll shoot." The command sounded ridiculous.

Fox looked to him, flinching as he saw the blue steel pistol and shaking hands. He cautioned with a wave of his free hand, careful not to move his own pistol, held now at his side. "Put it down, I'm a police officer . . . put it down."

"Don't move or I'll shoot."

"There's a man in here I'm after. He's wanted for murder," the Fox said fighting to control his breath.

"Drop . . . drop your gun."

"Look, goddamn it, I'm a police officer," the Fox pleaded as voices shouted and screamed behind him.

"You drop your gun first, then we'll talk." Banks warned, feeling a bit more in command.

An unseen female screamed in the back of the store. As Banks glanced toward the sound, Fox bolted through a checkout stand. Banks fired. A cigarette display near a checkout clerk several stands from where the Fox had stood collapsed. Screams and shouts echoed in the market. Banks ran after the Fox!

The Fox ran down an aisle lined with canned goods, then turned right, switched to another aisle, pushed by several partially filled abandoned carts, and slowed as he neared the long, open refrigerated-meat case that stretched the length of the market's rear. He looked cautiously up and down the shopping area in front of the meat display. Several butchers stood behind a glass partition to the rear of the display, open-mouthed, and staring. A child sat crying in an abandoned shopping cart.

"You can't get out," a voice called. "The police are coming." It was the manager. The Fox flattened his back to a soft drink display.

He sniffed and wiped at his nose with a forearm. Blood, lots of it. The soft mood-music designed to relax shoppers sounded insane to him as it mingled with the child's crying. Moon River, blood, and a crying abandoned child.

Raymond Blatts heard the manager's threat, too, as he squeezed closer to the end of the white meat cooler. More police had arrived. So if he didn't move soon it was over. He jumped and ran for the front of the market.

The Fox saw the movement. He jerked up the thirty-eight.

It was him. He was sure. He fired. The glass in a milk case exploded, sending a shower of white liquid and glass flying. The man disappeared up the aisle.

The Fox moved and the air in front of his face snapped. The blast stung his ears. A spider web of cracks flashed across the glass wall in front of the butchers. They disap-. peared beneath their benches. The Fox, darting to the cover of the next aisle, caught a glimpse of the manager taking aim at him again.

He rounded the corner where the man had gone. On the floor were rolling potatos, onions, apples, and pineapples. Several vegetable shelves lay empty on their sides. The man was nowhere in sight. He danced back and forth through the maze on the floor, moving toward the front, slipping, nearly falling as an apple smashed under his weight.

"Hold it," the manager warned, stepping from the front of the aisle, leveling the gun at him. The Fox saw the threatening muzzle. The muscles in the man's neck quivered, his fingers were wrapped securely around the trigger. The Fox dropped his gun to the floor as he watched a white-and-yellow city bus slide to the curb in front of the store.

He gave the manager a quick look of hatred as Raymond Blatts pushed into the bus along with several other people. The bus's door folded shut as it pulled away. The Fox shook his head in angry frustration. "You dumb-ass nigger," he grated.

"Just don't move, mister."

A black-and-white jerked to a halt in front of the market

and two officers jumped out. One carried a smoke-gray pump shotgun. In a moment they were inside. "Over there," a voice directed.

"Okay, mister," the black uniformed officer said coolly, leveling the shotgun. "Lay the pistol down on the floor and raise your hands."

"It's okay, Officer. I'm the manager."

"Just lay the gun down slowly."

"Taves," the Fox called, recognizing the brown face. "He got on the bus."

The officer eyed him. "Jesus Christ it's Fox."

"Come on," the Fox growled grabbing his gun from the littered floor, racing for the door.

"Go," the Fox screamed as he jerked the rear door of the patrol car shut.

The driver brought the car to life.

The passenger officer twisted in his seat, holding the shotgun upright between his legs as the patrol car roared away from the curb. "You okay?" he said, looking at the Fox's broken face.

"Yeah," the Fox answered, brushing at the clotting blood around his nose and mouth. "The son of a bitch hit me with something. I don't know what but I'm okay."

"Check right," the driver demanded as they neared a crowded intersection. Their electric siren was screaming. "Clear," his partner responded.

The car jumped ahead as the officer floored the accelerator.

Other traffic on the street pulled to the side as the black-and-white raced by, the sound of its siren echoing off the concrete canyon it sliced through.

"There it is." The bus pulled into the curb for waiting passengers at Forty-eighth Street.

Fox was out and running as the car slid to a stop. The bus began to pull away as he can alongside, banging at it with his gun. "Stop . . . stop, goddamn it, stop." The air brakes hissed and the big bus rolled to a stop in the street.

Fox scrambled onto the bus, the two officers close behind. The passengers stared in disbelief and cowered in their seats. "He's not here," Fox snarled. "He's not here." A teenage girl near the door began to cry softly.

Fox turned to the driver as he wiped at a feeling of blood on his lips. "I'm gonna ask you just once," the Fox breathed heavily. "Back at the market . . . at Fifty-first and Vermont

. . . a young dude and two women got on. I want that dude. Where's he at?"

The man swallowed. "Yeah . . . yeah, he got on. But . . . he, he didn't have any money. I . . . I made 'em get off at the next stop. At Fiftieth Street."

The Fox lowered his head.

One of the officers scrambled off. "Come on, Fox," the other said, taking him by the arm. "Motherfucker," the Fox mumbled in angry, painful frustration as he walked with head low to the waiting patrol car. The police helicopter clattered in a tight circle overhead. Passing cars slowed to stare. Small groups gathered on corners, pointing, watching. The Fox ignored them all. He pulled open the back door to the car and slumped into the seat. Sweat teased at his eyes as it gathered and raced down his face.

"That's a negative, Air-three," the black officer said. He was on the radio in the front seat. "Unknown what direction the suspect took. Bus driver advises only that he put him out at Fiftieth Street."

"Air-three, Roger." The observer's voice was heavy with the whine of the rotors. "We'll take a quick look in a wide three-sixty and advise."

Fox pulled at his tie and unbuttoned his shirt as he felt a wave of nausea sweep over him. He heard the car stop behind them, doors banging shut, but he didn't bother to look.

Reaching the patrol car, Lee knelt at the open door and Mattingly stood behind him. Fox and Hollister looked at each other for a long moment. The Fox could see Hollister had been shaken. He forced a grin. Hollister returned it. "Come on," he said, taking the Fox by the arm.

Mattingly produced a handkerchief. "It's clean," he assured, offering it to the Fox as Hollister walked him to the detective car.

"Thanks," the Fox said, pushing it to his nose.

"Mattingly," Hollister suggested, "you take over here. We'll be up at the California Hospital."

The Fox's stomach jerked as he opened the car door. It came without warning. He had no chance to fight it. The hot fluids gushed up his throat, filling his mouth with a bitter lumpy warmth. His jaws opened and the dark syrupy vomit poured to the pavement with a loud splatter.

Hollister, having started around the front of the car, raced back to him. The Fox steadied himself on the open door, his head low.

"Ya okay?" Hollister asked, laying a hand on his back. The Fox pulled away from his touch. "Lemme—" A second convulsion cut him short. This time he gagged. More vomit spilled out, splashing his shoes as it hit the warm asphalt.

Hollister and Mattingly stood silent as the Fox mopped his face with the handkerchief. Finishing, he climbed in the car and pulled the door shut.

"Give me a call as soon as you get something," Hollister said, moving for the car.

"Sure," Mattingly answered.

Hollister was quiet. He concentrated on driving. It was a fast ride, he was careful not to disturb the Fox, who was slumped beside him, resting his head with eyes closed on the back of the seat. The radio was filled with excited tense voices. Hollister listened as the area where the suspect was last seen was sealed off. A command post was being set up at Fiftieth and Flower. All units responding were advised to switch to Tactical Frequency-One. A field sergeant was asking the watch commander if the Special Weapons and Tactics Team should be called out for a house-to-house search. Air-three had a possible suspect in a backyard near Fifty-second and Hoover. He needed a ground unit to check it. One was responding, another added he was rolling. Hollister glanced at the silent Fox. He hoped they'd kill the son of a bitch when they got 'em.

Raymond Blatts lay frozen with fear, squeezed between the empty soft drink cases on the big truck. After getting off the bus he watched the black-and-white slide to a stop in front of the market as the officers raced in, guns in hand. He knew it wouldn't be long until they were after him. The truck was unattended beside him, the driver in the store behind him. He glanced up and down the sidewalk. All the eyes were on the patrol cars blinking red lights and the market front. He scrambled up the step-stacked cases and squeezed down between the center row and stretched out on the metal floor.

As Lee wheeled the Plymouth into the hospital parking lot, four miles south at the intersection at Vermont and Vernon Avenue, Jesse Walters slowed his soft-drink delivery truck for the officers standing in the intersection. They stood waving in a wide-legged stance, one held a shotgun at port arms. He double-clutched and slid the truck into second, pushing easy on the brake. Raymond Blatts could hear the unmistakable police radio squawk on a nearby patrol car's external speaker as it rolled to a stop.

"This about the market gett'en robbed?" Walters called down to the sober-faced officer.

"Yeah," the sweat-streaked face answered as he grabbed the brace of the rear-view mirror and pulled himself up onto the running board. He took a quick glance inside the cab. Walters smiled. "I got 'em hid in the back. Been planning it for months. We got forty-seven dollars and a watermelon."

Blatts could hear laughter and muffled voices mixed with the sound of the idling truck engine. Through the reflection of the rows of bottle necks he watched as the blue uniformed arms cradling the smoke-gray shotgun walked down the side of the truck.

"Got any cold ones?"

"Naw . . . they're all warm as piss."

"Okay, man, get your uncola truck out of un-street or get un-done."

The engine roared and the truck bolted forward. "Hope you get 'em."

The Fox lay on his back enjoying the cool dry air of the emergency room. It was bright and antiseptic. While he shifted the damp compress that covered his mouth and nose, he realized he'd have a set of black eyes, and nothing looked worse than a blue bruise on brown skin.

"Virgil, what's your date of birth?" Hollister called from outside the white curtain.

"August twenty-three, nineteen-forty," he answered through the wet towel. His moving lips pulled at the dried caked blood in his nostrils.

"Come on, Virg, it's for the hospital, not the yearbook."

"Nineteen-forty," he repeated.

"Thirty-eight, nurse," he heard Hollister say.

"Marlin," an unseen woman sobbed somewhere in the room. "Marlin, I can't stand the pain. Get the doctor." He heard a muffled male response. Then the woman again. "Marlin, get the doctor," she repeated.

"Shut up, bitch," the Fox ordered silently. "I'm laying here with a nose that'll take all the king's horses and all the king's men to put back together again and you can't stand the pain. Ten to one your diaphragm slipped."

Hollister pulled the curtain aside, the nurse followed. "Mr. Fox," she said sympathetically, "I'll need your signature."

The Fox took the clipboard she offered and scribbled his name near where she pointed; she smiled and moved away. The Fox caught her profile. Thirty-six D he guessed.

When the nurse was gone, Hollister dug out his cigarettes. After some search he found a match. "You know," he said, shaking out the match, throwing it under the bed, "I sure as hell could use a drink."

The Fox didn't answer. His eyes were closed now.

Hollister surveyed the cloth cubicle. No chair. He wished there was. "You wanna tell me about it?"

"Not now."

"Did you hit him?"

"I don't know. I thought I got 'em once."

"You're not sure?"

"I'm not sure."

"He have a gun?"

"Why'd you ask if I wanted to tell you about it now?"

"Well . . ." Hollister shrugged, "if you don't, just say so."

"I did . . . and I don't."

"Okay." Hollister knocked an ash from his cigarette, scattering it about the polished floor with a foot. He wished he could sit down, deciding in a few minutes he'd go out to the lobby. He drew on the cigarette again.

"Sergeant Hollister," the nurse called from outside the curtain, "there's a call for you."

The treatment room was nearly silent after Hollister left. Trying hard, while holding his own breath, occasionally Fox could hear the complaining woman's breath. He felt sleepy. He considered the possibility of his having a brain concussion, wondered if he did fall asleep if he would ever wake up. Raising a hand, he spread his fingers and silently counted one-two-three-four-five. Backwards, five-four-three-two-one.

He thought his vision was just a bit blurred. He closed his right eye. Clear. The other. There . . . there, see it's blurred. Son of a bitch, where was the doctor? Here he was lying, maybe dying as a small pin-sized clot choked off the supply of blood to a vital portion of his brain, while the doctor was locked in some small office unhooking a bra strap and Florence Nightingale stroked his joint. He had to stay awake.

"Is there some place I can get a coffee?" Hollister asked as the nurse led him to the reception desk.

"Sure," she smiled. "I'll show you as soon as you're off the phone."

Her eyes were light green and he guessed she was maybe two, three years older than he was. He had already decided he'd go to bed with her. Knew she had decided too and wished he knew her decision. There was something about a woman in uniform that excited him. They reached the desk. "The one on Hold," she said.

"Sergeant Hollister."

"Hollister, this is Captain Slack. I heard on the radio that a unit had gone to California Hospital. What's happened? Who's hurt?"

"The Fox," Hollister answered.

"Shot?"

"No . . . no, he got hit in the face with a board. He'll be okay."

"Do you think Fox is going to be admitted?"

"I don't know. He hasn't seen the doctor yet."

"Give me a call when you have some word."

Lee hung up, not really knowing how Slack felt. He was worried. He rubbed at a tight muscle at the base of his neck.

"Ready for that coffee now?" the nurse asked, returning to her desk with a stack of papers.

"Sure am," he smiled with effort.

He walked down the wide hall with her, enjoying the mild scent of her perfume. "You look tired," she commented, glancing at him.

"Thanks."

"No, I didn't mean it that way," she assured. "You just look tired."

"It's been a long night."

They reached the small lounge. A dark-haired, small-framed man worked at pouring himself a coffee. The white tunic he wore was soiled and wrinkled.

"We have two waiting in emergency, Doctor Marthouse," the nurse informed.

"Yeah, I know." He sampled the coffee.

"What are they?" His interest was mild.

"Policeman with a smashed nose, and a woman with gas pains." She handed Hollister a cup. "Help yourself."

"How's the little girl?" she asked the doctor as Hollister filled his cup at the urn.

"Dead," he answered dryly, moving to the door. "I'll be down in a couple minutes. I'm gonna wash off a bit."

The coffee was hot and welcome. Hollister enjoyed its taste. "What's the story on the girl?" he asked between sips.

The nurse folded her arms and leaned on the doorway. "She's a little black kid. Three years old. Cute as a button. Came in about an hour ago. She swallowed her mother's sleeping pills. Secobarbital. Fourteen of them, her mother thinks." Anger crept over her smooth face. "She waited a couple hours before she brought the kid in. Ignorant bitch. The little girl was in a coma when she got here."

"You call the police?"

"Yeah. They're here. I've gotta get back to my desk. You sit down and enjoy your coffee."

When she was gone, Hollister slid into one of the soft leather chairs, stretching his feet out in front of him. The coffee warmed and relaxed him. He thought of the little girl whom he had never seen or known. Three years old and now she was dead. It didn't change his life, or did it? While he thought of screwing the nurse, imagining her large bare breasts squeezed against his chest, the girl had drawn her last breath, and he hadn't even known it. He wondered if he would have cared if he had known. A lot of people would die today in Los Angeles, in California, in the nation, in the world. What the hell did he care? He only had to worry about the ones killed in his area. If someone was killed on Western Avenue north of the Santa Monica Freeway, he didn't care. That was Wilshire Division's responsibility. Why couldn't Ellen Shane have lived in Wilshire Division? Why in the hell did Dave Wilson have to know her? The whys didn't matter. It was his area and he'd have to find the son of a bitch.

Ellen Shane had been pretty. Even in her bloody nude death one could see that. He didn't blame Wilson for killing Shane. Understood it. He was sorry for Wilson that Shane hadn't deserved it. Wondered how Wilson would feel when he found that out. Wondered how Wilson was feeling now. Locked in a cell, booked for murder. Jesus Christ!

Murder was not the usual byproduct of rape. He knew from experience. He had learned that rape-related murder was usually the result of the girl knowing her attacker. Ellen Shane must have known this man. It was the rapist's usual motive to punish his victims, to violate their body forcibly. To show the hate and contempt he felt for them by taking from them the one thing that they gave to men to prove their womanhood. Letting them live on, he knew, was part of the normal rapist's continued punishment. "Normal rapist!" The thought provoked a childish laugh.

Two years of working sex crimes before going to homicide made him an expert, he guessed. An expert in the field of sex crimes. Jesus Christ. He smiled again, studying the cloud of cream in his coffee. He tried to remember how many rape victims he'd interviewed, how many vaginal slides he booked as evidence. He couldn't. They all blurred into one bloody-legged hysterical female who was too embarrassed to tell what had happened to her, or who had done it. What was the monthly average when he left? Between thirty-five to forty rape cases a month in Southwest Division alone, and that was just eleven square miles of this city of the Angeles. The yearly average for the city came in around twenty-one hundred. About six forcible rapes a day. That was just the ones reported. He, like every other experienced cop, knew that for every rape that was reported there were another two that weren't.

So in the City of Los Angeles each day there averaged six official rapes, and another twelve that never got reported. Eighteen each day in one city alone. The thought of how many there were in the state, and in the nation, each day, boggled his mind.

He knew that only about 47 percent of the rapes reported resulted in suspects being arrested. Of those, only a fractional 2 percent were convicted, and seldom if ever was a rapist sent to prison. Of course not. They needed help. They were sick men. Sending them to prison didn't help. He felt a surge of contempt for a system he had learned to hate.

His mind drifted to Janice and what she might be doing. He wondered if she was as horny as he was. Getting laid sure would be relaxing. Maybe the sandy-haired green-eyed nurse would come back, slip in, lock the door, and turn off the light. They could get it on right here on the cool tile floor. The smoldering cigarette with its long ash slipped from his relaxed fingers and fell to the floor. He was asleep.

Slack noticed Captain Judd, the patrol commander of Southwest Division, along with a uniformed lieutenant, enter the squad room from the hall. He was still at Purington's desk listening to the search efforts on the tactical radio.

"Anything new?" Judd asked as they reached him.

"No," Slack conceded, rocking back in the swivel chair. "Nothing yet."

Judd eased onto the edge of a nearby desk and removed a hand-carved pipe from his mouth. He wore a well-tailored blue suit, which to Slack made him look more like a young college professor than a police captain.

Judd studied the pipe after removing it from his mouth. "Bill, I'm going to have to call it off. It's been over an hour. I've got my entire watch down there and we've got nineteen calls backed up in communications. I can't justify any more time."

"We want this son of a bitch," Slack grated.

"You think we don't," Judd countered. "Wilson's one of our people, you know."

Slack dug out a cigarette. "Okay . . . okay, I understand." Judd glanced at the uniformed lieutenant and he moved away.

"There's more." Judd slid the pipe into his mouth and drew on it. It looked like it was out. "Dave Wilson's dead. Central jail watch commander called just before I came down here. They found him on the second cell check. He hung himself with his belt."

"Jesus Christ . . . Oh, Jesus Christ."

Judd relit his pipe. "I've got to go tell his mother." He shook his head, his eyes shifted to the floor. "I've made notifications before, but none like this. How do I tell his mother that her son killed a man, then hung himself?"

Slack shrugged his shoulders. "Christ, Jim, I can't believe what a fucking mess this thing has turned into."

"Captain." It was a graying detective from the desk. He approached with a slip of paper in hand.

"Yeah, Cliff."

"We got another homicide. Fifty-fourth and Crenshaw. At Fat Jack's Burger stand. Patrol's got a possible suspect in custody there."

Slack picked up a pencil and made a note of the address, then looked over the squad room. Several female clerks sat in a huddle at one desk. There were no detectives.

"Looks like they're all down on Vermont," the desk man suggested.

Slack rocked back in the chair. "See if you can get Purington on the air. Have 'em get a team over there."

"Summer must be here," Judd said sarcastically when the detective walked off.

"That's number forty-four for Southwest this year," Slack grimaced, glancing at the address. "Seven more than last year at this time."

"Sign of the times," Judd exhaled philosophically.

The Fox jumped as the nurse lifted the wet compress from his face. "It's all right," she assured with a quick smile. He blinked in the brightness as his sleep quickly left him. The doctor moved in beside him, studying the damaged bloody nose with a small chromed light. "I'm Doctor Marthouse. I'll be your captain for the flight. I specialize in broken bones, severed appendages, and wheel alignments."

The Fox smiled as much as his swollen upper lip would permit. "Just a minor tuneup will do."

"Un huh," the doctor said. "Lemme have some cotton and something to clean this blood away."

The nurse wheeled a tray near and the doctor went to work at washing and brushing away the layers of dried blood. The Fox closed his eyes. The pain wasn't bad. Most of his face was numb. "It's clotting nice," the doctor commented as he tossed aside several bloodied cottons.

"Open wide."

The Fox dropped his jaw. An index finger shook each front tooth independently. "That hurt?"

Rolling back the Fox's top lip, the doctor eyed it carefully. "You've got a laceration on the inside of your lip here. We won't stitch it. Tissue in there should heal fast." He let the lip relax. Reaching up, the doctor pulled the overhead light closer. "Cotton," he said. He wiped over the swollen nose carefully. "Looks like some pretty heavy splinters here around the nostrils. We might as well get those now. Get me a set of gloves."

The Fox glanced at the doctor as he leaned over him, slipping on the surgical gloves. "You want me to deaden this?" he asked, catching the Fox's look.

"No," the Fox answered. "I think it's already been killed."

"Okay," the doctor agreed. "Cover him with a towel and spray the nose with aerosol benzine. I'll need tweezers and a probe."

The Fox tensed, clapping his eyes shut as the nurse covered them with a dry white sterile towel.

"After we get all this wood picked out of you," the doctor said, "we'll ship you down to X-ray to see if anything's busted in there."

The slender pale nurse at the reception desk knew the four men were detectives when they came through the double doors. She continued her work on a chart until they reached her.

"Well, well," she said with a forced tight smile. "The four little pigs. I thought there was only supposed to be three." It was said without her looking up from the chart, but they heard.

Lieutenant Purington blushed, which made his blue eyes more intense. Mattingly and Collison said nothing. Perry, a short squat balding man, smiled back at her. "Pretty good, pretty good. You're right, there's only three little pigs. I'm a big one, and like my grandpappy taught me, it takes one to know one."

"Not bad," the brunette answered, sorting her papers. "I'll bet you're the one with the high school diploma."

"And ten to one you graduated from Berkeley," Perry countered.

"That's enough, Perry," Purington ordered.

"My, what a display of authority," the girl jeered.

Purington could take no more. He stepped closer to the counter, glancing at the nurse's name tag. "If you want to see a display of authority, Ms. Swartz, just offer one more insult and I'll stand you in front of the director of this hospital and let you repeat it."

The girl's makeupless face reddened with anger.

"When you put that uniform on," Purington continued, "like me, you put your personal prejudices aside or you don't wear it. I don't know what your problems are and I don't really care, but I'm not going to listen to your insults."

"The man you want to see is in X-ray. The other one's asleep in the lounge. Down the hall on your left.

"Pig bastards," she hissed as they moved away.

The reached the small lounge and eased the door open quietly. Hollister was slumped in the chair, sleeping soundly.

"Don't shoot!" Perry shouted.

Hollister jumped, instantly awake, eyes wide, heart pounding.

Purington shook his head as the others laughed.

"You no-class bastards," Hollister complained, rubbing his bearded face with both hands.

"Coffee. Great," Mattingly said, seeing the urn. Collison joined him at the pot.

"Did you get him?" Hollister asked, pushing up, stretching his arm as he stood.

Purington shook his head. "We searched for over an hour," he explained easing into one of the chairs. "Nothing, nobody saw nothing. The bastard just vanished after he got off the bus. How's the Fox?"

"He'll be okay. Busted nose I'd guess."

Perry chuckled. "Today in Southwest Division, officers in the line of duty shot and killed two walls, one cement, one wooden, one dairy case, and terrorized two elderly women, two butchers, and one bus driver."

"Shut up, Perry," Purington warned.

"Yes, sir."

"What are you going to do now?" Hollister asked Mattingly and Collison after they had filled their cups.

"He'll come home," Mattingly said.

"We got two units from the special operations squad sitting on his house," Collison added between sips. "John and I are going down to the D.A. when we leave here. Get a felony warrant for 'em. We'll get a teletype out by the end of the day."

"You hear about Wilson?" Perry asked.

"What about 'em?"

"He's dead . . . hung 'emself."

Hollister was stunned. His cheek twitched as his face flushed warm. He cleared his throat. "Poor bastard," he managed in a broken voice.

"What else could he do?" Collison offered.

"Ever hear of a cop living through the joint?" Perry said to no one in particular.

Hollister shook out a cigarette. His hand shook as he lit up. A chill swept over him. The room felt cold. He shrugged his shoulders to shake away the chill. He forced it away. He had to get organized. He was dog tired and hungry and the sooner he got things squared away the sooner he'd be able to get a shower and some sleep.

"Lee," Purington said, "we've got another homicide at Fifty-fourth and Crenshaw. Bud and Hutch are over there now. Perry and I are gonna take a run over and see what they've got. Could you get in touch when you find out what's going to happen with the Fox?"

"Yeah, sure," Hollister answered, taking a heavy drag on his cigarette.

"When you get done here go on home, get some rest. It's almost noon."

"I gotta couple more things that need done today." Hollister argued, studying his cigarette. It tasted bitter. He wished he could brush his teeth.

"Like what?"

"I was gonna go knock on some doors up on Montclair. See if I couldn't find someone who saw or heard something last night. The Fox picked up some license numbers up there this morning. They should be D.M.V.'ed and the registered owners run through R. and I."

"We can handle it. I can get a team to do that."

"I'll need the photos of the bloody footprint we got from the bedroom. S.I.D. should be able to give us a shoe size. Maybe even a type if we're lucky. If I get that, I wanna get out a teletype. Maybe this clown has pissed on some other broad that he's let live."

"Perry, you take care of that," Purington suggested.

"No argument," Hollister breathed, leaning a shoulder into the wall. "I won't be worth a shit today."

"Okay," Purington said. "Let me know how the Fox makes out."

"Take care, Lee," Perry smiled, slapping Hollister on the shoulder as he and the lieutenant headed for the door.

"Don't you say a word to the nurse," Purington cautioned Perry.

"I'll bet she has to tease her hair to keep her pants up," Perry answered.

"Not one word."

When he could no longer hear the two men, Hollister turned and sank into a chair. With a labored effort he crushed his cigarette butt in an ashtray, looking to Mattingly and Collison. Mattingly returned his look with a boyish grin. Collison had a silly smirk on his face.

Hollister shook his head. "What a mess you two clowns got us into."

Collison finished off his coffee with a quick gulp. "Well, if Wyatt Earp here would learn to shoot, it'd be all over now."

"Me," Mattingly defended. "Hell, I was in mud and flowers up to my asshole. All you had to do was aim and shoot. While I was sinking in that bed of flowered quicksand."

"You think Blatts is good for your caper?" Collison questioned, setting his cup aside.

"I don't know," Hollister shrugged. "Have to see what he has to say when we get him."

"Well," Mattingly suggested. "Let's get down to the D.A."

"If Blatts hits the bucket, you guys give me a call?" Hollister requested.

"Sure."

He slouched in the chair and listened to their footsteps fade and then disappear in the hallway. He knew if he got up and walked down the hall and asked about the Fox, one of the nurses would tell him he was in X-ray or with the doctor. Damned hospitals. He glanced at a tattered Newsweek on the stand beside him. "IMPEACHMENT'S EVE," the headline read, stripped across a sober-faced president. "We've all got our own problems," Hollister said aloud.

"That's a fact," the green-eyed nurse smiled in the doorway.

Hollister smiled with some embarrassment. "Just thinking out loud."

The nurse slid into a chair across from him. Hollister admired her legs as she stretched them in front of her. "Your friend should be ready in about five minutes. His nose wasn't broken. He's got some first-degree burns on his left cheek and neck. From coffee, he said. We took some splinters from his nose and cleaned him up. He's getting a tetanus booster and then he's all yours."

Chief of police James Peck stood at the rear of the elevator watching the green floor numbers flash on and off as the elevator made its climb.

The rectangular car was crowded with the noon rush headed for the cafeteria on the eighth floor of Parker Center, but like always when he was aboard, the other passengers were quiet. It was one of the small things about being chief of police that annoyed him. At times like this he felt more like the pope. Why people wouldn't talk to each other in his presence baffled him.

The elevator slid to a smooth stop on the sixth floor. The doors parted. "Out please," Captain Rosson, the chief's aide, announced from beside him. The crowd parted. "Excuse me," Peck said as he followed Rosson off.

They moved down the hall and into his office. Rosson went to his desk. Peck nodded to his secretary and went into the inner office, closing the door behind him.

Captain Rosson placed his briefcase on his desk and snapped it open. Pulling out several folders and placing them on the desk, he glanced to the dark-haired secretary. "What have we got, Jesse?"

Her brown eyes darted to a note pad on the well-organized desk. "Deputy Chief Spear from South Bureau called. He wants to talk to the chief concerning this morning's shooting." She spoke with a soft Mexican-American accent. "Commander Hogan has called twice, concerning press inquiries in regards to the shooting, and Councilman Hess called. He wouldn't say what the nature of his call was. You probably could return that."

The intercom on her desk buzzed. "Yes, sir."

"Jesse, could you have me brought down some lunch? I'll have whatever their dieter's special is today."

"Yes, sir. . . . Sir, Deputy Chief Spear is here."

"Then send him in and have Captain Rosson wait."

"Yes, sir."

Peck twisted the high-backed swivel chair toward the window. Los Angeles's skyline was shrouded in a bright glaring smog. The gray towering buildings in the distance took on a fuzzy, ghostly look. Be a hell'ava day to be riding motors. He grimaced remembering the many miles he had logged straddling a big black-and-white Harley Davidson, rolling over the sea of asphalt that covered the city. He could still remember the heat from the silver-ribbed cylinders melting the black polish on his high boots, making them so hot they blistered. Sometimes, he admitted to himself, he missed it.

He heard the door behind him, but didn't bother to turn. Deputy Chief Spear crossed the office and took a chair beside Peck's desk. "I'd say good morning, but it just wouldn't be true."

Peck glanced at him. Spear was a big man, fifty plus, but still had a full head of red hair and a rugged-looking face, accented by a square jaw. "I was just considering going down and checking out a motor," Peck kidded. "Go out on the Hollywood Freeway and blow out the cobwebs."

Spear slouched in his chair. "Think you could still ride one of those ball-bearing Jackasses?"

"Yeah, I think so."

"Hell," Spear huffed. "Anyone could. Hondas, Yamaha, all of 'em have electric starters. They look like ten speeds compared to our old Harlys."

Peck studied him for a moment. "Remember the night you got that bottle of J.B. from Barney's liquor, stuck it in your saddlebag? Then we got in pursuit of that dude and you ran over the curb and broke the bottle?" Peck chuckled, running a hand back over his graying hair. "You had the best-smelling motor in the city."

Spear smiled. "Seems like a hundred years ago."

"I think it was," Peck breathed.

"I was just downstairs . . . in the jail," Spear said, turning serious.

"Robbery-Homicide handling it. They're the ones that booked him."

"Uh huh."

"He did us a favor," Spear suggested as he shifted in his chair. "You know, Jim, the D.A. would have really gone after his ass. Anyone else would have slid by with a charge of manslaughter, but not Wilson, not a cop. No matter what the reason, the D.A. would have pushed for a murder one. Election next year, you know?"

Peck turned his eyes back to the smoggy skyline.

"If he hadn't done it," Spear added, "someone would have done it for him when he got to the joint. Those pricks love to rat pack a cop."

"I suppose," Peck conceded. "But, still . . ." His voice trailed away.

"I'm going to file a personnel complaint against the men that booked him and the jailor."

"Jesus Christ, Ben," Peck frowned. "You and your goddamned Marine Corps discipline."

"I didn't create the goddamned order," Spear countered. "But if it had been enforced—had his belt, like every felony prisoner's, been taken from him, he'd be alive."

"You just got done saying he did us a favor."

"My personal opinion hasn't got a damned thing to do with departmental orders or policies."

Peck knew his deputy chief was right. The men would have to be disciplined. He knew the system, knew tough discipline was the only thing that had kept the department clean for so many years. Still this time it seemed to defy logic.

They were quiet for a moment. Then Peck turned his chair to face Spear. "How about the shooting at the station? Could that have been prevented? That's a question everyone's going to ask."

Spear gave the question careful thought. He shook his head. "No, the investigators didn't do anything wrong. Hell, Wilson was at the other end of the station in the coffee room when he grabbed another officer's gun. We're just lucky he didn't hit anybody else. I don't think they could have done anything to prevent it. Hell, they couldn't foresee what was coming . . . although they'll be damned for not doing just that."

"Yeah, I agree," Peck answered thoughtfully, wondering what the mood was at Southwest station. "Now that this ex-husband has been shot and Wilson has hung himself, is the case closed?"

"No. Unfortunately it's not. It was learned after Shane's death that he no longer owned a VW like the one seen fleeing the scene." Spear's tone was apologetic.

"Jesus Christ. The press have this yet?"

"Yeah," Spear nodded. "Captain Slack, the commander of Southwest Detectives, has been very open with them. We've had a group of reporters down there all morning."

Peck pushed back in his chair again. "Well . . . there's nothing we can do, I guess. It's happened. All we can do is explain how and why. I think most will understand. We'll have to learn something from this, though . . . so it'll never happen again."

"I agree," Spear answered. "We've got another prime suspect. Couple detectives went out to pick him up this morning. He escaped, after hitting a black detective. We had some shots fired, but nobody got hit. There was an extensive search, but he got away."

· "Is the officer all right?"

"He's at the hospital now. From what I've been told, his condition's good."

"Do you think this case should be turned over to Robbery-Homicide Division? They've got the manpower and talent to handle this."

"No, not yet. I'm sure Southwest Detectives don't wanna give this thing up. Wilson worked patrol down there. The victim was his girlfriend. This other injured officer is one of theirs. I'm sure they want a chance to handle it themselves."

"I'm not saying they're not competent, but that's one of the busiest divisions in the city. Can they handle their caseload and this too?"

"They've got the suspect identified. They'll find him. You know ·the tradition. They want a chance to clean their own house. If they can't cut it, then we'll consider your recommendation."

"Okay, Ben, it's your area, but I want to be kept informed."

"You will be," Spear promised, pushing out of his chair.

Peck walked with him to the door. "How about stopping in Hogan's office and updating him on all this? I'm sure he's going to be besieged with calls from the press."

"Sure."

"Thanks, Ben." Peck opened the door for him. As Spear left, Peck motioned to Captain Rosson. "Come on in, Pat."

Rosson followed the chief back into his office. "Councilman Hess called," the captain smiled. "His wife's car was impounded on Wilshire Boulevard this morning."

"Well," Peck said angrily. "What the hell's he calling me for?"

"I'd guess he doesn't want to pay the seventeen-fifty it would cost to get it out."

"That's too goddamned bad."

Rosson drew in a breath. "Chief, I know we don't hand out favors, but I'd like to point out that the councilman's on the finance committee. And you have a meeting with them at two this afternoon concerning the proposed additions to Seventy-seventh Division's station."

Rosson stood in front of the chief's desk, studying his shoes, waiting. "If I may make a suggestion, sir. I think if we call the Wilshire Division community relations officer and explain to him what has happened, maybe he can contact the impound garage and make some arrangement."

"I don't want a dime of city money spent on this," Peck warned.

"I don't think that'll be necessary."

"My ass hurts more from that goddamned shot than my face," Fox complained, shifting in the seat beside Hollister as the Plymouth eased to the curb on Santa Barbara Avenue behind a black-and-white patrol car.

"I think you look better than when you came in this morning." A wide white patch covered the bridge of his nose above a swollen upper lip.

The Fox, not in the mood for kidding, ignored the remark. "What are you gonna do?"

"Get a pack of cigarettes from Fred. Need anything?"

"Naw."

"Think I'll get Fred to come out and take a look at you."

"Come on, man," the Fox pleaded. "I wanna get home."

"Be right back," Hollister promised, climbing out of the car.

"Hey, big time," Fred's coal-black lined face called from

behind the counter as Hollister entered the liquor store. Fred's hair was a tangled uncombed graying natural. His brown bloodshot eyes sat deep under two grayed brows. A pencil was jammed behind one ear, a cigarette behind the other.

"Hey, Fred," Hollister smiled to the small bony man. Moving along the counter, Hollister glanced at two uniformed officers standing at the rear of the store near the windowed refrigerators, drinking a Coke. He nodded to them. They returned it.

Fred rang up a sale on the cash register for an aging black woman. Hollister stood aside, waiting. "Four twentynine," Fred smiled to the woman, bagging her items.

The woman glanced over her shoulder at Hollister, then leaned close to Fred, speaking softly. Fred smiled, showing his wide, irregular yellow teeth. "Sure, honey, sure."

The woman pulled the sack into her arms and shuffled away. Fred pulled a pad from beneath the counter and made a note on it, then returned it.

"Fred," Hollister warned, moving up to the counter. "You're gonna go broke carrying the world."

"Shit," he smiled. "They always pay. May take 'em awhile, but they pay."

·Hollister pulled out a wrinkled dollar. "Two Marlboros."

"Hey," Fred shouted around Hollister. Two ten-year-olds were eagerly leafing through a display of books covered with a variety of nude females. "Get out of there. You wanna see some skin, go see a movie. Don't mess up my books. Go look at your daddy's."

The two youngsters scrambled for the door. "Damn kids," he frowned. "Should be in school."

"They're on vacation," Hollister smiled.

"That's no excuse," Fred shot back, producing the Marlboros. "They should still be in school." He took Hollister's dollar and rang up the amount on the cash register. The cash drawer opened with a ring. Fred inserted the dollar, took two half-dollars and slid them on the counter to Hollister.

Hollister eyed the change. "It's Friday. Don't you think it's about time I pay?"

"No, man. This is the first you've been in this week," Fred pretended to be insulted.

"See you guys . . . take care, Freddie." The two uniformed officers left.

"Catch a nigger by the toe," Fred called to them.

They smiled and waved.

"Nice kids," Fred said when they were gone.

Hollister picked up his cigarettes. "How's the horses treating you, Fred?"

"It's been a good week. I may go to Vegas and double my money. Hey, where you been? Where's that slick dresser Fox?"

"We've been crushing crime. It's been busy out."

"Hey, Lee." Fred leaned his elbows on the counter. "I was gonna give you a call. Could you check something out for me?" His face was sober.

"Run it by me," Hollister said, tearing open a pack of the Marlboros.

Fred produced a lighter from his trouser pocket. "On Wednesday . . ." He paused to light Hollister's cigarette. "On Wednesday these two dirt-bag lookin' paddies . . . no offense," Fred smiled, showing his teeth. Hollister thought he looked like a horse. "Anyhow like I was say'en, these two paddies, rented an apartment off of Mrs. Washington. She owns that build'en right across the street . . . see?"

Hollister gazed through the bright glare across Santa Barbara Avenue. The building was a four-story aging apartment house. Its red bricks were bleached orange and chipped. The brief lawn in front was littered and path-worn. Several black men lounged in the warm sun on the steps that led to the arched front entrance. "What about them?" Hollister asked, studying the building casually. "You afraid they're gonna hurt the neighborhood?"

"No, man, that ain't it," Fred defended seriously. "Mrs. Washington is a long-time friend . . . customer for many a year."

"Uh huh," Hollister exhaled, wishing Fred would get to the point. He knew the Fox would be pissed, waiting in the heat.

"She tells me that these two would only take an upstairs apartment facing the street."

"Yeah," Hollister said, taking a second look at the building. His interest stirred. He knew Fred was no alarmist:

"No, man, you know," Fred offered, "that they didn't want that for the view." He shifted his stance nervously. "Two paddies ain't rent'en noth'en down here for no good."

"You seen 'em?" Hollister questioned.

"Huh uh." Fred shook his head. "Only know what Mrs.

Washington tells me. She says they come in about seven in the morning and they leave about two in the morning."

"Wonder why?" Hollister asked, taking a final drag on his cigarette, dropping it to the floor to grind it out with a foot.

"I got it figured," Fred said in a hushed tone as if others were listening. "I think them two clowns are gonna rip me off."

Hollister studied his dark eyes for a moment. "Could be, Fred."

"What else, man? I'm the only attraction for two blocks in either direction."

"How much coin do you hold here?"

"Couple thousand on Fridays."

Hollister shook his head, giving Fred a hard look. "It's a wonder the mob from Chicago hasn't sent a team out here to hit you. It'd be worth it for them."

"Let 'em come. I ain't afraid of any motherfucker. I got Mr. Smith and Mr. Wesson and their six friends to help me out. Right here under the counter."

"How come you're telling me about these two paddies then?"

" 'Cause I don't wanna kill 'em here in the store," Fred bluffed. "It's bad for business, you know."

"Uh huh." Hollister studied the apartment building again. "They got an apartment upstairs there in the front, huh?"

"Yeah, second floor. The window on the far right."

"Okay, Fred, we'll shake 'em down. See who the hell they are. May take a couple hours."

"That's okay, man."

"Someone will give you a call, let you know what's happened. May not be me, I've got some other shit I've got to get done."

"Sorry." Hollister started the car. The steering wheel was hot to the touch. "Fred's got a couple paddies staked on him. He thinks they're gonna rip him off. That's what took so long."

"You discuss. that over a cold one?" the Fox asked as Hollister pulled from the curb.

"No, for real. I didn't have a drop, although I wish I had. Sure would go good right now."

"You think he's right about these crooks?" the Fox asked, fingering the tape on his nose carefully.

"Maybe," Hollister shrugged, slowing for a red light. "I'm gonna tell Robbery. Have them go shake 'em down."

"Tell Rainey," the Fox suggested. "He owes us a favor."

Hollister dropped the Fox at his car in the station parking lot. "You sure you don't want me to drive you home?"

"Naw, I'm okay. I gotta get this thing washed away." Fox pointed to his white Porsche.

"When do you think you'll be back?" Hollister asked as the Fox opened his door.

"Today, if you want. I just wanna go home and clean up a bit."

"No . . . no more today," Hollister said with a tired smile. "I'm gonna see how things are shaping up inside, then get out of here too."

"We're the 'on-call team' this weekend, so ten-to-one I'll see you before Monday," the Fox said with a twisted swollen smile.

"No doubt."

The Fox swung the car door shut and walked away. Hollister watched as he dug in his pockets for his keys. He knew he was hurting more than he would admit. He also knew the Fox was feeling a bit defeated, beaten, frustrated, from having Raymond Blatts floor him and then escape. It wasn't policeman versus criminal. It was a bitter personal insult that was hard for any man to accept. He hoped the Fox would go home and wash Raymond Blatts out with a bottle of Scotch. He made a mental note to call him later tonight. Lee secretly hoped the patrol cops would beat Blatts silly when they got him.

He parked the unmarked Plymouth in a vacant slot along with a dozen other detective cars at the east side of the station. Pulling at the keys he closed his eyes and laid his head back on the seat. A drop of perspiration gathered on his left temple and traced its way to his cheek. He felt it but didn't bother to brush it away. The car was warm, not hot. Sleep would come easy. Not a comfortable sleep, but sleep. It was hot, humid, and he knew he'd wake up swimming in sweat. Just sit for a minute, relax, then go inside. He remembered reading somewhere that this was called mini-sleep and was quite helpful when you were tired. Two minutes of mini-sleep, then he'd go inside.

Be good to get home. Get Carol to fix some breakfast—what time was it? One, one-thirty, something like that. Breakfast would still taste good. Then take a shower and slip into bed. Wake up about . . . Finally the error of his dream stirred him awake. Blinking his eyes in the brightness, he sat up. There was no going home to Carol. He'd left her. He rubbed at his tired eyes. He felt very old.

Digging out a cigarette, he lit up. It tasted bitter. His tongue felt coated and heavy. He climbed out of the car.

The squad room was cool and dim compared to the bright outside. Hollister welcomed its relief as he wormed through the tables to his desk. A little black girl with a bandaged face sat crying loudly at the front of the room. A uniformed officer worked at trying to get her to accept a Coke. The child cried louder, stretching her short chubby arms, pleading with a stream of heavy tears and frightened face to a handcuffed woman slouched in a nearby chair.

Lieutenant Purington noticed Lee as he slid into his chair. He had unlocked the desk and pulled out the bottle of urine when the Lieutenant and Perry reached him.

Perry slid a coffee in front of him. "Cream and sugar, isn't it?"

"Right," Hollister agreed. "Thanks." He picked up the styrofoam cup and sipped the hot liquid.

"How's the Fox?" Purington asked.

Hollister sampled the coffee again. "He's okay. Got a taped nose and a shot in the ass. He went home."

"You're gonna need a partner for weekend standby, right?" suggested Purington.

Hollister set the coffee down. "No. The Fox says he can handle it. Who knows, maybe we'll get through the weekend without another one."

"Ha," Perry laughed from the other side of the table. "And maybe it'll snow in Burbank this weekend too."

"So you and the Fox can handle it?" the lieutenant asked.

"Yeah, we'll handle it," Hollister answered dryly.

"Why in the hell don't you go home before someone orders an autopsy on you," Perry suggested.

Hollister ran a hand over his face. It was coarse with beard. He felt grimy and knew he must smell of perspiration. "I've got to book this," he said, picking up the vial of urine. "Make a crime report on both the homicide and the two-seventeen on the Fox."

"I can book that for you," Perry volunteered, reaching for the bottle.

Hollister willingly gave it to him.

"Who shall I book it to?" Perry asked, studying the cloudy

liquid. "The Pisser," he smiled, looking at what the Fox had inked on the label.

"The Pisser. That's a beautiful name for this son of a bitch."

"After you get the reports done, get your ass outta here," Purington ordered.

"Be glad to," Hollister agreed.

"Everything else is taken care of," the lieutenant advised. "Hanson and Gillmore have the autopsy results. They're up on Montclair now knocking on doors, looking for possible wits. We've got a teletype out on the homicide, requesting all info on similar M.O.'s. We've also got one out on Raymond Blatts. Mattingly and Collison got the warrant about an hour ago. One count four-five-nine and one count two-seventeen. They're at R. and I. now digging through his arrest package, trying to turn a few addresses or associates. Photo lab's still working on your pictures. When they're done, they're gonna hand-carry them to S.I.D. to come up with a shoe size. When we get that, we'll put out a supplement to our original teletype. I got Hall down at the building running Blatts's VW through Auto-F-I. If we rip off Blatts or if anything else develops, we'll give you a call," the lieutenant concluded.

Hollister nodded his agreement.

"Lieutenant Purington, line eight-nine," a female voice announced from the wall speaker.

The lieutenant moved away toward his desk.

"I'll get you the crime reports," Perry said, pushing out of his chair.

"Thanks, Dave."

"Sergeant Hollister, line eight-o," the wall speaker sounded.

Hollister pulled the black telephone to him and punched the blinking light. "Sergeant Hollister."

"Sergeant Hollister, I've called ten times today and you've never been there," the irritated black voice barked.

"I've been in the field, man."

"Uh huh, well don't you call in on them radios now and then to see who's been callin' you? I mean it ain't right that a person can never get hold of you."

Hollister rubbed a tired eye as the bandaged child several tables away reached a new high with its vocal protest.

"Is that a child cryin' there?" the caller asked.

"Yes, ma'am. Now I'm quite busy. What's this about?"

"Children shouldn't be neglected like that at the police station," the woman warned.

Hollister drew in a breath. "Ma'am, what do you want?" There was effort to control the anger.

"I'm Mrs. Doris Beechem. I'm calling from the General Hospital."

"Uh huh."

"I made a report on my husband on Thursday. He cut me on the leg with a butcher knife and got arrested. I got fourteen stitches in my thigh."

"Uh huh."

"That's an A.D. and W., isn't it?"

"A.D.W., ma'am?"

"Yeah, an A.D. and W. Anyhow, I called and they said you was the investigatin' officer."

"That's right."

"How come his bail is so high?" she demanded.

"What is it, five thousand?" he guessed.

"Yeah, and he hasn't got that kind of money."

"Mrs. Beecher . . ."

"Beechem," she corrected.

"The police department doesn't set the amount of bail. The courts do. It's high because he's charged with a serious crime and he's been convicted of a felony before."

"That was a humbug forgery that he didn't even do," she defended.

"Twelve people thought he did."

"Twelve people . . . he was only charged with two checks and they found him innocent on one. There wasn't no twelve people."

"I was talking about the twelve jurors, ma'am."

"Well, I don't know nothing 'bout no jurors."

"I suppose not."

"What?"

"I said there's nothing I can do about the bail, Mrs. Beechem."

"Well, then, I wanna drop the charges."

"You can't."

"I can't . . . what d'ya mean? . . . I said I'd drop the charges . . . I don't wanna go to court. I want 'em out."

"Even if you don't care, the state of California does. It's a crime to go around carving up people with a knife. The district attorney will have to decide whether or not you'll go to court."

"Screw the district attorney. Who in the hell does he think he is? Where was he when some motherfucker ripped off my house? How come that nigger never went to court?"

"I don't know anything about——"

"I want my man outta that jail. I said I ain't pressin' no charges."

"What happens the next time when he cuts your throat?"

"He was drunk. He didn't really mean to hurt me. It was a accident. That's what it was, it was an accidental assault."

Hollister, though weary, had to smile. "Mrs. Beechem, do you have any other questions?"

"No . . . but I want them charges unpressed. I ain't gonna testify against my man."

"We'll be in touch, ma'am."

"You better get it done, Sergeant," she warned.

He hung up the phone and pulled a note pad to him. He penciled on the pad, "Beechem ADW. Vict will not prosecute. D.A. reject/refer to City Attorney for Poss/Misd. or C.A. hearing." He studied the pad. "People are crazy . . . absolutely nuts," he said aloud.

"Lemme see," Perry smiled, sliding into a chair across from Hollister. "You're either Art Linkletter or a policeman."

"Neither," Hollister said sarcastically. "I'm a detective. I'm the toilet paper cops use to wipe the shit off of themselves after the fine citizens of this fair community throw it at 'em."

"Touchy . . . touchy," Perry said with an understanding smile. "What you need is a good stiff drink, a naked broad and a couple days off."

"Hollister, line eight-six," the box on the wall called.

"And a room with no phones," he growled, reaching for it. "Hollister," he barked into the mouthpiece.

"No need to shout," the Fox's voice answered.

"I'm sorry, Virg. It's just that this damn phone is . . ."

"I know . . . I know."

"What ya need?"

"A gun."

"Yours?"

"That'll do for a start."

"I've got it. We needed it for the shooting investigation."

"Okay. I thought maybe we left it at the hospital. Anybody talk to you yet?"

"No, I haven't even seen anyone."

Perry raised a finger. "Hold on a minute," Hollister said, looking to him.

"That the Fox?"

"Yeah."

"I.A.'s out taking pictures now."

Hollister nodded. "Virg, Perry says I.A.'s out at the scene taking pictures now. They won't get to us till Monday. I wouldn't worry about it."

"I'm not."

"It's not as if you hit anybody."

"I tried."

"How's the nose?"

"I can't smell my Scotch, but it tastes fine."

"Catch you later, Virg." Then, "Hey, Rainey," Hollister called to a dark-haired, smartly dressed detective entering the squad room with his smaller blond partner. "Could I see you a minute?"

"What can we do for you, Brother Lee?"

"You know Fred, that runs Blackie's Liquor at Brighton and Santa Barbara?"

"Sure," Rainey answered, parking his rear on the corner of the desk. "Ol' Freddy and I go way back. I ripped him off couple times when I was workin' Vice. Hellova bookmaker."

"Probably still is. But he's got another problem right now that sounds like robbery."

"Well, let's hear it. Robbery just happens to be my business. If somebody's gonna be robbed, has been robbed, is thinkin' of robbery, we wanna know."

"You know our motto," Berry, his younger partner chimed in, adjusting his mod glasses, which made him look like he belonged in the cockpit of an F-1-11. "If you can't do the time, don't do the crime."

Hollister wasn't really in the mood for all this verbal bullshit. "Across the street from Blackie's Liquor there's an apartment building. I don't know the address, but it's straight across, red brick, three stories."

"Uh huh," Rainey responded, with genuine interest.

"Two dirt-bag-lookin' paddies," Hollister continued, "rented an apartment on the second floor. They wanted one facing the street and they got it. As you face the building it's on the second floor righthand side. The landlady says they show up at seven in the morning and leave at two A.M.

Never leave the room other than that. Seven to two are the hours Blackie's is open."

"Very interesting," Rainey agreed.

"Fred tells me he holds up to two grand on weekends."

"Today's Friday," Berry reminded.

Rainey shifted on the edge of the desk. "Smells like robbery, don't it?"

"It's gotta be dope or a rip-off," Hollister agreed.

"Freddie give you a description of them or their car?" Rainey asked.

"No . . . none," Hollister yawned. "He got his info from Mrs. Washington. She manages the apartment building."

"Think she'll talk to us?" Berry questioned.

"I don't know," he shrugged. "I'd call Fred first."

"We'll do that," Rainey smiled, pushing off the desk.

"Thanks, Rainey."

"My pleasure. Thanks for the clue. We'll let you know what happens."

Hollister shook out a smoke after the two men walked away. Perry was busy working on the evidence report. Pushing back in his chair, Hollister decided to enjoy his cigarette and coffee before beginning the homicide report. Two uniformed officers walked in with a handcuffed black between them. They moved toward Hollister's desk. The handcuffed man was smiling, a look of defiance on his face. "Could you give us some booking advice?" one of the officers asked.

"What is he?" Hollister questioned with little interest, eyeing the youth.

"Two-eleven," the officer replied, pulling a chromed handgun from his waistband.

"See Rainey over there," Hollister said with a nod toward him.

"Thanks. Come on, Studley," the officer said, giving the man a stiff push.

"Hell, man, don't be pushin' on me," he protested.

"Sometimes, Dave," Hollister breathed, watching them move away, "I get the feeling that what we're doing isn't going to change things much."

Perry paused in his writing, glanced at Hollister as if to speak, then resumed his task.

Captain Slack sat quietly staring with a blank expression at the passing store fronts on Crenshaw Boulevard as Captain Judd drove. Lieutenant Bowen, the commander of the Morning Watch, and a black sergeant by the name of Johnson, sat in the back. Johnson had known the Wilson family for years and had talked Dave into coming on the job.

They had stopped at the scene of the homicide on Fifty-fourth Street. The sight and smell of death was still fresh in Slack's mind. His teeth were clenched tight. From what Linsay and Hutch has pieced together in the short time they had been there, it appeared that a gang of young blacks, "Crips," Linsay had guessed, came to the hamburger stand shortly before noon. They wanted credit. Fat Jack, a huge bulk of a man for his sixty-plus years, refused. For his refusal, he had been beaten to death with a ketchup bottle.

Linsay had speculated, in a matter-of-fact tone, that Fat Jack would have survived the beating, but after he collapsed behind the counter, his attackers had dumped several gallons of boiling grease from the deep fryer over his face and head.

Slack trembled with a chill remembering the open mouth that was filled with cooling white lard. The once black, gentle face was blistered and burned beyond recognition. He had grimaced and turned away when Linsay, standing near the body, picked up an uncooked hot dog from a pack on the counter and ate it.

Slack longed for the time when he'd be transferred to one of the city's white divisions. He was so sick of being called in the middle of the night to be told of another senseless homicide. "The suspect killed the victim because of an argument over what television show they would watch. The suspect shot her husband after he complained that his coffee was cold. The clerk was shot to death after being robbed for twenty-two dollars." The crimes were maddening and never ending. He was convinced Negroes would be the downfall of the nation. The black tide of violence was eroding the city that he had once loved to work in. He secretly hated them. It wasn't prejudice, he told himself. He didn't hate blacks. He just hated what they were, and how they made him feel. It wasn't prejudice, he reassured himself.

A burning, tingling cramp crept across the inside of his stomach. He massaged it casually. He had to calm down or within the hour his ulcer would have him doubled over in pain. As soon as he had the opportunity, he'd slip a couple of mints into his mouth. Second roll today. He had lived with his secret ulcer now for eleven months. Only Judy, his wife, shared the knowledge. Even she didn't know how severe it was. He envied attitudes like Linsay's and Hollister's. They could walk over half a dozen bloodied and dead bodies and sit down for lunch. Death to him had always been a trauma. In his eighteen years of service, he had always maneuvered around being assigned to Homicide.

"Turn right on Sixty-eighth," the Sergeant advised Judd from behind Slack.

"She a strong woman?" Judd asked, negotiating the turn.

"Yeah, she's pretty tough," the sergeant answered. "She lost Dave's younger brother in Viet Nam. She handled that well."

The four men were quiet for the last block.

"That's it on the right. The one with the white fence," the sergeant said.

Judd eased the car to the curb. The street was quiet and shaded by the trees that lined both sides. A neighbor pushing a lawn mower paused to glance at the foursome, then resumed his task.

Slack studied the green stucco house. The flower beds around it were fresh and well attended. It all looked peaceful and secure. "Son of a bitch," one of the men in the back breathed.

They climbed out, gathered on the sidewalk, and walked toward the house. The man mowing his lawn eyed them again. Leaving the mower, he walked to his house and went in.

The front door was open. A screen door covered it. Johnson, adjusting his uniform hat, straightened his stance and knocked lightly. Slack's mouth was dry. Bowen and Judd stood silently, waiting.

A dog barked sharply inside and a few seconds later flattened its woolly face on the inside of the screen, wagging its tail wildly.

"Hello, Buttons," Johnson smiled at the small dog.

"Is that you, David?" a voice called from the shadows inside.

"Oh, Christ," Judd muttered softly.

"No, Mrs. Wilson," Johnson answered, leaning near the screen, raising his voice. "It's Chuck Johnson."

Slack wet his lips, shifting nervously. The burning in his stomach was spreading up his throat.

"Oh," the woman answered, walked toward the door, toweling her hands dry on an apron she wore. "I . . . I thought maybe it was David," she said, eyeing the four. Her expression was puzzled. She unhooked the screen. "Get back, Buttons."

The dog moved away.

"Good morning, Mrs. Wilson," Judd said as he followed the others into the room.

"Sit down, please," she invited.

Johnson and Bowen, removing their hats, sat down on the couch. Slack eased into a velvet-covered easy chair and reached for his mints. "Go ahead, ma'am," Judd gestured to the one remaining chair.

"No," she smiled. "You sit down. I'll get one from the kitchen. We've been going to get another chair. We need it, as you can see," she said, moving to the kitchen.

Judd, sitting down, glanced about the room. On the end wall hung three eight-by-ten color photos. The fading one in the center was a smiling black man with slicked-down hair dressed in a wide-lapeled pin-striped shirt. On the right was a young man dressed in Army khaki. On the left was David Wilson, smiling, dressed in his L.A.P.D. blue.

Mrs. Wilson shuffled back into the room carrying a kitchen chair held by the back. She was a small woman, five-five, Judd guessed, thin with graying hair. Her face with its many soft lines showed the years, but her eyes were still bright and inquiring. "Could I get you some coffee?" she said, placing the chair.

"No thank you, ma'am," Judd spoke for the four.

"Mrs. Wilson," Johnson said, holding his hat in hand, "this is Captain Judd, your son's captain, Captain Slack, from Southwest Detectives, Lieutenant Bowen, Morning Watch commander."

"Nice to meet all of you," she smiled apprehensively. Her fingers worked at the apron in her lap. The dog lay down at her feet and closed its eyes.

Johnson cleared his throat and stared at the floor. It had been decided earlier that he would be the one to tell her of her son's death. "Mrs. Wilson . . ." he said in a broken tone as tears welled up in his eyes, ". . . there's no easy way . . . Dave . . . David is gone."

She tightened her lips and sniffed, straightening her head. Her fingers kneaded at the apron in her lap. She nodded her head slowly. "I'm sorry I'm not dressed very well. I was doing some laundry." Her voice was broken and choppy.

"We understand," Judd offered.

"Did . . . Did he suffer, Chuck?" she asked as a tear spilled down her cheek. She quickly brushed it away with a bony finger.

"No, Mrs. Wilson, he didn't," Johnson assured her.

The dog got up, yawned, and walked to Judd's feet, sniffed the leather and lay down again.

"He's always loved men's shoes," Mrs. Wilson said with a quick shaky grin. "David leaves a pair of boots out for him to sleep with when he's not home."

Judd reached down and patted the dog. "Is there anything we can do, Mrs. Wilson?"

She shook her head.

Pulling a tissue from an apron pocket, she mopped her eyes. "Did he die with honor?" she lowered her head.

There was an awkward pause.

Finally Lieutenant Bowen spoke. "He showed more courage than most men do in a lifetime, Mrs. Wilson."

"He was a good boy . . . a good son. If he dies with honor, I'm proud. His daddy would be too . . . he was a good boy."

"Could I get Lorie to come over with you until . . . until you get things organized, Mrs. Wilson?" Johnson asked.

"I'll be fine," she sniffed, looking up. Her face showed the heartbreak she was feeling. "I'll call my brother Eddie. He'll come over and help."

"Fine," Johnson agreed.

"David cleaned up his room yesterday before he went to work," she said with effort. "I said, 'David, what are you doing?' " A tear raced down her cheek. This time she ignored it. "He said, 'Just straightening up, Mama. Trying to get things in order.' "

PART TWO

The brown Plymouth moved slowly down the alley, stirring a light cloud of dust that hung in the hot summer air. "There's the van," the driver pointed to a blue Ford van parked in the shadows at the rear of the three-story apartment building.

His partner jotted down the license number as they passed the parked van. "Robert-one-one-seven-nine-four." When there was a brief pause in the constant radio chatter, he ran the number.

A female voice answered. "Three-William-twelve, Roger. Stand by."

The Plymouth reached the mouth of the alley and turned left. "Right where the manager said it would be, wasn't it?" the driver commented.

"Uh huh . . ." his partner agreed. "This just might be the same dynamic duo that smoked that clerk in West L.A. last week. Remember that? Think it was a Von's Market."

"Three-William-twelve," the radio called, and the officer readied his pencil over a small notebook. "California, Robert-one-one-seven-nine-four, no wants, no warrants, D.M.V. not in file."

"God damn it." Then with the mike keyed: "Three-William-twelve, Roger." He stuck the mike back on its clip. "What ya think?"

"I don't know." The driver was displeased. "Maybe they just bought it or something. That way the registered owner wouldn't be in file. In the process of being transferred. We'll set up in the alley again. Switch to Tac-One. Give Rainey the bad news."

Rainey lowered the black binoculars and passed them to Berry, who was slumped behind the wheel of their parked car. He picked up the mike from the open glove box. "This is Eleven, go," he answered, wiping sweat from his chin and neck.

"Three-William-twelve to Eleven. The van's where the manager said it would be. We ran wants, warrants, and

123

D.M.V. No hits, and D.M.V. not in file. We're set up in the alley. No activity at this time."

"Eleven, Roger," Rainey answered, releasing the mike button. "Goddamned crooks always have all the luck," he complained.

"One of 'em is back at the window again," Berry said in a hushed tone, pushing the binoculars tighter to his eyes. "It's the big one. . . . He's got something in his hands. Can't see clearly because the fuckin' curtains keep gettin' in the way . . . and he won't stand still. Wait a minute. . . . Yeah, there's the other one now. Both eyeballing the store."

"Give me the glasses."

Rainey, holding the binoculars, worked at readjusting them as he focused on the second-story window. "Okay . . . there, I got 'em. Yeah, I see. Fat boy has got something. Damned glasses . . . can't make it out."

"Gun, maybe," Berry suggested.

"Hell, I don't know. If these glasses were a thirty-ott-six . . . pow . . . pow . . . get both them mothers."

"That would get us out of this goddamned heat," Barry agreed, running a finger along his neck and damp collar.

Rainey watched the two figures until they moved away from the window and disappeared from sight behind the shifting lace curtains. He lowered the binoculars and wiped at his eyes. "Well, we can sit here until they make their move."

"Jesus Christ. They've been here since last Thursday. Maybe they won't make a move till next Thursday."

"I'll take it you vote 'no' on waiting."

"You took it right."

"Got any suggestions?"

"Yeah, let's go knock on their door."

"And if they don't answer?"

"Then we'll huff and we'll puff and we'll blow their door down."

Rainey shook his head. "Of all the people to get for a partner, I gotta draw Red Buttons." He picked up the mike. "Three-William-eleven to Twelve. Dit tight, Duff. We're coming around."

With both cars parked in the rear, west of the apartment house, the four men gathered and walked down the alley. Reaching the rear of the brick building, they climbed the three cement steps and opened a torn screen door. The hallway was dim and humid. A worn soiled carpet cushioned their walk to the stairs.

Rainey led the three men up to the stairs. On a cluttered landing where the stairs turned to the right, scrawled on the once-white wall, in a sloppy print, next to a vacant fire extinguisher recess was: "In case of fire, you're screwed."

They paused at the mouth of the corridor on the second floor. The sounds of the Jackson Five drifted through the air, and a toilet flushed above them. Rainey nodded and they moved cautiously down the hall.

Halfway down the hallway a door opened to their left and a smiling, laughing black face said, "Yeah, okay, man, take care. I'll be seein' ya." Pulling the door closed, the man turned and nearly collided with Rainey. The man's jaw fell, he jumped backwards, eyes wide.

Rainey put a finger to his mouth. "Sshhhhh . . . not a word, not a word."

The man ran a spread hand along the wall until he found the doorknob. Twisting it, he pushed the door open. "I thought you was leavin'," a voice said with surprise from inside.

"Shut up man . . . just shut up." The door swung shut.

Reaching the end apartment, the four men parted, two on either side of the door. Guns were drawn quietly. Rainey, kneeling to a knee, leaned an ear to the door. The others waited.

Cupping his hand, he placed it between his ear and the door.

A piece of furniture scraped along the bare floor. Chair, Rainey guessed. A cough. Then voices. "Will you put that damned thing away?"

"Pretty, isn't it?"

"Beautiful."

"Be glad when I get to fire it."

"Put it away."

Movement. Walking. Rainey tensed.

"Anything cold left?"

"Yeah, I think there's a Coke left."

A can popped open. More walking, then quiet.

"Sure as hell is hot."

"You noticed, huh?"

"Be glad when this is over."

"Tonight should do it."

Rainey eased away from the door and stood up. He pointed to his pistol and then to the door. "They're armed."

Taking Berry by the arm, they backed across the hall. "You and me, baby," he whispered to him. Berry gave him a nervous nod. Rainey looked to the other two men poised on either side of the door, guns in hand. "On three," he whispered to Berry. Drawing in a breath, he whispered, "One . . . two . . . three."

They dashed across the hall, turning their shoulders to the door. The hollow fiberboard door fell flat with a wallop, torn from the hinges and lock.

The two men inside sat at a table a few feet from the front window. The heavy one on the right turned his head with a surprised, shocked expression on his face. He never had a chance to move before Rainey, who hadn't broken stride, raised a foot and with a powerful kick sent him reeling to the floor.

The other managed to push to his feet before Berry reached him. Berry grabbed him by the chin and pushed the thirty-eight into his neck at the base of his ear.

Duff and his partner, moving in, pulled out their handcuffs. Duff moved to the rear of the man Berry held. "Don't move, bastard," Berry cautioned him, pushing on the gun in his neck for emphasis. He could feel the man trembling in the hand that held his chin.

"Hey, Berry," Duff said from behind the man. "He's carrying a pair of cuffs."

"Cuff 'em. We'll find out why."

Duff snapped on the cuffs, and Berry released the hold on the man's chin. "Sit down." Berry reholstered his pistol.

The man sank to the wooden chair. Duff pulled the handcuffs from the man's belt. "What are you doing with these, dirt-bag?" he said, dangling them in front of the long-haired man's face.

"I'm . . . I'm a cop," the man answered between gasps. "My name's Baskin. Serial number one-three-nine-eight-two. I work Internal Affairs, Special Problems Unit."

"Internal Affairs," Rainey growled. "Internal Affairs . . . what the fuck are you doing here?"

"I . . . I can't tell you that," the man answered without looking up.

Rainey pushed the table out of his way and grabbed the man by the hair. "Now look here, you ignorant son of a bitch. You could have got me or your own dumb ass killed."

Rainey pulled his head back. "So don't give me this cheap shit about not being able to tell me why you're here. I don't give a fuck if Christ Almighty sent you. I wanna know what the hell you're doing here."

"Hey, Rainey." Duff's partner was kneeling over the other man. "This one ain't waking up."

Rainey released the handful of hair he held. The man's head fell forward. "Internal Affairs," he snarled, wanting to smack the man.

Berry glanced to Duff. "Duff, go find a phone. Get an ambulance and then call the station. Get a lieutenant down here."

When Duff was gone, Berry turned to Rainey, who was examining the man on the floor.

"Let's set the door up." A crowd of curious onlookers were gathering in the hallway, peering inside.

Picking up the door from where it lay flat on the floor, the two men stood it in the opening and propped it up with a chair.

Finishing the task, Rainey wiped at the sweat gathering on his face. "Can you believe this shit? I've never seen anything like this. Internal Affairs. Jesus Christ."

"I see. I heard it, and it still hasn't sunk in," Berry agreed.

"Hey," the handcuffed Baskin called, shaking the cuffs that locked his wrists in the small of his back. "Could I get these things off? You guys know who I am."

"No," Rainey responded without hesitation, "we don't know who the hell you are."

"Look at my badge. It's on the couch over there with my piece. It's the same as yours, fella."

"No," Rainey glared at him. "It ain't the same as mine."

Baskin turned his head away. He sensed further argument would be futile. "You're gonna regret this, Rainey," he warned.

The man on the floor groaned. Duff's partner was still beside him. "Just relax, man. We got an ambulance on the way."

"His name's Williams," Baskin said with contempt. "Sergeant Williams. And you better hope he's not hurt."

Duff's partner glanced at him. "It's pretty goddamned obvious he's hurt, and it sure as hell isn't our fault."

Baskin didn't respond.

Rainey walked toward the window, stepping over the injured officer. Reaching the window, he grabbed a black briefcase that sat beneath it.

"I'd advise you not to tamper with that," Baskin cautioned. "It's evidence in an official police investigation."

"Like you said, Baskin, my badge is the same as yours." Rainey set the briefcase on the table and flipped open the snaps.

Berry moved in closer as Rainey pushed open the lid. The briefcase contained an assortment of thirty-five-millimeter cameras, telescopic lenses, film canisters, and notebooks. "They were watching old Freddie all right." He flipped open one of the notebooks. It was filled with an assortment of black-and-white photographs showing police cars, both detective and patrol, parked in front of Blackie's Liquor. More photos taken with the telescopic lenses showed the officers talking with Fred inside the store. Accepting items from him, over the counter. Bottles, cigarettes, magazines. "Now I get it," Rainey breathed. "They're gonna put the burn on these guys for accepting gratuities and that's why we weren't advised they were here. Not too goddamned clever of them," Rainey added.

Rainey knelt beside the injured officer again, studying his face. The man's eyes were closed and his breath came in short choppy gasps. Rainey shook his head. "I didn't know he was a cop."

A siren whined in the distance, growing more intense as it neared the apartment house. Berry and Duff lifted the small table to the side so the ambulance crew would have easy access to the injured officer. An open can of Coke on the table toppled and fell to the grimy floor.

The siren died abruptly in front, and shortly the ambulance crew thumped up the stairs.

"In here," Berry said, meeting them at the door.

"What happened?" the older of the two uniformed attendants questioned, walking quickly to the fallen man.

"He got kicked in the side," Rainey answered as the man knelt beside him, opening the black medical bag he carried.

"Could you move back a little?" the other attendant requested, squeezing by Rainey.

"Where'd he get kicked?" the older attendant asked, slipping on a stethoscope, moving it to the officer's chest.

"Just below the right armpit. Pretty stiff kick," Rainey admitted, feeling a flush of guilt.

"Pulse is weak," the younger attendant said to his partner

in a matter-of-fact tone. Releasing the officer's wrist, he reached and pulled back an eyelid. "Slow react . . . shock, I'd guess."

The older attendant pulled off the stethoscope. "Go get the oxygen and the stretcher, Bill."

"I'll help you," Berry offered.

"He's gonna be all right, isn't he?" Rainey asked in a worried tone, looking down at the man.

"We'll get 'em to the hospital just as quick as we can," the attendant promised with a quick glance.

"He's a policeman, you know," Rainey added.

"Yeah, I know."

Berry and the other attendant returned with the stretcher. Duff joined Berry at working loose the straps on the stretcher while the two attendants slipped the oxygen mask over the officer's mouth and nose. Then the chrome-wheeled stretcher was pulled in beside him and the four men lifted the officer gently onto it. Rainey turned away as an arm flopped limply from the stretcher to the floor.

Once the man was on the stretcher he was quickly covered with a red blanket and strapped in, the oxygen bottle tucked beside him. "Okay, let's go."

Berry, Duff, his partner, and the two attendants worked the bulky, awkward stretcher carefully down the stairs. Rainey stayed with Baskin in the room.

"Can you take these damn things off?" Baskin shook the handcuffs at Rainey.

Digging in his pocket for the key, Rainey moved to his rear. "Stand up."

Baskin pushed out of the chair. Inserting the small key, Rainey unlocked the cuffs and pulled them off.

"Thanks," Baskin grimaced, massaging his freed wrists.

"Don't mention it."

"Look, Rainey," Baskin said, "spying on policemen isn't my idea of a fun thing either, but I got a boss. He's a commander. I was just following orders."

Rainey gave him a look of contempt. "That's what Hitler's people said."

Lieutenants Milbrook and Purington entered from the hallway. "What happened, Rainey?" Milbrook demanded. "We saw the ambulance pulling away downstairs." He gave the long-haired Baskin a hard look.

"You know the info we got from Hollister and the apart-

ment manager?" Rainey answered. Milbrook was still eyeing Baskin, who was lighting up a cigarette. Rainey, noticing,
added, "It's okay, he's a policeman."

"A policeman," Milbrook frowned.

"Yeah," Rainey said. "A policeman. Internal Affairs. Special Problems Unit."

Milbrook was adding it up fast. "The one in the ambulance
a cop too?"

"Yeah. A sergeant named Williams. His partner."

Purington walked to the table and eyed the open briefcase. He understood. He glanced at Milbrook.

Berry and Duff returned from downstairs. "Ben went with
the ambulance," Duff said. "They're going over to Orthopedic
Hospital. It's the closest."

"Okay," Milbrook said, glancing around the apartment.
"Let's pack all this stuff up and get back to the station. Out
here's no place to discuss this."

"Lieutenant," Baskin said, "I'd like to go to the hospital.
Williams is my partner."

"Not now. There's a man with him. We'll call from the
station."

"Okay." Baskin was displeased. "Let me get my equipment together."

· "They'll get it. You come with me," Milbrook ordered.

"Lieutenant," Baskin protested, "I'm responsible for this
stuff. There's a hellava lot of city money invested here, and
I don't——"

"Look, Officer," Milbrook growled, stabbing a finger at
him, "I said you're coming with me."

Baskin shrugged. "Okay." He dropped his cigarette to the
floor and ground it out.

"Hey, Stu." It was Purington.

"Let's get the photo lab to come down and take overalls
of this place. I think we're going to need them."

"Good idea," Milbrook agreed. "Rainey, have one of your
people handle that. We'll need you back at the station."

"Sure," Rainey nodded. "Duff, can you stand by here?"

"Right." ··,

"Okay, Baskin, let's go."

Hollister turned the air conditioner to high. He'd found his
apartment warm and humid. Standing in front of the cool
breeze from the window unit, he pulled off his jacket and tie,

tossing them to the couch. After cooling his perspiration-damp shirt, he walked to the kitchen and flipped on the over-head fluorescent light.

Pulling open the refrigerator door, he studied the contents as he unbuttoned his shirt. Slipping out of the shirt, he hung it on a nearby chair. Unbuckling his belt, he pulled off the hol-stered thirty-eight and slid it on top of the refrigerator.

After a wide-mouth yawn and stretch, he chose what was left of a quart of chocolate milk and a piece of cold Kentucky Fried Chicken.

Adjusting the air conditioner to medium, he moved to the bedroom. Sitting down on the edge of the bed, he took a heavy drink from the milk carton. After downing the milk, he studied the chicken wing, grimaced, and tossed it to an ashtray on the night stand beside the bed. Setting the milk aside, he pulled off his boots and lay back on the pillows. The faint scent of Janice's Chanel lingered in them. Closing his eyes, he inhaled deeply.

Sex makes the world go around, he told himself. You name it and sex causes it. What was that theory Freud had? ... A gun was just a mechanical, contrived extension of the male penis, and the bullet acted as the ejaculation. What about when a woman shot a gun? Maybe Freud hadn't thought of that?

How about the Pisser? He hadn't used a gun. Razor or a sharp knife, Hollister guessed. Bled her out, then pissed on her. He wondered if Ellen Shane enjoyed her last act of intercourse. Was rape ever enjoyable? Yeah, he guessed it was. Remembering Sue, a girl he lived with for a couple months before he had met his wife. Sue loved to have her bra and panties ripped off, be forced to the bed, and then would scream and yell until he buried his erection deep inside her. He'd broken off with her after refusing to screw her girl-friend while she watched. He often regretted the refusal now.

Deciding he'd sleep until Janice called, he put off calling the Fox to see how he was feeling until he woke up. Maybe, if they got lucky, the stakeout on Blatts's house would work and they'd get the son of a bitch tonight. If that happened, he and the Fox would have to go in and in-terview him tomorrow.

He had a feeling about Raymond Blatts. He couldn't really put a finger on it, but it was a feeling he couldn't ignore. Now Blatts's M. O. fit that of the Pisser. Picking a young female who lived alone, he drove a car, a white VW, like Wilson had seen, and he ran like a rabbit when they went to get him. It all pointed at Blatts, but he didn't really feel Blatts was it. It was too easy, too logical.

"What's the condition of the officer in the hospital?" Deputy Chief Spear asked, drumming his fingers on the desk top, his anger showing plainly.

Captain Slack and Rainey exchanged a glance from where they sat in front of the deputy chief's desk. Slack spoke up. "As of our last call, which was about fifteen minutes ago, there was still no news. Only that he was still in the emergency room."

"Uh huh . . ." the deputy nodded, tightening his lips. "This could have been a lot worse . . . a hellava lot worse."

"Yes, sir, we agree," Slack responded. "We could have had a couple of officers killed if there had been a gun battle."

"I know . . . I know," Spear said. "You people sit still while I make a call. I may have some more questions for you."

"Bureau of Internal Affairs? This is Deputy Chief Spear. Give me Commander Stocker."

His fingers drummed the desk top again as he waited. He glanced at Rainey, who quickly looked away.

"Stocker, this is Spear from South Bureau. You sent two of your long-haired hippy-looking investigators from your Special Problems Unit down here to conduct some surveillance and damn near got 'em killed. In fact, they did such a goddamned sloppy job that a couple of our Robbery teams thought they were crooks and kicked their ass. You've got Williams in the hospital and I've got Baskin being held downstairs."

"Now wait a minute, damn it," Spear demanded, apparently not willing to be interrupted, "I've got here on my desk two cameras, a variety of telescopic lenses, a telescope, and a surveillance and photo log. What I wanna know, Stocker, is what the hell is this all about and why wasn't I notified?"

Speak looked exasperated. "Look, Stocker, I don't need to be reminded that you formally must report to the chief of police, but I am reminding you that you can play double-o-seven all you want so long as you don't jeopardize or interfere with my people. Today, however, because of your shabby work, you did interfere and so I'm making your investigation my business. If you won't give me any answers, I'll just hold onto this equipment until I talk with Chief Peck, and you can be sure that'll be damn soon."

After a short pause in which Spear seemed to virtually squirm in his chair: "I don't care how sensitive your investigation is, I'm not returning these materials to Baskin, and furthermore I will be the judge of what my officers should and shouldn't discuss among themselves. All you need to know, Commander Stocker, is that your man Williams is in Orthopedic Hospital and with that, may I say go to hell." Spear banged down the phone.

The deputy chief sat quietly for a moment, running a thumb along the line of his jaw. Then he looked to the captain and Rainey. "I'll have more to say about this later. For now, I want you, Sergeant Rainey, and everyone that was with you, to sit down and put everything you know about this incident on a fifteen-seven. And, Captain Slack, I'd like those reports on my desk on Monday morning. And one last thing. Let's keep this among ourselves for now. No discussions."

As Spear put a call through to Chief Peck, once the two men were gone, he flipped through the photo log taken from the apartment while he waited. Most of the pictures were of what Spear guessed were Vice officers entering Blackie's Liquor, conversing with the clerk, departing, entering their cars. Other pictures showed the same officers arriving at Southwest Station. The only logical conclusion he could make was that the officers were suspected of accepting gratuities. But he'd never known so much effort and secrecy to surround an investigation of some cop accepting a few packs of cigarettes or an occasional bottle. It baffled him, and thinking of Stocker, and his attitude, angered him. Well, Jim Peck, he was certain, would straighten this thing out and put a much-needed leash on Stocker.

The intercom on his desk buzzed. Pushing the photos aside, he keyed the instrument. "Yes?"

"Chief Peck on four-four, sir."

He picked up the phone. "Jim. Have I got a situation for you."

"I already know," the chief said in a flat tone. "I just talked with Stocker."

"That insubordinate bastard," Spear growled. "I told 'em I was going to call you."

"Listen, Ben, he had instructions to call me. I was aware of the investigation and Stocker was advised if——"

"You were aware. Jesus Christ. It seems like everybody knew but us down here in South end. What the hell's going on, Jim? We all suspects down here?"

"Now calm down, Ben. You touched on the issue a moment ago."

"What was that?"

"That nobody in the South end knew of the investigation."

"Why didn't we? Every other time Stocker's had to advise me of what his people were doing and where they were at."

"We couldn't do that this time."

"Why in the hell not? I can't be responsible for South Bureau unless I know what the hell's going on. If I were a principal in the investigation, I'd understand, but short of that there's no reason I shouldn't have been informed."

Peck didn't answer.

Spear slumped back in his chair. "Jesus Christ, Jim, don't tell me I'm suspect in something."

"That's exactly it, Ben," Peck admitted painfully.

Spear, shutting his eyes, massaged the closed lids with thumb and forefinger.

"What's the allegation?" Spear asked, his tone no longer angry, but flat and emotionless.

"Protection for major bookmaking," Peck answered. "Bought and paid for."

"The liquor store they were staked on?"

"Ben, I can't discuss it with you anymore now. I've already told you more than I should have."

Spear straightened in his chair, tightening his grip on the phone. "Jim, we've known each other since our first day in the academy . . . twenty-three years now. I thought we had established a mutual trust and loyalty, a friendship."

"We have, Ben . . . but our personal relationship can't be allowed to influence professional judgment."

"What the hell are you saying, that I'm a crook?"

"No, I'm saying we'll investigate a complaint against a deputy chief with the same vigor we'd use investigating a complaint against a rookie."

"Jim, if you're saying you don't trust me, you can take this badge and shove it right up your ass."

"If I didn't trust you, Ben, I'd pull you out of that office so fast your balls would rattle. Now, I want you to calm down and keep your mouth shut about this. I'll see you in my office on Monday morning." Peck hung up.

"There you are, gentlemen," Yesterday Phillips smiled, transferring the drinks from her tray to the oval table.

The two men smiled as she leaned over the table, exposing the cleavage between the ample smooth brown breasts.

"Yesterday," the older of the two men said, "when are you going to quit this place and become my maid?"

"Doctor," she smiled, glancing at him, picking up the money from the table, "I've been made too many times already."

They laughed.

She moved away. "Keep the change, honey," the doctor called to her.

"Thank you, sir," she smiled warmly.

Seeing another customer raise his glass in the corner, she moved to him. "Yes, sir."

"Another Christian Brothers with soda and a twist," he spoke softly and in the dim light of the lounge, all Yesterday could see was the outline of his dark face.

"Could I light the candle for you?" she suggested, placing a hand on the glass candle on the small table.

"No, thank you. I . . . I enjoy the darkness." His voice had a nervous quality to it that she found uncomfortable.

"Okay," she answered with her practiced waitress smile. "Have your drink in a minute." She turned and waltzed away.

"You beautiful whore," he whispered, watching her shapely outline in the soft light.

She paused and turned. "Pardon me, sir?"

"Make that a tall drink," he rushed the reply.

"Tall it is."

When she had turned and was moving toward the long bar, he slipped his hand beneath the table and grabbed his erection. "You'd like this, wouldn't you, bitch?" He squeezed the erection. A man like him, he told himself, had to have few regrets because if he doubted himself he could fail; they might catch him and that would be deadly. But he did occasionally acknowledge one regret, and that was that he couldn't tell others about the pleasure he had in his work. He understood that most would probably be repelled by the idea. Yet some might be able to understand the exquisite moments he had being in a woman's bedroom, a woman he didn't know, waiting for her. He enjoyed walking into their closets and smelling the clothing, stroking the silky things, going through the dresser drawers, fondling the bras and panties. It aroused him almost as much as having them struggling on the bed under his ropes. Yes, being in some-one's bedroom was always a particularly private experience; certainly nothing of the kind happened in their kitchen or living room. It even amused him to think that the laws for breaking and entering should allow for what specific rooms were "violated": what parts of the body of the house were broken into. But his greatest secret he knew none would know was realizing that the excitement of having a virgin for her first time couldn't match having sex with a woman for her last time.

"C.B. with soda and a twist," Yesterday said, reaching the service end of the bar, sliding the tray onto the polished top.

The red-jacketed bartender acknowledged with a nod.

"It's for Dracula over there in the corner," she added with a grimace to the shadow of the man across the dim room.

"Thought he'd want a Bloody Mary," the bartender teased, taking the glass, scooping some fresh ice.

Yesterday lit up a menthol cigarette from a pack at the end of the bar as a tanned, square-shouldered man with a well-trimmed full beard slid onto the end bar stool.

"What's a nice black girl like you doing in a place like this?" the man said, giving her body more than a casual look.

"What's a white dude like you doing in a nice place like this?" Yesterday countered, blowing smoke from her cigarette at him.

The man smiled, toying at his beard with a finger. "We've got to find you another job. You're getting a little rough around the edges in here."

"Who in the hell wouldn't?" she snapped, with a twist of the head that rippled the long black waves of hair that hung loose about her shoulders. It was not Yesterday's manner to be rude, and she seldom was, but with this man, Stu Miller, her agent, she could be unpretentious, and honest. He represented one of the few trusted friendships she had established in this sprawling concrete and asphalt oasis sandwiched between the polluted sea and the smog-banked mountains. It was hardly the rainbow's end Yesterday had hoped for.

She'd been in Los Angeles eleven months and twenty-two days. She remembered checking off the number on her calendar this morning. Somewhere she had picked the number five hundred. She'd stay five hundred days. If she hadn't got her foot into Hollywood's door in that time, it was back to Atlanta. This morning was number three hundred and fifty. More than halfway and not a hint of a chance yet.

Yesterday was twenty-two years old, and her physical attractiveness far exceeded her urban sophistication. She had been born and raised in Atlanta, Georgia, the daughter of a city garbage collector, youngest of six children, and the only girl.

By her eighteenth birthday she had learned that her beauty would open doors and provide opportunities where other blacks were turned away without consideration. She entered and won several local beauty contests. This led to her being hired by Dick Matson, the largest Ford dealer in the South, headquartered in Atlanta, to do a series of television commercials. She quickly became a popular and familiar face in five Southern states. Her wink and sensuous smile from the front seat of a Thunderbird, saying "Tell 'em Yesterday sent you," became a standard for late-night viewers, which brought her an abundance of fan mail, but little else.

Dick Matson, the car wizard of the South, had paid her a flat fee for the commercials with an option for more. As a result, other offers had to be refused.

After taping a new commercial one evening, Matson offered to drive her home. She accepted. As they drove into the outskirts of the city from the television studios, Matson, removing the cigar from his mouth, looked at her and smiled.

"Honey, I think you're damned pretty."

"Thank you," she replied, a bit embarrassed. He had never said more than two words to her before at the other taping sessions.

"You know . . ." he went on, "I don't think we pay you enough. I mean, with that body and all, you're worth a lot more."

She smiled a bit, not sure what was coming.

"Why don't we stop at Howard Johnson's up here? They got a nice bar. We'll have a drink and talk it over."

"You mean the Motor Lodge?"

"Uh huh."

Now she understood. "No thank you. I have to get home."

"You could be drivin' a car like this, you know, honey. Old Dickie takes care of his own."

"I have to get home, Mr. Matson."

His tone chilled. The cigar went back to the corner of his mouth. "You're kinda forgettin' who you are, aren't you, honey?"

Her heart pounded. She was frightened. She didn't answer.

"I mean, I ain't talkin' with no lily-white virgin. I know with them tits and that body you've been around the block a couple times. Would stoppin' with me be that bad? It's good business, honey. Just plain good business."

When he stopped for a traffic signal, she opened the car door and ran. "Hey . . . Come back . . . come back here. . . . You black bitch."

Four days later she received a certified letter from H.J. Ryerson, Attorney at Law, representing Richard Matson, Inc., advising her that due to a shift in advertising policies, her commercials would no longer be aired, but she was reminded that her option had seventeen months to run, and she was cautioned against seeking employment that would result in television broadcast and thus a violation of contract.

She felt defeated, and with the commercials gone from the air, what little she had gotten was quickly gone. How could the prettiest face in Atlanta go to work at a local shoe factory or bar? She just couldn't. The prospect of marrying her high-school love, Chad Pines, seemed more and more an acceptable face-saving move.

Chad was managing two dry cleaning stores and, by Atlanta's black standards, he was doing well. But Yesterday, in doing the commercials, receiving the fan mail, being recognized on the street, had tasted a life style her soul hungered for. Being Mrs. Chad Pines she knew wouldn't and couldn't fulfill it. There had to be another way.

It was in *Mahogany Magazine* she found what she hoped was the answer. Jazeman's Unlimited Black Productions in Hollywood, California, was searching for new talent, and those interested were invited to send a resumé and a photograph to Post Office Box Four-Four-Seven-O in Hollywood as soon as possible, Offer Limited.

She secretly mailed off the resumé and several of what she considered her best photos.

Within a week she received a letter from the president of Jazeman's Productions. He wrote that he was impressed with her experience and qualifications, explaining that he had already shown the photos to several producers, who expressed sincere interest. She was thrilled. The letter went on to state that one of the keys to success in Hollywood was exposure, and for three hundred and forty dollars he could reproduce and distribute her photos and resumé, which almost certainly would result in a job, a chance, a start.

She went to her oldest brother, Jordan. He was single and ran his own gas station on the south side of Atlanta. Jordan scoffed at the idea, warning that it was just a sham to make an easy buck. Yesterday argued that she had talent and knew that all she needed was the chance.

Unable to dim her enthusiasm, Jordan agreed to a compromise. Instead of sending Jazeman Productions three hundred and forty dollars, he'd loan her the money and she could fly out. "At least you'll get to see Hollywood for your money," Jordan sighed.

At the going-away party her mother gave, a handmade banner stretching across the living room read: "Tomorrow, Yesterday will be in Hollywood." The goodbyes were tearful, the plane trip fast, and the reality cold.

Jazeman Productions turned out to be nothing more than a post office box. Not listed in the telephone book, nothing with Directory Assistance. Her brother Jordan had been·right. She spent her first night in a motel on Hollywood Boulevard.

It was on that first night that she was reminded she was black. Leaving the motel wearing a white body shirt and blue bell-bottoms, she walked east on Hollywood Boulevard toward Vine, intent on seeing the famous corner. As she moved along the sidewalk, a warm breeze teased at the long black hair and she felt wonderful. If Jazeman Productions was a rip-off, she'd find someone who wasn't. Nothing could deter her. This was her town. She'd succeed.

Gliding along with her handbag slung over her shoulder, enjoying the sights and sounds of Hollywood Boulevard, she didn't notice the white Cadillac idling along the curb, following slowly. Finally the impatient aging driver honked the horn.

Yesterday glanced at the car. The man motioned to her. She stopped. He waved again.

She placed a finger to her chest. "Me?"

The man nodded, and, leaning across the front seat, he cranked the window down.

Yesterday moved a bit closer, careful to stay out of reach.

"You looking for a date?" the man asked with a sense of urgency.

"No . . . no, I'm not," she smiled, baffled by his bluntness.

The man studied the white shirt. "Fifty dollars for a half and half," he blurted. "Come on." He opened the car door.

She understood. Insulted and embarrassed, she turned and walked away.

"Whore," the driver cursed as the Cadillac roared away. She turned her face to the store fronts.

She was near tears when she heard another car slide to the curb behind her. Without looking back, she quickened her walk.

"Hold it up, honey," a male voice called. She didn't turn.

"Police officer. Now I said stop." He grasped her by the upper arm.

"Oh, I . . . I didn't know," she stammered, eyeing the young man suspiciously. He was blond and tanned, very California-looking. "I didn't know who you were. You don't look like a—"

"Yeah," the other officer smiled, "and we didn't know what you were either."

The officer holding Yesterday by the arm walked her to a closed clothing store entrance. "Haven't seen you up here before, have we?"

"No . . . I just got into town today," she answered nervously.

"Sure," the officer said, releasing the arm, taking her purse.

"Hey," she protested.

"Relax," the other cautioned.

"Got any dope or guns in here?" the tanned officer asked, pulling open the purse, shaking it, peering inside.

"Dope!"

"What's your name tonight?" the older officer questioned, giving her the once-over.

"My name's Yesterday Phillips," she responded, watching the man dig through her purse.

"Who's your pimp?"

"My pimp!"

"I didn't stutter."

"Look," she said, stepping back. "I told you who I am. I on't have a pimp. I just got here today from Atlanta, and don't like this at all."

The officers exchanged a smile. "Pretty convincing, huh?"

"Sure is."

"I want my purse," Yesterday demanded.

"What happened with the old Jew in the Cadillac? Couldn't he afford it?"

Her chest heaved and fell with heavy breathing. Tears welled up in her eyes.

"I'll bet she goes for a hundred a roll," the older speculated.

Yesterday spun away and covered her face.

"You have any ID?"

"What?" she sobbed.

"Identification . . . do you have any?"

"In my wallet."

They were quiet behind her for a moment, then: "Chuck, look at this."

"Uh huh."

"Yesterday Phillips, two twenty-seven South Burnside Way, Atlanta, Georgia."

"How about that?"

"And here's an airline ticket . . . dated today . . . Delta Airlines . . . Atlanta to L.A."

"Son of a bitch."

"Miss Phillips . . ."

"Yes," she sniffed, without turning to them.

"We owe . . . we've made a mistake. We owe you an apology."

"You're damned right you did," she snapped, mopping at her eyes.

The officer offered the purse. "We're sorry. We made an honest mistake."

She took the purse. "No, Officer, you're wrong. You didn't make an honest mistake. You made a bad mistake. You're worse than the people you're after."

The blond officer looked at the sidewalk. His partner turned to the street.

"May I go?" she asked in a tearful, angry tone.

"Sure . . ." the officer nodded, "and again, we're sorry . . . we thought . . ." He shrugged his shoulders.

She pushed by them and walked away. Reaching the

motel, she spent the rest of the night crying in her room, feeling very helpless and alone.

In the week that followed, Yesterday visited every studio she could find listed in the Los Angeles Telephone Directory. She spent eleven dollars on bus fares, got lost twice, and was turned away at every gate.

It was a sympathetic gate guard at Twentieth Century Fox who suggested to Yesterday, "Get an agent, kid. Nobody's ever gonna talk to you. You're pretty, but that won't get you in. You need someone that knows the ropes."

"I can't afford one," she answered.

"That's not how it works," he smiled.

"But how could I find someone?"

"I know a guy that might be able to help." He jotted the name and address on a card for her. "He's good people. Go see 'em. He'll tell if you're wasting your time."

Yesterday called the number as soon as she found the nearest telephone. Mr. Miller could see her in two days. Her heart sank, but she'd wait.

She arrived an hour early on Thursday for the meeting. Miller evened the score by arriving at his office an hour late.

The blonde receptionist introduced her to Miller. "Come on in," he invited, leading her into his office.

Pulling off his jacket, loosening his tie, Miller sat down behind his desk. "What can I do for you, miss?"

"I'd like to be an actress," she managed in a high-pitched nervous tone.

Miller studied her. Then, thoughtfully: "How long have you been in L.A.?"

"Eight days."

"You're from Miami, Atlanta, or Phillie," he speculated.

"Atlanta," she admitted.

"Let's see . . . in Atlanta you won several beauty contests, did some modeling, thought you were ready for Hollywood. Right?"

"I did some commercials."

"Uh huh . . . well, my advice is get on the next bus and go home."

"I won't do that," she said with a defiant look, standing up. "If you won't help, I'll find someone that will. I know I'm attractive, and I know I can act. I don't believe all this crap about 'It's a tough town, kid, you don't have a chance.'" She moved for the door. "Thank you for your time."

"Wait . . . wait a minute," he said with a wave of the hand. "Sit down. If I let you go, you'll wind up doing skin flicks or working as a topless waitress. We'll give it a try."

"Thank you," she sighed, brushing a tear from her cheek.

"Don't thank me yet. It may be a long time before we ever find anything for you. Perhaps never, but we'll give it a whirl. You look the part. That's half the battle."

"I'll be patient," she promised.

"Now," Miller said, rocking back in his chair, "tell me who and what a Yesterday Phillips is."

They talked for two hours. Then it was decided the first thing to consider was Yesterday's survival. She needed a job and a place to live. Not a motel. Miller asked if she would work as a waitress, explaining he knew the manager of a black bar called The Flying Fox on the south side. She wouldn't mind, she said, anything. She was excited.

The next day Miller introduced her to Leon, the manager of the bar. She got the job and Leon promised Miller he'd watch out for her. She liked Leon. He was lean, rugged-looking, fifty, with massive leathery hands. "I run a club for black people," Leon told her in his fatherish tone. "Not niggers. . . . Anyone that insults you, insults me . . . so we don't have it. I run a classy bar. You're gonna add to it."

A month later she had her own apartment only a dozen blocks from The Flying Fox, and with two hundred dollars she had saved and another four borrowed from Leon; she bought an aging yellow VW, promising herself she'd never ride another city bus.

In the months that followed, she was busy with work and the never-ending string of interviews and film tests Miller provided for her. She loved it, knowing that some day her chance, her time, would come.

The bartender, sticking the twist of lemon on the edge of the glass, slid the drink onto the bar.

Yesterday took a drag on her cigarette, then stubbed it out in an ashtray. "Be right back," she assured Miller with a wink.

She had nearly reached the table where the man was sitting before she discovered he was gone. She glanced about the lounge. Same customers. He hadn't moved. He was gone. She moved to the table. Two one-dollar bills lay on it. She picked up the money and returned to the bar.

"What's wrong with it?" the bartender asked, seeing her return the drink.

"Nothing, Casey," she answered with a puzzled expression. "He's gone."

Casey took the glass and dumped it behind the bar. "Probably got too excited to wait after seeing you," he teased.

"Oh, Casey!" she scolded.

"Stu," the bartender said, "what 'ya have?"

"Cutty and water, Casey."

"Well, agent-of-mine," Yesterday said with a smile, "what brings you to the ghetto?"

"I got you the lead in the new Walt Disney production called 'Mary Poppins Goes South.' "

"You bearded bigot." She stuck her tongue out.

"Seriously," he said, "I heard from a good source that Metro's gonna do another in the Shaft series. If they do, it'll be a chance for us. I know the producer. He's a liberal left-wing son of a bitch, got a guilt complex about something . . . anyway, he loves to use lots of beautiful black girls. That's where you come in."

"When will we know?" Her face was full of excitement.

"Should hear something next week," Miller smiled, enjoying her excitement.

"Great . . . oh, that's great."

Lee couldn't understand what the ringing was as he ran along the grassy river bank. Finally the thunder in the dark clouds died away as the ringing increased, and then the dream ended. Half asleep, he reached out in the darkness for the telephone beside the bed.

"Hello," he moaned, wetting his dry lips, rubbing at a sleepy eye.

"Hi. I hope I didn't wake you." It was Janice.

"It's okay," he yawned, swinging his feet to the floor to find he still had his socks and trousers on. "I had to get up to answer the phone anyway."

"What time did you get home?"

"About four," he answered, massaging the back of his neck. "What time is it now?"

"Twenty minutes to eleven."

"Damn it, why didn't you call earlier?"

"Because my dear mother drove in from Clairmont to see me and her granddaughter, and I invited her to spend the night. By the way, are you someone who just wants my body?"

"I'd say this is the beginning of a new understanding."

"I dislike endings but not beginnings," she purred.

"Well, how about starting something up over here to-night."

"I'd love to, but I can't."

He turned on the lamp beside the bed, squinting in the light. "Hey, how do I know you didn't bring home one of those jerks that are always trying to hustle you at work?"

"You don't," she giggled.

"Janice, I'm coming over," he warned.

"Fine. I want my mother to meet you."

"What time will she go to bed?"

"She always watches Johnny Carson."

"Christ."

"You wanna come over for a late breakfast in the morn-ing? Tomorrow's Saturday, you know. Mother's going to leave early."

"Yeah," he yawned. "I'd like that."

"I'll see that you do," she promised.

"Give me a call in the morning."

"Okay . . . I love you."

"Proves you have good taste."

After hanging up, Lee put out his cigarette in the ash-tray on the night stand, stood up, and slipped off his slacks, tossing them to a nearby chair.

Grabbing his cigarettes, he walked to the kitchen and flipped on the light. He thought of calling Virgil, but he realized it was too late, so he decided he'd call him in the morning before he went over to Janice's. He considered mak-ing some instant coffee, but gave up the idea when he found the only small pot he had was sitting on the range coated with dried vegetable beef soup. Instead he grabbed a bunch of grapes, switched off the light and moved to the darkened living room where he sat on the couch. His luminous dial showed that it was eleven-o-five.

As he sat quietly in his shorts and socks, eating grapes, he felt very alone. He wished he could see his parents. That, he knew, would help this nagging depression that attacked him every time he was alone. He longed to walk the open fields of his childhood home in New Carlisle, Ohio; to inhale the aroma of freshly mown hay and feel the dampness on his feet and legs as he pushed through the morning fields. Birds on the power lines. There no one got raped, no one got divorced. Maybe no one was lonely, and no one had to eat grapes in the dark.

The Flying Fox was packed with its usual heavy Friday night crowd. The amplified sounds of the Soul Train Express reverberated off the blue textured walls as they played and sang on the oval stage at the head of the lounge. The room was light blue and was thick with a haze of cigarette smoke.

"Carrie," Yesterday said as one of the other five girls working returned to the service end of the bar. "Could you cover my table for a couple minutes? I've gotta sit down. My legs are killing me."

"Sure, go ahead. Hell, in this crowd, who's gonna miss you?"

Yesterday pushed through a door marked "Private, Employees Only." As she moved down the narrow hall, the heavy drum pulse of the Soul Train Express and the crowds' noises dimmed behind her.

"Hello, Cookie." She waved to a huge fat black man in the kitchen who busied himself at a sizzling, smoking grill. The man brushed a hand on his grease-stained uniform. "Hey, baby, what's happening?"

· She paused at the entrance to the kitchen, stepping aside as a young man pushed by carrying a tray full of salads. "I just had to get out of there for a couple of minutes. It looks and feels like New Year's Eve out there tonight."

"I know what you mean," Cookie smiled, flipping several steaks with a long fork on the sizzling grill. "I feel like Ronald McDonald."

She giggled. "I'll see you later, Cookie."

"Be good, baby."

Reaching an office at the end of the hall, Yesterday slipped in and without turning on a light slid down on a soft leather couch. Leaning her head back, she stretched her long legs out in front of her. The office was cool and quiet compared to the lounge and she welcomed the relief.

She was nearly asleep when the overhead light flickered on. Blinking her eyes, she sat up.

"I'm sorry, honey." It was Leon. He was dressed in a long black jacket that Yesterday was certain he must have gotten from Johnny Cash. "If I'd known you were in here, I wouldn't have turned the light on."

"It's okay. I just had to get out of the noise for a few minutes."

Leon gave her an understanding grin as he moved to the desk at the end of the room. "I know what you mean." He looked tired. "I'm gettin' a little old for this crap too," he sighed, sliding into a soft high-backed chair at the desk.

"I've got to get back." Yesterday pushed off the couch, smoothing her long hair with a hand.

"Wait a minute," Leon said, digging in his cluttered desk, looking frustrated. "I wanna talk to you. Sit down."

She sat down on the edge of the couch.

"Ah ha," he said, finding the object of his search. Pushing the drawer closed, he set a small silver powder case in front of him and flipped it open. It was heaped with a snowy white powder.

"Leon. I wish you wouldn't while I'm here."

Ignoring her, he dipped the polished nail of his little finger into the white powder and raised it carefully to his nostril. He sniffed hard, then repeated the process with the other nostril. Finishing, he clamped his eyes shut, leaned his head back, and drew in heavily through the nose. Then snapping his head forward, eyes open, he folded the powder case shut and returned it quickly to the drawer. Yesterday watched him curiously.

Sniffing and rubbing his nose with a forefinger, he said, "I'm sixty-two years old. I've been married for twenty-seven years to the same woman, and I'm no alcoholic. I pay my bills, I work hard, and I've never touched a county check. I'm black and I'm proud, and I ain't going in the closet when I wanna horn a little toot.

"The good Lord knows I like coke and if He wants me arrested for it, I got my bail money ready."

Yesterday gave him an affectionate smile.

Leon sniffed again, wrinkling his nose. "I got a letter from your mother."

He pushed back in his chair. "She wanted to know how you were doing. Told me you've been writing, but she was still worried. She says they all miss you. Says it's been most of a year now and they'd like to see you."

"I know. I miss them too, but it's a lot of miles and a lot of money," Yesterday answered without looking up.

"Honey," Leon said, rocking forward, resting his arms on the desk, "me and my Mrs. . . . God bless her, never had any children of our own. If we had . . . we would have wanted a daughter like you. You're pretty, you're bright . . ." His voice trailed away.

"Thank you, Leon. You've been like a father to me . . . and I appreciate what you've done." Her words came awkwardly.

Leon nodded his head slowly as he studied the desk top. "I want you to go home. I want you to go see 'em. Go visit 'em. Spend a week or so at home."

"I can't . . . I just can't."

"I'll pay for it."

"I can't let you do that, Leon."

"Then I'll loan it to you. You can pay me back. I know you're gonna make it. Hell, girl, some day you'll be able to buy and sell me."

"Leon, I——"

"No argument." He slapped the desk top with a big hand. "Monday you're going. By damn, your mamma raised you . . . raised you and five other little niglets . . . and by damn she's got a right to see you now and again. You're going."

"Leon, I can't go this week," she bargained for time, having conceded she would go. "Stu, my agent, is lining up some really important interviews next week. I don't wanna——"

"That bush-haired paddy just wants in your pants."

"Leon," she barked.

"Well . . . damn it anyhow."

"Stu's been like a brother to me."

"Uh huh," Leon grunted, lighting a small black rope-looking cigar. "He's okay. I'm sorry," he puffed.

"I've got to get back." She stood up.

"You'll go after next week." It was more of a parental command than anything else.

"Maybe," she teased in little-girl fashion, moving to the door.

The cigar went to the corner of his mouth. He pretended to turn his attention to the paper clutter on the desk. "Be damn glad to get rid of you for a week or so," he mumbled, filtering through the papers. "Won't have to answer the phone forty times a day."

"Leon," she called from the door with a smile, "I love you."

"Get out there and push some whiskey," he warned. "Earn your keep."

He was back now. This time he sat at the far end of the bar toying with his glass. He had counted the five waitresses four times now as they moved in and around the tables. She wasn't there and he was disappointed. He was giving serious thought to the one in the blonde wig, whose name tag read "Carrie." She was probably a whore too. Except her tits were too big. He knew she'd have stretch marks on them, and stretch marks on brown tits were repulsive. He remembered the girl last night. Hers were firm and erect. The nipple small and tight. He remembered the warm moist smell of her body as she twisted and moaned beneath him. She had loved his touch, she would never have settled for another man after knowing him. He couldn't leave her wanting, longing. He couldn't leave her that way.

He wished the long-haired girl, Yesterday, were here. His dark eyes searched the crowded lounge once more as he shifted on the bar stool. He knew she wanted him. This afternoon when she stood in front of his table with her legs apart and asked, "Would you like your candle lit?" he knew what she meant. She had even smiled when she said it. The half erection stirred in his pants as he remembered quickly leaving the lounge, going to his car, and, in broad daylight, masturbating as he slouched behind the wheel. She would have moaned at the sight of the powerful hot eruption.

He knew she wanted to come out then. Wanted to suck his cock and fuck him right there in the afternoon sun in the parking lot. He waited for almost an hour, but she hadn't come. Her boss no doubt was watching close. Wanting to fuck her himself, the bastard. But she didn't want her boss, she wanted him.

The man downed his drink. The blonde in the wig with the big tits was out of luck. He didn't want her. He silently bet her cunt smelled worse than her armpits. He wouldn't eat a smelly dirty woman. Never again. He was grown now, his foster mother dead, the bitch. He was glad she was dead. She was fat with stretch marks on her sagging breasts, and a smelly cunt. He'd never have to eat another dirty woman. He wanted only those who wanted him for the man they knew he was. Some women, like the one he longed for now, knew what he was. She wanted him. He didn't have to. Never again would he have to.

Pushing his empty glass aside, he slid off the padded stool and gathered his change from the bar top. He was taking a final glance around the room when she pushed through the

*employees' door. Rolling the coins around the palm of his
hand nervously, he studied her shaded silhouette in the dim
light. There was no doubt, it was Yesterday.*

*Easing back onto the stool, he pocketed the coins. She'd
look for him in a minute, he was sure. Picking up his glass,
he shook the melting ice. Both bartenders were busying
themselves making drinks, but the one nearest him gave
him a nod. He wondered where she had been. It had been
nearly half an hour since he came in.*

*What could she have been doing? Well, it didn't matter.
She was here now.*

"What 'ya have?" the bartender asked.

*He wasn't paying attention. His eyes followed Yesterday
as she picked up a tray and moved smiling into the press of
mingling bodies.*

"Sir," the bartender repeated.

*"Oh . . . yeah. Ah, Christian Brothers and soda with a
twist. Make it tall."*

*He was digging in his pocket for a bill when the tall man
in the black jacket eased out the door at the end of the bar.
He was puffing on a small cigar clamped in the corner of
his mouth. Sweat glistened on his lined brown forehead in
the faint light. "Oh, no," the man moaned, studying him.
No, she couldn't have, not with this bastard. He watched as
the man with the cigar whispered to another at the end of
the bar. Soon they both laughed aloud. The one at the bar
slapped the cigar-smoker on the back and pumped his hand.
They were both smiling.*

*The son of a bitch. There was no doubt now. She'd been
in the back room with this cigar-smoking motherfucker and
she had fucked him. Look at him. See, you could tell. He
was smiling, sweating. They couldn't fool him. She probably
hadn't even undressed. Pulled down her pants from beneath
the short red miniskirt, leaned back over a desk, and laid the
meat to her.*

*The muscles in his neck grew tight as he sat glaring at the
man who continued to whisper into the ear of his smiling,
nodding companion. The son of a bitch was telling him how
good she was. How tight and warm. How she moaned and
groaned, and clung to him as she shuddered through orgasm
after orgasm. Why did she do it? She knew he'd return, he
told himself. Why couldn't she wait? Why'd she have to be a
whore? Just another dirty whore.*

The bartender slid the drink in front of him. He pushed a

five to him. Yesterday returned to the end of the bar with a tray of empty glasses. Eyeing her, he asked, "How does a person come by a name of Yesterday?" His tone was easy, the question casual.

"Yesterday?" The bartender smiled. "Says her mother named her that after she was a day late with delivery."

"She drives a white Porsche, doesn't she?" he asked.

"Naw, I know it looks like she should. But she doesn't. She's got an old yellow VW. Poor, like the rest of us."

"Thought I'd seen her in a Porsche."

As Yesterday stood waiting for the other bartender to fill her order, her eyes drifted down the bar. They met his. He looked away. His face flushed warm. To her, he was just another face, another customer, in the noisy crowd. Another forty minutes and the night would be over. She wanted to get home.

He waited until she had picked up her tray of drinks and moved into the crowd before pushing off the stool.

The bartender, returning with the man's change, found his spot at the bar vacant.

Walking casually to a narrow walkway that separated the Flying Fox and a men's shop east of it, the man looked over the cars in the parking lot, then disappeared into the darkness between the two buildings.

Moving carefully in the blackness, he inched along the rough wall, concentrating on the shaft of light that filtered in from the rear. He kicked a can and it rattled and banged, colliding with others in the dark clutter. He paused. There were some laughing voices in the parking lot behind him. Customers moving to their cars, he guessed. Soon he heard the sound of closing doors, followed by the whine of a starter. He relaxed and inched on.

Passing just short of where light spilled into the narrow passage, he listened intently. The muffled sounds of the band filtered through the heavy walls. Cars rolled by on Santa Barbara, but there was no movement, no sound, from the rear.

He found five cars parked at random angles in the small space posted "Employees Only." A white highly polished Mark IV, several older Cadillacs, a small battered MG, and a yellow VW. Again his eyes searched the lot. A large yellow cat chewing on something he couldn't make out was the only movement.

Carrying his car keys in hand, he strode into the light

coming from the globe above the rear door. Passing the other cars, he walked to the Volkswagen as if he were about to climb in and drive away. The yellow cat stiffened, then darted for cover in the shadows between several trash cans.

Reaching the VW, he moved to the driver's side and tried the door. It was locked. He pushed on the wing window, using the back of his hand, and it twisted open without resistance. Slipping his arm in up to the elbow, he pulled the handle and the door clicked open.

Leaning into the open car, he reached for the glove box. The faint smell of perfume flared his wide nostrils. He sniffed the lingering odor. Popping open the glove box, he pulled out what papers he could find.

In the faint glow from the small dome light, he examined a white tattered envelope with canceled stamps that bore the name Miss Yesterday Phillips, 4127 South August, #18, Los Angeles, California. It was from C. Pines, 907 Carlton Walk, Atlanta, Georgia. He jammed the envelope into his pocket, returned the others to the glove box, closed it, and pulled out a handkerchief.

Using the folded handkerchief, he buffed the glove-box door and the window. Pushing out of the car, he finished by locking the door and then made a final wipe of the window and moved away.

By 2:00 A.M. the bulk of the crowd was gone. Glasses pinged and rattled as the two bartenders put the finishing touches on the night's cleanup behind the long bar. The Soul Train Express worked at fitting their polished amplified instruments into the black cases on the stage. Several boys from the kitchen wandered through the disarrayed tables gathering dishes and cluttered ashtrays. Yesterday, along with the other girls, sat at the long cushioned bar.

There wasn't much talk because they were all tired. Yesterday worked with little interest at smoking a menthol. Then Leon came in from the kitchen. "Come on, my little beauties." He smiled, slapping his hands together. "Time to walk you out."

The dark morning air was crisp and clear. Yesterday enjoyed its touch and taste. It pushed the drowsiness from her eyes and mind.

The VW coughed and came to life with its familiar garbled growl. Backing out, she gave Leon a final wave and pulled away.

Reaching the mouth of the alley, Yesterday rolled to a

stop. Reaching to the middle of her back, beneath the white shawl she wore, she pulled down the zipper of her blouse and unhooked her bra.

Shrugging her shoulders to loosen it, she gave a sigh of relief. She pushed the car in gear and headed home, a few short blocks away.

* * *

He'd expected to have to remove the louvers from the bathroom or kitchen window. She saved him the trouble by leaving the bedroom window open an inch. The window faced a wide alley and after cutting the screen expertly over its four hooks, he removed it, climbed in, and replaced it. It took twenty seconds.

Once inside, he had stood silent for several minutes in the darkness of the bedroom.

Certain he was undetected, he relaxed. Moving to a closet and with a gloved hand he eased the sliding door open and inhaled deeply, drinking in the smell of silks, cottons, straw purses, and leathery shoes. Pulling off a glove, he ran his fingers over the hanging garments, moving from one to another.

At one point he pulled a long silk nightgown to his face and rubbed it over his neck, chin, cheeks. Burying his face in it, he inhaled deeply, letting the breath out slowly through the smooth silk.

Then he unzipped his trousers and pulled at his half-erected penis. With his stiffening erection swinging in the darkness, he eased the silk gown toward it. He could feel a dampness growing across his forehead. The silk touched the head of his penis. "Oh, God," he rushed in a heavy whisper, pulling it away.

Closing his eyes, he again eased the gown toward the now-throbbing erection. It touched him again. His body convulsed. He moaned. Using both hands, he buried the exposed erection in the smooth silk as he balled it into his crotch. He pumped his buttocks back and forth, nearly losing his balance in the darkness.

He could feel the tightening high in the back of his legs. His neck curled back as the feeling raced up his spine. The powerful thrusts into the silk quickened. Climax was only a brief second or two away.

The key in the door shot an icy bolt of fear through him

like the flash of a camera. He dropped the gown. Several coat hangers rattled to the closet floor with it. Flattening his back to the wall just inside the bedroom door, he pulled the long slim folding knife from his back pocket and opened it.

The door opened. "Yesterday," a voice called. The door was now half open. The light flooding in spilled across the living room and into the bedroom. Holding his breath, he watched the light and shadows on the bedroom carpet.

Yesterday turned to the voice. "I don't have any mix, Vickie."

"No, I don't wanna borrow anything. Just bring your body over here. I've got a few friends over who want you to meet 'em."

"Not tonight. Thanks."

"Come on."

"I'm tired."

"Have a headache too?" Vickie teased.

"I look a mess." She was about to give in. "Let me freshen up first."

"Oh, come on. You look fine."

"In a few minutes."

"Look, damn it," Vickie warned, "when you look your worst, you make me look like a dog. So I ain't gonna let you come over here looking like Diahann Carroll. Now come on."

A broad-shouldered black man appeared behind Vickie. "Come on, Yesterday. Get over here."

"Okay, Leman," she smiled. "Just a second."

Stepping inside the apartment she sat her purse on the couch. The door was still open a few inches. In the dim light of the living room she pulled off her shawl, ran the zipper down on her blouse, pulled out her arms, and pushed the blouse to her waist.

The man stretched to the edge of the door as she slipped the unhooked bra off her shoulders and pulled it away. Square in the light of the window he could see the smooth outline of her naked breasts and the distinct swell of her nipple.

Tossing the bra to the couch, Yesterday slipped her arms back into the blouse and pulled it up. After zipping, she smoothed her hair with a hand, dug her keys from the purse, and slipped out the door, locking it behind her.

When she was gone, the man moved quickly to the living

room. Kneeling beside the window, he eased back the edge of the curtain. His eyes searched the courtyard outside. It was bathed in green and red night lights. Beds of ivy and wide-leafed green plants dotted the stucco walls and twisting cement walks, but there was no movement. She was gone. He was angry, frustrated. She had been so near, so close, and they had called her away.

He paced the dark apartment like a caged animal, moving from window to window, peering into the darkness.

An hour went by. He checked his watch constantly, continuing to return again and again to the living room window. Leaning onto the couch he found her bra in the darkness. He buried his face in the hollow of the cups, inhaling deeply. He rubbed it over his face and neck, moaning with delight. A wet tongue flicked out and licked at the loose straps. Finding the cool touch of a metal clasp with his tongue, he drew it into his mouth and chewed at it savagely.

The sound of footsteps in the courtyard drew him back to the window. It was a man walking to the front. He stuffed the bra into a pocket.

He snacked on a banana he found on the small kitchen table and drank from a quart of milk he took from the refrigerator. He decided he'd wait another fifteen minutes. When they were gone, he added another ten.

When another half an hour had passed, he gave up. "Filthy bitch," he growled, taking a powerful kick at a cocktail table, sending it and a glass ashtray spinning with a splintering crash into the darkness.

"I'll show you," he threatened. "I'll show you, whore." He moved to the bedroom. Stepping onto the bed, he grabbed the satin spread and jerked it away exposing the pillows. Centering himself on the soft mattress, he unzipped and pulled out his penis. "I'll show you."

He was on the verge of flooding the bed with warm piss when the sound of a siren reached him. He stiffened, tensing, to listen. There was no doubt the siren was growing closer. A neighbor had heard him kick the cocktail table, saw him at the window, a thousand thoughts raced through his frightened mind.

"Ahhhh," he hissed when the zipper on his trousers ripped pubic hair from its roots as he hastily pulled it up in jumping from the bed. Pushing the curtain aside, he stabbed at the thin screen. Its soft aluminum frame buckled and fell away. He climbed into the window and disappeared into the darkness.

The curtains swayed gently in the night air through the open window as the sound of the siren faded.

The best way to start any Saturday morning was with a shower and shave, Hollister told himself as he washed the traces of shaving cream from his face with cool water. Toweling his face dry, he studied his image in the mirror. He was pleased. He felt good, and he was convinced it showed in his face. Looking good, he believed, was directly related to how one felt, and this morning he felt good. Twisting the cap from a bottle of after-shave, he splashed some on his hands, rubbed them together, then patted it gingerly onto his face and neck. Today was a day off. His day. The Pisser, Raymond Blatts, the entire city of Los Angeles, could go to hell. Today it was someone else's problem.

He was slipping on his shirt when the phone rang. Walking to the night stand, he picked the receiver up on the third ring. "Good morning, beautiful."

"Well, good morning to you, too, big fella."

"Who the hell is this?" Hollister smiled.

· "Let's get to know each other a little better first," the caller teased.

"Ray Dance, you bastard," Hollister growled, recognizing the voice. "Come on, what's on your mind? You're on my time."

"We got Raymond Blatts."

"Where? How'd you find him?"

. "Well," Dance teased, "I was filtering through some reports here at the desk and these two guys walked up to the counter. I said 'May I help you,' and the ugly one said 'I'm Raymond Blatts.'"

"He surrendered? Who's with him?"

"His attorney."

"Son of a bitch."

"Yeah, I agree," Dance breathed. "Been nicer if the bastard had been ripped off out in the street. You know . . . put up a little resistance. Surrendering takes all the fun out of it. Anyway," Dance continued, "Hall's got 'em in the squad room. All we've done is tell 'em he's under arrest. We haven't advised him or anything. Thought we'd call you first."

"Okay, Ray. I'll be in. Be about twenty minutes or so."

He hung up the phone. "Son of a bitch," he breathed, fighting with a sleeve button. For the moment he really hated his job.

He reached the station shortly after ten. The drive in the smog and heat combined with Janice's anger when he called to cancel their morning did little to improve his mood.

The squad room was cool and quiet. The rows of desks were covered with their usual paper clutter, but the room had a relaxed atmosphere. Even the dozen-plus telephones seemed to acknowledge and accept it was Saturday morning. Hollister found it comforting. Here, behind these walls, he was safe. This was his world. Here, he wasn't Lee, but Detective Sergeant Hollister. Here, he was a professional. Here, he was master.

Two detectives sat with a black man near the front of the room. "Morning." It was Ortiz, a stocky short-necked Mexican sergeant who worked the Gang Squad. "Meet 'Bad Man Blatts.' " Ortiz's voice was edged with a soft Spanish accent.

"We've met." Hollister looked directly at Blatts.

Blatts held his glance for a moment and then dropped his eyes to the floor. He sat slumped in a chair pushed back from the desk, arms folded, feet stretched out in front of him. Hollister tried to read the expression on his face, but couldn't. His hair was combed in a neat tight natural. His slacks were double-knit, and he wore a pair of high-heeled boots that added two inches to his height.

"He's all yours," Ortiz said, pushing at his chair.

Blatts flashed the sergeant a heated look. Ortiz caught it and smiled. "I told you I'd go get you a club and let you try it on me, sucker."

Blatts sniffed, shifted in his chair, and looked away. Ortiz mumbled, *"Su madre es una cabrona,"* as he moved away.

Hall, the other detective, leaning on the desk, said, "Time of arrest was nine-twenty. We'll be at the desk if you need us," and moved to join Ortiz.

Hollister shook out a cigarette and lit up. "Follow me."

Blatts followed him across the room, where Hollister opened the door to one of the interview rooms. "Inside."

Blatts balked, eyeing the small room. "I wouldn't try nothing, man. My attorney's outside."

"I said inside," Hollister ordered in a slow, deliberate tone.

Blatts, watching him closely, moved into the room.

"Sit down," Hollister said, pulling the door shut.

The room was small, with acoustical blocks covering the four walls and ceiling. A small wooden table with two chairs was the only furniture centered on the carpeted floor. A single shaded white light washed all shadows from the room, giving its features a stark, hard look. Blatts slid into a chair on the far side of the table. Resting his elbows on it, then pulling them away, he looked uncomfortable.

Hollister took the chair across from him. "Do you smoke?"

"Yeah," Blatts answered, reaching for his shirt pocket.

"Ah," Hollister said with a wave of the hand. "I'm sorry, I forgot. Can't smoke in here." He gestured to the carpet.

Blatts shrugged and slumped in his chair.

Hollister took a long drag on his cigarette.

"What am I under arrest for?" Blatts demanded, pushing straight in his chair.

"We'll get to that."

"Just get me booked, so I can get out of here."

"Bail's all ready, huh?"

"That's it. I ain't spending three days in your filthy jail on some humbug arrest."

Hollister stiffened with anger. "I wanna advise you of your constitutional rights."

"Hey, man, don't bother. I ain't saying shit to you. I know my rights. I've been hummed into jail before. A bunch of lying motherfuckers sent me to the joint before, and this dude ain't going back."

"You have the right to remain silent," Hollister continued. "If you give up that right, anything you say can and will be—"

"Man," Blatts laughed, shaking his head. "Your mother gave birth to a dumb one."

Hollister's lunge cut him short. Grabbing the man's wide-lapeled shirt at the collar and twisting, he pulled Blatts into the table; drawing back his arm, he clenched his fist. Blatts grimaced and pulled at Hollister's hand on the shirt. "Go ahead, man . . . go ahead. You hit me and I'll have my attorney in here in five minutes."

Hollister was breathing hard through clenched teeth. He held his arm cocked, wanting to strike him, wanting to beat his black face bloody. He looked deep into the glazed brown eyes. He hated this man. Hated him enough to kill him. "Some day . . . some day," he threatened, releasing his hold.

Blatts pulled away, pushing back in his chair, massaging

his neck, straightening his shirt. "Never. The day's gone when you imported white pigs can beat a black man and get away with it."

"You're no black man. You hit a black man with a board yesterday, you yellow-backed son of a bitch. If you'd faced him, man to man, he'd killed you . . . and some day some black man probably will. You lawless bastard, you and ten thousand others like you, run over this city ripping off your own kind and when you're caught, you blame your problems on anything that's white. You're black, but it's not from being a black man. It's from the dirt inside you."

"I want my attorney."

"Fuck what you want, dirt bag."

"I gotta right to have—"

Hollister stuck a finger in his face. "I've got a couple rights too. Like having four hours to book you after your arrest. You came in at nine-twenty, so I'll book you at one o'clock."

"Come on, man, my attorney can't stay that long."

"Tough shit. That's the law. The same people that gave you all your rights gave me a couple too."

"That ain't right. You'll pay, man, you'll pay."

"I think your bill's a little higher than mine," Hollister answered, pushing out of his chair.

Opening the door to leave the room, Hollister found Sergeant Ortiz and Hall standing outside. "What the hell are you two doing?" he asked, pulling the door shut behind him.

"We were just hoping," Ortiz smiled.

"He won't. He knows all the angles, the son of a bitch."

"His attorney wants to know what's going on," Hall advised.

"Tell 'em we're gonna book him."

"Now?"

"Yeah," Hollister breathed. "The longer I wait, the longer I'll be here. The prick ain't worth my day off."

"He's gonna bail 'em right out."

"I know . . . I know. What the hell can I do about that?"

Hall shrugged and moved away.

Hollister flipped for coffee and then bought the three-man desk crew each a cup. After finishing his coffee, he walked Blatts down the rear hall to the jail and booked him. "I knew my attorney wouldn't let you set on me for no four hours," Blatts told him. "I'll be bailed out before you get the reports done, turkey." Blatts was booked for attempt murder of a police officer, assault and battery on a police officer, assault with a deadly weapon, evading arrest, and burglary. Thirty-seven minutes after being booked, Raymond P. Blatts walked out the front door. Hollister was still working on the arrest report.

"You know what I was wondering?" Ortiz said as he walked to the desk where Hollister sat working.

"What's that?"

"I wonder if Blatts's bail is higher than the Fox's hospital bill?"

It was almost noon when he finished the reports. He walked to Records and dropped them in the repo box. Returning to the squad room, he sat down at his desk and called Janice. There was no answer.

The thought of returning to his apartment to spend Saturday alone didn't appeal to him at all. He nearly gave in to an impulse to call his wife, then dismissed it. He waved to the desk crew and headed for the door.

"Stay near the phone," one of them called. "This is your weekend. But don't call us, we'll call you," Ortiz added.

He stopped at a liquor store several blocks from the apartment, bought two frozen dinners, a six-pack of beer, and a *Playboy*. After nearly rear-ending a car at a red light, he gave up looking at the Playmate of the Month until he got home.

Parking in the subterranean garage, he pulled a can of beer from the pack, popped the top open, sampled it, and picked up the magazine. He leafed through it while working on the beer.

Dropping the empty can into the sack along with the magazine, he climbed out and walked to the stairs that led to the courtyard.

Skirting the edge of the pool, he noticed several women who were sunbathing around it. His half-erection quickly vanished when he collided with a folding chair and nearly fell. He cursed his clumsiness.

Reaching his apartment at the far end of the pool, he pushed the key in the lock and let himself in. Sliding the grocery sack onto the kitchen bar, he walked toward the bath in the bedroom. He entered the bedroom and stopped suddenly. "I thought you'd never get back," Janice smiled from the bed.

A soft light filtered through the drawn curtains. Her face was framed by the almost studied effect of long blonde hair fanned out carefully on the pillow. Her body was peach colored on the blue bedspread.

"I . . . I thought you were—I thought you'd gone to your mother's," he stammered.

"I didn't." She stretched her arms outward to him. Her breasts quivered, nipples erect. She wasn't smiling.

"I'm dressed," he said in a boyish tone, hesitating.

"You're also embarrassed, but come here, I'll help you undress." He found the fold across her stomach that particularly excited him. He sat on the edge of the bed while she unbuckled his belt, unsnapped the pants, and ran the zipper down. As she slipped a hand under the band of his jockey shorts, he slid a palm over her flat stomach, running his fingers into the fluff of hair between her thighs. Much to his surprise she then lowered her head and took his now-throbbing penis in her mouth. He wondered whether she would let him come right then, but he thought not.

"Does this mean every time you hang up on me I can come home to this?"

"H-mm." She took his hand and placed it on what Lee felt was her clitoris and slowly rotated it. He felt both aroused and mildly put off by her boldness, but he said nothing. He never talked during sex.

They slept into the early evening after their lovemaking, wrapped in each other's arms and legs. It was about seven-thirty when Janice got up and fixed them dinner. They ate in the nude at the kitchen bar.

After eating half his dinner, Hollister surrendered to the impulse to kiss her breasts while she sat nude on the bar stool. Pushing her plate aside, Janice moved a hand to him and he responded. They moved to the cool tile floor.

Dinner was followed by a twosome shower. Once they had toweled one another dry, the television was rolled into the bedroom and they settled in for the night. "I should call the Fox," Lee said, with a yawn, resting his head between Janice's breasts. "In a minute," she whispered, cradling him. Closing his eyes he wondered where his children were. It had been so long since he had seen them. He hoped they loved him, hoped somehow they knew he loved them. He squeezed and pushed harder into her breasts with his cheek. She held him tight.

He woke early in the morning and much to his surprise he found he wanted her, not so much to race to a climax, but just to enter her and enjoy the warmth, the nearness. He gently placed his hand on her breast, kissed her lightly on the neck and she began to be stirred. Shifting his body, his erection pushed between her buttocks. Without opening her eyes, she turned and raised a leg. Sliding a hand beneath the sheet, she guided him in. He pushed. Her neck arched back into the soft pillow as he entered.

After a few minutes of slow movement, his half-erection became full. He wished he had brushed his teeth because he wanted to kiss her. It was difficult for him to get really turned on without kissing her. Their movement stopped when the telephone rang. Janice, stretching, picked it up from the night stand and handed it to him. He pushed to keep the fading erection inside her and took the phone.

"Hollister? This is Hall from the desk. We've got a dead body in a garage over on Stocker Avenue. Patrol says it looks like a suicide. He may have let his car run in the garage on purpose, but they're not sure."

"Who found him?" Hollister asked, wiping at his face as if to brush the sleep away.

"His wife. About thirty minutes ago."

"Ambulance roll on it?"

"Not yet. . . . The patrol officers tell me he's slumped behind the wheel of his car in the garage. It's locked, the key's in the ignition."

"How do they know he's dead?"

"They said his tongue's hanging out and his eyes are open. They beat on the windows, shook the car. He's dead. They know what they're doing."

"Uh huh."

"You want us to take a run over and look? Give you a call back?"

"No, it's okay. That's what I get paid for. I'll be in."

"Okay."

"You call the Fox yet?"

"No . . . will he be working? I thought he'd be off a while."

"He told me he'd be working. Give 'em a call. See if he feels like coming in."

"Right."

"How about calling Prints, the photo lab, and the coroner. Give 'em the address. Tell 'em I'll be there in about thirty minutes."

"How come thirty minutes?" Hall questioned. "You've always claimed you could make it in twenty minutes."

"I have the right to remain silent," Hollister said, and hung up.

"You really want me again?" Janice said, taking his face in her hands.

He nodded. "Do you mind?"

"No," she assured, slipping a hand beneath the sheet to find him.

He pushed on top of her and began a steady rapid thrusting. She held him tight with her legs. A light sweat dampened his brow. He paused, and through the tangle of her hair and pillow he asked, "Can you?"

"I don't think so. I'm not a morning lover. Can you?"

"Close," he said breathless, resuming his movement. With several more thrusts he finished, pushing her wide-legged into the sheets, muffling his cry in the pillow. She brushed at the short hair on the back of his neck as he sighed and relaxed.

"You know," he said, turning his head to the side, strands of her hair clinging to his sweaty forehead, "it's crazy."

"What's crazy?" she asked.

"I just made love to you. Now I have to go look at a dead body."

She said nothing.

It was a little after nine when he got on the freeway. It looked like a Sunday morning should, he decided. The air clear, the sky blue, dotted with white puffy clouds, and the traffic was still light with mostly campers and boats. He switched on the radio, then gave up when all he could find was rock music or hymns. Moving to the outside lane, he lit up a cigarette and cracked his window open to draw out the smoke.

He hoped the Fox was coming in. If he didn't, he decided, he'd take one of the desk crew out to the scene with him. Suicide shouldn't take too long. Hour maybe. Afterwards, with Janice gone to Clairmont to pick up her kid, he decided he'd call his wife. See if he couldn't come down and see the kids. Maybe take 'em and get an ice cream.

He got off the freeway at Santa Barbara Avenue and turned west. There was little traffic on the streets. A few older black women sat on a bus bench at Figueroa, a man in soiled coveralls worked at opening his service station, a jogger in a red sweat suit looked directly at him as if the man knew what he was. It seemed to him that one of the first things a black child learned was to spot the man, the police. They were always looking for them.

At Normandie Avenue a large black crow pecked at a scrap of discarded food in the center of the street. "A crow," Hollister laughed, seeing the bird as he rolled toward it. "Hi ya, Jimmy." He sounded his horn and the crow leaped into the air. "You stay down here, bird. You'll wind up being served with some grits and greens."

He turned into the station's parking lot from La Salle Avenue. A black officer assigned to station security, leaning against a small guard shack, only glanced at him and returned to reading a Sunday paper.

Hollister stopped his car beside the man. The officer's uniform hung slack on his frame, his shoes were highly polished. Recruit, Hollister guessed. The officer looked up over his paper at him.

"Do you know who I am?" Hollister questioned in a sober tone.

The young man quickly lowered his paper. "No . . . no, sir, I don't."

"Uh huh," Hollister said, looking him up and down. "You let anybody drive in here?"

"No, sir." The officer straightened his stance, not sure what to do with the paper.

"If you don't know me, how come you didn't stop me?"

"Ah . . . well, sir, you look like a policeman."

"What's a policeman look like?"

"You know, sir. You're white and you drove in like you knew where you were going."

"Uh huh," Hollister frowned, enjoying his game. "I'm white. You mean if I was black, you'd stop me?"

"Ah, well, if I didn't recognize you. Yes, sir."

"But if I'm white it's okay to just drive in."

"Well, no sir, that's——"

"I think you're prejudiced, Officer." Hollister put the car in gear and rolled on.

To his pleasure he found the Fox sitting at their desk in the squad room with Sergeant Ortiz and Dance.

Ortiz glanced at his watch as Hollister took a chair across from the Fox. "Thirty-two minutes."

"I'll bet our call disturbed his piece," Dance added.

"Man's got a right to his privacy," Hollister answered.

"Had to be a woman," the Fox smiled. "He's wearing a tie, and it's got a knot in it that looks like it was made by someone who had an opposable thumb this time."

"Fox, be careful! Your education is showing," Lee responded, wishing at that moment he had the formal education Virgil had.

"Well, you don't look too bad," Lee added after a pause. There was a wide strip of white tape over the bridge of Virgil's nose. His eyes were still puffed, and near the tip of his nose Lee could see several small scabbing punctures.

"No, it's not too bad. Feels a helluva lot better today."

"You know your friend Blatts' here?" Hollister asked.

"Yeah. Walked in and surrendered, I understand."

"He didn't want you shooting at him anymore. Probably figured you could only miss so many times."

"His day will come. Come on, let's go do some police work." The Fox pushed out of the chair and stood up.

"Keep your nose out of things," Dance laughed.

"Dance," the Fox suggested, "why don't you go empty the ashtrays in the captain's office?"

Stocker Place was a wide tree-lined street. The houses and apartment buildings were Spanish in style and all a sleepy soft brown ringed with wide spaces of grass and flowers.

"Some ghetto," Hollister snorted as they rolled down the quiet street.

Fox glanced at him as he drove. "My, we're in a good mood today, aren't we?"

"Hasn't a damn thing to do with mood. It's just that I'm tired of hearing what a terrible place this so-called ghetto is. Hell, look at these places. It's nicer than the town I grew up in."

"Uh huh," the Fox agreed. "But where is it written a ghetto has to be dirty?"

"Come on, you know what I mean."

"I know what you mean. You're surprised that the neighborhood is all black and still looks good."

"No, that's not it. A ghetto is poor and run down."

"In your mind."

"Yeah, in my mind."

"Well, to these people, this is a ghetto."

"Well, they're wrong."

"How many times did you get stopped by the police while walking to school?"

"Never, but that was different."

"Anybody in your school ever get cut or shot? Did you have three locks on every door in your house? Ever get stopped for having a taillight out?"

"No."

"All that and a helluva lot more is true down here."

"Don't talk down to me," Hollister cautioned. "I know it's true, but we didn't cause it."

"Who caused it isn't important. The fact it's true is. It's a ghetto all right."

He studied the Fox for a moment, realizing he'd touched a nerve. When he thought of him, he realized he didn't think of a black face. "Do you think of yourself as black?" Hollister was immediately sorry he had asked the question.

"Yeah, I think of myself as black. I get reminded too often to forget. Do you think of yourself as white?"

"No. But you do mind being black."

"Mind being black? Hell, my mother probably wouldn't love me if I wasn't."

"Des looks like da place," the Fox said, spotting the black-and-white patrol car at the curb ahead sandwiched between several other cars.

They moved down a walk that led to the rear of the two-story stucco apartment. A uniformed officer stood in the shade of an elm near the side door of a garage that faced the alley.

"He's in here." The officer led them into the cramped one-car garage where the heavy odor of exhaust fumes still filled the air. The '68 Cadillac sat quietly with its hood up, a whisp of vapor drifting from the cooling radiator. A single unshaded hundred-watt bulb overhead washed what little color there was from the gray, unpainted cluttered walls.

Fox moved to the driver's door. The man lay with his head back over the seat. His tongue was a distinct blue, which Virgil assumed was caused by the poisonous carbon monoxide. It rested on his lips as if his mouth were full of blue tongue. His eyes, open and reddened, had a film over them. His arms hung limp at his sides, palms out. The light brown slacks he wore were wet in the crotch.

"I think he's dead," the Fox said, continuing to survey the interior of the car.

"Very good, Watson."

"There's rags stuffed along the bottom of the garage door," the officer said from the doorway.

"Uh huh." The Fox moved to the rear of the car and nudged the rags with the toe of his shoe.

"That shit'll give you a headache," Hollister said, complaining of the lingering odor.

"It'll go away after a bit," the Fox answered, working his way around the other side of the car. "If you don't believe me, ask our man in the car."

They moved outside and into the shade of the tree. The morning air was growing warm.

"Where's your partner, Smith?" Hollister asked the officer as he lit up a smoke.

"Inside with the bereaved."

"How is she?"

"Pretty good . . . you know, not the usual basket case."

"When'd she find him?" The Fox was toying with the bandage on his nose.

" 'Bout eight-thirty this morning. Said they had a fight last night, and he split about ten. She came out with some trash this morning and heard the car running. She got a key, unlocked the garage, and found him."

"What do ya think, Virg?" Lee asked, with a glance at him.

"Murder." The Fox's answer was matter-of-fact in tone. He pulled a twig from a low-hanging branch.

"Murder!" the officer exclaimed. "I don't see it. I mean, I've been here for over an hour . . . and all I saw was some dude that climbed in his car and gassed himself."

"That's why we're detectives, boy," Hollister smiled. "Let's go talk to your crook, Virg. Smith, Prints and Photos are coming down. Let us know when they get here."

"Sure . . . You guys really believe it's murder, huh?"

The back door was open. They moved through the small kitchen into a living room, where they saw a middle-aged woman on the telephone. Hollister smelled the aroma of freshly brewed coffee. A stocky black officer, who had been sitting across from her, hat in hand, rose out of his chair as the two entered.

The officer took a few steps toward them away from the woman. "How ya feeling, Fox?"

"Fine. Who's she talking to?"

"Her brother," he whispered.

"She looks like she's taking it pretty good," Hollister offered. She was a tall woman, maybe 5' 10", whose high cheekbones were highlighted by the fact that her hair was drawn back and tied. Lee thought her eyes were unusually large and that her long red gown accented her blackness.

"According to her, they were gonna get a divorce," the officer whispered. "They've been separated a couple times.

She said he came home drunk last night and she told 'em to get out. That was the last she saw of 'em."

"Okay," the Fox nodded. "We'll see what she has to say. Why don't you go out with Smith?"

The woman ignored their presence as she continued to talk softly into the phone, cupping the mouthpiece with a hand. Hollister took the chair the officer had vacated. Fox sat down on the other end of the eight-foot velvet couch.

To Hollister's left, on the top shelf of a metal bookcase, sat a ten-gallon fish aquarium. Air bubbles streamed to the top in a continuous line from a small filter buried among the green wavy plants anchored in the sand. He wondered if his son still had his aquarium. He smiled as he remembered a Saturday night when he and Jeff had lain on his small bunk watching the live-bearing, swelled black molly streak again and again to the water's surface, then dive away sharply as a pinpoint of life, freed from its mother's body, wiggled through the water.

When the woman hung up the phone, the Fox said, "Mrs. Carson, I'm Investigator Fox, and this is Sergeant Hollister. We're the officers assigned to investigate your husband's murder."

"Mur—murder!" she stammered with wide-eyed fright, clutching the neck of her robe with both hands.

"Yes ma'am. Before you say anything, I must advise you of your constitutional rights."

"My God." She pushed to the edge of the couch.

"You have the right to remain silent." Fox looked directly into her eyes. She did not hold his gaze. "If you give up the right to remain silent, anything you say can and will be used against you in a court of law. You also have the right to speak with an attorney and to have the attorney present during questioning. If you so desire and cannot afford one, an attorney will be appointed for you without charge before questioning. Do you understand each of these rights I've explained to you?"

"Yes—but—"

"Do you wish to give up the right to remain silent?"

"My God, you think I've done something."

"Do you wish to give up the——"

"Yes, yes, I'll talk to you. I haven't done a thing."

"Mrs. Carson," the Fox cautioned, "my partner and I are homicide investigators. We're professionals. We don't do this as a hobby. It's our specialty, and we're good at it. We're going to investigate this incident completely, and we're going to find the truth."

The woman was visibly shaken. Her hands were clamped in fists held in her lap.

"I . . . I thought he committed suicide," she said with effort.

The Fox gave her a hard look. "You found him locked in the garage this morning."

She nodded.

"The door only locks from the outside, Mrs. Carson." Fox spoke in a slow accusing tone.

Hollister tried to remember the lock on the garage door. It had looked like a common dead bolt to him.

"You were the last one to see him alive, Mrs. Carson," Fox continued. "Now, we know he couldn't have locked himself in, and you're the only other person with a key. You're not a bad person, Mrs. Carson." Virgil's voice was now sympathetic. "You're no murderess. There must be something behind this. Why don't you tell us about it? Believe me, we'll understand."

"I . . . I can't."

"You see my nose," the Fox gestured. She gave him a tearful nod. "I wanted to kill the man who did it. I would have if I'd had the chance. So I can understand how some drunken husband harassing you week after week could push you into something like this."

Lowering her head, she brushed a tear away. Fox glanced to Hollister.

Hollister took the cue and straightened in his chair. "Let's take her down and book her. She's not gonna say shit. We've got enough evidence."

"No, wait. Give her a chance. There's a big difference between murder and something like this where she had no choice."

"Choice, shit," Hollister growled. "She's good for murder one. Let's go."

"Now, look. I told you what I thought and I'm running this case. If you don't like it, get out."

"Glad to," Hollister snapped, pushing out of his chair, stomping out of the room.

Fox waited until Lee had closed the door.

"What do folks call you?"

"Jackie," she answered.

"Jackie, he means what he said."

She shook her head. "I didn't wanna do it," she sobbed. "I knew it wouldn't work. I told him."

"You told who, Jackie?"

She shook her head. "I can't . . . I just can't."

"You know we'll find out. It's easier if you tell us."

"It was Reeves's idea . . . he wanted to do it." She bent her head lower.

"Who's Reeves?"

"Reeves Gateman. He's my boyfriend."

"Why'd he want to do it?"

"Johnnie wouldn't give me a divorce," she sniffled and raised her head.

"Did he know you had a boyfriend?"

"Yes . . . yes, he knew. That's why he wouldn't give me a divorce."

"You wanna tell me about last night?"

"I hadn't seen Johnnie for about a week. He was like that. I work every day and all he does is whore around, spending my money on a bunch of pigs. Reeves and I went out last night. When we got home, Johnnie was here drunk on the couch. We took 'em out to the car. I was hoping the bastard would get killed driving, but he passed out again in the car. That's when we decided to . . ." Her voice trailed away.

"Who stuffed the rags under the door?"

"We . . . we both did."

"Where does Reeves live?"

"On Hyde Park."

"What's the number?"

"Do you have to bother him? It was my fault. The motherfucker deserved it anyway."

"Yeah, I'm gonna have to talk to him." Fox was amazed at her cold-blooded attitude.

"Sixty-one thirty-three Hyde Park, number six."

She gave him a tearful nod. "Am I going to be arrested? I don't wanna lose my job."

Fox stood up. "We'll talk about that."

Walking to the kitchen door, keeping an eye on the woman, he called to the black officer. "Hey, Blake. Come on in and baby-sit this broad. She's under arrest but don't cuff her yet. I want her attitude good until we get her statement on tape."

"She do it?"

"Half of it."

After Blake was inside, Fox joined Hollister in the garage. He was watching a small-framed man in horn-rimmed glasses work at dusting powder with a small brush along the inside of the driver's door of the Cadillac. The body was gone.

"Simon says he's got some good lifts," Hollister advised as they watched the man work.

"Who says?" Fox smiled.

"Simon says."

"Oh, how'd you get in the car?"

"Smith opened it with a coat hanger."

"Did you get some pictures before you took 'em out?"

"Yeah. Photos have been and gone. Coroner left maybe two minutes ago."

"Did you insult him this time?"

"No," Hollister grinned. "I was very nice. Plus this one wasn't a faggot."

The Fox rubbed at his bandaged nose. "Damn thing really itches."

"Your bluff work?" Hollister smiled.

"How's that?"

"The door . . . it locks from either side."

The Fox smiled. "I'll be damned. I didn't know that. I was betting on the car windows being rolled up. If it was suicide, he wouldn't have let them up."

"Uh huh." Hollister grinned, pleased with his partner's cleverness. "She go for it?"

"Yeah, she and her boyfriend did it. A dude named Reeves Gateman."

"How about that!"

"Smith," the Fox said.

"Yeah?"

"When we leave here, we'll take the snake. You go down to sixty-one thirty-three Hyde Park, apartment number six, and get us a dude named Reeves Gateman."

"Arrest him?"

"Arrest him," the Fox assured.

"My pleasure."

"I'll go back in and get this broad to get dressed," the Fox said. "We should be ready to roll soon, right?"

Hollister shrugged. "Simon, how about it? How long?"

"Ten minutes," the voice answered from inside the car.

"Simon says ten minutes," Hollister smiled.

It was almost noon when the Fox wheeled the Plymouth into the station parking lot. Hollister was riding in the back seat with the woman. The Fox braked sharply when the young black officer stepped out and threw up a hand. "Jesus Christ," the Fox growled.

Moving to the side of the car, the officer, using his Academy-taught tone, said, "May I see some identification please."

The Fox was shocked. "God damned, man, are you blind? This is a police car I'm driving."

"Yes, sir, it appears to be, but it's unmarked."

Hollister smiled.

The Fox shook his head. "It's an old custom that L.A.P.D. detective cars aren't marked, junior."

"I'll have to see some I.D., sir," the officer stood firm.

"Jesus Christ!"

Hollister chuckled softly. "Show 'em some I.D., Fox."

The Fox pulled open the front of his suit jacket, revealing a silver-and-gold badge pinned to a strap on his shoulder holster.

"Thank you, sir," the officer said. "You may enter."

The Fox opened his mouth to speak. He was near rage.

"Virg," Hollister cautioned from behind.

The Fox took in a long breath and let it out slowly. Shaking his head in disbelief, he let the car roll ahead.

The Fox escorted the woman to one of the detective bureau's small interview rooms while Hollister went to the cramped tape control room. With the Fox guiding her through every detail of the past twelve hours, Hollister recorded her every word.

When the interview was finished, Fox got her a coffee and one of Hollister's cigarettes. He and Hollister were sitting at their desk enjoying a cup when Smith and Blake brought in their handcuffed suspect.

"Meet Reeves Gateman," Smith said, pulling out a chair for the man at the desk beside them. "Sit down," Smith ordered.

The man wasn't what the Fox expected. Jackie Carson was a big woman and he expected her lover to be the same. Instead, he was a small, thin black man with a receding hairline and a full beard. His face was set in an angry, defiant expression.

"Has he been advised of his rights?" Hollister asked, studying him.

"That won't be necessary, officer," Gateman responded in a voice that the Fox found fitting for his size. "I have no intention of making any statements, and I think you'll find this arrest will be a rather costly one since I'm not guilty of any wrongdoing."

"Is that a fact?"

"Yes, that's a fact."

"Blake," the Fox suggested, "why don't you take Mr. Gapemon—"

"It's Gateman," the man corrected.

"Oh, yes," the Fox agreed with a smile. "Take Mr. Gapemon over to the interview room on the left and introduce him to the young lady in there."

Gateman did not appear alarmed.

After Blake ushered the man into the room, Hollister and Fox moved quickly to the tape room.

There Hollister depressed the play and red record buttons on the machine.

". . . only from outside he told me," the female voice pleaded.

"You dumb bitch. You stupid dumb bitch. He lied to you, and you fell for it."

"I'm sorry, Reeves," she cried. "I love you, baby, I'm sorry."

"Love me. . . . If you loved me, what am I doing here? You told them about me, didn't you?"

The woman sobbed now. "I had to. They knew everything."

"Shut up."

"Insurance money. You . . . you wanted the insurance money more than me. Reeves, why? Why did we do it?"

"Shut up, god dammit, just shut the fuck up."

"That's enough," Hollister said. "We've got his nuts tied in a square knot. Go tell 'em."

After Fox left, Hollister continued to listen to the speaker.

"I loved you, Reeves. I truly loved you."

"You're too dumb to love anything."

"Oh, Reeves, don't, please don't."

"Pardon me for interrupting," the Fox's voice broke in.

"Get 'em, Fox," Hollister said to the speaker.

"I don't know what you're trying to do, Officer," Gateman complained. "Putting me in here with this woman I've never seen before."

"What was that?"

"I said I don't like being in here with this woman I've never seen before."

"I'm sorry, sir," the Fox said. "You're going to have to speak up or the tape recorder won't pick it up."

"What!" Gateman shouted.

"I said you'll have to speak——"

"That's illegal. You can't do that." The confident defiant tone was gone. "I know my rights. I'll sue you smart mother-fuckers. You can't do this."

"Well, sir," the Fox answered coolly, "the California Supreme Court decided it was legal to record conversations between principals in a conspiracy in the case of the people versus Calhoon."

"Fuck the people and Calhoon. I'll sue all you—" Hollister switched the machine off.

While Smith and his partner booked the two suspects, Fox worked on the death report. Hollister phoned the coroner's office and scheduled the autopsy for Monday at nine.

"Either we have dumb crooks or we're damned good detectives," the Fox said, finishing the report.

"I think you know which it is," Hollister said, glancing at his watch. It was ten minutes of one.

"Wanna come over and share a steak?" the Fox invited.

"You're gonna do the steaks?"

"No. I got this little teacher that lives next door. Loves to mother me. She's coming over. Even bringing the steaks."

"I wouldn't wanna interfere with your love life."

"No problem. She's got a foxy blonde roommate. Tells me she's part mink. Do you good to get exposed to some wild-life."

Hollister considered the invitation. "I was gonna call home. Maybe go by and see the kids."

"Uh huh. I know who you wanna see, and it's not the kids."

"No way."

"You're homesick," the Fox teased.

"I just wanted to see how the kids were."

"It's a sunny summer afternoon in June. Every kid in the world is fine. You call now and you're landing in the middle of their day. When they need to hear from you is when there's nothing else to do."

"It's been a while," Hollister countered.

"Call 'em," the Fox urged. "If they're not home, you might as well come over."

Hollister tried to build a mental image of what the blonde-

haired schoolteacher looked like. The thought stirred a bit
of excitement in the back of his mind. A slice of guilt
brought Janice to his mind's eyes. Hell, what was he hurting? She'd never know. He pushed away the thought of
Janice, not wanting her image to share in his thoughts. "Let
me give 'em a call. If they're not home, you got a deal."

Lee's heart quickened as he dialed the number that had
been his for . . . he couldn't remember how many years.
Virgil got out of his chair and walked away. Hollister silently thanked him for his consideration.

As the telephone rang in his ear, he could almost hear it
in the house that had been home for so many years. "I'll get
it, Mom," Cathy would shout. He smiled, remembering how
she'd race to the phone and be utterly destroyed when it
wasn't for her. Jeff never would answer it unless ordered to
and then he'd complain.

"Get the phone, Jeffrey," Carol would order. It was always
"Jeffrey" when used with a command.

"Hello." The voice was fresh, crisp. He wasn't ready.

"Uh . . . Carol?"

"Yes, who is this?"

"It's me."

"Lee?"

"Yeah."

"Hi, how are you?" she asked, as if hearing from an old
friend. He found it unnerving.

"I'm fine." He refused to ask how she was. "How are
the kids?"

"Fine. Jeff went to see the Angels this afternoon with Bill
and little Bill."

He was jealous. "Isn't that cozy."

"I think it's thoughtful," Carol cautioned, catching his tone.
"It fills the gap, Lee. Jeff needs the company of a man at
this age."

"Jeff's not the only one," he shot back, wanting to tell her
he knew.

"I'm not going to listen to your insults, Lee. Those days
are gone."

"Okay . . . Okay, where's Cathy?"

"She's over at the Klines'. Its Becky's birthday."

There was an awkward pause. He wanted her to speak,
wanted to hear she missed him, wanted him to come home.
She said nothing.

"Okay," he said, breaking the silence. "Tell the kids I said hi. Maybe I'll see 'em next weekend."

"Okay, take care of yourself," she answered. It was still the distant cool voice.

"Goodbye."

"Bye, bye."

"What's it gonna be?" the Fox asked, snapping him back from his daydreaming blank stare at the telephone.

"Huh? . . . Oh, you got a date. Let's get the hell outta here before another homicide goes down."

"No chance. We won't get called again till the steaks are just about done."

"Here's to the Pisser." Virgil raised his glass as he looked out over the balcony's rail at the fading sun. "May his life be short and his justice quick."

"I'll drink to that." Lee felt a little drunk already. They both raised their glasses and drank.

"And here's to Dave Wilson. One hellava man."

"One hellava man." Lee realized he didn't know him at all.

"And here's to Raymond P. Blatts. May the day come when I have the chance to meet the son of a bitch head-on."

"Virgil?"

"What?"

"I'm sorry I wasn't there, partner."

"No need to be sorry. Hell, you couldn't help it."

"Well, God damn it. I should have been." The alcohol was making him very melancholy. "I'm your partner and I should have been there."

They were quiet for a few minutes watching the lights blink on across the city as the waning sun fell below the horizon. A gentle breeze stirred the evening air.

"Hey, Lee? Remember when we kicked in Blatts's front door? Did you see what was on TV?"

"No, I was busy."

"Password was on."

"Terrific."

"You know how they flash the word on the screen for the home audience? Well, when we crashed in, the word on the screen was 'door.' "

"Uh huh."

"Don't you get it?"

"Get what?"

"The word was door."

"Oh."

"You know what the odds on that were?"

"No."

"I don't either," the Fox admitted. It just didn't seem as funny now.

They were quiet again for a while. The movement and conversation of the two women behind them in the apartment occasionally drifted out into the night air.

"He's out there, Virg."

"I know."

"Think we'll get him?"

"If we're lucky."

"Maybe we should call Banacek, Colombo, or Ironside. They'd catch 'em in sixty minutes or so."

"Let's call McCloud," the Fox suggested. "Then when we find 'em, we won't use tear gas. We'll throw horseshit at him. If he doesn't come out, the flies'll eat him to death."

"You think Blatts did it, Virg?"

"Naw. I looked at your arrest report. He's only five-seven and weighs one fifty-five."

"So?"

"So, I figure, at the most, he'd wear a nine and a half shoe. The Pisser's is, I'd guess, ten and a half, from what we saw in Ellen's bedroom."

Hollister nodded his agreement. "He wears a nine. I checked when I booked him."

"Think we'll turn any wits?"

"Doubt it."

"Then it's a dead end."

"Uh huh."

"Till he does it again," the Fox breathed.

"Till he does it again," Hollister agreed.

"Gentlemen, dinner is served." She was blonde and wore a yellow halter with lime-green shorts. Hollister gave her a longing look. Smiling, she held out a hand to him. "Come on. I think you'll like this."

"I'm sure I will," he answered, admiring her heavy breasts. Lee learned that she was thirty-one, but he thought older. He also would have preferred a thinner woman, but her seemingly sincere interest in almost everything he had to say pleased him more than he thought possible at the time. His heavy tongue warned him to go easy on the booze. Too much now would mean too little later.

The only light in the room was what little filtered through the curtains from the parking lot outside. He realized he was drinking too much, but he still remembered enjoying dinner pretty much and the company of Paula and Judy. He had kissed a black woman, Paula, for the first time when they played spin the bottle with an empty wine bottle. He was sorry he was drunk. He wished he could remember it more clearly. He knew he hadn't disliked it.

Turning his head, he could see a slice of bright light beneath what he guessed was the bathroom door. Moving his wrist to within several inches of his face, he tried to focus on the luminous dial on his watch. Ten-fifteen.

The light at the base of the bathroom door disappeared, casting the room in virtual darkness. Lee tried to focus on where he guessed the door was. "Judy?"

"Yes?" He felt her weight on the bed.

"I just wondered what you were doing."

"Getting comfortable." As she moved in beside him he turned toward her and his cheek brushed her breast. "Oh," he exclaimed, moving a hand to a bare leg.

"Why don't you get comfortable?" she said, covering his face and eyelids with soft kisses, moving a hand to his crotch.

"What about the coffee?" He felt his zipper go down, and a hand pull at parting his trousers.

"First the dessert, then coffee."

"Judy, I'd like to, but I—"

"I know . . . I know. Don't worry. You just relax."

. He felt cool with his trousers and shorts gone, but imagined he looked a little ridiculous being nude only from the waist down. Judy solved the problem by skillfully unbuttoning his shirt and pulling it away.

The large breasts he had longed for earlier were now just mounds of warm jelled flesh that made his breathing difficult as Judy forced them again and again into his face. He tried to reach an erection but without any success. He wished somehow he could satisfy her and end it. He felt strangely more like a spectator than a participant in what seemed like an adolescent sexual fantasy.

Shifting in the darkness, Judy's warm kisses moved down his chest, across his stomach, and then she took him in her mouth.

Lee awoke to find his left arm buried beneath her. When he pulled, she groaned and rolled to her stomach, pulling blanket and sheet with her. He moved his fingers while massaging the numb arm. His mouth was coated and tasted foul. The musty smell of a woman loved and unwashed reached his nostrils. He wondered if women found the smell of men as distasteful. He wished he were anywhere but here with this strange naked schoolteacher. He didn't remember falling asleep and that bothered him. He never liked staying overnight with a woman he didn't know at all. Squinting in the darkness, he could see that it was a quarter of six. It would take him a good forty-five minutes to get dressed and drive home, and on Mondays it was a standing rule that he and Virgil got in at seven instead of the usual eight. There was no way he could make it if he went home.

Easing off the bed, he stood up and searched for his clothes. Once when he thought he had everything except one sock, a pocketful of change rained to the floor from the bundle of clothes he held to his chest.

Head pounding and angry, he gave up the search for the missing sock.

He dressed in the light of a small aquarium in the living room. He felt dirty and wrinkled, and his headache added to the misery. He was sorry he hadn't just gone home yesterday.

He considered leaving a note, then decided not to. She already had one of his socks. Maybe she'd got up in the middle of the night and hid his sock. He shook his bare foot in his boot, which felt strange and cold, and then he reached for the door. It was five minutes to six and the morning light was growing on the curtains.

Virgil was half shaven when he heard the quick knock at the door. He had the radio on and the water running in the sink, so he wasn't sure of what he heard. He turned the water off and listened. There was no doubt there was someone at the door. Drying his hands, he moved from the bath into the kitchen and pulled his two-inch from the top of the refrigerator. Holding it hidden in the small of his back, he walked to the door.

"Who is it?" Fox stood to the side of the door.

"It's the Avon Lady. Open the goddamned door."

"Don't say a word," Hollister cautioned as Fox opened the door. "Just go finish shaving. I wanna use your razor."

"How'd you enjoy your night with the schoolteacher?" the

Fox smiled, sliding his gun onto the breakfast bar and walking back to the open bath.

"She's a real cop-sucker."

"Get yourself a coffee," the Fox called from the bath. "It's fresh."

"Got any juice?" Hollister opened the refrigerator.

"Yeah, should be some tomato in there. Look in the bottom."

Finding some glasses in a top cupboard, Hollister filled two of them and added a sprinkle of salt and pepper. The taste was cool and fresh.

"You got a pair of socks I can borrow?" he called to the Fox as he poured himself a coffee.

"Where's yours?"

"I lost one in action."

"I'll rent you a pair. Fifty cents a foot."

"I thought you were black, not Jewish," Hollister countered.

"Fine line." Fox appeared in the kitchen. "Get with it. Bathroom's all yours. We got crime to crush."

Taking his coffee with him, Hollister headed for the bathroom. "You want some breakfast?" the Fox called to him.

"Yeah. Two Bufferin over easy."

By twenty minutes to seven, they were ready to leave. Hollister, showered and shaven, was feeling much better.

"You wanna leave your car here?" the Fox said, pushing his four-inch thirty-eight into his belt holster.

"Might as well," Hollister agreed, finishing off a second cup of coffee.

"Let's do it."

Hollister set his empty cup in the sink. "What if Judy's coming out at the same time? I don't want to see her."

"Why? You do something you're ashamed of?" the Fox asked with a knowing grin.

"No. It's just I left without saying anything."

"She'll live. Anyway, she's got your sock to remember you by."

The squad room was milling with detectives and the incessant ringing of the telephones and the static of the squawk box.

"Hey, look," a gravel voice called as Hollister and Fox came in from the rear hall. "Sanford and son are back," he continued.

"Hey, Fox, how's the nose?"

"Fine, beer barrel. Can't smell a thing I eat . . . fell in love three times over the weekend."

"Hey, Hollister." It was a detective from the auto-theft table. "You and the Fox have been assigned to the Special Homicide Investigation Team until the Pisser is captured."

"What the hell's that?"

"You mean you haven't heard of the Special Homicide Investigation Team?"

"No."

"It's the S.H.I.T. detail. You and the Fox are the men from S.H.I.T."

Half the room laughed. Hollister blushed. "Go to hell, Axelrod."

"Oh, there's been a murder," a voice mocked in falsetto. "Well, stand by, ma'am. We'll get the men from S.H.I.T. right out there." More laughter.

The Fox gathered a stack of reports and teletypes from their assignment box and dropped them on the desk in front of Hollister. "Welcome to Monday."

Lieutenant Purington had requested they receive a copy of every sex crime occurring in the city, hoping that if the Pisser struck somewhere else they would catch it in a similar M.O. During the long hot weekend there had been many.

The Fox, after getting them each a cup of coffee, took a chair across from Hollister.

A slender graying detective with a well-trimmed black moustache approached their desk. "Here's your autopsy results."

Hollister flipped open the manila folder.

The cuts and slashes on Ellen Shane's body were penciled in on a preprinted nude body. Arrows led to the various wounds, giving length and depth and damage inflicted. At the bottom of the report was the deputy coroner's name who had performed the autopsy and his opinion of the cause of death. Hollister studied it for a moment, then spun it around and pushed it to Fox.

"Thanks, Hanson," Hollister said to the man.

"Oh, I'll get even. You know how I feel about autopsies. I thought I wouldn't eat for a month."

"You'll get used to it."

"No way," Hanson shook his head. "You can have it. I don't like watching those butchers make canoes out of people, even crooks. It just ain't my bag."

Hollister knew how Hanson felt. It had taken him many trips to the coroner's office till he learned to steel himself against the initial repulsion of having to watch the top of a man's head be sawed off and his brain pulled out and weighed.

"We didn't do any good up on Montclair Friday," Hanson said. "We checked every apartment in the court, and then up and down the street. Nobody saw nothing."

"No one ever does."

They spent the next hour reading through the stack of reports. A male Nego had been booked in Seventy-Seventh Division for "crime against nature" after being caught in the laundry room of an apartment house having intercourse with a large collie. He admitted a prior arrest for the same offense in Texas. The suspect was twenty-seven years old and married.

In Wilshire Division another suspect had been arrested for indecent exposure after running through an Akron store with a Playtex Living Glove stretched over his erected and exposed penis. The report said his penis had been inserted into the thumb recess of a left-handed glove. A tube of Vaseline was recovered from his pocket at the time of his arrest. He had four prior arrests, same offense.

In Hollywood Division, a forty-seven-year-old suspect and his wife were arrested after his twelve-year-old stepdaughter walked into the police station and reported her father had hurt her. A doctor's examination at Hollywood Receiving Hospital revealed the girl had been the victim of rectal intercourse which had caused a tear in her anus requiring three stitches. She told the doctor her mother made her do it. In a statement after her arrest, the mother said, "Anal sex opens up Julia to a whole new area of pleasurable sensations to be relished by her and used to increase her personal experiences and give her better insight into herself and others." The woman's other three children were taken into custody and placed in Juvenile Hall. She had two prior arrests for maintaining an unfit home.

A suspected rape victim was found nude, bound, and gagged in the trunk of a car in Newton Division. She had been beaten to death with a wire coat-hanger. Identification pending. Hollister penciled a "maybe" on the corner of the report.

A few minutes before eight Fox noticed that Grant West, a black Burglary detective, came in the squad room.

"Hey," the Fox said to Hollister. "West just came in. Purington said he and his partner worked on a similar rapist back in seventy."

"Okay," Hollister said without looking up. "Go talk to 'em. I'll finish these."

The Fox took his coffee and worked his way through the crowded room to West's desk. "You got a minute?"

West, making some marginal notes on a report, paused and looked up at him. "Sure, sit down."

The Fox knew the story behind West, that he had once been one of the South Side's best homicide investigators, and that his personality had been warm and friendly.

But all that ended with the death of his white partner several years ago. West had apparently blamed himself and now quietly worked his job in Burglary, refusing other assignments, keeping pretty much to himself.

The Fox settled into the chair across from West. "You remember working on a rapist couple years ago who pissed on his victims?"

West studied the desk top for a moment. "Yeah, I remember him," he answered without emotion.

"He's back."

"Figures."

"What 'ya mean?" Fox sipped his coffee.

"Stryker . . . my partner and I figured he went to jail on some other charge. He quit too sudden for it to be anything else. You know," West continued, leaning onto his desk, "no hot prowl homicidal rapist is going to hit four times in one year and then just stop. It was either he was dead or went to the joint."

"Makes sense."

"You check with the Adult Parole Authority," West suggested. "See who's been put on the street in the past month or so. May be worth your while."

"I'll do that," the Fox assured him. "You guys ever have any worthwhile leads, any evidence?"

West shook his head. "No, just piss. Never a fingerprint, footprint, nothing. He's a slick son of a bitch. Victims were all young, attractive, divorced, or never married, living alone."

"Uh huh, ours are the same."

"You got anything solid on him?"

"No," the Fox admitted, "just a bloody foot, and not a very good one."

"Hope you get the crazy motherfucker." West went back to his paper work, signaling for Fox to leave.

"We got two in custody this morning," Hollister said, pushing the reports to the Fox as he sat down. "One for wife-beating, the other for firing shots into an inhabited building."

"How thrilling," the Fox smiled, turning the reports to him.

Hollister glanced at his watch. "It's eight-thirty now. Let's get 'em interviewed and then after the autopsy we can swing by the D.A.'s office, file these two and the one eighty-seven on Carson and Gateman from yesterday."

"Okay," Fox agreed.

"What did West have to say?" Hollister asked, loosening his tie.

"Might be the same asshole that was hitting a couple of years ago. Same M.O."

"Where's he been?" Hollister questioned, "or does he only get a hard-on every couple years?"

"West, like you, figures the Pisser isn't gonna hit, hit, hit and then quit. So he figures if now he's back after a couple years, he might have been in the joint. So when we get caught up today," the Fox went on, "I'll drop a dime on the Parole Authority. See who's hit the bricks before Ellen got ripped off."

"Sounds good," Hollister nodded. "Come on. Let's get these turkeys interviewed."

Deputy Chief Spear and his adjutant, Lieutenant Sayles, arrived at the chief's office at eight-thirty sharp.

"Is he in?" Spear barked at the secretary.

"Yes, sir," she replied with a shaky smile. "He's expecting you."

"Come on," Spear said to his adjutant.

"Sir," Captain Rosson said, standing up at his desk across from the secretary's.

"What?" Spear gave him an irritated look.

Rosson smiled diplomatically. "The lieutenant will have to wait out here, sir. Chief Peck thinks that would be best, sir."

Spear considered, then: "Have a seat, Bill. If I need anything, I'll be out."

The lieutenant nodded and moved to a cluster of chairs off to the side for waiting visitors.

Spear rapped on the inner office door and then opened it without waiting for further invitation.

Commander Stocker was seated in a chair facing the chief's desk. Peck, as usual when in his office, was without jacket. "Ben, come on in."

Spear chose a chair beside Stocker, shifted it an inch or so, and sat down. "All right," he said, making no attempt to mask his displeasure or suspicion. "Let's have it."

"Okay," Peck nodded, agreeing to get into the matter quickly. Spear noticed that the chief looked tired and worried. "Commander," Peck said, "why don't you lay out what you have, and then we'll go from there?"

"Very well." Stocker unsnapped the latches on an attaché case beside his chair. Reaching inside he pulled out a small blue folder, laid it on his lap, and flipped it open to several typed pages. Spear shifted in his chair.

"On June twenty-four of this year," the commander began in a tone Spear thought belonged to the foreman of a jury bringing in a verdict, "at fifteen hundred hours Sergeant Raymond R. Cox, serial number one-two-one-seven-o, Southwest Division Patrol, then on loan to Southwest Vice, came to the office of Internal Affairs and requested a conference with the commander thereof. At approx——"

"Come on, Stocker," Spear growled. "Knock off this cheap dramatic bullshit and get to it."

Stocker lowered the paper, looking to Peck, ignoring Spear. "Shall I continue, sir?"

"Ben," Peck said, eyeing his longtime friend, "be patient. It's important you understand the complete chain of events."

"Go on," Spear urged Stocker.

"During a subsequent conversation with Sergeant Cox, he advised me he was on temporary loan to Vice, filling in for a sergeant who was off I.O.D. He stated that earlier that afternoon at about twelve hundred he was riding with Lieutenant Tilden when the lieutenant stopped at Blackie's Liquor Store at thirteen hundred West Santa Barbara. He told me the lieutenant advised him to wait in the car while he went inside. Approximately three minutes later the lieutenant returned and they drove to Southwest Station.

"After arriving at the station, the lieutenant, still in the company of Sergeant Cox, went to the office of the deputy chief, commander of South Bureau, your office, sir," Stocker said with a glance at Spear. "The sergeant said the lieutenant approached your open door and asked where lieutenant Sayles was."

Spear was listening intently now, trying to recall the incident.

"The sergeant, waiting in the outer office, heard you reply, 'He's downtown.' The sergeant then observed the lieutenant remove an item from his shirt pocket and state, 'I think you know about this. It's the money from Blackie. Could I leave it with you? Lieutenant Sayles knows how to divide it up.' He then heard you reply, 'Sure, I'll hold onto it. Is our cut in there?' "

"All right . . . all right," Spear interrupted. "I remember it. So that's what all this bullshit is about."

"It's not bullshit," Peck cautioned, moving to rest his elbows on the wide desk. "It's a very serious allegation."

"It's bullshit," Spear scoffed. "It's completely out of context."

"All right, explain it," Peck snapped.

"This—this, what the hell's his name?" Spear was shaking.

"Who?" Stocker said coolly.

"The one who owns the liquor store."

"I didn't say who owned the liquor store."

"Don't try to make a fool of me, Commander," Spear shot out a finger at him.

"I don't have to make a——"

Wham! Peck's fist smashed into the top of his desk. "Now, God damn it, I've had it. If there're any more of these personality clashes, I swear I'll suspend both of you indefinitely right here and right now. Is that clear?"

"Yes, sir," Stocker answered without hesitation.

"Ben," Peck said, looking to him.

Spear nodded that he understood.

"Go on," Peck urged.

"That person," Spear started over, speaking to Stocker, "whatever the hell his name is, the one who runs the liquor store, is an informant for Vice. He recently gave them three back rooms in one week. They requested four hundred dollars from the secret service fund to pay him. I approved the request and the money was gathered from Seventy-Seventh, Newton, and Southwest to meet the amount. Two days after the payment was made the informant called Vice and stated he wanted to return the money."

"He wanted to return the money?" Peck questioned with a raised eyebrow.

"That's right. It's unusual, but it's true. He just didn't want it. Maybe guilt, who knows. Vice didn't know what to do, so the question came to my office. We're always short of secret service funds, so I made the decision to take it back. The Vice lieutenant picked it up and when he brought it to my office, my adjutant, who handles these things, was out, so I accepted it. The dividing it up talk was about what division got what. That's the whole thing." It was when he finished talking that he realized he was sweating. He wiped his brow with what he hoped was a casual move.

Chief Peck and Stocker said nothing.

"If there's any doubt in anybody's mind, let's take a look at the books. All of these transactions are thoroughly documented."

Peck picked up a yellow pencil from the surface of his desk. "It's not that simple anymore, Ben."

"Why the hell not? How long could an accounting take? One day, two days?"

Peck gave him an examining look. "The effectiveness of an accounting was compromised when that robbery team from Southwest kicked the shit out of Brocks's surveillance team."

"Are you saying there's doubt?"

"Ben, I'm saying in a situation like this every instrument available to eliminate doubt must be used."

"You mean the polygraph," Spear said, glaring at him.

Peck laid his pencil down carefully. "I've known you for damn near a quarter of a century, Ben. You've given me an explanation for what happened and I'd go to hell defending it as the truth. The people we have to convince in a situation like this is the sergeant who reported it, the men who conducted the surveillance, and the Police Commission, because that's where the results of the investigation are going. I'm too biased to pronounce a fair judgment this time."

"Then a polygraph examination will be a part of the investigation?"

"I don't see how it can be avoided."

"Jim, for Christ's sake, I've given you the truth," Spear pleaded, leaning forward in his chair. "How can I command the respect of the men in the three divisions under me if I'm submitted to a lie detector test? The shadow of doubt would be cast."

"Ben, the shadow of doubt has been cast."

Spear studied Peck's face for a long moment. "You do believe what I've said?"

"No doubt at all, Ben."

The deputy chief slowly rose out of his chair. "My office will be empty in the morning. I'll say it's because of health." He turned and walked to the door.

"I'm sorry, Ben," Peck's voice trailed after him.

Spear nodded, then opened the door and was gone.

Hollister lit up a cigarette as the white-gowned coroner's deputy checked the name tag on the ankle and made a notation on his clipboard. "Johnnie Carson," the deputy smiled. "Rather an interesting name for a black man."

"You feel better if it was Jefferson Davis Jones?" Fox snapped.

The coroner blushed. "Well . . . I didn't really mean anything."

Hollister's cheek twitched as a bone saw came to life several tables away from them in the examination room. Its high-pitched whine softened as the blade met its target. He drew on his cigarette.

The coroner's deputy seemed to enjoy the feel of his surgical gloves as he slipped them on, smoothing every wrinkle away. Hollister wished he hadn't drunk last night.

When the coroner picked up his scalpel, Hollister walked to Fox, hoping it appeared casual.

"What's wrong?" the Fox said softly. "Don't you wanna watch any anatomical dissections today?"

"Screw you and your diploma," Hollister exhaled.

After exposing the outer rib cage, the deputy picked up what looked like a pair of small-jawed hedge clippers, centered them over the flat sternum, and with several quick cuts severed the man's chest in two. Laying the bone-cutter aside, he pulled at the gap which folded away with little resistance, exposing a myriad of gray and yellow tissue streaked with a thousand veins. Again with scalpel in hand he reached into the gaping cavity and began cutting. Hollister glanced to the dead man's face. The eyes were closed, the expression relaxed, lips set in a straight line.

The deputy coroner lifted out a dripping gray lung and sat it on a scale beside the stainless table. Wiping his hand on his white apron, he noted the weight of the lung on the clipboard. Moving the jellylike lung back to the stainless table beside the body, he took scalpel in hand and carefully dissected the lung, leaning close to study the discolored inner tissue.

"Sergeant Hollister." Hollister turned. It was one of the girls from the reception desk. "I'm Hollister."

"I have a telephone call for you. The caller said it was urgent."

"Okay. Virg, I'll be back."

"I'll be here. I wanna watch slick here finish his canoe."

Hollister followed the girl to the windowless double doors, and they pushed into the hallway. He welcomed the fresh air and breathed deep for the first time in twenty minutes.

"Doesn't that bother you in there?" Lee thought she was nineteen at the most.

"Doesn't what bother me?" the girl asked.

"Never mind."

"Line seven-four," she said when they reached the counter at the end of the polished hall.

He punched the blinking light and picked up the phone. "Hollister."

"Hollister, this is Welty from Wilshire Detectives."

"That doesn't sound too urgent."

"Okay, it was nice talking to you. Good——"

"Wait, wait a minute, Welby."

"Welty, W-E-L-T-Y."

"Welty. Okay, I've got it. What can I do for you?"

"I was going over my reports from the weekend. I work Burglary and I think your rapist may have hit in my area."

"What makes you think it's him?" Hollister questioned. He was being deliberately speculative.

"Well, from what I've heard of his M.O., it fits right down the line."

"Lay it out to me."

"The victim is a female Negro by the name of Yesterday Phillips. She's twenty-two, and according to the patrol officers that took the report, she looks like an escapee from a Playboy Club. She's single, lives alone down on South August. Saturday night, no, it would have been in the A.M., Sunday morning, this guy removed the screen from her bedroom window and climbed in."

"Was she home?"

"No, she works at the Flying Fox on West Santa Barbara. It's a black club. Kinda for the upper-class blacks. No dirt bags, you know? It's just west of Crenshaw on the south side of the street."

"Uh huh."

"She got off work about two A.M., Sunday morning. Says

she went home. And listen to this, as she unlocked her door, a girlfriend invited her over. She agreed, but first went into her apartment, just to take off her bra. My kind of woman. Anyway, she told the officers she didn't go any further than her living room. Tossed her bra to a couch after taking it off and left her purse behind too. Never turned a light on. Probably saved her life."

"How do you figure that?" Hollister hadn't heard anything yet that sparked any real interest.

"I figure this dude, the Pisser, was waiting on her."

"What makes you think that?"

"That his M.O., isn't it? I mean, to pick a snake, then crash in and wait on her?"

"We think that's it. None of the victims have lived to tell us."

"Well, from the way it looks here, this cat spent a lot of time in her apartment. He ate some fruit from the kitchen table, moved her purse from the couch in the living room, chewed up the straps on her bra, knocked down a bunch of clothes in the bedroom closet, and tore up the bed. He didn't take a goddamned thing. Now that spells only one thing. Rape. He was after her."

Hollister now was interested. "Did you get any prints?"

"I called Prints before I called you. They got nothing but smudges. Nothing readable."

"Have you talked to this broad yet?"

"No, I called her at home. No answer. I called the Flying Fox. They said she'd be in today at four."

"I'd like to talk to her," Hollister said. "Can you give me her address and number, Welty?"

"Okay. She lives at forty-one twenty-seven South August, number eighteen. Telephone two-nine-two-seven-one-four-six."

"Welty, Jack Webb would be proud of you."

"It's nothing," Welty assured him. "Just another amazing piece of police work by a big-city detective. All in a day's work."

"We'll let you know if anything develops."

"Do that." ·

Hollister wished he didn't have to go back into the examination room. He slipped the notebook inside his jacket and walked down the hall toward the double doors. What a way to start a week, he told himself. Watching some medical school reject slice up a human body like it was a dead cow, just to find out why it was dead. Jesus Christ, he knew that. Why didn't they ask him? The man died of asphyxiation. He took a deep breath and pushed through the door.

"Death by a combination of asphyxiation and carbon monoxide poisoning," the Fox said softly as Hollister reached him.

The district attorney's office was located on the seventeenth floor of the Criminal Courts Building just across the street from the coroner's office. They checked in at the D.A.'s reception desk and then sat down in the waiting room with a dozen other policemen.

The Fox found a tattered two-day-old copy of the Los Angeles *Times* and leafed through it.

Hollister, slouched in a chair beside him, was working on a story to give to Janice to explain where he'd been all last night. He'd never lied to her before and he found the thought of it distasteful.

"Says here," the Fox said from behind his paper, "that the panel of tape experts have concluded the gap in the presidential tape was deliberate and required repeated efforts of erasing and rerecording."

"I knew that," Hollister answered.

"I wonder who did it?"

"The butler?"

"You guys from Southwest?" a detective beside Hollister asked, leaning toward him.

"Yeah," Hollister answered.

"How come Deputy Chief Spear quit? Is it true he was on the take?"

"What!" Hollister was shocked.

The Fox lowered his paper. "Where'd you hear that?"

"From a good source. You mean you guys don't know about it?"

"No, we've been at the coroner's office since nine. We don't know a thing about it," Hollister explained.

"From what I heard, some Robbery team from Southwest ripped off a couple dirt-bag paddies Friday night that were staked on a liquor store. Got in one helluva fight with 'em. The two paddies were cops from I.A. One of 'em is in the hospital. That blew the whole thing open. Deputy Chief Spear was called to the chief's office this morning, and Peck fired him on the spot."

"Jesus Christ." Hollister fully realized that it was Fred's clue that had led Rainey to the two men. It had to be the same deal. He turned to the Fox. "You see Rainey this morning?"

"No, come to think of it I didn't. You mean he's the one that—"

Hollister walked from the waiting room to a small office off the main hallway. "Day," he said, entering the open door, "I wanna use your phone."

Day was a broad-shouldered, dark-haired man assigned as liaison officer to the D.A.'s office. "Sure, go ahead."

Hollister picked up the phone. "Could I ask you to wait outside?"

"You could ask," Day balked.

Hollister turned to another man at a second desk in the office. "How about you too?"

The man paused in his work and glanced first at Hollister and then at Day. "Is this important?"

"Yeah, it's important," Hollister grated.

"Hollister," Day said, "I wouldn't do this for just anybody. If I hadn't personally broke you in on the job, I wouldn't do it for you either. Come on, Chuck."

"That's what I like about you, Day. You're all heart."

When the two men were gone, Hollister pushed the door shut and dialed the station.

"Good morning, Southwest Detectives. Sergeant Risher. May I help you?"

"Cliff, this is Hollister. Did Deputy Chief Spear get fired?"

"I heard he quit."

"Why?"

"There's a lot of rumors. Running from bribery to an affair with his secretary. I worked for him when he was a sergeant in Newton. He couldn't be bought, so I don't know what to believe."

"You seen Rainey today?"

"No, but I heard he's down at I.A. Berry and Duff are there too. They're the ones that ripped this whole thing open Friday night."

"Is the skipper there?"

"No, he's downtown. I'd bet he's with Rainey."

"Okay, thanks, Cliff."

Another twenty minutes went by before they got in to see one of the deputy district attorneys. Hollister was quiet. He was worried about what he'd got Rainey and his men into. He wondered, since he supplied the information that blew I.A.'s surveillance, would he therefore be a suspect? Did they follow him last night? Was his phone tapped? Could they tap phones for a deal like this?

The deputy district attorney they were assigned to wanted to talk about the shooting at the station. Had they seen it? Did they know the officer who did it? Why did they think he hung himself? Hollister felt contempt for the small-framed mousey-looking man, silently thinking that if he saw a man killed, he'd faint.

The deputy was entranced with the tape-recorded statement of Mrs. Carson and her lover, Gateman. He played it three times. "These people are real killers," he said finally, turning off the machine. "Well," he said, picking up his pen, "we'll put 'em where they belong."

Hollister could take no more. "How long have you been with the D.A.'s office?"

"Ah . . . this is my fourth month," he answered, adjusting his horn-rimmed glasses.

After Hollister's question, the deputy's questions and comments ceased. He worked quickly and quietly. They finished just before noon.

"Why'd you have to embarrass the poor kid?" the Fox asked Hollister as they walked to the elevators.

"He probably never filed a one eighty-seven before. You gotta keep 'em humble. Plus I don't like attorneys."

"Occupational hazard."

Hollister filled the Fox in on the information he'd received from the Wilshire detective as they drove back to Southwest. They decided they'd go to the Flying Fox at four and interview this Yesterday Phillips. The Fox liked her name. Hollister guessed only a black woman could be named Yesterday.

They glanced at Blackie's Liquor as they rolled west on Santa Barbara Avenue. "Wanna stop for some smokes?" the Fox teased.

"No, I'll pass today."

At the station Hollister went to work on finishing the paper work for the cases they'd been assigned while Fox got the number for Central Parole Index from one of the detectives at the Auto table.

Returning to his desk, he picked up the phone and dialed the number.

"Good afternoon," a high-pitched female voice answered. "Central Parole Index. Name please?"

"Fox."

"First name?"

"Virgil."

"Middle initial?"

"None."

"One moment please." The line clicked and he was on hold.

The Fox shifted in his chair seeking a comfortable position.

The line clicked. "We show no record of a Fox, Virgil."

"That's my name."

"Oh, I see. Well, what parole officer are you assigned to, sir?"

"None, I'm a police officer."

"Well, sir, you didn't tell me that." The voice was chilled.

"I didn't have a chance to, ma'am."

"Well, what can I do for you, Officer?"

"I'd like some information on recent parolees."

"Very well. May I have the names please."

"I don't have any names. I wanted——"

"Well, how will I search the index if you don't know the parolee's name?"

"I was hoping I could get the names from you."

"What name would you like, sir?"

"I don't have the names, lady."

"Well, we file alphabetically. Just pick a name, sir, and I'll pull the index card."

"No, that won't do, ma'am. I wanted to find out how many recent parolees there have been to Los Angeles, say, in the past month."

"I'd have to have their names, sir."

"Yes, okay, I understand that. Do you know who I can call to get that information?"

"Try the Central Parole Coordination Office at six-seven-nine-o-o-four-one."

"Thank you, ma'am."

"You're welcome, sir."

"What the hell was all that?" Hollister asked as the Fox hung up the phone.

"I'm not sure."

The Central Parole Coordination Office quickly supplied him with the names of three individuals released on parole within the past twenty-eight days. The Fox penciled the information onto a tablet in front of him as the girl read it off:

1. Richard W. Webster
   Male/Negro: D.O.B. 1/14/47
   27 Yrs. 5'8", 160 lbs.
   Reported address: 9347 S. Denker, L.A.
   Offense: Possession of heroin for sale
   Sentenced 12/70
   Released from Chino: 6/4/74

2. Edward NMN Branch
   Male/Negro: D.O.B. 5/11/41
   33 Yrs. 5'11", 185 lbs.
   Reported address: 1747 S. Packard, L.A.
   Offense: Forgery
   Sentenced 10/70
   Released from Chino: 6/12/74

3. Franklin R. Comstock
   Male/Negro: D.O.B. 9/27/43
   31 Yrs. 6', 180 lbs.
   Reported address: 1444 W. 43rd St., L.A.
   Offense: Assault with a deadly weapon
   Sentenced 9/70
   Released from Folsom: 6/20/74

After hanging up the telephone, the Fox spun the tablet
around for Hollister to view. "That's our three candidates,"
he said.

"Wouldn't it be nice if one of them had a white VW?"
Hollister said, studying the names, descriptions, and addresses.

"Let's go see," the Fox suggested.

"That's no good. The white VW is just a maybe anyhow.
We should stake these three night and day. Live with 'em.
See what the hell they're doing."

"Let's lay it on Purington. See what he's got to say," the
Fox said.

Hollister picked up the tablet with the three names on it,
and he and the Fox walked to the Lieutenant's desk.

"Please God," Purington said as they approached, raising
his eyes to the ceiling, "let it be good news."

"Your morning been that bad?" the Fox asked.

"You haven't heard?" Purington sighed.

"About the deputy chief?" Hollister guessed.

"Hell," Purington snorted, rocking back in his chair. "That
was nothing. I'm talking about Axelrod and Beer Barrel."

"What happened to them?" the Fox questioned.

"Oh, nothing," the lieutenant said, running a hand back through his short black hair. "They're both fine. We won't see Axelrod till tomorrow morning at nine-fifteen when the time lock on the vault opens, but other than that he's fine."

"How the hell did he get in a vault?" Fox was smiling.

"The Bank of America down on Fifty-fourth and Western called to report several safe-deposit boxes appeared to have been tampered with. Axelrod and Beer Barrel went down to look them over. Axel was inside looking at the boxes when Beer Barrel closed the door to see if the lock had been tampered with. It hadn't and it locked. It won't open until tomorrow morning. Now half of the press in Los Angeles is down there. Taking pictures, doing interviews." Purington shook his head. "Really adds to our professional image, locking each other in bank vaults."

"Axelrod okay in there?" Hollister asked with some concern.

"Yeah. Hell, it's air conditioned, good lighting, and he's got a twenty-four-year-old teller in there with him."

"There's an intercom, too," Purington said. "Axel knows he's in there for the night."

"Hope he had breakfast," Hollister added.

"He'll have to piss in his boot with that broad in there," the Fox said with a grin.

"What do you two need?" Purington leaned his elbows onto his desk in an exaggerated manner, suggesting that he was near exhaustion or simply exasperated.

Hollister offered the yellow tablet. "We think one of these three may be the Pisser."

Purington took the tablet and read over the names. "What do you want me to do? Pick the right one?"

"You give us the manpower, we'll pick the right one."

The lieutenant pushed the tablet back to him. "You two can have all the overtime you want."

"We need two other teams. We wanna cover all three suspects."

"I can't do it," Purington apologized. "Hutch and Linsay have identified three of the gang members who beat the old man to death down at Fifty-fourth and Crenshaw. They've got four men from Burglary helping them. Ski and Al are working on an attempt murder over on Ellendale. Autos are going out to help Narcotics on a surveillance and buy where ten grand's going to be flashed, everyone's up to their ass with Monday's workload, and Axelrod's locked in the goddamned vault. We just don't have anyone we can spare to baby-sit those three assholes."

"So what do we do?" Hollister argued. "Sit back and wait for him to score again?"

"Find out which of the three he is and put 'em in jail."

"You know we don't have a case on any of the three."

"You don't even know it is one of the three," Purington said, stabbing at the tablet with a finger.

"It's the only possibility we've got."

"Look," Purington said squaring his shoulders, a tactic Hollister knew he used when switching from friend to lieutenant. "If I put a policeman in each bank or liquor store in the division, I could cut robberies by seventy percent too, but I can't do it. We just don't have the manpower."

"The answer is no?" Hollister asked with a hard look.

"The answer is we don't have the capability," Purington defended. "If your suspicions were stronger, if you had a shred of evidence . . . maybe then."

"We do nothing, and I'm sure we'll get more evidence, in the way of another dead body." Hollister grabbed the tablet from the lieuteant's desk and walked away.

Purington looked at the Fox. The Fox opened his mouth to speak. "No," Purington said flatly.

The two men got a coffee from the urn in the corner of the squad room and returned to their desk.

"Well," the Fox said, sliding into his chair, "Plan A is out."

Hollister shook out a cigarette and lit up. "What do you think?" he exhaled, shaking out his match.

The Fox sipped his coffee. "It's like you said. We don't have a case, not even a clue on any of these three turkeys, but they're all we've got."

"We can't follow three of them."

"Valid point."

They sat quietly for the next few moments. Each searching their minds for a workable strategy. "I've got it," the Fox said, breaking the silence.

"Go ahead," Hollister urged, setting his coffee down.

"We can't follow three suspects, and we don't know which of the three it is."

"Hell, I know that," Hollister frowned.

"So," the Fox went on, "we'll let him come to us."

"Just how the hell are we gonna do that?"

"The Pisser never missed before, did he?"

"Not that we know of."

"So he missed this time. Now, that had to frustrate him. Really pissed him off, so to speak."

"Very funny."

"My point is he may come back."

"Maybe he will, maybe he won't."

"Look," the Fox argued. "He picks his targets carefully. That means he's got a lot of time invested in this Yesterday Phillips. Really has a hard-on for her. I'll bet he'll be back."

Hollister gave the suggestion careful thought. "You may be right. Plus now that we've got names, we can go to R. and I. and pull some mug shots. Maybe this snake will recognize one of them."

"Could be," the Fox agreed.

"Well, get the horses, Tonto, and let's get riding. It's one-fifteen already."

They stopped at a McDonald's for lunch and then drove on to Parker Center. The temperature had climbed into the high eighties. At R. and I. Division, they each read the three suspects' arrest packages cover-to-cover. None of the three had any prior arrests for sex offenses. Fox pocketed a mug shot from each package.

Leaving Parker Center, Hollister suggested they drive by each of the three reported addresses. The chance of a white VW. was one they couldn't afford to ignore.

The last address to be checked was that of Richard Webster at ninety-three forty-seven South Denker. The address was one of three in a one-story stucco triplex. There was no white VW.

"Son of a bitch," Hollister complained as they rolled by slowly.

"Only in the movies," the Fox added sarcastically.

Hollister bitched about the heavy afternoon traffic as he wormed the Plymouth north on Crenshaw Boulevard. The Fox entertained himself by searching the bus benches on every corner for attractive women. They reached the Flying Fox at three forty-five.

"You ever been in here?" Hollister asked as they left their car and walked toward the entrance.

"Couple times. The place got a class name."

They paused inside the front door to let their eyes adjust to the dim light. The air was cool and fresh. There were several men at the long curved padded bar and a sprinkling of customers spread across the carpeted lounge. It looked white to him. He silently bet a Jew owned it.

The Fox led them to the bar, and they slid onto cushioned stools.

"What will it be, gentlemen?" a red-jacketed bartender asked as he moved down the bar to them. His bald head reflected the soft light from above.

"It'll be a Cutty on the rocks with a little water back," the Fox responded.

"Tall V.O. and seven."

As the man went to work on the drinks, the Fox surveyed the room. A busty black waitress with frosted hair leaned into the bar at the far end talking with a customer. "Yesterday Phillips here yet?" the Fox asked the bartender as he slid their drinks onto the polished bar.

"Not yet. You here about her apartment gettin' ripped off?"

"Uh huh," the Fox answered, sipping his Scotch. "My name's Fox. This is my partner, Hollister."

The bartender extended a meaty hand with a smile. "Fox, huh? Nice to meet you. My name's Casey." He shook hands with both men. "Yesterday should be here in a couple minutes. I'll let you know."

Hollister, checking the wide frosted mirror behind the bar, found he was the only white face in the place. It made him a little uncomfortable. "You know," he whispered to the Fox, "I'm the only paddy in here."

"It's okay. They won't say anything if you don't."

"Thanks," Hollister blushed.

The first drink went quickly and the Fox bought a second round. "Beats the hell outta that chocolate malt we had with lunch," Hollister said, picking up his drink.

"Better McDonald's than nothing."

"I know." Hollister paused to light a Marlboro. "But it's degrading for a big-time city detective to eat a big Mac for lunch. I mean you never see Mannix or Cannon eating Big Macs. It just isn't good for our image."

"Be like Kojak," the Fox suggested. "Carry a pocket full of lollipops."

"You know he carries those so at lunch he sneaks into the park and gives them to little girls."

"Did you gentlemen want to speak with me?" a voice behind them broke in.

They twisted around. Her hair was coal black and hung

straight in long gentle waves over her shoulders. A small pixielike nose separated the dark eyes which were set deep under heavy lashes. The high cheekbones gave her soft brown face an aristocratic elegance. "I'm Yesterday Phillips."

Hollister usually let the Fox speak first in interviews, but this time Fox said nothing. Hollister took the initiative. "I'm Sergeant Hollister; this is my partner, Virgil Fox. We're from Southwest Detectives. We'd like to talk to you about the burglary of your apartment."

"All right, would you like to sit down at a table?" she suggested.

"Sure," Fox answered, picking up his drink.

Fox walked behind her, enjoying the soft scent of her perfume and admiring the Coke-bottle figure as she led them through the tables to a corner booth.

She slid into the cushioned booth and Fox followed. Hollister took the other side. "We won't draw so much attention over here," she said.

"Could we get you a drink?" the Fox offered.

"No, thank you," she smiled. "If I drink, I find the night seems much longer." She toyed nervously with a ring on her little finger.

"Miss Phillips," Hollister said.

"Please," she said with a quick grin. "Call me Yesterday. Miss Phillips sounds like I'm getting a call from the phone company or something."

"Okay." Hollister felt a bit self-conscious about looking at her. The body shirt she wore cut low across her bosom, exposing the half globes of her breasts. "Do you have any idea who may have broken into your apartment the other night?"

She shrugged her shoulders. "I just don't know. The most expensive thing I have is my stereo, and it's from Sears."

"Has anybody here at the club been trying to hus . . . tried to . . . has anybody been trying to date you who may have followed you home?" the Fox asked, trying to phrase it softly.

"I catch a remark now and then, or a pat on the bottom." She worked at the ring on her finger again. "But nothing heavy. Nobody's ever insulted me or got pushy."

Hollister put his cigarette out in an ashtray. "Anybody ever followed you home that you know of?"

"No, not that I knew."

"How about your neighbors?" the Fox questioned. "Any

problems with them, or maybe you've seen someone hanging around who didn't belong there?"

She considered the question. "No, I haven't seen anyone. My neighbors are all nice. We look out for each other, you know? Just last week Mr. Green, he's the manager, had his car stolen from the carport. I've been afraid they'd steal my old VW. I heard they take them to cut them up for dune buggies."

Fox reached into his jacket, pulled out the mug shots. "Yesterday, I've got some pictures here I'd like you to look at. If you recognize any of these men, let me know. You may have seen them here in the club, on the street, at a store, almost anywhere." He spread the pictures on the table in front of her.

Pulling the red-shaded candle closer to the pictures, Yesterday studied them carefully. As he watched a polished nail straighten one of the pictures, Fox thought that the flickering soft light of the candle added to her beauty.

"I'm sorry. I don't think I've ever seen any of them."

"That's okay. We just wanted to be sure."

"Is the man who broke into my place one of those men?"

"We think so."

"Is he some kind of a creep or something?" She grimaced. "I mean, he chewed up a strap on one of my bras." Her eyes lowered with embarrassment.

Fox gave Hollister a questioning look which Hollister acknowledged by nodding.

"Yeah," Fox said, turning to Yesterday, looking directly into her eyes. "He's some kind of a creep. I don't wanna frighten you, but he's a very dangerous man."

"What . . . what's he want?" she stammered.

"You." Fox fingered his glass. "He's a rapist."

Yesterday moved a hand to her neck. Her eyes were wide. "Will . . . will he come back?"

"We don't know," Hollister said flatly.

"My God, I'm scared."

"We've got a favor to ask, Yesterday," Fox said.

"What is it?"

"Have you got some place you could stay for the next couple of nights?"

"I . . . I've been staying with a girlfriend of mine since it happened. She lives just a couple doors away. I don't think she minds. Why?"

"Well, like I said, this dude is dangerous. It wouldn't be

fair to tell you otherwise. We have reason to believe he may come back. You know what a stakeout is?"

"Uh huh." She held her hands together on the table now. Fox wished he could move his hand to hers, as if offering his personal protection.

"My partner and I, with your permission, would like to stake out your place for a while, wait inside, and give this character the kind of welcome he deserves."

Fox could hear her now-pronounced breathing, and it excited him strangely. He could understand why this man wanted her. "I . . . I guess it's okay."

"Can we start tonight?"

"I suppose," she answered. "But the place is a mess. I wasn't expecting. . . ." Her voice trailed away.

"Don't worry about it," Fox offered.

"Will you stay all night?"

Fox looked to Hollister. "I'd guess until about three. If he hasn't shown by then, I don't think he will," Hollister answered.

"The TV's got a bad tube, but it still works pretty good."

"That's okay," the Fox smiled. "We won't be using it. We want to look like you're not home."

"You mean you'll just sit in there in the dark for hours?"

"Uh huh," Fox grinned. "It's okay, he's white, but he still makes pretty good conversation."

"Detective Fox," she scolded.

"Virgil."

"Virgil is your first name?"

"No, it's my middle name. My parents were so poor they couldn't afford a first name for me."

Hollister closed his eyes and shook his head slowly as he raised his glass.

Yesterday giggled, moving a hand to her mouth. "You know," she said, pointing a finger at him, "my grandfather's name was Virgil. He was a fire-and-brimstone shoutin' Southern Baptist minister."

"I'm a Baptist," the Fox said.

"Small world," Hollister smiled.

The two didn't hear him. "Are you from L.A.?" Yesterday questioned.

"Where are you from?" the Fox countered.

"Atlanta. I've only been out here eleven months."

"You're kidding." Fox shifted a bit closer to her. "I'm from Georgia too."

"Oh Christ," Hollister said under his breath.

"You're not," she smiled warmly.

"Sure am. Little town way down in the corner of the state called Dearmont."

"Dearmont . . . I don't think I've heard of it," Yesterday smiled, realizing Fox's soft Southern diction was a put-on.

Neither has anyone else, Hollister said silently, knowing Fox had been born and raised in Indiana.

"Oh, it's just a wide spot in the road, but it's home," Fox said, toying with his glass as if the mention of it brought on a wave of nostalgia.

"Do you miss it as much as I do?" Yesterday asked, moving a hand to his.

"Look," Hollister interrupted, working hard to keep a straight face, "if you two will excuse me, I'll go phone the station."

"Sure, go ahead," the Fox urged.

"I'll let Purington know what your plan is," Hollister said, sliding out of the booth.

When he returned, Fox had an arm placed casually on Yesterday's shoulder. They were smiling and talking softly. Hollister went unnoticed until he slid into the booth. "Okay, we're all set."

"Good." Fox self-consciously removed his arm. Picking up his drink, he finished the trace that was left in the glass.

"Yesterday," Hollister said, shaking out a cigarette, "we think we know this guy is one of the three we showed you." He paused to light up.

"But," he exhaled, "there's an outside chance we may be wrong. Let's say that's true. That means it could be anybody. A neighbor, a regular customer here, an employee, someone you've dated. There's no way to know. Because of that possibility, we'd like to keep the stakeout quiet. There's no one that needs to know, other than the three of us."

"I promise," she said soberly.

"Fine. That'll improve our chances."

Hollister glanced at his watch and then at Fox. "It's almost five. Let's get some chow. Move in just after dark."

"Why don't you have dinner here?" Yesterday suggested, looking to the Fox. "You can't beat Cookie's steaks."

The Fox glanced to Hollister. Hollister shrugged. "You got a deal, lady."

"Fine. If you'll let me out, I'll order them for you."

"Promise you'll come back."

"I promise."

"How would you like your steaks, gentlemen?"

"I'll have mine medium rare," the Fox answered. "John Wayne there likes his well done."

Fox stood and watched as she moved away. "Sit down, your tongue's showing," Hollister said.

Fox eased into the booth with a silly grin on his face. "I feel guilty."

"Why?"

" 'Cause the city's paying me to do all this and I'm enjoying the hell out of it."

"You mean you're impressed with that snake?" Hollister teased.

"Snake?" the Fox defended. "She's a fox."

"Your body's in love, that's all."

"Grant you that. She's packaged like a Christmas toy, but beneath all that smooth warm flesh there's one helluva nice girl."

"I didn't know there were any left."

"I didn't either," the Fox agreed.

The steaks were delicious and they took their time eating. It was Hollister's first good meal since he and Janice had gone out for dinner last Friday night. He assumed that most restaurants made their profit off of single or divorced men.

As Yesterday worked at clearing away the dishes from their table, Fox took her by the hand and said, "Miss, could I have the key to your apartment?"

"But we've just met," she teased with a surprised look.

"I know," the Fox answered, cupping her hand in his. "But this time I know you're the real thing."

"You mean I'm a bottle of Coke."

"They're both originally from Georgia, aren't they?"

"I guess they are." She reached deep into the shadow between her breasts. The Fox and Hollister watched. Her fingers searched. "It was here a minute ago," she said, continuing to probe deeper into the bra.

"Would you like some help?"

"Virgil," she scolded. "Here it is." She pulled the silver key out and handed it to the Fox. "You know where it's at."

"Sure do. Do I get to put the key back when we're done with it?"

Yesterday shook her head with a soft smile. "It's an extra. I'll get it back after you've caught this terrible man."

Hollister noticed she spoke as if there were no doubt about their suspicions or their ability to catch the man. He had doubts, he knew the odds weren't in their favor. She probably, like millions of others, was brainwashed by the tube. The television cops always got their man, and wasn't that the way real cops did it? Who knew a real cop? People don't know cops, they just call them. The only ones who know cops are just other cops.

Fox promised he'd call her Tuesday morning and let her know how the night went. She gave him Vickie's number and explained she'd only be three doors away after she got off at two. He said he'd watch for her when she came in.

They paid their bill and walked to the door. Yesterday was with them. "You're welcome to anything that's there," she said. "I think there's some Coke in the refrigerator. Maybe some potato chips on the counter."

"Thanks," Hollister answered.

"Please be careful," she said with a worried look.

"We always are," the Fox assured with a smile. "I'll talk to you in the morning."

"Good night."

"Wow," the Fox shouted to the sky as they walked to their car.

Hollister lit up a smoke. "Never thought I'd see the day," he exhaled.

"For what?" the Fox asked as they reached the car.

"That my partner, the sly Virgil Fox, the great cock hound, would fall in love at first sight."

"Oh, I could," he answered, unlocking the door on the passenger's side. "I could real easy. That's the type of girl that every man dreams of. Beautiful, good personality, I mean she's got it all. She's what makes being black beautiful."

"Yeah," Hollister agreed. "She's pretty."

Starting the car, Hollister glanced at his watch. "It's only seven-twenty. What 'ya wanna do till dark?" It was still bright and warm.

"She wants to be an actress," the Fox answered, staring ahead.

"Fox!" Hollister growled. "What 'ya wanna do?"

"Do what Kojak would do in a situation like this."

"Go to a commercial?"

"Point for Lee Hollister."

"Let's go check the three addresses again."

"I was just gonna suggest that," Fox said.

Neither of the two really expected to find a white VW at any of the three addresses, but it was a way to pass the hour or so of daylight that remained. The evening was cooling, and the afternoon shadows were stretching across the avenues. With the dinner hour over and the temperature dropping, the street corners were filling with blacks. The tempo of activity on the police radio hidden in the car's glove box reflected it. "THREE-A-NINE, A WOMAN SCREAMING. TWENTY-SEVEN, THIRTEEN ELLEDALE. CODE TWO . . . NEWTON UNITS AND THIRTEEN-A-ONE, A TWO-ELEVEN JUST OCCURRED AT TWO-TWO-NINETEEN SOUTH CENTRAL. TWO MALE NEGROES, NO FURTHER. THEY USED A GUN. LEFT IN UNKNOWN DIRECTION. THIRTEEN-A-ONE, CODE TWO . . . WILSHIRE UNITS IN THE VICINITY AND SEVEN-A-FORTY-TWO, A MAJOR FOUR-FIFTEEN WITH SHOTS FIRED, AT THE JACK-IN-THE-BOX AT PICO AND CRENSHAW. SEVEN-A-FORTY. TWO YOUR CALL IS CODE TWO."

"Poor patrol cops take it in the shorts on a night like this, don't they?" the Fox said in a matter-of-fact tone. He was gazing out the window.

"They eat it up," Hollister answered, slowing for a traffic signal. As they rolled to a stop, two white-helmeted motorcycle officers pulled up on the Fox's side of the car and braked to a halt. They too waited for the light to change. The Fox eyed the polished idling machines.

The officer closest to the Fox caught his look. He smiled from beneath the sunglasses that added to his Gestapo look. "It's almost sunset," he said over the rumble of his motor. "I thought all detectives were home in bed."

"Don't you sometimes wonder who with when you work every night?" the Fox answered quickly.

"Not anymore," the officer smiled. "I'm divorced. Wife ran off with some detective."

"Serves him right," the Fox agreed.

The light switched to green.

"You wanna trade places for the rest of the night?" the Fox asked.

"Hell, no," the officer said, shaking his head. "People get killed in cars." He shifted the machine in gear and the two cycles rolled ahead simultaneously.

A black prostitute wearing a blonde wig sat down on a

bus bench and tried for an innocent look as they rolled by
her near Adams Boulevard. Fox smiled at her. The girl ignored him. He counted three more whores before they
reached Western Avenue. As the evening's darkness gathered, the neon glitter of the iron-gated storefronts flickered
on. A group of six young blacks loitered near a liquor store
at Thirty-sixth Street, waiting for a sympathetic customer
who would buy them the six-pack they'd pooled their
money for. An ambulance raced by, northbound, its red
lights flashing, siren screaming. The cars on the street
yielded, people on the sidewalks payed no attention. Fox
nodded to a patrol car that had a pink Cadillac stopped near
Vernon. A tall slender black wearing a wide-brimmed hat
and cape stood beside it with a white girl in a short miniskirt.

After they made their rounds of the three widely scattered
addresses, the sun was gone and the street lights blinked on.
"Make a left at the next signal," the Fox said, guiding
Hollister into the tangle of winding streets and cul-de-sac
where South August was located. "How close are we?" Hollister asked.

"Four blocks. Why?"

"I figure if you drop me in front and I go in alone, it'll
draw less attention. Then," Hollister continued as he negotiated the turn, "you park and lock this thing about a block
away and walk back."

"Coming up on the right," the Fox said after guiding him
through several more turns.

Hollister studied the numbers on the stucco apartment
buildings on the south side of the street. "There it is, forty-
one twenty-seven." He eased the Plymouth to the curb just
west of the building.

The Fox dug in his pocket. "Here's the key."

"See ya soon." When Hollister had crossed the street, Fox
put the car in gear and rolled away.

Lee pulled off his tie and stuffed it in a pocket. "No Solici-
tors," a sign on the glass double doors announced as he
pushed through them into the enclosed court. There was a
blue well-tended pool in the center of the courtyard bor-
dered by a wide pastel concrete walk lined with blooming
bird of paradise plants. He heard the sound from a mixture
of stereos and TV's coming from behind the screened curtained windows as he strolled casually around the pool searching for number eighteen.

The apartment was at the rear of the court in the center of the four that formed the south wall. To his pleasure, there was a light on inside. If the man was already waiting in the alley on the other side of the building his suspicions wouldn't be aroused by Hollister having to turn on a light. He unlocked the two locks on the door and went inside.

Inside the door Hollister pulled his thirty-eight from its shoulder Standing in the living room, he could see into the kitchen, which was separated by a small breakfast bar. A shadowed doorway led into what he guessed would be the bedroom and bath.

With the light at his back now, Hollister felt vulnerable as he peered into the dark bedroom. His eyes strained, studying the faint outline of the window. The pleated beige curtains hung straight, motionless. He inched into the room that smelled of powder and perfume.

Satisfied no one was in the room, Hollister moved cautiously to the closed bathroom and gave the door a push with his foot, the thirty-eight leveled at the darkness. The door swung open without resistance and banged against a glass-walled shower. He jumped.

Reholstering the thirty-eight, he went back to the living room and pulled off his jacket. Fishing his cigarettes from a pocket, he tossed the jacket to the couch. Sitting down in a chair across from the couch, he shook out a Marlboro and lit up.

"Who is it?" he called to a knock on the door, expecting Fox.

"You like to buy some stereo tapes?" a young voice called through the door.

Hollister got up, moved to the door, and peered through the glass peephole. A young black, sixteen or seventeen he guessed, stood in front of the door holding a black case.

"What are you selling?" Hollister asked through the door.

"I gots some fine tapes here. I got the Jackson Five, Sly and the Family Stone, Marvin Gaye, I got it all, and I'm sellin' them for a buck a piece."

Hollister opened the door. The young man's jaw dropped as he stared wide-eyed at the shoulder holster and gun. "Youngblood," Hollister threatened, "now that I've seen you, you better get those tapes back in the car they came out of."

"Er, ahh . . . I . . ."

"Get your ass outta here."

The youth quickly disappeared into the shadows. Seeing

Fox approach, Lee returned to his chair, leaving the door
open a few inches.

"What was that all about?" Fox asked, closing the door
behind him, twisting the locks closed.

"Some punk selling hot tapes."

"You set his mind straight?"

"You can bet he's out of door-to-door tape sales."

"Nice," the Fox said, looking around.

"Figured it would be. Didn't you?" Hollister said with a
glance.

"Uh huh."

Hollister glanced at his watch. It was a quarter of nine.
"Take a look around," he suggested. "See where the bathroom is, so you don't piss on the floor later. Then we'll shut
off this light."

"All the windows closed?" the Fox asked.

"Yeah. After you look around, crack open the one in
the bedroom. Make it easy for this son of a bitch. I wouldn't
wanna do anything to discourage him."

Virgil moved into the bedroom, where Lee heard the window slide open. Shortly after that the bathroom door banged
against the glass shower for the second time. Hollister smiled
as he heard Virgil curse quietly.

Returning to the living room, Virgil turned off the table
light at the end of the couch. The room fell dark. Removing
his jacket, he hung it carefully on the back of one of the two
stools at the kitchen bar just as Hollister figured he would.
He guessed his taste for expensive clothes and the care he
showed in handling them came from having to wear raggedy
hand-me-downs throughout the young years of his life.

"What did that jacket cost, Virg?" Hollister asked.

"One sixty-five," Fox answered, adjusting it on the chair.
"Why?"

"I don't remember what any of mine cost. Why do you?"

The shadow in the kitchen stood silent for a moment.
Hollister was sorry he had asked. The silence was awkward.
"I guess it's a symbol of making it in a white world," Fox
answered.

Lee said nothing.

"Kinda like the dude that makes seventy-five a week at the
local gas station," Fox went on, "and buys a new Cadillac. Its his way of showing he's made it . . . it's the only way
he'll ever be able to show he's made it."

Hollister didn't respond.

Fox chose a spot along the living room wall where he could see into the courtyard through the front window plus into the bedroom where the light from the alley framed the window with a faint grayness in the otherwise dark room. He sat down on the carpet and leaned back against the wall. "You figure three o'clock, huh?" he said to Hollister, whose white face reflected the light from the glowing tip of his cigarette.

"She gets off at two," Hollister exhaled. "Gets home maybe ten minutes later. If he's not here by three—that's an hour after she gets off—he isn't coming."

"You really think it's him?" the Fox questioned.

"Uh huh."

"And that he'll come back?"

"You saw her. What do you think?"

"He'll be back."

They sat quiet for a few minutes. Hollister enjoyed the still darkness, not allowing his mind to pick any worrisome thoughts.

Finally Virgil broke the silence. "Wonder if Axelrod's asleep."

"He's gotta be some kind of a first," Hollister smiled. "It's not likely any other L.A.P.D. detective has ever spent a night in a bank vault."

"Especially with some snake," the Fox reminded.

"Axelrod's luck, she's a virginal Jehovah's Witness."

"He'll change that," the Fox chuckled.

"I tell you about the broad that was in that extortion deal couple weeks ago?"

"Don't think so."

"Most of the victims in that were Jehovah's Witnesses."

"Yeah."

"So, I'm interviewing this one lard ass and I said, in my official police voice, 'Ma'am, are you a Jehovah's Witness?' and she answers, 'No Officer, I wasn't even there, and I don't know the man.'"

They both laughed. As their laughter died, Virgil said, "It's been a heavy week. The Pisser's back, Wilson's dead, Axelrod's locked in a vault, and a deputy chief fell."

"When it rains, it pours."

"You think Spear is dirty?"

"Is John Wayne a fruit?"

"Why'd he pull the pin then?"

"I don't know," Hollister shrugged. "Maybe Rainey'll have some answers. If he'll talk to me."

"Think he's pissed?"

"Hell, I don't know."

"Real can of worms, all right," the Fox agreed.

"Who's gonna give a shit next year?"

"What 'ya mean?"

"I mean who cares?" Hollister answered. "How is what we're doing tonight going to change the world? Does anyone in San Diego really give a shit about what we're doing in L.A.? Twenty years from now who'll know about what we're doing tonight?"

The Fox considered what Hollister had said carefully. Then, looking to the dark shadow slumped in the chair, he said, "I think it was Shakespeare who said, 'Man has seven ages. In his fifth age he reflects on his sense of being and identity, and considers his value as a person in what he can contribute to his fellow man, and what impact it will have in the overall history of mankind itself.' "

"What?"

"I said I think you're in your fifth age."

"How come you're a cop, Virgil?" Hollister asked in a serious tone.

"It paid more than teaching."

"Tells you something about our society, doesn't it?" Hollister snorted.

"How come you're a big-city detective?"

"Got shit-canned from flight school at Pensacola. Spent the next four years leading a bunch of skin-headed high school dropouts through Viet Nam rice paddies. This was the only job I could find when I got back."

"How come you got dumped from flight training?"

"Buzzing some broad's house. I had already soloed. I was logging a few hours in a T twenty-eight when I saw this young thing sprawled next to a pool in her back yard. She waved to me. I made a low pass to wave back, just one. Her old man was an admiral."

"Just once and they dumped you?"

"I think it was hitting their TV antenna that did it."

"That low?"

"I was a good pilot," Hollister argued. "I wanted to fly. A bunch of fuckin' draftees that didn't want to, made it. Just didn't make any sense, one goddamned admiral."

"You sorry now about being a cop?"

"No, it's a living. I like it."

"Here we sit," the Fox smiled. "A grounded pilot and a would-be schoolteacher, waiting in the darkness for a rapist."

"Maybe he'll be an admiral."

Occasionally a door would close and footsteps would echo in the courtyard. Or keys would jingle as a tenant came home and unlocked a door. There was little else to mark the passing hours.

A few minutes after 2:00 A.M. the Fox asked, "You asleep?"

"Was."

"My ass went to sleep," the Fox complained, massaging his thigh, shifting his position.

The spurt of a match Hollister lit punctured the darkness. Cupping his hand around it, he drew on his cigarette and then shook it out. "You know," he exhaled, "the Pisser's probably been asleep since eleven o'clock."

"Yeah, I know. And here I sit with my ass numb. When we get 'em, I'm gonna beat him like I owe him."

"Someone's coming," Hollister said in a hushed tone.

The Fox twisted to the window beside him. He found the approaching footsteps moving along the far side of the pool. He recognized the long-haired figure. "It's Yesterday," he whispered. He watched until she neared the rear of the courtyard, where he could no longer see her. "If he's coming, it should be soon."

The man didn't come.

The Fox got up and went to the bathroom. Returning, he sat down on the couch. "Wilson's funeral is today," he said, leaning his head back.

"What time?" Hollister asked.

"Ten."

"You going?"

"Yeah, I think so. How about you?"

Hollister hunched forward in the chair. The thought of a funeral didn't excite him. He was tired, and he could visualize a bunch of wailing black women clinging to one another around the grave site. "No, I don't think I'll make it."

"What time we gonna do it tomorrow?" the Fox asked.

"Same," Hollister answered, glancing at his luminous watch. "It's ten minutes to three. Let's go home."

The Fox closed and locked the bedroom window. "Wanna leave the same way we came in?" he questioned, slipping on his jacket.

"Yeah." Hollister considered going by Janice's, but he thought that she might not appreciate being awakened at three-thirty in the morning.

"Pick you up out front in five minutes," the Fox said, opening the door.

Hollister took a last look around the apartment. It frustrated him to know that the Pisser had moved through these rooms in the darkness as he did now and then fled leaving no clue to his identity. A faceless black rapist. He really hated this son of a bitch. He hated rapists in general, but this one was a savage. A subhuman animal that pissed. He hoped they had to kill him.

Driving northbound on Western Avenue after he and the Fox parted at the station, Hollister decided with a yawn that Janice should sleep the rest of the night undisturbed.

His turn onto the freeway was reflex. He lit up another smoke. It tasted bitter. He coughed, and stabbed it out in the ashtray. Damn things. That was it. No more smoking. He could do it. He was certain of that. He hoped he had some Bufferin at home. Feeling sleep pulling at his eyelids, he cracked the window open. The rush of cool morning air erased the fatigue for the moment. He realized that by the time he got to bed, which would be 4:00 A.M., his day was going to be twenty-two hours old. The city got its money's worth today. He was lighting up another cigarette when he noticed that he'd just passed his off-ramp.

He awoke swimming in sweat and tangled in the sheets. The room was stuffy and humid, and his eyes ached. He squinted at he gazed at the clock radio beside the bed. "One-eleven, goddamn it." He ran a tongue over his coated teeth and swung his feet to the floor.

Pulling a pair of faded levis from the closet, he danced on one leg while pushing the other into the pants. He sat down on the edge of the bed to put in the other, having had to struggle hard with the first. He stood up to zip them and found they were tighter than he remembered. Gaining weight, he thought. Have to watch it.

Moving into the living room, Hollister turned on the air conditioner and stood in front of the rush of cool air until he got goose bumps. It was one in the afternoon . . . what day? Tuesday . . . yeah, it was Tuesday. Staying up all night always screwed up his biological clock. It seemed to him he'd slept through an entire day somehow. The past two days blurred into a fuzzy image that he found hard to clarify. How in the hell did Morning Watch cops do it? Working every night from midnight to eight. They had to be nuts. Having slept late gave him the feeling he should be somewhere else, and wherever that was, he was late. A shower and shave would set his mind straight, he told himself.

Walking to the refrigerator, he got a bottle of Dr. Pepper, Janice's own personal stock, and a pear. After picking up the morning paper from outside the front door, he settled on the couch to enjoy his breakfast.

He finished off the bottle of soft drink and pushed off the couch. A shave and shower would rid him of this sticky, sweaty mood that seemed to melt through his body and into his soul. Get some fresh clothes on and get busy with something that would shake this unidentified gloom hanging in the back of his mind.

What was it the Fox had said? His fifth age. He was in his fifth age and he was searching for his purpose in life, what was he worth, how would his life affect all mankind. Was that why he'd left Carol? Was he searching for who he was? No, he told himself. He knew who he was, and what he was. What he wasn't was a drive-home-every-night suburban Joe Doe who would grow old living in a cookie-cutter house forever fighting crab grass and the local P.T.A. He was bored with a wife who screwed only on her back and only in bed, so he left her. Anyone who didn't understand or agree could get screwed. Anyway, when he was dead, what would it matter who remembered what?

He was certain the only thing that the future generations of mankind would remember of these years was that the people were governed by an unindicted coconspirator. Here he and the Fox were trying to rip off a few crooks in the Los Angeles ghetto while the White House employed spies and burglars. His efforts seemed so futile. The mood, the very character, of the country seemed shaken and wounded ever since that hot day in Dallas so many summers ago. The rifle bullet had killed more than a young president. He was certain within a few years, maybe a decade, the system would fall riddled with corruption and the incurable cancer of self-righteousness.

The ring of the telephone brought him back from his analytical daydream. He quickly rinsed the traces of shaving cream from his face, picked up a towel, and headed for the phone. He hoped it was Janice.

"Sorry if I woke you, Lee." It was Purington.

"No, you didn't." He sat down on the edge of the bed and pulled a cigarette from a pack beside the phone. "I've been up for about an hour."

"I called to let you know you and the Fox have court tomorrow."

"What case?"

"Raymond Blatts."

"We'll be there," Hollister assured him.

"So will Mattingly and Collison," Purington added. "The D.A. subpoenaed all four of you."

"What court?"

"Division thirty-four, eight-thirty."

"Got it."

"How'd last night go?"

"Quiet."

"You and the Fox had two people in jail this morning."

"Yeah."

"I assigned them to Rondino and his partner."

"Thanks."

"You still think this thing is worthwhile?" Purington questioned.

"It's all we've got, Tom. Now the son of a bitch has killed five women in the past four years. I think that justifies a little concentrated effort on any clue we have, and this stakeout is all we've got."

"Okay . . . okay. It's just that Lieutenant Blake doesn't like his Burglary people handling our arrestees and that's what Rondino and Rollenhagen are doing this morning."

"Tell Blake to get screwed."

"I did," Purington answered.

"Rainey back yet?"

"Yeah, he's here today. He's in the field right now."

"We in any trouble over that deal?"

"I don't think so . . . but I'm not sure. They're interviewing a helluva lot of people."

"Somebody'll take it in the shorts."

"We've got a new deputy chief," Purington advised.

"Who?"

"Deputy Chief Richard M. Yearling."

"Jesus Christ."

"Thought you'd be overjoyed to hear."

"Of all the people . . . Yearling."

"He asked Captain Slack this morning to update him on

the status of your case. The skipper told him about your stakeout, and the three parolee-suspects."

"What'd he say?"

"You don't wanna know."

"Come on, Tom. What the hell did he say?"

"That stakeouts were straw-grabbing efforts and shouldn't be substituted for good solid detective work."

"That worthless prick," Hollister growled. "What the hell's he know about good solid detective work? I'd like——"

"Now calm down. The skipper defended what we're doing. He told Yearling if he wanted to run the Detective Bureau, he could have it. Otherwise, it was hands off. Yearling agreed."

"Got any other good news?"

"That'll have to do."

"Thanks."

"Good luck tonight."

"You get a chance, come by. We'll leave the bedroom window open a crack. Just push it open and climb in."

Much to Hollister's delight, Janice had left her daughter in Clairmont. He apologized four times for not calling Sunday evening or Monday. Finally, she warmed and agreed to dinner.

He picked her up at five-thirty at her apartment, and they drove to the Whaler's Cove on the pier at Redondo Beach for a seafood dinner.

"Lee," Janice warned as she picked through a shrimp cocktail, "I lived for nine years with another policeman." He didn't like being reminded of her ex-husband. It made him feel uncomfortable, guilty. "My biggest bitch with Chuck was that eighty percent of the time I didn't know where he was."

"I promise it'll never happen again," he answered with a glance.

"Your promise is too casual," she cautioned. "I'm being very serious."

"I promise. Would you like me to kneel beside your chair and say it again?"

"You'd promise anything just so you can come over when you get off in the morning."

"I promise—I mean, that's not true," he smiled.

Janice laid her fork aside. "Lee, you're treating this whole matter as a joke."

"Look, I——"

"You look," she threatened. "I invested too many years in one of you so-called crime fighters to get burned again. If you want my opinion, I think you're all on an ego trip. TV and the movies all paint you people as steely-eyed six-footers who are able to leap over all buildings in a single bound and run around with a constant hard-on. You're all out to live up to that image, and when the wife or girlfriend treats you as just a human, you drop her like a hot rock. You're all parasites. You bleed a woman dry, and when she's got nothing else to give, you move on. Well, this is one woman who has a few needs of her own, and I'm not going to get shit on again."

Lee searched her eyes. She glanced down to her salad.

"Janice," he said, reaching for her hand, "I'd like to believe I don't belong to that club. I think I'm different. If you'll give me half a chance, I'll show you. I can't help it if this damn job keeps me away from you. I wish it didn't. I want nothing more than to be happy with you. All cops aren't the same. No more than all women are the same. We both have our needs and I think you and I can fulfill them. All it'll take is effort. I promise mine."

He met Fox at the station at a quarter of eight, where they went through the new teletypes and crime reports but found nothing new on the Pisser. Hutch and Linsay were still in the squad room working on a homicide that had occurred late in the afternoon. It seems that a Mrs. Gloria Parks from South Budlong had accidentally run over her crippled husband in their driveway . . . three times.

The Fox told Hollister that he and Yesterday had shared an early dinner in Chinatown at Madame Wong's . . . just so he could fill her in on how the case was developing. Hollister smiled wryly. "Your case is developing fast."

It was twenty minutes to nine when they arrived at the apartment, where they used the same procedure on entering. After Fox parked a block away and let himself in, Hollister told him to look at the kitchen counter. There was a setting for two, set expertly on the small bar. Silverware and crystal glasses and blue napkins rolled in silver rings. A tray of cut sandwiches and assorted crackers and cheeses sat covered in the center with a small note attached. Fox picked up the note.

To whom it may concern,
I didn't know what you guys like so I made both ham
and egg salad. In the frig you'll find some coke, and
the pot of coffee is fresh.
Good luck and be careful,

                                    Yesterday.

The highlight of the night was the telephone ringing at pre-
cisely twelve-ten. The first ring jolted both men from their
drowsiness.

"What 'ya think?" the Fox asked in the darkness as the
phone rang for the second time.

"She wouldn't call here, would she?"

"I told her not to."

The Fox slept through Yesterday coming home, and that
angered him. Oh, well, he'd call her in the morning. They
left at three-ten. Both were worried about the telephone
call. Hollister suggested the Fox talk with Yesterday about
it. Maybe she'd have some idea who it was.

It was ten minutes to four when Hollister slid into bed with
Janice. "Good morning," he whispered, moving an arm under her head and drawing her toward him. "Hello," she
yawned. Her flesh was almost feverishly warm.

"You have the alarm set?" he questioned, cupping a breast
in his hand.

"Uh huh, for six-thirty," she purred.

"Your honor," the black defense attorney said, pushing up
out of his chair, "on behalf of the defense, may I make a motion that all the prosecution's witnesses be excluded."

The graying, seemingly uninterested judge looked up from
his bench. "Call your witnesses," he said mechanically to the
young deputy district attorney.

The district attorney stood and picked up a file from the
long desk in front of him. He studied the paper. "Detective
John Mattingly."

Mattingly pushed from the bench and stood.

"Detective Douglas Collison."

Collison stood.

"Detective Lee Hollister."

Hollister pushed up.

"And Detective Virgil Fox."

"That's all, your honor," the D.A. said, turning to the
judge.

"Wait in the hallway until you're called and do not discuss the case among yourselves or with others," the judge ordered.

"Your honor," the D.A. added, "may Detective Mattingly remain and act as the investigating officer?"

"Mr. Pernell," the judge said with a glance to the defense attorney with the large natural.

"No objection, your honor," the man answered with a tight smile. Raymond Blatts sat slumped in a chair beside the attorney, calmly studying his nails.

"Call your first witness," the judge ordered, rocking back in his high-backed cushioned chair.

"The people call Detective Mattingly."

Mattingly pushed through the small double doors at the bar and moved toward the witness stand.

"Raise your right hand," the elderly clerk of the court called, raising his own. Mattingly faced the man and raised his hand.

"You swear to tell the truth and nothing but the truth in the matter now pending before this court, so help you God?" The clerk's voice was rapid, practiced.

"I do."

"Take the stand."

Hollister, the Fox, and Collison moved into the crowded wide hallway and were fortunate enough to find space on one of the cushioned benches that lined the walls. A heavy black woman with huge sagging breasts and a bulging stomach sat beside Hollister constantly burping while take large bites out of a sweet roll.

"How's the stakeout going?" Collison asked from the far end of the bench.

"We're still at it," the Fox answered, leaning back against the wall, brushing at some lint on his trouser leg.

They sat quietly for a while. Hollister played eyes with a blonde prostitute, the Fox wiggled his toes in his left boot, silently damning the wrinkle in his sock that crowded his little toe. He considered walking to the restroom, pulling off the boot, and straightening the sock, but decided to wait. It wasn't that uncomfortable.

The Fox wondered what Raymond Blatts was thinking. Several days ago in a dirty hot alley they had tried to kill each other. Each thinking his cause just. Now here in the courtroom they would sit within a few feet of each other while a judge decided if there was sufficient evidence to hold a man for trial in superior court.

He wondered if he'd kill Blatts now if he had the chance. He fantasized centering a gun to Blatts's head and slowly squeezing the trigger. Blatts's eyes clamped shut as death neared. The pistol barked and jumped. Bits of bone and flesh splattered as the soft lead flattened, impacting the skull bone. No, he wouldn't do it. He couldn't kill him that way. He would beat him bloody in a fair fight, but he couldn't kill him without provocation.

He planned on calling Yesterday when they got out of court. He looked forward to that. Maybe, he reasoned, instead of calling he'd stop by the Flying Fox and see her before meeting Hollister at the station tonight. He had to talk to her—might as well be in person. He savored the memory of their dinner at Madame Wong's. She had been so beautiful. He knew it was against departmental policy to develop on-duty contacts into off-duty social relationships, but in this case he thought that he was just going to have to overlook that little regulation.

He thought of sleeping with Yesterday, yet ironically had yet to kiss her. Yesterday was special. She was a lady, and that's how he intended to treat her. Slow and easy. This time, he allowed himself to think, this time it could be the one he'd been waiting on. Jesus, he thought, death and violence had led to love. It was the first he could recall that the word love seemed appropriate regarding his feelings toward a woman. It excited him.

"Deputy Chief Yearling came down to the squad room this morning," Collison said in an effort to start conversation.

"What did he want?" Hollister asked.

"He gave us a little pep talk on being professionals."

"You know what a professional is, don't you?" the Fox questioned.

"What?" Collison said.

"An amateur who takes money," the Fox smiled.

"Timely joke," Collison agreed, then added, "Yearling told us not to be shaken or embarrassed by all that we were seeing in the papers and on television. To hold onto the faith that we were working for the best police department in the world, and that in time our reputation would be our salvation."

Fox shook his head.

"Hanson offered to pass the hat after Yearling left," Collison added.

"Bet that went over big," Hollister smiled.

"Lieutenant Blake tole 'em to watch his smart remarks. We all gave Blake a round of applause."

"Yearling should have been an evangelist," the Fox suggested.

"That prick thinks he is," Hollister grated.

"Chief Peck thinks he's a good man," the Fox said.

"Peck just fired the only good deputy chief we had," Hollister answered.

"I hear he and Spear were academy classmates," Collison added.

"Helluva way to go after thirty years," Hollister breathed.

"What's he done for us lately, as Joe Citizen would say," the Fox added sarcastically.

"Think they'll make public the results of the investigation?" Collison asked.

"Why should they do something different this time?" Hollister's tone was bitter.

"In the interest of justice," Collison argued.

"Justice!" the Fox scoffed. "Why the hell expect justice? Why should Spear be thrown to the wolves when a vice president can get off by pleading no contest to a goddamned misdemeanor? Why expect justice from the courts that lock up juries for eight to ten weeks while the crook is out on bail? As long as we have revolving doors on the courts we're gonna have to live behind locked and bolted ones."

Collison gave the Fox a puzzled look. "You got my vote, Virgil, but what the hell does all that have to do with Deputy Chief Spear?"

"The original draft," he answered, giving Collison a hard look, "said, with justice for all . . . even deputy chiefs."

"I'd bet my next check Spear is clean," Hollister offered.

"You still owe me one for Agnew," the Fox reminded him.

The courtroom door opened. A black marshal in a well-tailored tan uniform stepped out. Holding the door open, he said, "Detective Fox."

"Tell 'em the devil made you do it, Virg," Hollister smiled.

The marshal held the door until the Fox moved inside. The courtroom benches were filled with policemen, victims, witnesses, all waiting for their cases to be called. Mattingly sat beside the deputy district attorney at the long desk just inside the courtroom bar. The court clerk stood waiting at the end of the judge's raised bench.

The Fox pushed through the small gate at the bar and walked toward the witness stand.

"Raise your right hand, please," the clerk said.

The Fox raised his hand just short of the witness stand.

"Do you swear to tell the truth, the whole truth, and nothing but the truth in the matter now pending before this court, so help you God?"

"I do." Fox glanced at Blatts, who sat chin in hand beside his attorney, a slight smile teasing at the corners of his mouth.

"Take the stand and state your full name, and please spell the last."

"Virgil Fox. F-O-X."

When Virgil was seated, the marshal adjusted a microphone in front of him and moved away. The court reporter, a thirtyish-looking brunette in a tight sweater, sat in front of the witness stand, her fingers poised above the keys of her machine.

He had testified a thousand times or more in the past nine years, and this time like all the others he had butter-flies in the pit of his stomach. He guessed a pilot must feel the same way every time his airplane left the runway and took to the air, or a football player when he ran from the bench into the game. He knew the feeling would vanish when the D.A. asked his first question.

From the corner of his eye he could see the judge beside him was doodling with a pencil. He wondered if the judge's mind was already made up. Hoped he wouldn't say anything that contradicted what Mattingly had already testified to.

"Investigator Fox," the district attorney said, looking to the papers spread before him, running a hand back through his straw-colored straight hair, "what is your occupation and current assignment?"

The Fox straightened in his chair. Mattingly winked at him. "I'm a police officer for the city of Los Angeles, currently assigned to Southwest Detectives."

"Were you so assigned on June twenty-first of this year?"

"Yes, sir."

"In the course of your duties on that day, Detective Fox, did you assist some other detective with an investigation?"

"Yes, sir."

"Could you tell the court who those other detectives were, and what the nature of their investigation was?"

"My partner, Sergeant Hollister, and myself, accompanied Investigators Mattingly and Collison to twelve-o-two West Fifty-second Street to conduct a burglary investigation."

"Would you please tell us what occurred when you arrived at the address?"

"Upon arrival we observed——"

"Your Honor, I object," the black defense attorney barked, pushing out of his chair. "The witness is testifying to what *we* observed, what *we* saw. Would the court please advise him to restrict his testimony to his own observations, and not to the vague conclusions he makes as to what others may have seen or heard."

"Sustained," the judge said. "Officer, just testify to what you saw or did," he cautioned.

If he'd had more than three hours' sleep, he wouldn't have made the mistake, the Fox told himself.

"Just tell us what you saw or did, Detective Fox," the district attorney said, rephrasing his question.

"I had been advised we were seeking a man by the name of Raymond Blatts," the Fox answered, regrouping his thoughts, "who resided at twelve fifty-two West Fifty-second Street, and drove——"

"Objection, your honor," the defense interrupted, again standing up. "The officer is now testifying to hearsay."

"Your honor," the district attorney defended, "this is for the purpose of probable cause only."

"Overruled. You may answer the question," the judge answered.

"——and that this Raymond Blatts drove a white Volkswagen sedan."

"What did you observe when you arrived, Detective?" the district attorney went on.

"I observed a white VW sedan parked in a driveway on the east side of the residence and a female Negro in the front yard."

"Detective Fox, did a white Volkswagen sedan have any particular significance to you?"

"Yes sir."

"What significance was that?"

"Several hours earlier a witness in a murder investigation told me he had observed a white Volkswagen going away from the scene of a homicide."

"I see, and you were considering that this white Volks——"

"Your honor," the defense attorney pleaded, slapping the table in front of him and again standing up. "I object to this line of questioning the district attorney is pursuing." His tone was angry. "My client is not charged with murder, and I must strongly oppose the district attorney attempting to inflame and inflate the allegations that have been made with these vague, ambiguous remarks about a white Volkswagen that may be related to a homicide investigation. And even, your honor, if this phantom VW does exist, there is no evidence that the one parked at Mr. Blatts's residence was the one they were seeking."

The judge considered the objection while probing his sagging jowl with the eraser of a wooden pencil. Glancing to the district attorney, who stood waiting, ready to respond, he said, "Mr. Seaman, how is this relevant?"

"Your honor, it's for the purpose of probable cause only. I think it's important the court fully understand what this officer's state of mind was when he approached that house."

"I see. Very well, overruled. Proceed."

The defense attorney sat down.

"Now," the district attorney said, adjusting his tie, "as you approached this house and observed the white VW, what were you thinking?"

"I gave consideration to the fact that this Raymond Blatts may also be a suspect in the homicide I was investigating."

"Tell us what you did next, Detective," the district attorney urged.

"Detective Collison identified himself as a police officer to the woman by displaying his badge and asked if she lived in twelve-o-two."

"What did she answer?"

"She stated her name was Rosey Blatts and that she did live there."

"What occurred next, Detective?"

"Investigator Mattingly was asking Mrs. Blatts about the ownership of the white VW, when the defendant appeared in the open doorway of the house."

"When you refer to the defendant, Detective Fox, do you see that individual here in the courtroom today?"

"Yes, sir," the Fox answered, raising a hand to point a finger at Blatts. "He's seated just to the left of the defense counsel."

"Let the record show the officer pointed out the defendant," the judge advised.

"What did you do after observing the man, Officer?"

"I called to him. I said 'can I talk with you for a minute?' "

"Did he answer?"

"No, he just remained standing in the open doorway."

"What did you do next?"

"I walked toward the front porch. I was approximately thirty, thirty-five feet away."

"What did the defendant do?"

"As I moved toward the porch, the woman, Mrs. Blatts, shouted 'it's the police, baby. They want you for something about the car.' "

"Did she shout loudly?"

"Yes, sir."

"What happened next?"

"After the woman shouted, the defendant stepped back from the door and slammed it shut."

"What did you do then, Detective?"

"Fearing the defendant was about to arm himself to resist arrest or flee, my partner and I approached the front door and forced it open."

"After you forced the——"

"I object, your honor," the defense interrupted, pushing to his feet. "The officer with his testimony admits that there was no compliance with section eight forty-four which requires a police officer knock, identify himself, and state his purpose in being there. None of the three were done, your honor. As he just said, they raced to the door and kicked it in. No knock, no announcement, no identity. I don't think, your honor, that it's written anywhere that it's unlawful to slam a door in the presence of a police officer.

"Detective Fox tells us he called to the man, 'hey, can I talk with you,' and admits he got no answer. I think it's possible that Mr. Blatts didn't hear the officer, or if he did, didn't realize he was talking to him. He claims he knew Mr. Blatts's name. I would wonder then, your honor, why he didn't use it?

"Further, your honor, I must point out that Detective Fox testified that he feared Mr. Blatts was about to arm himself or flee. Quite frankly, your honor, I don't know how one can escape by closing a door. Flee out the back? I don't think that's reasonable. There were four seasoned police detectives present. Certainly deploying two men to the rear would have quickly sealed off any possible escape.

"As for the possibility of Mr. Blatts arming himself . . . really, your honor, I think that's grasping at straws. Are we to assume all black men are armed? I thought that the day was gone when every suspected black man was considered a disciple of Huey Newton and armed with a submachine gun. Mr. Blatts does not own a firearm, and has no criminal record that reflects any activity with firearms.

"Isn't it conceivable that Mr. Blatts closed the door to slip on his shoes, pick up his cigarettes, but how did the police react? By racing to the door and kicking it in without a word. The detective said nothing about the man running, just the opposite. To quote the officer, your Honor— 'the man stepped back and slammed the door.' Nothing about his running away from the door. No suspicious moves, just stepped back and closed the door.

"We've heard testimony from Detective Mattingly about an alleged burglary, we've heard testimony from Detective Fox about an alleged homicide, but there has been no burglary victim to testify, no homicide revealed. My client is not charged with burglary, with homicide. He's charged with attempted murder of a police officer.

"Your honor, I'm a reasonable law-abiding citizen, but placed in the position Raymond Blatts found himself in, I'm afraid I may have reacted the same way. Here he was just out of bed and he's confronted with two gun-wielding men who kicked in his front door without identifying themselves. Was his reaction so unreasonable?

"What I think we have here, your honor, is a classic case of police overreaction. I temper that suggestion with the knowledge that these men have dangerous jobs. It is quite possible one of them, or all of them, have been in a similar situation where violence did erupt and officers were injured, but I must point out that my client is not charged with similar situations. He's charged with the felonious crime of assaulting a police officer, and this case must be judged on its own merits.

"I believe in this case, your honor, that the court must find the officers, by their own admission, did not comply with section eight forty-four of the penal code, and in failing to do so poisoned any police action made after their illegal entry into the home. Based on this, your honor, and the other points I've already made, I move for a dismissal on the grounds of insufficient evidence."

Raymond Blatts flashed an arrogant smile at the Fox. The Fox returned the look with a threatening gaze.

The judge moved his forearms onto the edge of his high bench. He looked to the district attorney. "Mr. Seaman, I tend to agree with the points Mr. Pernell has made, but I'll listen to your argument before I rule on the motion."

The district attorney accepted with a nod. "Your honor, I too would be impressed with Mr. Pernell's argument were I not an attorney. But since I am, I realize that court decisions and judgments are based on fact, not emotional arguments or alleged facts, that have yet to be offered as evidence in this case.

"In Mr. Pernell's view what we have heard the officers testify to is to be considered a classic case of police overreaction. I think the facts of this case illustrate how asinine that assumption is.

"The facts of the case are, your honor, as Officer Mattingly testified, that when the four detectives went to the house on West Fifty-second Street, they already had enough probable cause to effect the arrest of Raymond Blatts for the crime of burglary.

"Upon their arrival, there they met and had a brief conversation with the defendant's mother in the front yard. Then the defendant appeared at the open front door. The police didn't open that door. It was already open, and it was to remain open until, as Detective Fox walked toward the house, the defendant's mother called to him . . . 'it's the police. They want you for something about the car.' . . . It was then the defendant slammed the door, after he knew the men were police officers.

"Mr. Pernell suggested two officers could have been deployed to the rear to block escape. In testimony to come, your honor, we will reveal that was attempted, but before the officers could reach the rear of the residence, the defendant escaped . . . just as Detective Fox feared he might.

"In this case, your honor, I think it's been established that the officers were identified to the defendant . . . by his own mother, and after that identity was made, it was then he slammed shut the door and fled out the rear. He knew who they were, and he was attempting to escape." The district attorney sat down.

The judge inhaled deeply as his eyes swept over the

crowded courtroom. He finished with a side glance at Virgil. He pulled the sleeves of his black robe up on both arms, exposing the white shirt beneath. Virgil thought it looked as if were about to wash his hands. Pontius Pilate himself.

"Dismissed," the judge snapped in an unemotional matter-of-fact tone.

"What night is this?" Hollister asked from his reclined position on the couch.

"The third," the Fox answered, turning from the window, glancing to the dark shadow on the couch where Hollister lay.

"No, I mean what day is it?"

"Thursday morning."

"It's really starting to blur. I mean, it seems like it's Tuesday. I lost Wednesday somehow."

"Yeah, so did I."

Hollister caught the tone. "Hell, Virg, don't let it bother you. Blatts's day will come."

"I know, but it still smarts. I wanted to kill him when the son of a bitch smiled at us when he left the courtroom."

"Wonder if Judge Morrison's sleeping?" Hollister asked the dark ceiling.

"I hope someone breaks into his house and rapes his old lady in front of him."

"She would probably enjoy it 'cause he doesn't have any balls."

"You know," the Fox said thoughtfully, "the courts would be better if once a day some dude was pulled off the corner and sat on the judge's bench. By damn, we'd see some justice."

"Uh huh," the shadow on the couch agreed.

"I mean, what's Morrison know about justice?" the Fox went on. "Ten-to-one he was born and raised somewhere like Santa Barbara, attended law school at U.C.L.A. in the early fifties, when the only black there was the one who swept the halls, practiced law for five or six years, and then got appointed to the bench because his uncle is the vice president of Standard Oil and was a big contributor to Governor Brown's campaign."

"Yeah, he knows a lot about life and justice in the Los Angeles ghetto. I'm sure he knew the reason why the schoolteacher from Leimert Park wasn't there. Because the last time her apartment got ripped off she lost six days of work going down to court and sitting in the hall all day. Because there's no place to park, she got two ten-dollar parking tickets, because after six days of waiting and coming back, she saw the smiling nineteen-year-old defendant walk out of the courtroom free, because the judge didn't believe the officers properly advised him of his constitutional rights. I'm sure her opinion of justice is a little different than Judge Morrison's."

The Fox tried to visualize this man who wanted to rape Yesterday. Now that he knew her he knew how Dave Wilson felt when he found Ellen's body in her bedroom. Now he understood fully why Wilson had killed Shane.

Hollister lit a cigarette and propped his feet up on the cocktail table. Fox leaned his head against the wall next to the window and turned his eyes back to the shadows in the courtyard.

The shimmering water of the kidney-shaped pool looked cool and inviting. He pictured himself and Yesterday swimming in it, she in a small yellow bikini, her brown skin glistening in the light.

After having a sandwich at the Flying Fox earlier in the evening, Yesterday had walked him to his car, which was parked at the rear with those of the employees.

"Be careful," she cautioned, taking his hand. "I'll see you tomorrow." There had been no discussion of seeing each other on Thursday. She assumed they would, and by her tone he knew she wanted to. It thrilled him. He kissed her, intending for it to be a gentle, casual, I-care kiss. But the embrace had been long and passionate. When they parted, she squeezed his hand and went back inside. Neither one said anything.

A hint of movement in the dark shadows at the head of the courtyard snapped him from his dreaming. He caught it in the corner of his eye. Not enough to identify it as a man, just movement. He was certain it wasn't one of the swaying plants. After three nights he was familiar with their patterns. This was something else, and it didn't belong.

"Lee," he whispered, turning fully to the window.

"Where?" Lee moved carefully to the window in the darkness.

"Up near the front to the left of the pool, near the palm."

Hollister, kneeling beside the Fox, stared into the darkness, searching for movement. After a few moments he said, "Virg, I don't see a goddamned thing."

"I know I saw it."

Fox continued to watch the unmoving shadows. He hoped it was him. His pulse quickened.

"There he is," Hollister hissed as the figure stepped from the shadows near a clump of tall wide-leaved plants at the front of the courtyard.

The Fox tensed. "Come on, bastard, come on."

Hollister unholstered his thirty-eight as the dark shadow of a man moved slowly along the curved walkway to the right of the pool. His image faded as he moved through the darker shadows from the tall palms that ringed the walk.

"What the hell's he doing coming in the front?" the Fox whispered, pushing up on his knees.

"What the hell does it matter if he comes down the chimney, as long as it's him."

The figure moved slowly as if walking on noisy gravel. He wasn't a big man. Five-eleven, the Fox guessed, with a large Afro. The Fox silently cursed the darkness, wishing he could see the man's face. Halfway down the side of the pool the figure paused, then turning to his left, moved toward an apartment on the east wall.

"Not that one, you goddamned idiot," Hollister grated.

"Simple bastard's lost."

Moving to the door of the dark apartment, the man stood motionless in the shadows for a long moment.

"What the hell's he doing?" Hollister whispered.

"Making sure they're asleep."

Finally the figure stepped from the walk in front of the door into the plants around the wide-screened front window.

"Here he goes," the Fox said, realizing he was breathing hard.

The man ran a hand around the aluminum frame of the screen, pausing now and then when his experienced fingers found a hook. Soon he lifted the screen away, setting it carefully among the tall plants. With the screen gone, he dug in his pocket, removed what the Fox guessed would be a knife, and turned his attention back to the window.

"How do you wanna handle it?" the Fox asked without taking his eyes off the man.

"When he's inside we'll go over," Hollister answered quietly. "I'll get on the phone and get patrol to back us up."

"One of us will have to cover the back," the Fox said. "If we get over there and hear him doing a number on some broad inside, we're gonna have to go in. If we do, the son-of-a-bitch might get out a back window."

"Goddamn it," Hollister complained, "why couldn't he follow our plan."

With the suspect going into a different apartment, he felt the two of them just weren't enough. "I'll take the back. If we have to go in, Virg, he's all yours. Don't fuck with 'em, just kill him." Hollister didn't like being separated. When they were separated chasing Blatts, Fox had been hurt. Now with the Pisser they found themselves in the same situation.

"I'll be careful. Get on the phone."

Hollister took a final glance at the figure who still worked at the window, and then moved for the bedroom.

The dial tone sounded loud to him in the quiet apartment. Hollister quickly dialed the number on the lighted receiver.

"Police department, may I help you?"

"I'm a police officer," Hollister whispered, cupping the receiver with his hand. "I'm at forty-one, twenty-seven South August. I'm white, my partner is black. We're in plain clothes. We've got a burglary in progress on the east side of the interior courtyard. The suspect is a male Negro, six foot, in dark clothing. No further description. When the crook is inside, my partner and I are going after him. We're gonna need some assistance."

"What's the address again?" the officer at the complaint board asked.

"Forty-one, twenty-seven."

"Got it."

"I'll be covering the rear. My partner will be in the front," Hollister advised.

"Right . . . could I have your name, serial and division?" The officer was being cautious of a setup.

"Hollister, Sergeant, Southwest Detectives, one-one-four-nine-six."

"Help's on the way, Sergeant."

"He's got it open," the Fox whispered in an excited tone as Hollister knelt beside him.

"Cavalry's on the way," Hollister said, straining to find the figure again in the darkness.

"He's going in," the Fox said as the man raised a leg and lifted it into the open window. In another second he was gone.

"Let's go," Hollister whispered, pushing up.

"WILSHIRE UNITS IN THE VICINITY AND SEVEN

ADAM SIXTY-THREE, OFFICER NEEDS ASSISTANCE, FORTY-ONE, TWENTY-SEVEN SOUTH AUGUST. USE CAUTION, PLAIN CLOTHES OFFICERS INVOLVED WITH FOUR-FIVE-NINE SUSPECT BREAKING IN NOW. SEVEN ADAM SIXTY-THREE, YOUR CALL IS CODE TWO."

The Fox closed the door quietly behind them as they stepped into the cool morning air.

"Watch your ass," Hollister cautioned. With his gun in hand, he moved away into the darkness, skirting the far side of the pool, heading for the exit.

Fox, watching the open-curtained window, moved quickly along the curved walk to the apartment the suspect was in. Leveling his thirty-eight at the window, he inched up the walk and flattened his back to the stucco wall beside the door. The wait was on.

Outside Hollister found the space between the buildings was not a cement walkway as he hoped, but a dark slot crammed with litter, dense high weeds, and the pungent smell of wet earth and decaying garbage. He waded into the darkness.

Fox listened intently. If the man were raping a woman there had to be some noise, some movement. There wasn't a sound. He hoped Hollister was in position.

Hollister paused in the slime to study the dark wall of the building but he couldn't tell what window belonged to what apartment. Neither could he remember if the suspect had gone into the second apartment on the east wall, or the third. He decided to move on a bit further.

It felt like a Coke or ketchup bottle under his left foot, he wasn't sure. As he began to slip, he shifted his weight to the other foot and it slid on the damp weeds. He grabbed for the wall, but it was too late. He fell, hitting the ground with a soggy wallop. "Aw, shit."

Fox tensed as he heard movement inside. A second later, the curtain in the open window parted and a small nine-inch portable television appeared. A black hand lowered it carefully to the ground and then disappeared inside.

Fox smiled. He was thoroughly enjoying his secret presence. He thought God must feel very much the same way: watching a man doing something he wanted no one else on earth to see. He had to fight the urge to laugh. "Just you and me, God," he whispered.

Soon the curtain parted again and the hand pushed out a portable radio, lowering it carefully to the ground.

A siren whined in the distance, two blocks away and coming on fast, the Fox guessed. At the same time the curtains parted and a leg popped out followed by arms and head.

Fox was three feet from the man and unnoticed. The suspect gathered up the television and radio. Tucking the radio under an arm, he moved down the walk. Fox followed, still undetected.

As the men reached the point where the walk met the wide cement deck that surrounded the pool, the Fox lunged forward and gave him a stiff shove between the shoulder blades.

"Awwww," the suspect screamed as he stumbled forward and fell face first, arms flailing at the air, into the deep end of the lighted pool.

Fox moved to the side of the pool. It was obvious the suspect wasn't an expert swimmer. He struggled and thrashed, trying to reach the surface. His shirt and pants were swelled with water, giving him a cartoon look. Fox offered no assistance.

Finally the suspect reached the surface. "I can't swim," he cried, thrashing in the water. He began to sink.

The whine of the siren died abruptly in front of the apartment. Seconds later two uniformed officers burst into the courtyard. "Over here," Fox called.

The two officers raced toward him. "Everything's okay," he assured them as another team arrived.

"Put out a code four," one of the first to arrive called to the officers just entering the courtyard.

"I see you got 'em," a uniformed officer smiled, reaching the Fox.

"Yeah," the Fox grinned, watching the figure beneath the water as it struggled toward the surface again. "He thought he was Jesus Christ and tried to escape across the pool."

"Do you think he's drowning?" another officer asked, joining them.

"I think so," the Fox said in a matter-of-fact tone.

"Shouldn't we do something?" the officer said as a hand broke the water's surface. A desperate gargled cry followed.

"Someone should call the police," a voice among them teased as more officers arrived.

Fox could tell the man was in serious trouble now. His

struggle was weakening. "Next time he comes up, let's pull 'em out."

"What if he doesn't come up?" a voice asked.

"That's his tough shit," the Fox grated. He was disappointed. The man looked much too young to be the Pisser. Just a goddamned burglar, the Fox told himself.

Lights blinked on inside the apartments that ringed the pool. The tenants pulled back their curtains to peer out at the commotion. Others, wrapped in robes and gowns, gathered in small clusters to watch the group of officers huddled near the pool.

One of the uniformed officers, with his partner hanging onto his gun belt, leaned over the water, dangerously off-balance, and extended his night stick to the suspect. "Grab it . . . grab hold of it."

A hand grabbed the black stick as the face sank beneath the water. "Pull," the officer urged his partner and they struggled backwards. In a moment the exhausted man reached the edge, choking and gagging.

One of the men grabbed the suspect by the collar, another by the arm. They pulled the man up and laid him on the cement decking.

"You're under arrest. Don't move," a voice chuckled.

Fox watched as the man's back heaved with deep lung coughs between his gasps for breath. His body shook as if he'd just been plucked from an ice-filled pond.

"Here comes Ironsides," a uniformed officer warned.

A uniformed sergeant entered the courtyard and walked toward the men.

"Someone stole the strawberries."

"Watch this . . . I think a code four was broadcast, men."

The sergeant reached the group. "I think a code four was broadcast, men. Let's get back on the air. Everyone but the car that got the call."

As the group broke up and moved away toward the exit, Hollister approached, leaving a trail of wet footprints behind him. His entire right side was covered with mud.

"Everything under control?" the starched-looking sergeant said to the Fox.

"Yeah," the Fox smiled as Hollister reached them. "What the hell happened to you?"

"I fell," Hollister grated.

"In what?" the Fox laughed.

"What happened in here?" Hollister said, ignoring the

Fox's remark. He glanced at the wet suspect on the cement who groaned as if he were about to vomit.

"He came out about a minute after I got over there," the Fox explained. "He tried to get away, we struggled, and he fell in the pool."

"He bring anything out?"

"Radio and TV."

"Where are they?"

"In the pool," the Fox smiled.

"They fell in the pool during the struggle?" the uniformed sergeant questioned.

"It was an intense struggle," the Fox answered soberly.

Hollister and the Fox then went over and knocked on the apartment door where the suspect had gone in. A sleepy-eyed, middle-aged black man opened the door. His name was William Martin, he worked for the city, street maintenance division. He was shocked when the Fox pointed out the open window and missing screen. He'd been asleep in bed and hadn't heard a thing.

Martin was upset when the two uniformed officers, using a rope from the sergeant's station wagon with a twisted coat hanger, fished his portable television from the bottom of the pool. The radio was more difficult to snag.

"It ain't the Pisser," Hollister said to the Fox as Martin worked at replacing his screen, muttering about how bad the neighborhood was becoming.

"I know. The dumb shit has got all of L.A. to rip off. Four million homes and apartments, and this clown has got to pick the place where we're staked out."

"Shame, isn't it?" Hollister said, lighting up a smoke. "Can't do any police work because of all the crooks in the neighborhood."

After the suspect vomited twice and sat up, Fox gave one of the uniformed officers the nod to handcuff him.

While the Fox walked to get the car, Hollister worked at washing the mud from his clothes at the shallow end of the pool. When he finished, he decided the mud had caused less discomfort than being wet did.

Hollister squeezed as much water out of his pants as he could. They still clung to his legs. He gave up and walked out front to meet the Fox.

He was taking a final drag on his cigarette when the Fox rolled up. He flipped his butt away and climbed in the car. They were pulling away when the yellow VW rounded the corner. The Fox saw it and knew it was Yesterday. He wondered if she noticed. He was tempted to sound the horn. Oh well, he could call her in the morning. He glanced at Hollister.

"Yeah," Hollister smiled, "I saw her."

The two Wilshire Division officers booked the suspect for them. The Fox went to work on the arrest report. Hollister walked to the coffee room and got them each a cup. Pushing the Fox's to him, he said, "I'm freezing my ass off with this air conditioning."

"I imagine our crook's a little cold too," the Fox smiled, tasting his coffee.

Hollister penciled out an evidence report and tagged the television and radio while the Fox finished the arrest report.

It was 4:10 A.M. when they finished. Hollister centered a copy of the arrest report on Lieutenant Purington's desk, and they left.

Captain Slack finished reading the arrest report and pushed it aside. He rocked back in his chair, staring blankly at the desk top. "Any prints on the first burglary over there, Tom?" he said with a glance at Purington, who sat waiting quietly.

"No, nothing readable."

"How about M.O.?" Slack questioned, tugging at an ear lobe.

"Different," Purington answered. "On the first entry he went in through a bedroom window. Ransacked, chewed up a bra, messed up the bed, nothing taken."

"This time in through the front," Slack said, thinking out loud.

"Uh huh."

"Could it have been the same man on both, Tom?"

Purington considered. "It's possible—he may have been frightened away on the first one. That would explain why nothing was taken."

"Let's for the minute say the first entry was by the Pisser. Do you think he'll come back?"

"I don't know, skipper. I don't know how to judge it. Every time you try to apply logic to one of these idiots, they defy it."

"This girl's apartment is located in Wilshire Division, right?"

"Yeah, on South August."

Slack looked troubled. He shifted in his chair. "Days like this I wish I was a patrol cop, just handle my calls, let the brass worry about everything else."

"You're thinking about ending the stakeout," Purington speculated.

"That's right. We've given it three nights now. They bagged a good burglary . . . he could be good for both jobs. Commander Cockran is putting pressure on us to solve that ice-pick murder of the R.T.D. bus driver, we've got one of our three teams on vacation . . . I don't see how we can go with it on maybes. They could spend another week there with nothing. We have to draw the line. Perhaps Wilshire detectives can take it over."

Purington said nothing.

"Call 'em up, Tom. Tell 'em it's over. Be in at eight tomorrow morning."

"Yes sir."

Hollister was awake when the phone rang a little after three. He'd been awake for a half an hour or so. He'd slept well, and felt good. He'd just about decided to slip into his trunks and sit in the sun for a while, hoping there'd be something around the pool to look at.

Picking up the phone, he lowered his voice and said, "Good afternoon, Forest Lawn Mortuary, we'll move the earth for you."

"I'm . . . I'm sorry, I have the wrong number."

Hollister recognized Purington's voice. "No you don't, Tom. It's me. What 'ya need, leader?"

"There's trouble in River City."

"I was out back when the crook fell in the pool," Hollister defended.

"No, it's not about that. We're gonna have to put the lid on the stakeout."

"No," Hollister said flatly.

"It's not a suggestion, Lee."

"Your order, Tom?" Hollister was angry. "What happened to the tradition of investigators running their own case as long as the job got done?"

"Nobody's telling you how to run your case. Last night down on Slauson Avenue a bus driver got an ice pick buried in his ear right up to the handle. Ferrand and Lumis are on vacation, Bud and Hutch are tied up with a jury trial, and we're hurtin' for help. We need you and the Fox back on days."

"And what about the Pisser, Tom? Just forget him and hope he doesn't come back . . . what about him?"

"Maybe Wilshire detectives will take it over."

"Shit. They've got their own problems."

"Tomorrow morning at eight, Lee."

"What about the girl, Tom? What the hell do we tell her?"

"Tell her to lock her windows, leave lights on——"

Hollister banged the phone down.

Yesterday raced to Fox when he came into the lounge at about five. She was all smiles. "I've got something to tell you," she said eagerly. Taking him by the arm, she led him to a booth.

"I've got something to tell you, too."

"Let me be first, Virgil." She moved in beside him and took his hands.

Her mood was contagious. "Okay," he said, squeezing the soft hand. "Go ahead."

"I got a part in a picture," she announced proudly, squaring her shoulders, raising her chin.

"Fantastic. What film, where at?"

"They're not sure of the title yet, but it's another in the Shaft series. MGM's going to do it, and I've got a role as Black Rose. She's a big-time prostitute in Harlem."

"That role's gonna require a lot of practice," the Fox teased. "And I'll be glad to help."

"Virgil, you're terrible," she scolded.

"Seriously, woman," he said, weaving his fingers around hers, "I think it's great. You're on your way."

"Thank you," she said with a warm smile and squeeze of the hand.

"When did you find out?"

"Stu, that's my super agent, called me about two. I've been yelling and shouting, and kissing everyone ever since then."

"You missed me," the Fox said with feigned insult.

She slipped a hand behind his neck and moved to him. "Hmmmm," he said as the kiss ended. "More."

"I can't in here, Virgil."

"Let's go outside then."

"Work comes before play."

"Story of my life."

"I'm off Saturday and Sunday, Virg. Could we celebrate on Saturday night?"

"We can and will. We'll make it a night we'll never forget. Saturday L.A.'s going to meet Yesterday."

"You got a date, Officer." She touched the tip of his nose with a finger. "Now what did you wanna tell me about? If it's about catching that man in Mr. Williams' apartment, I already know. Vickie told me all about it."

"It's related to that."

"Was he the one that was in my place, Virgil?"

The Fox shook his head. "I don't think so. This guy's just a rip-off artist. He's no rapist."

"You think the rapist is still free?" Her smile faded.

"Uh huh."

"Is that what you wanted to tell me?"

"I want you to move."

"Oh . . ." she caught the icy tone in his voice. "But why?"

"Because Hollister and I won't be there anymore."

"Why not . . . if the one you caught isn't the rapist?"

"For a lot of complex reasons that don't make a lot of sense, but it's a fact. The stakeout is over."

"Could he still come back, Virgil?" Her eyes searched his face for reassurance.

"It's not likely, but I'd feel better with you living somewhere else."

Her eyes moved to the red tablecloth. She pushed at a bread crumb with a polished nail. She'd been comfortable for the past few days, had even slept well. Now she felt the same fear as the night she found the apartment ransacked.

"If you're off Saturday, I could help you look for a place," Fox suggested.

She managed a smile. "Okay, that would be nice. I . . . I don't know where to look."

"Let me worry about that."

She snuggled to him. "Virgil, what would I do without you?"

"You'll never know, Yesterday, you'll never know."

Janice was engrossed in the Thursday night movie. Hollister lay, eyes closed, with his head in her lap. He had already figured out that the building security officer was the one who killed the man when he was caught stealing company secrets. He couldn't understand why the hell the Snoop Sisters were having such a tough time of it.

"Lee," Janice said when a commercial interrupted the show.

"Hmmm," he said without opening his eyes.

"Do you love me . . . I mean really love me?"

"Uh huh."

"Are you going to marry me?"

He opened his eyes. "Is that a proposal?" he said, looking up at her.

She ran a finger along his eyebrow. "It's an invitation."

"One I gladly accept."

"Just wondered if your intentions were honorable."

"You been talking to your mother. That's mother talk if I ever heard any."

"Know-it-all," she quipped.

He closed his eyes again.

"Lee."

"What?"

"We'll be the same as we were. You with a wife, me with a cop-husband."

"It *won't* be the same, Janice, I've promised you that." The program resumed, and she turned her attention to it.

What was happiness, he asked himself. Happiness was the first time you held your first-born, the first house you bought, your son catching the football he had to hold in both hands. Happiness was payday when there was no gas left in the car or milk for the kids. Happiness was waking up at night in your own home because the baby coughed, and then going back to sleep after looking at the woman beside you. Happiness was the companion who accepted your failures without question. Happiness was gone. He knew he missed it, ached for it, longed for it, but realized it was gone. "I love you, Janice."

"I love you too, Lee."

Yesterday's night had been long and busy and although she was still excited about the weeks to come, a dull ache had settled into the back of her head. She knew it was tension, and all she hoped for was to get home, get into the tub, and soak in hot water.

She lit up a menthol waiting for a traffic light to change, trying to ignore the stare from the car idling beside hers. The light changed to green and she put the car in gear. Being so excited, she didn't know how she would ever sleep this night. If it were morning, she could call home. Thinking that since it's 2:15 A.M. in Los Angeles and that it would therefore be 5:15 in Atlanta, she decided to call home at four. That gave her two hours to bathe, and then she could use the phone in her apartment so that she wouldn't bother Vickie. Besides, she needed to get some clothes for tomorrow.

After parking the VW in the street, Yesterday strode into the quiet shadowed courtyard practicing her best prositute walk. She smiled remembering her first night in Los Angeles when she'd been mistaken first by a man cruising in a Cadillac as a prostitute and then by two vice officers. "I'm a natural for the part," she smiled to herself, hoping no one was watching.

Skirting the pool, Yesterday glanced at her mirrored reflection on the still water. Interesting camera angle, she thought, as she dug in her purse for her keys.

The light was still on in the living room, she noticed with a glance at the window as she unlocked the door. She wondered if Virgil was asleep, wondered if he slept in the nude as she did, wondered what it would be like to make love to him. It was his masculine gentleness that attracted her to him. He was strong, self-confident, but not overbearing. She was also sure that his interest in her was sincere.

Dropping her purse to a chair, she pushed the door closed with her butt.

"Run my bath water first," she said aloud, reaching to the middle of her back for the zipper as she headed for the bathroom.

She was still struggling with the reluctant zipper when she reached the darkness in the short hallway between the bedroom and bath.

The movement on the shag carpet was her first hint that she wasn't alone. She stiffened and looked up and caught only a glimpse of a hairy nude man before he struck her. She could feel the carpet against her cheek; her stomach was a knot of fire. He struck her again, this time on the side of the face. "Unfaithful bitch."

She curled instinctively to protect herself. "Filthy unfaithful whore." He kicked her in her stomach and her mouth opened in a silent breathless scream.

Grabbing his still erection, he stood over her and strained. Soon the urine twisted in a steady heavy stream. "There, bitch." The urine matted the long black waves of hair and filled her stinging ear.

"Now you're clean. Now you're ready." He knelt beside her and unzipped the high boots. She groaned as he straightened a leg. "Shhh. You'll be fine." He pulled a boot away and went to work on the other. "You'll be fine. I'm going to love you. I'm going to fuck your beautiful body, and you'll love it."

When the boots were gone, he reached under the miniskirt and curled his fingers over the top of her panty hose, jerking them down. His breath quickened as he pushed the nylon down her legs.

When he grabbed her throat, her tongue pushed out between her teeth. "I know you have to pretend you don't like it." He tightened his grip. "I know that, but don't yell, baby, don't yell." Yesterday was a little girl again. In her mind's eye she was racing for her daddy across the sidewalk when the bicycle hit her. Her stomach burned, and her face smarted. Her father knelt over her. "Don't cry baby . . . don't cry. You're going to be all right."

When she was nude, he rolled her on her stomach and tied her hands behind her back with her panty hose.

Turning her over again, he pushed a hand between her thighs. He probed until he found her and then forced a finger deep into the warm soft wetness. After working the finger back and forth slowly several times, he removed it and put it in his mouth, sucking it.

She remembered bouncing on the bed when he dropped her after he carried her in from the hallway. She felt her legs being forced apart and even through the pain that masked her mind, she knew what was coming. She kicked with what little fight was left in her. "Bitch." He punched her stomach and her face, leaving her nose bloody.

"I don't wanna hurt you," she heard him say through the ringing in her ears. "I just wanna love you, then I'll leave."

Her knees were bent and drawn up, arms bound behind her back. He shifted on the bed, parted her legs, and lowered his face between them. He rubbed his face against her, twisting it right and left, and then his tongue sought her. She scarcely felt the sensation because of the pain. "Oh, God, don't let him kill me . . . please let me live, God . . . please don't let him hurt me anymore."

"You're so sweet, baby. You're so clean . . . so very clean . . . not like her at all.

"I know you've wanted this." She felt his weight settling on her stomach and chest. His hot breath filled her nostrils as he kissed her face. Then he thrust his penis between the lips of her vagina. "Oh God," he groaned.

"Looks like we've been gone for a month," Hollister complained as the Fox set the stack of reports on the desk.

"You know," the Fox said, easing into his chair, "if we could get it turned around somehow . . . so that the crooks had to do all this damned paper work, I'll bet we could cut crime in half."

"You're right. What this country needs is a good ten-cent do-it-yourself crime-and-arrest report."

"Nice of you guys to drop in on Friday morning," Sergeant Rainey smiled as he passed their desk. "Helluva team you two are. Foundation of our fine police division."

"Hey, Rainey," Hollister beckoned. "I wanna talk at ya."

"Everything's okay," he winked. "All under control. I've got someone waiting at the desk right now. I'll catch you later. Maybe share a little lunch."

"Hollister eight-seven," the intercom on the wall announced.

Hollister punched the blinking light on the console and picked up the phone. "Sergeant Hollister, may I help you?"

"Hollister, this is Knott from Wilshire Homicide.

"I understand you and your partner are working on this homicidal rapist that likes to piss on his victims."

"That's right," Hollister tightened the phone to his ear.

"And I understand you had a stakeout here at forty-one twenty-seven South August, number eighteen."

Hollister straightened in his chair. "Are you there now?"

"Yeah. Been here for about ten minutes now. She's dead. Girlfriend found her this morning."

The Fox saw Hollister's face turn pale.

"What is it, Lee?" Fox asked, leaning onto the desk.

"Are you still there?" the voice on the phone asked.

"Yeah . . . yeah, I'm still here."

"I thought maybe you people would be interested in looking at the scene before we went to work on it. You're more familiar with this turkey's M.O. than we are. Maybe you can point out a few things to us."

"Yeah, okay. . . . We'll . . . we'll be over."

He carefully placed the receiver on the cradle.

"What the hell is it?" the Fox said.

Lieutenant Purington walked up and paused at the end of their desk. "I wanna see you two when you get a minute."

Hollister stood up abruptly, pulled his jacket from the back of the chair and slipped it on. "We're going out," he said without looking at the lieutenant.

"I'd like to see you first," Purington added. "Only take a minute."

"You go to hell, Lieutenant," he said in a slow deliberate tone. "I told you we're going *out*."

The squad room fell quiet. Purington's face flushed red with anger.

"Come on, Fox."

The Fox pushed out of his chair and followed. The only sound in the crowded room was the police radio on a desk near the head of the room.

"You wanna tell me what the hell this is all about?" Fox questioned, sliding into the car as Hollister started it up.

"In a minute, Virg, in a minute."

Fox rolled down a window as Hollister drove west on Santa Barbara.

When he turned on the left-turn signal at Buckingham Road, Fox straightened in his seat. He didn't like this waiting. "What the hell's going on, Lee?"

Hollister didn't answer as he negotiated the turn.

Fox sat rigid and silent as Hollister twisted the Plymouth through several more turns and then onto South August. There was a black-and-white patrol car parked in front of the apartment. The gray county coroner's station wagon sat in line behind it.

"What the fuck is this, Lee?"

Hollister eased their car to the curb behind the other detective unit and turned off the ignition.

The Fox's chest heaved. He wouldn't allow the thought in his mind.

Hollister wiped at his face with both hands as if trying to reach some deep hurt. He drew in a breath and looked to the Fox. "Yesterday is dead, Virg."

The Fox sat rigid, unmoving. Tears welled in his eyes. "No, she's not."

Hollister stared at the windshield. The tree-lined street looked peaceful and cool.

"She's not dead," the Fox repeated. "There's been some mistake."

Hollister sniffed. "I don't think—"

The Fox cut him short by jerking open the car door, scrambling out, and racing for the other side of the street.

"Virgil, no," Hollister shouted, jumping out, running after him.

When Hollister burst into the courtyard, Fox was pounding the far end of the pool at a dead run.

"Virgil, don't . . . stop." Hollister spotted a uniformed officer leaning in the open doorway of the apartment. The officer straightened as Fox ran toward him. "Stop him," Hollister screamed. "Stop him."

Fox hit the officer at a hard run. Uniform hat and flashlight went flying as the officer fell backwards into the apartment, but he had grabbed Fox around the legs and held on. "Let go, you son of a bitch," the Fox cursed, struggling with the man.

The two detectives inside and another uniformed officer pounced on Fox, grabbing him around the neck, twisting his arms. "You crazy bastard," one of them growled.

"Easy . . . easy," Hollister ordered as he reached them. "He's my partner."

Hollister knelt beside the Fox. "Come on, let him go." They released their holds carefully.

"Take it easy, Virg," Hollister said, laying a hand on his shoulder. The other men stepped back. Hollister helped him up off the floor. "Come on, Virg, let's go outside. You don't wanna see."

Fox buried his face in both hands. Violent sobs shook his hunched shoulders. Hollister put an arm around him and led him out the door.

"Is he Virgil Fox?" She was a tall attractive black girl in a bathrobe, standing at the head of the walk as Hollister helped Fox down the three steps. Hollister nodded.

"I'm Vickie Washington," she sniffed. "Yesterday told me about him. Would you like to sit him down in my place? It's right there."

Hollister didn't like the crowd of curious tenants standing around the inside of the courtyard staring at the Fox. "Yeah, that would be fine." The girl turned to lead the way.

"Take it easy, Virg," Lee said, guiding him with an arm around his shoulders. He moved like a drunk man.

The girl held the door open while they moved inside. Lee led Virgil to a couch and he sank on to it. "I'll . . . I'll be okay." He kept his head down. "Just leave me alone for a while."

"You sure?" Hollister asked in a guarded tone, looking down at him.

The Fox nodded as he dug out a handkerchief.

"I'll be back in a minute, Virg."

"I'll sit with him," the girl whispered to Hollister. He took a final look at him. He was mopping his face with the handkerchief. He'd never seen him look so bad, not even after Blatts had hit him with the board. "Keep an eye on him?" he said to the uniformed officer in the doorway.

Outside, Hollister lit up a cigarette, hand shaking badly as he held the match. He shook out the match, took a deep drag, and walked toward apartment number 18.

The living room looked familiar to Hollister after having spent three nights in it. Knott paused in the living room with Hollister. "No use of all us going in. We haven't been over the floor yet, so be careful where you step."

"Sure." He eased by Knott and into the hallway. The morning sunlight was spilling into the bedroom. He drew in a deep breath, checked the floor where he intended to step. "My God," he grimaced as he entered the bedroom.

Yesterday was sprawled on her back, arms beneath, with her legs spread, impaled with a three-foot section of broken broom handle.

Hollister turned and steadied himself on the door frame. Swallowing again to clear his mouth of the bitter taste, he inhaled several times deeply and held it. It's just a body, he told himself. You've seen hundreds of them. They don't feel any pain. It's just a body.

Opening his eyes, he turned back slowly. Her eyes were wide and staring at the ceiling. Her open mouth was stuffed with what he guessed was a pair of panties. Her long black hair was wet and matted, clinging to the once long, elegant neck which was now covered with scarlet globs of blood from the slash just beneath her chin. The ample brown breasts stood firm, their walnut-colored nipples relaxed. On the flat of her stomach, and in her navel stood the drying yellow urine. The once-white sheets surrounding her bore a distinct yellow stain. His eyes moved back to the broom handle. He silently prayed Yesterday was already dead when the man made his final sadistic assault on her in an effort to assert his masculinity. He turned away, sorry he had wanted to see.

A chill swept over him. He was frightened of the human animal that had made this attack. He felt sick and helpless.

"What 'ya think?" Knott asked as Hollister joined them in the living room.

"It's the Pisser's work all right," he answered in what he hoped was a casual professional tone.

"You see what was on the pillow?" Knott questioned with a glance at the bedroom.

Hollister dug out his cigarette. "No, I didn't go any further than the door."

"There's a contact lens on the pillow to the left of her head."

"Oh," Hollister said, lighting up. His cigarette tasted bitter. He wished he had something to rinse his mouth with.

"You know if she wore 'em?"

"No, but it shouldn't be too hard to find out."

"After the photo lab gets here and gets what pictures we need, we'll take a look at it."

"If this caper is anything like last Friday's," Hollister exhaled, "that contact lens is our second clue."

"What was the first?"

"The urine."

"Can it be typed?"

"I don't know, but we'll find out. That's what we've got a lab for."

"I'll get a sample before we move her."

"I understand you guys staked this place out for a while?" Knott's graying partner said.

"Yeah," Hollister admitted painfully. "Until last night."

"Jesus," Knott said, shaking his head.

"I'll be next door," Hollister breathed.

Fox was still sitting on the couch, elbows resting on his knees. A cup of untouched coffee sat on the cocktail table in front of him. He glanced up as Hollister came in.

"Would you like a coffee?" Vickie asked from where she sat at the end of a small but comfortable room.

"Yes, please."

Lee sat in a chair across from the couch. "You gonna be all right, Virg?"

The Fox, staring blankly at his coffee, nodded. "Yeah, I'm okay." His voice was low, but Hollister was pleased. He seemed rational, in control.

Vickie returned with the coffee. "Would you like cream or sugar?"

"No, black is fine, thank you."

After the girl sat down, Hollister asked, "Do you know if Yesterday wore contact lenses?"

"No, she didn't. She didn't even have glasses. Her eyes were fine."

"Are you sure? I mean, could it be possible she wore them and you didn't know?"

"She slept here. If she'd worn contacts, she would have had to take 'em out at night. You can't sleep with them in. I'm sure she didn't."

The Fox looked up. "You find a contact over there?"

"Knott says there's one laying on the pillow . . . on the bed."

"Is it the Pisser's?" the Fox questioned.

"If it's not hers."

They sat quietly for a few minutes as Lee drank his coffee. Fox didn't move. His blank, expressionless stare worried Hollister.

Fox inhaled deeply and let the breath out slowly through his nose. "Can they get a urine specimen over there?" he said, looking to Hollister.

"Yeah, I think so. Why?"

"Let's get a specimen and the contact lens and go," Fox suggested with a side glance at Vickie. Hollister understood he didn't want to talk in front of the girl.

He sat his cup on the table. "I'll be right back."

Knott and his partner had already collected the urine specimen in a prescription vial they found in the bathroom.

The photographer was still working in the bedroom.

"Has he got a picture of the contact lens yet?" Hollister asked Knott and Oakes. They stood in the short hallway watching the photographer, directing his shots.

"Yeah," Knott answered.

"Could we borrow it?"

"Why, did you lose one?"

"We may know the son of a bitch that did."

"Lemme check." Knott disappeared into the room. Hollister noticed that as the apartment warmed, the heavy bitter smell of stale urine was growing. In a moment Knott reappeared, carrying the small convex lens on his fingertip. He squeezed by his partner to Hollister and pulled a small brown envelope from his jacket pocket. "Here, open this," he said, handing the envelope to Hollister. Hollister opened it, and Knott carefully dropped the clear lens inside. "Will we get it back?" he asked.

"Yeah. Along with the one that matches it."

The Fox was waiting outside, standing staring at the pool. "Come on. I got it," Hollister said when he reached him.

As the two men neared the exit, a deputy coroner in a gray suit entered the courtyard pulling a wheeled chromed stretcher. The bearings on the wheels squeaked as the stretcher was pulled along behind him. Fox looked away.

When they reached the car and climbed in, the Fox said, "Find us a phone booth."

"What have you got in mind?" Hollister asked with a glance at him, starting up the car.

The Fox dug in his jacket pocket, pulling out a small notebook. "I'm gonna call Central Parole Index. Find out who the parole officers assigned to these three assholes are and see if any of 'em wears contacts."

They found a public telephone booth at a Standard station at the corner of Buckingham Road and Santa Barbara. While the Fox went to the phone booth, Hollister headed for the men's room.

When Hollister returned, he walked to the booth. The Fox was holding the door open. "Okay, thank you very much," he hung up. "Strike one," he said picking up another dime from the change he had spread on the metal tray beneath the phone. "Webster doesn't wear glasses."

"Who's next?" Hollister asked, lighting up a cigarette.

"Edward Branch," the Fox said, dialing the number he had penciled in his notebook.

"Good morning, Mr. Brush's office, may I help you?" It was a secretary.

"Is Mr. Brush in?" the Fox asked.

"Who's calling please?"

"Investigator Fox, from Southwest Detectives, L.A.P.D."

"One moment, sir."

The line clicked. He was on hold. He didn't want to be on hold. He didn't want to wait. He didn't want time to remember, time to think. He wanted to keep moving, keep doing. Keep busy.

"Mr. Brush," the line answered.

"Mr. Brush, this is Fox from Southwest Detectives. I got your number from Central Parole Index. They tell me you have a recent parolee by the name of Edward Branch."

"Yes, that's correct. Eddie was just in my office yesterday." The Fox grimaced. The word tore at his guts.

"Are you still there?" Brush questioned.

"Yes, sir, I'm here."

"I hope Eddie's not in any trouble. He's been trying real hard. He has a job at Bacon's Office Maintenance Service on Pico. He works every night except Thursdays and Fridays."

"Does he wear contact lenses, Mr. Brush?"

"Gee, I couldn't really tell you that. If he does, I haven't noticed. Hold on, officer, let me check his file. I've only had him for about a month. Just a minute please."

In a moment he was back. "Okay, I've got the file here in front of me. Let me see." A page turned . . . another. "Here we are. Physical impairments. Eyes: must wear corrective lenses. Currently wearing contact lenses. I guess that answers your question."

"Yes sir, it does. Is his address current?"

"You mean the one at seventeen forty-seven South Packard?"

"Yes, sir."

"I last checked . . . oh, about ten days ago. It was a valid address then. Could I have some idea of what he's suspected of?"

"Rape and murder," the Fox said flatly.

"Well," Brush went on, his tone unchanged, "if what you suspect is true, I'm sorry, but be assured I'll assist you in any way I can."

"Thank you."

The Fox hung up the phone.

"Well?" Hollister said.

"He wears contacts, and he works nights, but," the Fox snarled, "he's off Thursdays and Fridays. Last Friday is when he got Ellen Shane, and last night was Thursday."

"Sounds right, but what about the first time he went into the pad on South August, that was on a Saturday night?"

Fox considered it. "I don't know. Maybe the prick had a night off. He works for Bacon's Office Maintenance. We'll call them and check."

"How about our third candidate? We'd better call. He may wear contacts too."

".The son of a bitch better not," the Fox warned, picking up another dime.

"Good morning, Mr. Tatum's office."

"Is Mr. Tatum in?"

"No, sir, he's not. Could I take a message please?"

"Maybe you can help me. This is Investigator Fox from Southwest Detectives. I'm calling about one of his parolees. A Frank Comstock."

"Oh, yes," she said, "are you the one handling his case?"

"What case?" The Fox was puzzled.

"The possession of marijuana. He was arrested last night by Newton Division."

"What time?"

"Let's see . . . ten last night."

Fox hung up. "Comstock was in jail last night." He gathered his change from the phone tray and stuck the notebook back in his jacket.

"Virgil," Hollister said as they drove north on Crenshaw toward Pico Boulevard. The Fox sat quiet with a fixed stare at the windshield.

"Yeah?"

"I'm not gonna let you arrest this Eddie Branch."

"What?" He gave Hollister a heated look.

"I've been watching you. You're a powder keg looking for a place to explode. I let you near this asshole and you'll kill 'em. I'm not gonna do it, Virg. You're not gonna pull a Wilson on me."

"Don't worry about me. I'm fine," the Fox snapped.

"Well, I'm not gonna worry about you. If it turns out this Branch didn't work last Saturday night, I want him arrested too. But we're not going to do it, Virg. You're too close this time, Virg. You're personally involved, and I don't wanna see you go to the joint for shooting this asshole's eyes out."

The Fox studied him for a moment. "You're right. I agree. We'll get someone else to rip him off."

Bacon's Office Maintenance, Office Upstairs, the sign read. At the top of the stairs they found a closed door. A frosted glass in the door showed there were lights on inside. "Good, they're open," Hollister said, twisting the knob.

"Anyone here?" he called.

"Yes, just a moment," a male voice called from inside, then added, "and see if you can find that file on the Jenkins account, Julia."

"Yes, sir," the girl answered, and then opened the door. "Hello," she smiled to Hollister and the Fox. She was a thirtyish dishwater blonde with blue eyes and large breasts that hung braless under her blue sleeveless sweater. She seemed to be adjusting her skirt.

"We're police officers," the Fox said. "We'd like to talk to the manager."

"Of course," she smiled. Her chest heaved, nipples erect.

"Phil," she called, twisting her chair to the open inner office. "These two men would like to speak with you."

Hollister had half an erection and it was becoming a problem. The blonde noticed as she turned back to her desk, giving him a quick smile. He eased onto the edge of the other desk, raising a leg in an effort to camouflage it.

"What can I do for you gentlemen?" The man smiled as he came out of his office. He was short, balding, and Jewish.

"We're police officers," the Fox said again, feeling a bit like a broken record. "I'm Investigator Fox, this is my partner, Sergeant Hollister."

"Phil Bacon," the man said, extending a chubby hand.

Hollister nodded to him and went back to playing stare-at-the-secretary's-breasts. She didn't seem annoyed.

"Could we talk to you in private?" The Fox asked with a glance to the woman.

"Julia's my sister-in-law," Bacon smiled. "We can talk in front of her."

"Do you have an employee by the name of Eddie, or Edward Branch?"

"Yes, we sure do."

"Could you tell us if he worked last Saturday night?"

"Last Saturday . . . Julia, could you check your book on that?"

"Of course," she smiled, pulling a blue ledger to her from beneath the clutter on her desk. She folded it open and leaned into the desk. Hollister watched her breasts swell as they pushed against the desk. Her finger ran down a line of dates. "Here it is . . . no, he didn't work. We have him marked off sick that day."

"I got one more favor to ask," the Fox said to Bacon. "I've got a picture in the car I'd like you to take a look at, just so we know we're talking about the right man."

"Be glad to," Bacon smiled, trying to discreetly tuck in his shirttail.

"I'll be right back," the Fox said, moving for the door.

When he was gone, the woman glanced to Hollister. "Would you like a coffee, Sergeant?"

"No, thank you," he smiled.

The telephone rang and Bacon turned to his office. "I'll get it, Julia."

"Do you work around here, Sergeant?" She ran a hand back through her hair which raised her breasts and then let them relax again.

"Not too far away," he answered with an I-want-you look.

"Most of the day I'm here alone. Phil goes out to collect and sell accounts. It's a big old office," she smiled. "Any time you want a coffee or something, you're welcome."

"I'll do that."

"I keep the door locked when Phil's out. The neighborhood you know. When you come, just knock. I'll let you in."

"You can bet on it."

"Has Eddie Branch got himself in trouble or something?" she said, brushing a wrinkle from her short skirt.

"Yeah, I'm afraid so."

"This picture your partner went——"

"What picture?" Hollister exclaimed, pushing off the corner of the desk.

"The . . . the one your partner went down to get." She was puzzled.

"Son of a bitch." He ran to the door, raced down the wooden stairs, nearly falling at the bottom and out onto the sidewalk into the bright morning sun. No Plymouth. Fox was gone.

Fox drove by the address first, rolling south on Packard. He didn't turn his head. He knew the plain Plymouth fooled no one. The only people who might not recognize it as a police car were the California Highway Patrol. Seventeen forty-seven was a small one-story bland-colored stucco house on the west side of the street about mid-block. It blended so well with the homes on either side of it that he nearly missed the number. It was only a quick side glimpse, but all looked normal. Several children played in the yard.

He parked around the corner, and slipped off his jacket and tie. He laid both carefully in the back seat. Unbuckling his belt, he slid it off, freeing holster, ammo pouch, and handcuff case. He pulled the blue steel thirty-eight from its holster; twisting, he shoved the empty holster and ammo pouch under the jacket on the back seat. By now he knew Hollister had discovered his ruse and would be on his way. He hoped Hollister understood. This one had to be his. He owed her that.

Climbing out of the car he pulled his shirt out of his pants and let it hang over his belt. He slipped the thirty-eight under his belt in the small of his back and smoothed his shirt over it.

After locking the car door he pocketed the keys and headed up the street.

He hadn't yet decided what to do after he killed the man. It really didn't seem to matter. Whether or not he ran or waited didn't seem to make much difference. Perhaps, he thought, after he killed him, he'd go get a drink.

Reaching the house he turned in the walk. He watched the front windows as he approached. There was no movement, all looked quiet.

"Police Department, may I help you?"

"This is Hollister from Southwest Detectives. I'm at the corner of Pico and Ridgely. I need a car here right now."

"Are you okay?"

"I'm fine . . . get me a car."

"What's the number you're calling from?"

"Get me a car here," he growled in angry desperate frustration. "Get me a car."

Fox picked an envelope carefully from the mailbox beside the door. He glanced at it. Occupant, Seventeen forty-seven South Packard. Holding the envelope to his side, he knocked on the door.

Aware of the glass peephole in the door, he relaxed his stance and pretended interest in an elderly man several doors away who fought a losing battle with getting his likewise aging mower started.

A long thirty seconds passed. His ears strained for any movement inside. He felt a trickle of sweat tracing down the center of his back.

He sniffed, ran a finger by his nose, and knocked again, this time sharply, four, five times. He could hear the heavy footsteps approach the door. He fought the urge to stiffen, move away.

"Who is it?" An irritated voice inside demanded.

Fox raised the envelope addressed Occupant and pretended to read it. "Mr. Edward Branch, Seventeen forty-seven South Packard."

"Yeah."

"Telegram."

"Put it in the box."

"I'd like to do that, man. I'm sorry to disturb you, but I need a signature. You know."

"Shit," the voice inside hissed. A safety chain rattled, a lock snapped open.

Fox faced the door and slipped a hand to the middle of his back for the cool metallic touch of his thirty-eight.

"I was sleeping." The door swung open. He was about thirty and he was wearing only a pair of faded levis.

The man's jaw fell open as Fox jammed the barrel of the thirty-eight into his sagging stomach just above his navel. "Inside, motherfucker."

Hollister had the patrol officers shut off the electronic siren two blocks away as they raced toward South Packard. A second black-and-white patrol car fell in line behind.

"There's his car." Hollister gave the parked detective car a quick once-over as they turned onto Packard from the south.

"What's the number?" the officer driving called over his shoulder.

"Seventeen forty-seven."

"There's fifty-one," the uniformed driver said, braking the patrol car to a sharp halt. His partner pulled the twelve-gauge shotgun from its rack in front of the seat. Tires screeched on the pavement as the second black-and-white slid to a stop behind them.

"Two of you take the rear," Hollister ordered as the five of them raced across the street. The old man working with the lawn mower stopped to stare.

Cutting across a lawn, Hollister neared the corner of the house, gun in hand. Two of the four officers darted for the rear. Hollister paused, out of breath, leaning a hand on the warm stucco. He studied the curtained windows and listened. There was no sound, no movement inside. By now the officers were in position at the rear. His heart was pounding. He damned himself for letting the Fox trick him so easily. He drew in a breath. "Virgil . . . Virgil, it's me, Hollister. Open the door."

No response.

"Virgil, open the door."

Footsteps sounded inside. One of the officers beside Hollister dropped to a knee, shouldered the twelve gauge, and took quick aim at the front door. Hollister bit into his lip.

"Lee?"

"Yeah, Virgil, it's me."

"Hold your fire . . . everything's fine," the Fox answered.

"Open the door, Virg."

The knob turned and the door swung open. "Come on in." It was Fox.

The officer with the shotgun led the way, his smoke-gray weapon still poised. Hollister gave an audible sigh of relief when he saw the man lying on the floor, hands cuffed behind him, staring up at them. Fox sat at a nearby cluttered table. He shrugged and glanced to the man on the floor. "I wanted to kill the son-of-a-bitch, but he's not worth it."

Hollister reholstered his pistol. He felt weak, shaken. He moved to the table and sat down across from the Fox.

The suspect stared blankly at the ceiling, as if no one else were in the room and he lay there handcuffed only by choice. "You scared the hell out of me, Virg."

"I'm sorry."

The two officers who had gone to the rear of the apartment came in from the kitchen. "You guys wanna get 'em the hell outta here," Hollister asked.

"Sure, where to?"

"Southwest."

"Okay, asshole, get up." A foot nudged him in the shoulder.

"Where am I going?" the man asked, looking up at them from the floor.

"Home."

Drawing up his knees, the man rolled onto his stomach and stood up. "Can I have a shirt, and shoes? They're in the bedroom." The dirt and grit from the floor clung to his sweaty hairy chest.

Hollister nodded his approval.

Two of the officers moved down a hall to the bedroom. In a moment they returned, one carrying shoes and socks, the other a pullover knit shirt.

"Come on." They took him by the arm.

The man balked. "I wanna put 'em on."

One of the men gave him a stiff shove. "I said come on."

When the four men and the suspect were gone, the Fox reached among the dirty dishes on the table, picked up a small rectangular plastic case, and offered it to Hollister.

He flipped open the plastic case. Inside, resting in one of two concave depressions, was a clear contact lens. He closed the case and slipped it inside a jacket pocket. "Where'd you find it?"

"On the coffee table in front of the couch. He probably sat down there to take 'em out when he got home."

They were quiet for a moment. The familiar whine of the police car starters sounded out front, and then the cars moved away.

"He wears a ten and a half shoe," the Fox said when the sound of the cars was gone.

"Find any with blood on 'em?"

"No. He's got eight pair. I checked them all. Nothing."

"Probably got rid of them."

"There's a pair of dirty shorts in the bathroom with piss stains all over them and what looks like maybe a blood stain."

There was an awkward pause.

"You talk to him at all?" Hollister asked, breaking the silence.

"No, not a word."

"He ask what it was about?"

The Fox shook his head. "He didn't have to . . . he knows."

"Maybe we can get a statement from him," Hollister said, knowing it was wishful thinking.

"Lee, I . . . I wanna go home."

"Sure, Virg."

While the Fox walked to get the car, Hollister took a quick look around the small house. In the bedroom the sheets were pulled back on the bed, wrinkled and stained, looking as if they hadn't been changed in quite a while. The curtains were drawn, and a small table lamp on a night stand beside the bed illuminated an array of tattered paperback nudist books, an open jar of Vaseline, several balled Kleenex, a cluttered ashtray, and a pack of matches.

Hollister moved around the bed to the night stand. More paperback books lay on the floor between the bed and the wall. He nudged them with a foot. *Shaft of Hot Lust . . . The Willing Waitress . . . Balls of Fire.* A half-empty bottle of Pepsi with a cigarette butt floating in it sat beside the books. Stepping over them, he picked the pack of matches from the night stand.

The match cover was a deep black with a red running fox in the center. He tucked the matches in his pocket.

In the bathroom he found the dirty stained shorts the Fox had mentioned lying in front of the toilet bowl. When he probed at them with a natural comb he picked from the counter, he found some spots, deep dry brown in color, on the front of the shorts near the fly.

He bundled the shorts in the sports section of the Los

Angeles *Times* which was scattered on the floor between the toilet bowl and the bathtub.

Fox slid over to the passenger's side as Hollister climbed in and dropped the bundle to the floor in the back. Fox took a final glance at the house as they rolled away.

"Your car's still at the station," Hollister said as they rolled into the subterranean garage of the Fox's apartment house. It was the first they had spoken since leaving South Packard.

"I'll get it later."

"Virg," Hollister called as the Fox climbed out.

"Yeah."

"You're gonna be all right, aren't you? I mean, you wouldn't do anything dumb?" The question embarrassed Hollister, but he was worried.

The Fox gave him a shaky grin. "I'll be okay. I just wanna be alone for a while."

"I'll give you a call later."

"Okay." Fox swung the car door shut and walked away.

After dropping Fox, Hollister drove to the Vernon Eye Clinic at Vernon Avenue and Vermont. It was nearly noon and it was hot. He pulled at his tie knot, loosening it as he eased the car to the curb. Unlike the sense of satisfaction he'd known after most arrests, this one left him with a hollow, defeated feeling. It seemed that all they did now was in vain. The Pisser had won. He was booked by now, but what did it matter? He felt someone was wrong, someone had caused it, someone was to blame, but he couldn't focus his anger. It left him feeling frustrated and helpless.

The eye clinic waiting room was jammed with waiting patients. Several of the children were crying. Hollister could feel the stares as he neared the reception desk, because he was the only white in the place and he was certain they knew what he was.

After he had shown the receptionist his badge, he had to wait only a minute before the girl returned, followed by a handsome black man in a spotless, seemingly starched, white tunic.

"I'm Doctor Fields," he said, reaching the counter.

"Could I see you in private, Doctor?"

"Sure, come on in." He opened a small gate at the end of the counter.

Hollister followed him down the hall and into a small examination room. The room was lined with optical instru-

ments, and in the center of the room was a cushioned examination chair with a gray polished viewer hanging at eye
level. The doctor sat down on a swivel stool. "What can I
do for you?"

Hollister dug in his jacket, pulling out the contact lens
case and the brown envelope. "I've got two contacts, Doctor.
One was found at the scene of a homicide and the other
from a suspect. Could you tell me if they're both the same?"

The doctor took the envelope and case. "We might be
able to learn if they could possibly belong to the same individual." He opened the envelope, shaking the contact into
his palm. Laying the envelope aside, he turned the stool to
the counter and slid the lens under what looked like a
microscope with a light beneath it. Picking up a chromed
probe he centered the lens on the glass slide and then he
removed the second lens from the contact case and placed
it beneath the viewer, again centering it with the probe.

Studying the two lenses, the doctor made a few adjust-
ments with a knob on the side of the instrument. Hollister
took a final drag on his dying cigarette and put it out in an
ashtray on the examination chair.

After a minute or two the doctor switched the scope
light off and turned to him. "The prescription for both
lenses is for a nearsighted person. From the tool marks on
the perimeter of them, it *appears* both were ground and
polished on the same machine, which means that *maybe*
they both belong to the same person."

"Could two different people have the same prescription?"

"Uh huh. About everyone in a hundred is the same . . . or
is very close. It would take the doctor who made the examination and the technician who ground the lens to really
make a positive identification on them, and even then it
would be an educated guess on their part."

"How about brand, Doc? Can you tell what brand they
are?"

He shook his head. "There's no brand identification on
contacts. Did these come from a black man in south .Los
Angeles?"

"Yeah."

"If he went to a clinic here in south L.A., the lenses are
probably from Apex Optics in Thousand Oaks. They contract with just about every reputable clinic I know down
here."

His answer was less than Hollister had hoped for, but it

was something. "So the best we can do is establish they were both ground by the same machine, which means maybe they both belong to the same person."

"Plus," the doctor added, "they're both from a near-sighted man. That's the best I can do. Sorry."

"Hey, Hollister," a voice called as he stepped off the elevator on the third floor of Parker Center. It was Knott, from Wilshire Detectives. "What's that?" Knott asked as he approached, eyeing the bundled newspaper under Hollister's arm.

"Pair of bloody shorts we got from the crook's house."

"Good. I heard you got 'em. He have anything to say?"

"I haven't talked to him yet."

"You been by Southwest since I saw you this morning?"

"No."

"I called there about an hour ago. They seemed a bit concerned about where you and your partner were."

"Screw 'em."

"I told them what had gone down. The lieutenant I talked to said he understood."

"Purington?"

"Yeah, that's it. Lieutenant Purington."

"I'll give them a call in a while."

"How's your partner?"

"He's okay."

"You gonna get a blood type on the stains?"

"Hopefully."

"I was just picking up the photos from this morning," Knotts explained. "I'll go with you."

"Two days is the best I can do," the chemist defended. "Your suspect is already in jail so I have others who are going to have priority over yours."

"This guy has killed six women in the past four years," Hollister argued.

"Sergeant," the chemist answered, pulling off his horn-rimmed glasses, "I'm working on a case from last night where the suspect beat a family of four to death with a claw hammer. One of them was a three-year-old girl. The suspect isn't in custody. Now, like I said, Monday is going to have to do."

As they left the lab it was decided that Knott and his partner would meet Hollister and the Fox at Southwest on

Monday morning and the four of them would go to the district attorney's office to file their case on the Pisser.

The drive back to south Los Angeles irritated him. It seemed he'd spent half the day driving from one place to another. It was late in the day and he had much work left to do. Interview the Pisser. Complete the arrest report, book the evidence. He wished the Fox were here, but understood why he wasn't. He hoped he was all right. He decided he'd go see 'em on the way home.

"Hey, Lee, you got the Pisser, huh?" It was one of the men at the Auto table in the squad room.

"Yeah, we got 'em," he answered with a wave, not wanting to elaborate on the story now.

"You know how they got 'em, Berry?" Rainey smiled, pushing back in his chair as Hollister passed.

"No," Berry answered, pausing in his work on a report. "How'd they get him?"

"He lied about belonging to the Knights of Columbus and the Masons."

"How'd that get 'em caught?"

"He was going around telling everyone he was a masonite."

A splattering of laughter rippled across the squad room.

Hollister smiled and as he sat down at his desk he saw Purington approaching.

The lieutenant sat down across from him. "I'm sorry about the girl, Hollister."

Hollister knew it was sincere. "Hell, it isn't your fault, Tom. Who would have guessed she'd go back. The Fox told her not to. I don't suppose we'll ever know why she did."

"Where is Fox?" Purington asked with a glance around the room.

"Home," Hollister answered casually. "He thinks he ate some bad bacon or something. It's giving him stomach cramps and the runs. He's gonna take the rest of the day off."

"How good a case do you have on this Eddie Branch?"

Hollister paused to light up a cigarette. "There were four women ripped off by the Pisser in nineteen-seventy," he exhaled.

"Yeah," Purington agreed.

"None after that until last Friday."

"Right."

"That's because in October of seventy, Edward Branch

went to the joint for four years for forgery. He was paroled on the twelfth of June . . . nine days before Ellen Shane got ripped off."

"Go on," Purington urged.

"This morning in Yesterday's apart— in the victim's apartment," he corrected himself, "we found a contact lens. The Fox checked with Branch's parole officer and found that he wears contacts. The parole officer also told us where he worked. It's an office cleanup outfit over on Pico. We checked with them and learned he works nights, except Thursdays and Fridays. Friday was when Ellen Shane got it, and last night was Thursday."

"Sounds good," Purington agreed.

"It was a Saturday night," Hollister went on, "when he made his first attempt on Yesterday Phillips and missed . . . that night he reported off sick from work.

"When we arrested him we found he wears a ten and a half shoe. That's the same size as the footprints found in Ellen Shane's bedroom. He also had a pack of matches from the Flying Fox. That's where Yesterday Phillips worked as a waitress.

"It just so happens he's missing one of his contact lenses. The one he had was setting on the coffee table in his pad when he was arrested. I had an optometrist examine them, and he says they were both ground to fit by the same machine, and that they both belonged to a nearsighted man.

"The lab is working on a bloodstain on a pair of his shorts. Ten-to-one it's gonna match either Ellen Shane's or Yesterday Phillips's. We'll know Monday morning."

"Good piece of police work," Purington said when Hollister finished.

"Yeah. As they say, 'the operation was a success but the patient died.' "

Purington stood up. "I'll fill the skipper in. I'm sure he'll be pleased."

Hollister shoved the contact lens into the desk, got a cup of coffee, and walked down the hall to the jail. Outside the wire-mesh-covered jail entrance he pulled out his thirty-eight and locked it in a small wall gun locker, pocketing the key.

"Coming in, Leonard," he said to the khaki-clad heavyset jailor behind the gray wire mesh. The electric lock buzzed as the jailor pushed a release button, and Hollister pulled the heavy metal door open.

"I'd like to see one Edward Branch," he said as the metal door slapped shut behind him with a heavy thud.

"He's back in the celebrity room," the heavy dark-haired jailor said to a younger officer. "Bring 'em out."

"Where's that slick-dressin', two-hundred-dollar-a-suit partner of yours?" the jailor asked as they waited.

"He's off sick."

"Sick of what?" the jailor smiled as if he had some secret knowledge.

"The system, I suppose," Hollister answered, half-serious, leaning on the cool gray wall.

"Can't let the system get to you." The jailor sat down at a wooden paper-cluttered desk and rocked his chair to a comfortable position. "You have to learn to move with it. Not to fight it. In here I see 'em come, I see 'em go, and I don't let it touch me."

Hollister was toying with the idea of what it would be like to be a jailor when Branch and the other jailor returned. Hollister took two steps toward the prisoner. "Follow me, Branch."

He led Branch down a short dim hallway off the main jail corridor and opened the door to a small interview room. The flat of his hand found the light switch and the overhead light washed the shadows from the small room.

"Sit down." Branch chose one of the two chairs at the small wooden table in the room. Hollister pulled the door closed and sat down in the other. There was a scant two feet between the two men.

Branch was a man about his own size, a few pounds heavier at the most. His brown face was smooth shaven, and hair cut short in a tight natural. The knit shirt he wore stretched tight around his biceps. Lifting weights in the joint, Hollister guessed. His face was set in a sober worried expression, eyes fixed on his hands, which were folded on the table in front of him. Hollister wasn't really sure how he felt about him. He had been easy to hate when he was a faceless murdering rapist, but now that he sat across the table from him, looking worried and scared, he felt almost sorry for him.

"Branch, my name is Hollister. I'm the investigator assigned to this case."

The man didn't move.

"You understand what you've been booked for?" Hollister's tone was firm, but friendly.

Branch looked up at him. "I know what the charge is, but I don't understand it."

"I'll explain everything to you, but before we go any further, I have to advise you of your constitutional rights."

Branch nodded, as he worked at dirt under a fingernail.

"First, you have the right to remain silent. If you give up the right to remain silent, anything you say can and will be used against you in a court of law. You have the right to speak with an attorney and to have the attorney present during questioning. If you so desire and cannot afford——"

"That's what I want," Branch interrupted.

"What?" Hollister questioned.

"An attorney. I want an attorney."

"You don't want to give up your right to remain silent?"

"No. I want an attorney." He worked at the fingernail feverishly.

Hollister leaned into the table. "Let me explain something to you, Branch." His tone was cooling. "We're not making a movie, this isn't some two-bit TV show, this is right here and right now, fella. What we're talking about is the rest of your life.

"Being a detective isn't my hobby, it's my profession. It took me many years of hard work, and I'm damned good at my job. Before I'm done with you I'm gonna know how many times a day you take a shit and where at.

"You know why you're here and I know why you're here. You know we didn't pick you out of the yellow pages. We found you because we've got evidence that links you to the murder of six women."

"What evidence?" Branch took the bait.

"You know what evidence. You know what you left in that girl's apartment last night."

"I can prove where I was last night," Branch defended, twisting in the chair. "And it wasn't nowhere near South August."

"Who said anything about South August, Branch?"

"You did," Branch shot back at him.

"No, I didn't." The words came in a slow deliberate tone.

"Yeah . . . well, someone else did. One of them other cops did. That's where I heard it. They told me about it."

"You're lying. Look at you. Your eyes are watering, your lips are dry—"

"Sure . . . sure they are. Cause I'm nervous, but I ain't

done nothing and I ain't saying nothing. I want an attorney."

"You've already said enough, Branch."

"I ain't said nothing. Just because a bunch of filthy black whores get killed you come hassle me . . . just 'cause you know I'm on parole. It's just a bunch of shit to get me violated and sent back to the joint. Bunch of motherfuckin' whores ain't sendin' me nowhere. Whores get killed everyday, who gives a shit? Not me. I ain't never touched a whore. I'm a man. I don't have to buy no ass. I don't touch filthy whores. They're dirty."

"Where'd you lose your contact lens, Branch?" Hollister needled.

"I wanna go back to my cell," his voice was near a shout. "I wanna remain silent. I ain't saying nothing."

"I'm going to put you back, and I won't talk to you again, and you'll get a public defender to represent you. But when you're laying back there in your bunk, I want you to know I found your other contact lens."

Branch stiffened slightly, but didn't look at him.

Fox, sitting with his shoes off, feet propped up on the cocktail table and drink in hand, ignored the knock at the door.

The caller pounded on the door again. "Virgil, open the goddamned door. It's me, Lee."

Fox parked his drink and walked to the door. "Sorry, I was asleep." He squinted in the light from the hallway. The curtains were drawn in his apartment, the lights out.

Hollister was holding a small blue gym bag in his hand. "Come on, man, get your shit together. We're gonna go up to the academy and play some handball."

Fox shook his head as he walked away from the open door. "No . . . no thanks. I just don't feel up to it."

"I don't remember asking you how you felt." Hollister stepped inside and swung the door shut. "And I don't really give a shit. Now, get your gear and let's roll."

"Come on, Lee, goddamn it."

"Virgil . . . get your gear."

They played four fast and furious games of handball. That was followed by a two-mile run through the now-dark hills of Elysian Park that spread for hundreds of acres around the police academy. The summer night air was cool and clear and from the hills Los Angeles extended in all directions like thousands of sparkling diamonds on a blanket of black velvet.

They came down the last hill, sweating heavily, gasping for breath, and collapsed on the cool grass of the P.T. field.

They lay on their backs a few feet apart. The only sound was that of their heavy breathing as they studied the night sky.

After a long moment Hollister broke the silence. "Man, that sure is pretty, isn't it?"

"Sure is."

They were quiet again for a while, then the Fox said, "Lee."

"Yeah."

"Thanks."

"Sure."

            WU TLX
WUB 145 ICS IMPRNCZ CSP
7145229114 TDRN LOS ANGELES CA 13 6-27/0327 EDT

PM JOHN PHILLIPS / 912 WALNUT ST. ATLANTA GEO / DELIVER ASAP

DEAR SIR WE REGRET TO INFORM YOU OF THE DEATH OF YESTERDAY PHILLIPS THIS CITY 6/27 PLEASE CONTACT L.A. COUNTY CORONER AT 213 974 1749 REGARDING REMAINS. SINCERELY

T. NAGANO
L.A. CO/CORONER

Saturday night was the hardest for the Fox. As evening neared he drew the curtains, locked the door, and took the phone off the hook. After fixing a drink he picked the *Sand Pebbles* from among his paperback library in the living room. He had already read it twice but with the death of his parents in an automobile accident several years ago he discovered the novel had an unexplainable therapeutic effect on him. No matter how bad his troubles were, they seemed less than those of the men of the San Pablo. He sat down on the couch and opened the book.

Sunday Hollister picked up his two children and drove to Huntington Beach. They walked for miles along the oceans' edge, chasing gulls into the air, collecting seashells, and getting soaked to the knees. It was like so many other Sunday mornings, but something or someone was missing. Even the children sensed it. Although there was no mention of any problem, the laughter and conversation died as they trekked back to the car. One parent makes it a small hollow family, and Lee was relieved when he was back on the freeway headed home.

Hollister breathed a bit easier when Fox came into the squad room at a little after seven on Monday morning. He had recaptured his Harris and Frank look. Hollister was eager to tell him of the black man waiting in the lobby. When he arrived at six-forty-five, Cliff told him someone was waiting on the Fox. Hollister had walked to the reception desk and introduced himself as Fox's partner. The man, who Lee judged to be six-four and a heavily muscled two hundred pounds, thanked him but stated, "I'll wait on Virgil Fox."

"How's it look this morning?" Fox said, reaching their desk, pulling off his jacket, hanging it carefully on the back of his chair.

"Couple of cut-'em-up family disputes and a guy that shot out fourteen street lights," Hollister said with a glance at the array of reports spread in front of him.

"Fourteen street lights! Why?" The Fox said, sitting down.

"Cause before he got the fifteenth one the police———"

"I guessed that." The Fox smiled with a white grin. "Why any of them?"

"The bad guy worked for the Department of Water and Power," Hollister explained. "Until Friday, that is."

"They fired him?"

"Right."

"He's just trying to create enough work so they'll rehire him," the Fox suggested.

Hollister studied him for a long moment.

"What are you looking at?" Fox said with a puzzled expression.

"I was just trying to figure out whose husband is waiting in the lobby to see you."

"Someone's here to see me?"

"Uh huh."

Fox pushed out of his chair and walked to the head of the

squad room into the front office where the reception counter was.

The man was sitting outside the counter on a wooden chair. Hollister was right, Fox noted. He was a big man.

"I'm Virgil Fox, can I help you?"

The man stood up with his hands clasped in front of him. He was in his early thirties, the Fox guessed. He wore a blue suit that was just a bit too small, which added to his muscular look. His brown face looked grim. "I'm Jordan Phillips from Atlanta, Mr. Fox. I'm Yesterday's brother."

Fox took the hand. It was a firm handshake. Phillips's brown eyes showed the pain of the past few days. "Call me Virgil, Jordan. And I'm pleased to meet you. I'm just sorry it had to be the way it is—"

"Yesterday talked about you in her last letter to Momma," Jordan said with a soft Southern accent, releasing the Fox's hand. "She said you were a good friend and that she liked you."

"Yeah. We were good friends."

"Did you get the man that did it?" Jordan asked with a hard look, spreading his palms flat on the counter.

"Yeah, we got 'em."

"I'd like to see the man." Jordan looked explosive.

"I can't do that, Jordan."

"I won't hurt him."

"It's not that. No one's permitted to visit our jail."

"Do you have a picture of him? I've got a right to see the man that killed my sister." It was as if the family honor depended on him seeing the man.

"Yeah, I've got a picture."

"Could I see it please?"

Fox nodded and walked back into the squad room. Activity was increasing to its usual Monday morning level of chaos. He moved through the press of busy detectives to his desk.

"Who is it?" Hollister asked.

"Jordan Phillips, Yesterday's brother," he answered flatly, leafing through the papers on their desk.

"From Atlanta?"

"Yeah, from Atlanta." He found the mug shot of Edward Branch and walked back to the counter.

Jordan studied the picture for a long moment. It showed a front and profile exposure. "What's gonna happen to him?"

"We're going down to the district attorney this morning,"

Fox explained as Jordan continued to study the picture. "He's the one who files the criminal complaint. Then tomorrow morning he'll go before a judge to be arraigned."

"Could I see 'em then?" he asked, still not looking up from the picture.

"In court?"

"Yeah."

"Yes, I guess so. The courtrooms are open to the public."

"I'd feel better," Jordan said, looking up, pushing the photo back to the Fox, "if I saw 'em before I took Yesterday home."

The Fox nodded.

"When will you be back from this District office, Virgil?"

"District attorney's office," the Fox corrected. "Hour or so, I'd guess."

"I'll wait."

"Jordan," the Fox said in a friendly tone, "you don't have to wait. I can give you a call. I'll even——"

Jordan interrupted. "Am I allowed to wait here in the lobby?"

"Yes, but——"

"Then I will. I wanna know what this district attorney does. I'll wait here until you come back."

The Fox knew further argument would be futile. "Could I get you a coffee or something?"

"No thank you. You just go on about your work like·I wasn't here. I'll be fine."

Knott and his partner, Oakes, from Wilshire Homicide, arrived at Southwest a few minutes past eight. Knott had called the crime lab earlier. The blood on the Pisser's shorts was type O. The same as both Ellen Shane's and Yesterday Phillips's. The chemists were noncommittal on the urine specimens. At the best it was a maybe that they had both come from the same man.

At eight-thirty they finished their coffee and headed for the D.A.'s office.

It took Hollister and Knott some forty minutes to carefully lay out the history, and the case that was built against the Pisser. Fox looked to the floor when the pictures of Yesterday were presented.

Deputy District Attorney Mark Seldeen listened intently, made a mass of notes, studied the pictures and diagrams.

"And the lab advised this morning," Sergeant Knott said

as he laid out their final evidence, "that the bloodstains on the suspect's shorts is type O, the same as victims Shane and Phillips. We've established from his prison records that he's a type A."

Seldeen slouched in his leather chair, holding his chin in hand. His blue eyes studied the array of notes on his desk. He looked deep in thought.

"He's a guilty insane son of a bitch," Seldeen blurted, pushing up in his chair. "I know it, you know it, but we'll never get into a courtroom."

"What!" Hollister grabbed the cigarette from his mouth.

"Now, wait," Seldeen cautioned, raising a hand as if to ward off his anger. "Before you jump all over me let me explain how the court is going to view all this."

Fox gripped the arms of his chair.

"First," Seldeen said, picking a pencil from his desk, "when I'm done, we'll bring in my boss and get his opinion. If it's different than mine, hooray. If it's not, we'll go a step higher, right to Joe Bush himself, if that's what you want."

"Go on," Hollister urged.

"Number one, the suggestion that Branch being in the joint for four years pins him as a suspect will be dismissed by any judge without a second thought. You and I know it makes sense, but no judge in L.A. county will give a fuck about it.

"The contact lens . . . again, you and I know where they both came from and who they both belong to, but can we prove it beyond reasonable doubt? And don't expect that word reasonable to mean a damned thing in front of a judge. You know if there's any doubt, who's going to get the benefit of it.

"Next, the shoe size. How many men in this city wear a size ten and a half shoe? Any judge will laugh at it.

"As for the job, sure the son-of-a-bitch is off Thursdays and Fridays and he was off sick the night he first went in on South August, but can we prove that? Do we have wits who saw him at or even near any of these places? No, we don't.

"He screwed up when you talked to him, Hollister. Said he was never on South August, but like you said, that was after he said he wanted to remain silent, wanted an attorney. You all know what the hell that means. Not admissible.

"The book of matches from the Flying Fox. We all know

that's where he picked Yesterday Phillips as his next target. Knott, you went in there and showed his mug shot. Did the bartender recognize him? Did any of the waitresses?" Knott reluctantly shook his head.

"You know what his defense would be. He cleans offices. He just picked them up somewhere. Who knows where? Again, we can't prove he was there.

"Type O blood on his shorts when he's a type A. What is it . . . three out of every four people in the world have type O. He'll say he screwed some broad the night before that was having her period. I know it's Yesterday Phillips' blood, but we can't prove it.

"What we've got is a lot of circumstantial evidence that points to this Edward Branch. I know you guys, and I've got no doubt he's the Pisser, but none of what we've got can be proven. Just the contrary, it's all very easy to disprove. Here he is, The Pisser, six women dead, and we can't touch the son-of-a-bitch. The system sucks . . . to protect the innocent; I could throw up."

The argument that followed lasted another hour and a half and took them all the way to the assistant district attorney. The opinions remained the same. Insufficient evidence.

Hollister lit a cigarette from the one he was about to discard, as he wheeled the car onto the southbound Harbor Freeway.

"We'll start the stakeout tonight, Virg," Hollister exhaled, moving into the fast lane. "We'll live with him night and day. He'll move again and when he does we'll be there." He was talking fast, angry. "No matter where he goes we're going with him. We'll be there when he gets up and we'll be there when he goes to bed. We're gonna get him, Virg."

Virgil Fox was studying a line of puffy cumulus clouds and wondering what it was like to be something other than a policeman.

Jordan Phillips was still sitting outside the counter at twenty minutes past eleven when the Fox returned.

Jordan buttoned his jacket as if he stood before a judge about to receive sentence. He studied the Fox's face. "It's not good, is it, Mr. Fox?"

"No, Jordan. It's not good."

"Is he going free?"

Fox nodded.

"What kind of justice is that?" he asked with a bewildered, hurt look; his brown eyes were tearing.

"It's no kind of justice, Jordan."

The big man's eyes moved to the floor. "Go on home, Jordan," Fox said softly. "Take Yesterday and go home. Something will be done."

Jordan turned and walked away.

Edward Branch walked out the front of Southwest Station into the bright summer afternoon just after one o'clock. He stood on the steps and drew in a deep breath of fresh air. He felt more than relieved, he felt triumphant. He had beat them. He'd been right. Nobody cared about whores. Even he scarcely remembered them.

He walked west on Santa Barbara Avenue two blocks to Western Avenue, where he caught a northbound R.T.D. bus. One transfer and thirty-five minutes later he got off the bus a block from the seventeen hundred block of South Packard.

Digging in his pocket, he found he had enough money for a six-pack of malt liquor. He picked up the six-pack at the Cotton Brothers Liquor Store on the corner and headed home, deciding when he got there he had to call Bacon's Office Maintenance and see if he still had a job. Should have, he reasoned, only missed two nights. Yeah, he told himself, he'd still have the job. He knew the big-titted blonde secretary liked him.

He checked the mailbox—nothing there—dug out his keys, and unlocked the door. Parking the six-pack on the table, he pulled out a can, popped it open, and drank heavily. The taste cooled his throat and stomach. He wiped his mouth on his forearm, set the can on the table, and walked for the bathroom. He had to piss. He massaged the half erection. Maybe, he thought, after taking a leak he'd strip down and jack off. It'd been awhile.

He pushed the bathroom door open and reached for the light, holding his penis through his open zipper in the other hand.

The first blow struck him savagely in the front of the neck, sending him sprawling backwards into the hall. He tried to scream, but his throat felt as if an apple had been forced down it. He was grabbing for the strange feeling in his neck when he felt a terrible blow between his legs that quickly swept him into a deep buzzing blackness.

As the fuzzy light of the bedroom crept into his eyes the

fire in his groin sent wave after wave of hot nauseating pain through him. A dry dusty rag held his mouth open and pulled at his cheeks. He could feel the knot in the material at the back of his head. He gagged, again and again. His arms were bound beneath him. The bed bounced and squeaked as the big man moved on it. Branch grimaced with a muffled scream as his legs were jerked apart.

Using a torn sheet, the man tied one end of a wooden broom handle to Branch's left ankle and then followed by tying the other end to his right ankle, leaving him bound and braced in a wide-legged sprawl on the bed.

The man moved alongside the bed, slipped a hand under Branch's neck and jerked him to an upright position. Branch's eyes were wide with fright, his breath and muffled pleas escaped from around the gag that bound his mouth.

Branch shook his head, eyes wide. He struggled with the cloth that bound his wrists. The man released his hold and he fell backwards on the bed.

"Awww," he screamed through the gag as the man tore away his pants and shorts. He stiffened and arched his back as he felt the fingers gather his balls. The man squeezed and pulled them. Then he saw the knife and jerked. What he felt and heard sounded like strings breaking. The feeling reached high into his stomach. He gagged, vomit bubbled from around the cloth gag. His eyes rolled back and all fell black.

"Fox, eight five," the squad room intercom announced.

Fox laid aside the report he was reading and punched the blinking light on the phone. "Investigator Fox."

"He's home. He won't be botherin' any more women. I'm sorry I had to do it." The next thing Virgil heard was a dial tone.

Fox hung up the phone, paused for a moment, and then picked up the report he'd been reading.

"Who was that?" Hollister said, looking up.

"Wrong number."

CRIME AND DETECTION NOVELS
FROM CORONET

FRANCIS DURBRIDGE

☐ 21302 7 A Game of Murder 60p

JOHN GODEY

☐ 18772 7 The Taking of Pelham One Two Three 50p

GEORGE V HIGGINS

☐ 21786 3 A City on a Hill 80p

MICHAEL LEWIN

☐ 23843 7 Night Cover 95p

NICHOLAS MEYER

☐ 21316 7 Target Practice 60p

ROBIN MOORE and MILT MACHLIN

☐ 21525 9 The Set Up 95p

All these books are available at your local bookshop or newsagent, or can be ordered direct from the publisher. Just tick the titles you want and fill in the form below.

Prices and availability subject to change without notice.

CORONET BOOKS, P.O. Box 11, Falmouth, Cornwall.

Please send cheque or postal order, and allow the following for postage and packing:

U.K.—One book 19p plus 9p per copy for each additional book ordered, up to a maximum of 73p.

B.F.P.O. and EIRE—19p for the first book plus 9p per copy for the next 6 books, thereafter 3p per book.

OTHER OVERSEAS CUSTOMERS—20p for the first book and 10p per copy for each additional book.

Name ....

Address ....

....